"WE THAT ARE LEFT"

"WE THAT ARE LEFT"

TONY SQUIRE

CONTENTS

I dedicate this book to all who have served in the armed forces, whether in a combat or support arm, each person being part of a well oiled machine, each dependent on one another. When you were needed you were ready. Let no man put asunder.

Cover design by Tony Squire.

Cover photograph is courtesy of The Australian War Memorial, Canberra.

Front Cover:

Accession Number - E05925.
Maker - Unknown Official Australian Photographer.
Place Made - France: Picardie, Somme, Amiens Harbonnieres Area, Villers-Bretonneux Area, Villers Bretonneux.
Australian War Memorial Description - French children tending graves at Adelaide Cemetery of Australians killed in battle on the Western Front.
Copyright - Item copyright: Copyright expired: Public Domain.

FOREWORD

As this final instalment of *The ANZAC Chronicles* reaches your hands, I find myself reflecting not only on the journey of the Taylor boys but on the broader silence that still surrounds the Great War in our national memory. Despite the scale of sacrifice - nearly ten percent of Australia's population volunteering to serve - our school curriculum continues to skim the surface and thus the deeper story remains largely untold. This series has always aimed to illuminate the lesser-known chapters of our wartime history. "WE THAT ARE LEFT" follows "OUR LAST SHILLING" in tracing the path of two Queensland regiments - the 9th Battalion and the 2nd Light Horse Regiment - through the brutal campaigns of 1918. These units may not feature in every text book, but their contributions were no less vital. Through Archie, Percy and Rueben Taylor, I've tried to capture the hardship, fear, and camaraderie that defined their experience. War, after all, is not a grand narrative - it is a daily fight for survival. To ground this story in truth, I've relied heavily on two exceptional sources: *'History of the 2nd Light Horse Regiment A.I.F. - 1914-1919'* by Lieutenant Colonel G.H. Bourne, DSO, and *'From ANZAC to the Hindenburg Line - The History of the*

9th Battalion A.I.F.' by Norman K. Harvey, BA, AACI. These firsthand accounts have been invaluable, offering not just facts but the voices of those who lived them. Wherever possible, I've included real soldiers from these regiments placing my fictional characters beside them - not to share their glory, but to honour it. The battles, dates, and locations, are historically accurate, and I've done my best to portray the physical and emotional toll of a soldier's life in that era, whether trudging through mud or riding into fire. To those who've followed this series from the beginning, thank you. Your support has meant more than you know. If this book moved you, please consider leaving a review and sharing your thoughts. You can also follow me on Facebook at https://www.facebook.com/TonySquireAuthor/ to stay connected. Lest we forget.

CHAPTER 1

The Year Turned Without Applause

The summer sun was already high by mid-morning, its warmth drawing a shimmer from the paddocks and painting a familiar glow across the dry Queensland earth. It was January 1918, and although the rains had been patchy, they had been kind this season, and the land had responded in turn - the creeks were running strong, the pastures around Sandy Creek still held a tinge of green, whilst the cattle grazed lazily under the broad blue sky and the cicadas screamed from the gums, the scent of dry dust and eucalypt carrying on the breeze. Life at Doriray Station continued in its steady rhythm, far from the war but never free of its shadow.

Out at the back of the homestead, a barefoot boy with a mop of ginger curls stood in the dust, squinting into the distance with one hand shading his eyes. Frank Taylor, now six and a half, had grown tall for his age, but there was something in the way he stood - quietly, thoughtfully - that made him seem older.

"Will he remember me, Mummy?" he asked without turning around.

In the laundry, bent over the old porcelain sink, sleeves rolled up and apron tied, Lil looked up from scrubbing shirts and paused to listen. The cicadas hummed their endless tune, and somewhere beyond the cattle yards a windmill creaked with the breeze. She wiped a damp hand across her forehead, leaving a streak of suds.

"Who, love?" she called gently, though she already knew.

"Daddy," said Frank, "when he comes home...after the war".

Lil stepped out into the yard, drying her hands on her apron. Her dark eyes found her son's worried face.

"Of course he will, Frankie. He talks about you in every letter. Says he can't wait to see how tall you've grown, and that he reckons you've probably got faster legs than Uncle Roo by now".

Frank smiled at that, just a little.

Inside the house, Doris, humming softly to herself, set a plate of scones down on the table and glanced out of the kitchen window, watching Lil cross the yard. At fifty two, Doris had the same dark curly hair she had always had, though it now carried threads of silver. Her face still wore that open, cheerful expression that made people feel welcome even before she spoke. At five foot eight, she moved with the energy of a woman half her age.

Ray sat nearby, long legs crossed, a newspaper folded in his lap. He was a tall man, thin as a sapling, with a narrow face and sharp cheekbones. His dark hair, streaked with grey, was brushed back from a furrowed brow. He looked out across the land he and Doris had carved from scrub over three decades ago. His eyes - narrow, watchful - lingered on his grandson in the yard. He said nothing at first, just took in the stillness - broken only by the occasional bellow of a cow from the far paddock or the slap of a screen door.

"For a small lad he certainly thinks a lot," Ray said softly.

"I think we all do," Doris replied, pouring tea, "the war has been going on for four years now. You can't blame a lad for wondering if his dad's coming home, and when he does if he'll remember him or not".

Ray said nothing for a long moment. Then he reached over and plucked a scone from the plate.

"Archie and Percy *will* come home, and so will Roo, and when they do, they'll need steady work and a quiet place to help them get back to normal life".

Doris looked at him and nodded.

"And they'll have it here as they always have. Clancy and Pip too, if they want it. Percy already said they'll be working this land when it's all over. There's certainly plenty to do, and more than enough land and cattle to go around".

Ray gave a quiet grunt of agreement, and then added, "And Alfie".

At that, Doris looked toward the window. She caught a glimpse of Lil, crouched beside Frank now, brushing dust from his cheek.

"Yes," she said softly, "Lil's been trying not to show it, but I think she's quietly thrilled. Percy's letters say Alfie's stuck to him and the others like glue. A brother for Frankie, *and* nearly the same age. She's probably already thinking about making a bed for him in Frank's room".

On the mantle above the hearth, tucked beside a small vase of wattle, stood a photograph - sun-faded and well handled. It showed Percy, Archie, and Roo standing side by side in uniform, rifles at their sides, grinning beneath the Egyptian sun - a photograph taken before Gallipoli, before things changed. They looked like boys playing at being men, though they were already soldiers. Lil often paused by it when the house was quiet. She would run a thumb along the edge, whisper something under her breath, and move on.

As she sat on the ground next to Frank, Lil's auburn hair was pinned up under a faded straw hat. She paused for a moment, smiling quietly to herself as she thought of the news that Percy had written last - that young Alfie, just eight years old, would be coming back with him after the war. Lil couldn't explain it, but the thought of Alfie living with them gave her a warm feeling in her chest. Frank would have someone to play with - a kind of older brother, or perhaps something more like a shadow. They were only a year and a half apart in age after all.

Lil's thoughts about what might be soon faded as her gaze turned to Frank, who was now pretending his stick was a sword, slicing through the grass. Her hands lingered on the dusty ground, her mind taking over again as her thoughts drifted thousands of miles away to a tent somewhere in Palestine, or maybe the Jordan Valley, where Percy and Alfie might be sleeping under canvas - dusty, weary, and waiting for it all to end.

But her heart didn't stop there. It pushed further still, past deserts and date palms, to the frozen trenches of France, where Archie and Roo would be shivering under layers of damp wool and mud covered greatcoats. She imagined them standing silent in the pre-dawn dark, breath misting in the icy air, rifles resting cold and heavy in their hands. Maybe Roo was saying something cheeky to lift their spirits, and perhaps Archie was staring hard across the wire, thinking of home. The chill crept into her bones just imagining it, and she pressed her palms into the warm earth, as if that might somehow send a little comfort their way.

On the Western Front, New Year's Day 1918 had not been a day for celebration for the 9th Battalion, for it was back to the line for them. The weather was bitterly cold and wet and rations were scarce. Messines, however, was for that moment a quiet sector and well known to the troops as they had occupied the area in December of 1917, spending yet another Christmas Day at the front.

"I reckon I'd have forgotten when Christmas Day *is* by the time we get home," said Roo shifting his weight side to side to keep warm, and blowing into his cupped hands.

"I think the last real Christmas Day I ever had, or can remember, was in the orphanage when I was a young lad," Pip added as he rubbed his hands together for warmth.

Roo glanced sideways.

"Did you get any presents?"

Pip gave a wry smile.

"The nuns weren't *that* generous. We were lucky to get a few more lumps of meat in our soup...at least I think it was meat".

"Well, you just wait. Christmas back home was always made special by Aunty Doris and Uncle Ray. Big roast, pudding, and presents...you'll love it," said Roo.

Pip looked up, a small grin creeping across his face.

Roo went on, the cold seemingly forgotten for a moment.

"One year, Uncle Ray thought it'd be funny to swap the name tags on all the presents. Archie opened a box of bloomers meant for Aunty Doris, and I ended up with a teapot...best laugh we'd had in years...he's definitely a bit of a card is Uncle Ray".

Pip smiled.

"That sounds like a *proper* Christmas".

"It is mate," Roo said, "first Christmas after this mess is over...sunshine, a feed you don't have to chew with your eyes closed, and not a trench in sight".

They both laughed quietly, as they pulled their coats tighter in the freezing temperatures, the sound of distant guns muffled under the weight of grey skies and happy memories.

"I'm sorry you had to have that life mate," Stowie added, as he touched Pip lightly on the shoulder.

"Eh? Oh don't worry about that pal...it wasn't so bad. The nuns were good to us...except when they weren't," said Pip.

Roo thought for a brief moment.

"Yeah, I reckon I know what you mean. Stand by your beds in the morning and beatings if you spoke out of turn".

Although Pip was aware Roo's childhood he was still surprised when he spoke of it.

"It's funny how even on the other side of the world things are so similar like?" he said, shaking his head.

"I suppose," replied Roo, "same terrible people, just a different country. Anyway, that's all gone now".

Pip nodded as a stray enemy shell whined and shrieked overhead, crashing harmlessly in the rear, but managing to toss soil and debris their way.

"An angry nun, or Fritz's artillery? No contest really...I hate those bloody nuns," laughed Pip.

As each man joined in the laughter, their outburst of joviality was interrupted by Clancy, as he and Captain Ponsonby arrived on one of their inspection tours. Pip, ever the former British soldier, braced up in acknowledgement of the two men.

"Alright sirs? How are you this fine day?"

Clancy looked visibly annoyed and somewhat indignant at Pip's unusual greeting.

"What do you mean, am I alright, you flamin' bludger? Do I look bloody sick or something?" exclaimed the CSM.

Pip was a little taken aback by Clancy's response.

"No sir. Sorry sir. It's just something us Scousers say...you know, a greeting," Pip explained.

"Yeah, old Taff was much the same...what is it he used to say...oh, I know...'alright Stowie, 'ow's it goin', alright?'...good memories," said Stowie.

Captain Ponsonby gave Clancy a sideways glance.

"Yes, well, good morning Pip. I am well. Thank you for enquiring".

"Enquiring? Bloody hell mate I thought you were learning to be a proper Aussie, *and* to speak like one," growled Clancy.

The captain cleared his throat.

"Yes I am old boy but, what is it they say? You can't teach an old dog new tricks".

"I understand what you're saying sir. These fellas speak a foreign language like. I can't understand them half the time, what with their fair dinkums, bonzas and bloody oaths," Pip added.

"Pot...kettle, mate," said Archie.

The front lines had been relatively quiet for a few weeks now except for the occasional stray round here and there, not to mention the odd recce by enemy aircraft.

"So, what's happening sir? Where's Fritz? Is the war nearly won do you think?" asked Stowie.

Captain Ponsonby and Clancy sat down on some ammo crates, as Roo filled their mugs with hot tea.

"If only it was corporal, but no I think the Germans have something big up their sleeves," replied the captain.

"Well I wish they'd hurry up...this is year five for some of us, and it would be just dandy if we could pack up and go home," said Stowie.

"Yes, it would indeed," replied Captain Ponsonby.

"What? The war is over?" asked an excited Ten Bob, who had just stirred from a quick nap.

"Huh?!" Clancy scoffed, "no, far from it mate, but we *are* packing up and moving to some farm or other for some training".

"And work parties?" asked Archie, hoping for the answer no.

"Yes mate...and work parties," Clancy confirmed.

"Bugger me!" said Stowie.

There was certainly no let up for the Light Horse either. January 1918 arrived without fanfare. No bugle call, no raised glasses - just the steady clip clop of hooves and the rustle of equipment as the men of the 2nd Light Horse Regiment moved out from Neby Kunda on the 4th of January. Their orders were clear - relieve the 4th Light Horse Brigade and take up position in the rough country near Midieh and Nalin, eight miles east of Ludd, and thirty miles from Esdud.

'C' Squadron, Percy Taylor's mob, was assigned the left flank, in touch with the 75th Division. The terrain was unforgiving - steep ridges, dry gullies, and stone that defied the pick. It was a place that seemed to resist occupation, as if the land itself had grown weary of war.

Percy rode in silence, his eyes constantly scanning the horizon. Behind him, Davo was trying to light a pipe with matches that were repeatedly extinguished by the wind.

"Bloody January," he muttered, "too hot for comfort, too cold for a decent sleep at night".

Boggy shifted in his saddle and grumbled.

"Comfort? My arse has been sore for years".

Percy didn't look back.

"I reckon you should have joined the infantry mate".

"What and miss this wonderful scenery?"

They laughed; the kind of laughter that came easy among men who had seen too much. Chugger rode beside Rachel, his fiancée. She wore her slouch hat with pride and carried her curved scimitar over her shoulder like a talisman. She had become part of the regiment - not officially, but in every way that mattered. Chugger and the boys had scrounged bits of uniform for her, and she wore them with a quiet dignity that made her seem taller than she was.

Alfie, the bootblack boy, trotted along on Bow, his donkey, the reins looped loosely in his small hands. He wore a pair of Percy's old boots, stuffed with rags, and a khaki shirt that hung off him like a tent.

Digging was impossible. The ground was stone and shale, so the men built sangars - dry stacked walls of sandbags and rocks that offered some protection from snipers and the wind. It was hard, dirty work. Hands blistered, tempers frayed, but the sangars rose, squat and defiant.

Percy oversaw the construction in his sector with quiet efficiency. He didn't shout orders - he didn't need to. The men respected him, not just for his stripes but for his steadiness. He worked alongside them, sleeves rolled up, sweat streaking the dust on his face.

Once they had completed their defences they turned their attention to carving a zig-zagging road down the steep slopes. The Generals praised the engineering skills of the men, admiring the road which twisted and dipped like a dropped ribbon, clinging to the terrain with an almost stubbornness.

When the sun dipped low and the hills turned gold, Percy's thoughts drifted to Doriray Station, nestled in the folds of Sandy Creek near Kilcoy. He imagined Lil standing on the verandah, her hair catching the light, her eyes full of that quiet, innocent beauty that had never left her. He pictured Frank, six years old and full of questions, helping Ray with the cattle or chasing chooks through the yard. The boy had his mother's smile. Percy wondered if he would remember him when he came home.

At night, the squadron settled into a rhythm. The small cooking fires were extinguished as darkness fell. Rachel sat crosslegged, sharpening her blade with slow, deliberate strokes. Chugger watched her with a mix of pride and awe.

"She's got more guts than a lot of blokes I know," he said, kicking sand over the flames of the dying fire.

Alfie curled up beside Bow, using the donkey's flank as a pillow. Percy had begun teaching him to read, using scraps of newspaper and old army forms. The boy was quick, always asking questions no one wanted to answer.

"Why do the Turks run when they see Rachel?" he asked one evening.

Percy paused.

"They believe if a woman kills them, they won't go to heaven".

Alfie frowned.

"That is silly Mister Percy".

Percy nodded.

"War is full of silly things mate".

On the 20th of January, the Canterbury Mounted Rifles arrived. The Kiwis were lean and laconic, their horses well groomed, their equipment immaculate. The handover was smooth. Percy exchanged nods with a sergeant, and then led his men down from the hills to the Division Bivouac Area at Richon.

Richon was a different world. The land flattened out, the air softened. The sea wasn't far, and the scent of salt hung in the breeze. The men relaxed, but only slightly. War didn't allow for true rest.

Training resumed with a vengeance. Officers and NCOs attended refresher courses in new mobile tactics - the kind that changed with every battle. Percy found himself leading drills, his voice steady, and his movements precise.

Chugger and Rachel practised mounted manoeuvres together, drawing curious glances from other units. She rode like she was born to it, her scimitar flashing in the sun.

In the quiet moments, Percy wrote letters about the hills, the sangars, Rachel and her sword, and the boy with the donkey. He wrote about the way the men laughed, even when they shouldn't, about hope, and how in the folds of that dusty bivouac, beneath the slouch hats and the weight of war, a strange kind of family had formed. Not by blood, but by choice. By survival. By mateship.

By late January, the men of the 9th Battalion, along with the other three battalions, were once again on the move. As was typical of the winter months, January meant relocation. First, they shifted to Gable Farm, then, on the 21st, marched on to Ramillies Camp at Kommel, where the 3rd Brigade took up duties as Divisional Reserve. The rest didn't last long however, and two days later, the entire brigade was ordered forward to relieve the 2nd Brigade, with the 9th taking over the Oosttaverne Sector near a sluggish stream known as the Wambeek.

The position was quiet - eerily so - and after just a week of trench routine, the battalion was pulled out again. But this time, there was a small blessing - instead of a foot slog through frozen mud, they were bundled onto a narrow-gauge light railway and shuttled off to Neuve Eglise.

Neuve Eglise, just fifteen kilometres south of Ypres, had felt the full weight of war. Caught along the shifting front lines of 1917 and 1918, the village and surrounding countryside bore the scars of constant shelling, trench digging, and bitter engagements. Situated in the heart of West Flanders, it sat on the line that once divided the German and Allied forces - changing hands more than once, and each time leaving it more battered than before.

The journey was far from glamorous, but compared to marching, it was luxury.

As the train clattered along the battered tracks, the men made the most of the moment.

"I thought I was dreaming when they said no marching," Stowie grinned, leaning back on his pack.

Pip, who had curled up on a pile of sandbags, cracked open one eye.

"Don't tempt fate mate or we'll probably end up pushing the bloody thing or something".

"Still, better than trudging through ankle deep slush with frozen toes and a fifty pound pack on your back," Stowie muttered, tugging his coat tighter.

Roo laughed.

"Keep the noise down boys or at this rate, they might start charging extra for the first class service".

"First class? You call this first class?" Ten Bob exclaimed, "I've seen better seating in a cattle train".

The carriage jolted, sending a few helmets clanking together.

"Ey up...you've upset the train now," laughed Pip, as he winked at the others.

Despite the cold and the filth, the mood among the men was lighter than usual. A train ride, no matter how rough, meant a brief reprieve from the endless march of war - and that was enough to lift their spirits, if only for a while.

Following their quiet time on the front line, February was about to get quieter, except for more training, drilling rigorously in preparation for the expected German Spring Offensive, and even more sports.

Christmas Day 1917 came later again, this year falling on the 15th of February 1918. The celebration was followed by sports, and yet more sports for the remainder of the month, with *some* training thrown in on the side. The 9th Battalion had quite a successful time of it, managing to defeat both the 1st Field Artillery Brigade and the 1st Field Ambulance at rugby, which the Aussies insisted on referring to as football, or footy for short, whilst their British counterparts insisted that football was a different sport altogether, with a round ball. But ball sports weren't their only triumph, having beaten the 3rd Division tug of war team, as well as being the undefeated champions at soccer...the *other* ball game. There was one downside, however, when the battalion tug of war team were defeated by the 1st Pioneer Battalion in the divisional finals...c'est la vie!

It was a different story for the Light Horse. The sun had barely cleared the horizon when the 2nd Light Horse Regiment upped sticks and moved out from Richon the 16th of February, bound for Jerusalem. The morning light was pale and sharp, casting long shadows across the dry earth, whilst the air was dry and restless, the kind that clung to the skin and turned every breath into a mouthful of sand. Already the heat was rising, shimmering off the stony ground in waves that blurred the distance, whilst the dust, kicked up by horses' hooves, was settling into every crease of uniform and every corner of thought. The road ahead wound through low hills and stony valleys, the kind of country that tested both horse and rider.

Horses snorted and stamped as the column formed, the men settling into the rhythm of the ride - backs straight, eyes forward, minds wandering. The column stretched along the track like a slow moving serpent, hooves kicking up more dust that hung in the air like smoke. The land was hard and treacherous, the road to Junction Station dry and rutted, the kind that jarred the bones and wore down the patience.

Percy Taylor rode near the front of 'C' Squadron, his mount picking its way along the dusty track. The land rolled gently at first, then dipped into gullies and rose again into low, stony ridges and terraces, with the odd fig tree clinging here and there to the hillside. Olive groves flickered past, their leaves silvered by the wind, and the occasional stone house stood silent in the distance, shuttered against the heat.

Behind him, Davo wiped his brow with a sleeve.

"Bloody hell, it feels like we're riding through a baker's oven".

Nobody disagreed with him.

They reached Junction Station at around 1530 hours, the sun casting long shadows across the railway lines and telegraph poles. The bivouac was rough but serviceable - canvas stretched between trees, horses tethered in rows, the scent of sweat and leather thick in the air.

As the men settled in, Percy sat with his mates around a low fire, the billy steaming gently.

"I can't believe we're going to Bethlehem," Johnno said, poking at the embers, "I never thought I'd be riding into a place we learned about at Sunday school".

Boggy chuckled.

"Yeah...I hope there is room at the Inn for us".

Davo puffed on his pipe.

"I'll settle for a bit of shade and a quiet corner".

Percy looked out toward the hills, their edges softened by the haze.

"Funny, isn't it? All the stories we grew up with - shepherds, stars, wise men...and now we're riding through it".

Alfie, curled up beside Bow, looked up.

"Will there be angels?"

Percy smiled.

"If there are, they'll be keeping their heads down like the rest of us".

The fire crackled. The horses shifted. Beyond the hills, Bethlehem waited - quiet, ancient, and full of stories yet to be written.

The next day they were on the move again, the next stage of their journey to Bethlehem involved them passing through the ancient villages of Zakaryya and El Khudr. The column slowed as the terrain changed again. The village of Zakaryya lay ahead, its domed roofs catching the light like old coins. Rachel, who had slotted herself into the column beside Chugger, rode with the confidence of a seasoned veteran; sitting easy in the saddle, her eyes fixed on what lay ahead. The two exchanged a loving glance as she rode quietly, her slouch hat pulled low, the curved scimitar slung over her shoulder in the leather scabbard Chugger had given to her. Alfie and Bow trotted along behind, the donkey's ears flicking at flies, its hooves thudding rhythmically against the dry track as the boy whispered encouragement to the animal, urging it to keep pace with the horses ahead.

The regiment passed through Zakaryya, a sleepy village of stone houses and olive trees, then on toward El Khudr, where the land began to rise and the air grew thinner. The sun beat down without mercy, and the men rode in silence, each lost in their own thoughts.

Percy slowed his horse and glanced sideways at Rachel, who was riding with her eyes half closed, as if listening to something beneath the wind. He wiped the sweat from his brow and glanced at the hills, then back to Rachel. He, like the rest of the men, had heard these names before - Zakaryya, El Khudr, and Bethlehem - not in dispatches, but in Sunday school.

"Do you know this place?" he asked.

She nodded.

"Zakaryya. It was named for the prophet Zechariah. He prayed many years for a child. Was old man when son came...John...the one who baptised".

"Baptised? So his son was John the Baptist?" asked a surprised Percy.

Rachel thought for a moment then nodded.

"If that is what you call him...then...yes".

Percy looked again at the village, its quiet lanes and shuttered windows.

"Well...I didn't know that".

"Many do not," she said softly, "he was a holy man. Guardian of the one you call Mary. She lived in temple before...before angel came".

She paused, eyes tracing the stone path that led to a well.

"In our book, she is Maryam...chosen above all women. The angel brought word of a child...though no man had touched her".

Percy turned to her, unsure what to say.

"You mean...Jesus?"

"Yes," Rachel said. "We call him Isa. He was born by God's will. A prophet. A sign".

Percy hesitated.

"Christians believe he is the Son of God," he said quietly, "born to save".

Rachel didn't flinch.

"I know," she said, "we see him in a different way, but still with honour".

Percy nodded slowly, eyes drifting to the hills.

"It's strange," he murmured, "the same story...almost, but told in a different voice".

Rachel smiled and placed her hand on her chest above her heart.

"Sometimes the voice changes, but the truth still reaches here".

They rode on, the horses picking their way through stony paths. Ahead, the land opened toward El Khudr, where the hills seemed to lean inward, as if guarding something.

"El Khudr," Rachel murmured, "it is named for Al-Khidr. Green One. He walk with Moses, teach him things not easy to understand".

Percy glanced over.

"Is Moses part of your faith too?"

She nodded.

"Yes...all of them... Zechariah, Maryam, Yahya, Musa...Khidr. My mother told me their stories when I was small. She say they teach us how to wait, how to trust".

Percy was quiet for a moment.

"Funny. We were told some of the same things. Different names, maybe".

Rachel looked at him, her expression soft.

"Then perhaps we ride same road, just from different ends".

He smiled.

"And meet in the middle".

The wind stirred the dust, and the olive trees whispered above them.

"Some say Khidr still walks," Rachel added, "he help those who are lost....or...those who listen".

They passed through El Khudr as the sun dipped lower, casting dark shadows across the valley. The men rode quietly now, the weight of old stories settling over them like a second saddle. Somewhere ahead lay Bethlehem, and beyond that, Jericho. But at this moment, they moved through sacred ground, guided not just by maps, but by memory.

Percy shifted in the saddle, the rhythm of the ride steady beneath him. The hills rolled past, ancient and indifferent, but something in Rachel's words had stirred a memory.

"When I was a boy," he said, "Lil and I used to sit in the back row at School. She'd whisper the answers before I could think of them. Smart as anything".

Rachel smiled.

"She sound very...er...how you say...clever".

"She was. Still is."

He paused.

"I remember around Christmas time, the teacher talking about Mary and Joseph travelling through these hills. Said they walked for days, maybe weeks. Looking for shelter. I used to imagine it like a painting...you know...stars overhead, donkeys, lanterns swinging".

Rachel nodded.

"We have same story".

Percy glanced at her.

"But the feeling's the same, isn't it? That someone walked here once, carrying hope."

She looked out across the valley.

"Yes...and maybe someone still does".

The horses moved on, their shadows stretching long across the dust. The sun dipped lower, casting a golden hush over the land. Percy felt it then - not awe, exactly, but something quieter. A kind of belonging, as if the road itself remembered every footstep, every prayer, every whispered promise.

He turned to Rachel.

"Thanks for telling me".

She met his gaze.

"'Afwan," she said, the word soft, almost musical, "it means you are welcome".

They came into Bethlehem as the day waned, the sun laying its last light across the stone. The New Zealand Mounted Rifle Brigade was already bivouacked on the outskirts, their horses tethered, their men resting in the shade. The Australians joined them, setting up camp in a dry field bordered by olive trees.

Canvas was stretched between low walls, providing a decent shelter for the night. The horses drank deeply, and the men moved slowly, conserving energy. The bivouac was quiet, the kind of quiet that comes after a long ride and before something unknown.

That evening, as the light faded and the stars began to prick the sky, the boys sat in a semi circle, watching the fading embers of their camp fire. The talk turned to the coming operation - Jericho, they had heard. The 53rd and 60th Divisions, along with the ANZAC Mounted Division, were preparing to move. The objective apparently was to push the Turks back across the Jordan River, secure the valley, and take the ancient city.

Boggy stirred the embers.

"Jericho...another name from the old stories".

Johnno leaned back.

"I used to love the hymn...that line about the walls coming tumbling down when they blew their trumpets".

Chugger laughed.

"I think it will take more than just a trumpet mate".

Rachel listened, her brow furrowed.

"We go there soon?"

Percy nodded.

"Soon...east, toward the valley".

She looked toward the hills.

"I ride with you".

Chugger gave her a quiet smile.

"Only if you are sure...and soon we will be married...yes?"

Rachel smiled and grasped his hands tenderly.

"Yes...very soon".

The next day, they were on the move again. The sun rose hard and fast, burning off the morning haze before most had finished tightening girths. The track ahead was narrow, winding like a scar through the hills - steep, sun-blasted, and inhospitable. Loose shale slid under hooves, and more than once a startled horse skittered dangerously close to the edge, sending a spray of stones clattering into the ravine below. Percy's horse danced sideways at one point, ears flat, and nostrils flaring. He reined in sharply, heart thudding.

"Easy Sandy, easy boy".

One wrong step and it would've been a long, brutal fall.

They rode in single file, heads down, sweat streaking faces and flanks alike. The heat was relentless, making the men quiet and the horses irritable. At 1400 hours, they reached Beit Obeid - a cluster of stones and scrub - and halted for water. The relief was immediate and unmistakable. Men slid from saddles with groans, stretching stiff legs. The air smelled of dust and leather and something ancient.

Foraging parties were quickly deployed, with Percy's section locating some ancient cisterns up in the hills. Chugger dismounted and pulled up the leather bucket, which had hung in the well for years, perhaps decades. A quick taste proved the water to be good and clean, and it was possible to water the horses using the canvass buckets that each man carried.

On the 20th the troops were woken by the rumbling of artillery in the distance as the Royal Artillery gunners pounded Jebell Ekteif and Talat-Ed-Dumm, to the north, prior to the infantry assault.

They waited for a few hours, giving their horses a longer rest and feeding time, before pushing on another two miles toward Muntar, recently taken by the infantry. There they paused again, drawing rations under a sky that was beginning to darken with dusk. The night was now their enemy. The cliffs loomed like sentinels, and the track narrowed further, forcing movement in half sections. Every echo felt like a threat.

"You've got to admire old Joshua when he attacked Jericho," whispered Boggy, "it's hard enough for us *now*, let alone thousands of years ago".

He wasn't wrong. The terrain was perfect for an ambush - tight gullies, blind corners, and high ground everywhere. If the Turks had left a rear guard, they would have had the advantage. But luck held. With information being received of the existence of another track further south, the 1st Brigade pushed along it, reaching the east side of Nebi Musa before daylight on the 21st. The New Zealand Mounted Rifle Brigade had also pushed on during the night from the west side of Nebi Musa and found it deserted. The plan had been for the 3rd Light Horse Regiment to attack Nebi Musa from the east, with the 2nd giving them protection, but the vacant Nebi Musa changed things. The most northerly troops, a patrol of the 3rd Light Horse Regiment and 'C' Squadron of the 2nd Light Horse pushed into Jericho together, entering the town just after first light.

Jericho lay quiet beneath the dawn, its ancient stones catching the first gold of morning. The air was still, heavy with history. Crumbling walls and date palms whispered of centuries past - of prophets and conquerors, of blood and belief. Percy felt it as they rode in; the weight of time pressing down, as if the town itself remembered every footfall.

The streets were narrow and crooked, lined with low buildings of sunbaked mud and stone. A few goats wandered, indifferent to the war. The silence was eerie, not the silence of peace but of something waiting.

Boggy looked around.

"This place smells like ghosts".

Chugger snorted.

"More like shit".

Percy dismounted near a half collapsed archway, brushing dust from his sleeve. He glanced at the others - tired, wary, eyes searching every rooftop and every window. They were soldiers, yes, but also intruders in a place older than memory.

CHAPTER 2

The Ground Was Not Yet Quiet

The Wadi Kelt was running strong - its waters fast and brown from recent rains, carving through the gorge like a blade. The regiment briefly watered there, horses plunging their muzzles deep, flanks heaving from the morning's march. The men drank too, grateful for the coolness, even if it tasted of silt and stone.

From there, patrols were pushed out - north to Wadi Obeideh, four miles beyond Jericho, and eastward to the Jordan. The land flattened as they neared the valley floor, but the danger didn't ease. Every rise could hide a rifle, every shadow a sniper. The regiment took up the outpost line from El Ghoraniyeh to the mouth of Aujah - a stretch of roughly eight miles, exposed and tense.

Aujah, or Wadi Auja, twisted through the land like a snake, descending from the highlands to spill into the Jordan River. The stream carved a deep gorge in places, flanked by cliffs and dotted with ancient aqueducts and crumbling stonework from

25

long-dead empires. It was ambush country - quiet, deceptive, and steeped in history. The mouth of the wadi, where it met the Jordan, was a natural choke point. If the Turks were going to dig in, this was the place.

Daylight patrols under Captain McLean and Lieutenant King made contact with the enemy - brief, sharp exchanges that left no doubt that the Turks were watching.

Sergeant Schmidt and Percy took out a joint patrol to the Jordan, tasked with investigating enemy guns rumoured to be hidden near the river. They dismounted near a stand of tamarisk and left the horses with the rest of the patrol, then moved forward on foot - just the two of them, low and quiet, the river to their left and the scrub brittle underfoot.

They didn't speak. Percy crouched behind a low rise, surveying the bridgehead through his binoculars. The enemy position was well laid out - sandbags, wire, and a dug-in line that spoke of preparation, not panic.

Schmidt watched the horizon, rifle resting across his knees. He gave a low whistle - not alarm, just a nudge. Time was ticking on.

Percy pulled out his note book and pencil, writing with a steady but quick hand. There were no artillery pieces. He marked the trench lines, the angle of the riverbank. No flourishes, just the facts; enough for command to see what they were up against.

He tucked his note book into his tunic pocket and the two men slipped back the way they had come, careful not to leave tracks. The sun hung low in the sky, its light spilling thin across the valley. There may have been no guns, but the bridgehead was strong, and they had seen all they needed to see.

Back at the horses, Schmidt gave Percy a look - half approval, half weariness.

"Nice and fast drawing there mate," he said.

Percy shrugged, brushing dust from his sleeve.

"Well...I didn't fancy staying for tea".

Schmidt snorted, mounted up, and turned his horse toward the outpost line. Percy followed, the sketch safe in his tunic, the river fading behind them.

On the 22nd, the 2nd Light Horse Regiment established new outposts along the forward line - bare ridges with little cover, chosen more for necessity than comfort. The ground was hard, the wind sharp, and the enemy watchful. By midday, the shelling began. Sporadic at first, then deliberate. The posts were bracketed with shrapnel and high explosive, forcing the men to lie low and wait out the storm

At 1800 hours, with the light fading and the shelling still probing, the regiment withdrew. Orders came down for the Brigade to begin their return to Bethlehem once darkness fell. They moved out in silence, horses strung in single file, the column stretching long and thin across the valley floor.

It was a miserable night. Cold crept in early, settling into the joints and lungs. The wind came off the Judean hills like a knife, and the path was rough - rocky, uneven, and rugged. Men wrapped scarves over their mouths, pulled tunics tight, and rode with heads bowed. There was no singing, no chatter. Just the sound of hooves, the occasional stumble, and the low murmur of orders passed down the line.

Percy rode near the centre, his horse limping slightly, breath steaming in the dark. He could hear Chugger somewhere behind him, whispering something to his horse, coaxing it forward.

They reached their bivouac area near Bethlehem at 0430 hours, the sky just beginning to pale. The men dismounted stiffly, legs numb, faces drawn. There was no ceremony - just the quiet relief of arrival and the ache of endurance.

The regiment had suffered no casualties in the operation, but the horses told a different story.

Two had been killed outright. Four were wounded - shrapnel mostly. Three had died from exhaustion, collapsing on the trail and never rising, and seventy nine were lame or too spent to stand. The farriers moved among them like field surgeons, assessing, tending, and deciding.

Percy stood beside his horse, stroking its neck, feeling the tremble beneath the skin. Sandy had carried him through the shelling, through the night, and now he stood with his head bowed and eyes dull.

"Good lad," he whispered, "you did well mate".

Nearby, the quartermaster was counting prisoners - thirty-seven in total, young and cold, their faces blank with fatigue. One of them looked up at Percy and nodded, just once. Percy nodded back.

There was no triumph in it. Just survival.

On the 24th the regiment was granted a rare reprieve. Each man was given leave to sightsee in Bethlehem and Jerusalem - no orders, no patrols, just a few hours to walk where history had walked.

Percy, Chugger, Davo, Boggy, Rachel, and Alfie set out together, walking the ancient roads and pathways, the dust of the valley still clinging to them. Alfie rode high, taking turns on Percy's and Chugger's shoulders, his small hands gripping their collars, eyes bright with the kind of wonder only children carry.

They started in Bethlehem, where the Church of the Nativity stood solemn on the site where Jesus was born. Boggy immediately noticed a wrought iron chain wrapped around the handles of the small wooden door, and secured with a rusty padlock.

"No room at the inn again I see".

It was indeed strange to see a locked church, but the priests had resorted to this under Turkish occupation due to theft and vandalism.

The friends moved on, naturally disappointed.

Later, in Jerusalem, Rachel guided them through the old city. She wasn't from here, but she knew the stories, and she carried them with care.

At the Western Wall, Percy placed his hand on the stone.

"I've read about this place. It's supposed to be the last bit of the temple. I think they call it the Wailing Wall".

The group stood and watched as the locals bobbed backwards and forwards whilst they prayed, some placing handwritten messages and prayers into cracks in the stonework.

Boggy stepped forward and pressed his palm to the wall.

"It really feels...well...alive...as if it knows us".

Chugger laughed.

"You'd better watch out mate or we'll be thinking you have suddenly become religious or something".

"It's not that I don't believe...because I do...I just don't believe in the way things have been done in the past".

At the Church of the Holy Sepulchre, the group moved slowly, reverently. Alfie was now on Chugger's shoulders again, his head resting against the man's slouch hat. Inside, the air was dim and still. Candles flickered in alcoves. The men didn't speak much.

"This is Calvary, where they reckon He was crucified," said Percy.

Each of the friends paused for a moment, their thoughts and hopes of getting back home in one piece now stronger than ever.

Outside, the sun slipped low behind the domes and spires. They found a quiet hill overlooking the city. Alfie sat between Percy and Chugger now, legs stretched out, chewing on a piece of dried fig Rachel had given him.

Chugger was sketching something in the dust with a stick - a rough outline of the star in the church floor. Davo watched, silent, whilst Boggy sat with his arms around his knees, eyes on the horizon.

Percy leaned back, the ache in his legs forgotten.

"You know...this war has brought us a lot of things...but I never thought I'd see this place," he said, "all those stories and hymns; and now we've walked it, maybe even in Jesus's footsteps".

For the next two days they rode hard, the dust rising behind them like smoke from a battlefield, until at last they reached their old bivouac near Richon-Le-Zion. The place welcomed them not with a blast of trumpets, but with familiarity - a balm to men wearied by war. Each rider felt the tension ease from his shoulders, as though the land itself had reached out to cradle them. It was not just the return of their tents and long-abandoned baggage that lifted their spirits, though that too was a comfort, it was the land - God's own garden, it seemed.

The almond trees had burst into bloom, their pale petals drifting like snow across the tracks, softening the hard edges of the campaign. Orange groves stretched in orderly ranks, their fruit glowing like medals pinned to the earth. Vines, pruned with the precision of a quartermaster's ledger, marched across chocolate-brown ridges in perfect formation, as if nature itself had taken up soldiering.

The lanes were hedged and humming with birdlife, a chorus of whistles and chirps that reminded the men of spring mornings far from this foreign soil. Fields spilled over with snowdrops, their white heads nodding in the breeze, and among them bloomed flowers of such vivid colour - scarlet, yellow, purple - that even the most hardened among them paused to take in the sight. And there, rising like giants, stood the blue gums - tall, graceful, and unmistakably Australian - a whisper of home in a land that was not theirs.

Sadly, for the 9th Battalion their belated Christmas and sporting events soon, like all good things, came to an end, with the battalion departing on the 28th of February to relieve the 16th Battalion in "supports" at 'Crater Dugouts' in the 'Spoil Banks' at Hollebeke, a short distance from Hill 60. On the 1st of March they relieved the 4th Brigade on the front line, and within days, all four battalions - the 9th, 10th, 11th, and 12th – were together again at Hollebeke. Their task seemed never ending; repairing trenches, reinforcing wiring and preparing defensive positions across the British front.

The battalion eventually took its place on the "Left Front Line," positioned just north of the railway and the Ypres-Comines canal, its headquarters situated in a pill box in dead ground in Fusilier Wood.

"Here we go again lads," said Pip as 'B' Company settled into their trench.

As usual the duty rosters were arranged with at least a quarter of the company on rest, or sleep, whichever one they could manage. The CSM, along with the Q staff, ensured that there was plenty of ammunition and mills bombs at hand in the forward trenches, and more stored in saps as close to their front line as possible, for quick and easy replenishment.

By the 5th of March, the 2nd Light Horse had been reinforced - fresh men, fresh horses, though none truly fresh in spirit. War had a way of grinding down even the newest recruit. Still, with the brigade bolstered and orders in hand, they moved once more, this time toward Beitin, a hardscrabble village nestled in the hills north of Jerusalem. The dusty road wound through rocky terrain and ancient olive groves that had seen more armies than any man alive.

Three days it took, the column snaking its way through the high country, dust clinging to uniforms and the sun beating down like a hammer. The horses bore the weight with stoic grace, their hooves striking the earth in rhythm with the men's thoughts – steady and resigned.

When at last they reached destination, the brigade was ordered to hold back, forming the reserve. It was a strange kind of limbo: close enough to hear the distant crack of rifle fire, to smell the smoke curling on the wind, yet far enough to feel useless. The men waited, sharpening bayonets, checking weapons, and watching the horizon with the wary eyes of soldiers who knew that being held in reserve was no guarantee of safety - only a delay of the inevitable.

The next morning brought fresh orders, sharp and sudden as a bugle call - the regiment was to be ready to move to Tel-Asur at a moment's notice. No explanations, no promises - just readiness. A few officers were dispatched to conduct a reconnaissance of the route, their eyes checking every ridge and wadi for signs of Turkish movement, or terrain that might turn against them. Two days later, on the 10th another recce was sent out, this time toward the River Jordan and the hills that loomed beyond it. It was a clear signal - an attack was brewing.

The intelligence gathered was valuable, but not comforting. The Turks held every ford, every crossing, their positions dug in like ticks on a dog's back. The river itself was swollen with spring rains, and surged with a fury that mocked any attempt to tame it. On the 13th the regiment was ordered back to Bethlehem, where they were ordered to vanish into the olive groves like ghosts. Fires were forbidden. Movement was minimal. The troops huddled beneath the twisted branches, their breath misting in the bitter air, the rain falling in sheets that turned the ground to a mire. The Jordan and its tributaries were in full flood, and the high command's plans - so carefully drawn - were now sodden and torn.

Rachel, as usual, slept curled beside Chugger beneath a shared goatskin. She was no stranger to hardship, having followed the regiment through dust and thunder, and into battle, her presence a quiet defiance of the chaos around them. Chugger found in her a rare peace, and the love they felt for each other, and her hand in his, gave him hope for the future.

Despite the weather, despite the river's wrath, the brigade moved out under cover of darkness on the 20th, their destination the Jordan Valley. They arrived at Nebi Musa the following night at 2100 hours - a place sacred to many, believed by some to be the resting place of Moses himself. But there was no time for reverence. The engineers had failed to span the river; the floodwaters had made a mockery of their efforts.

So the regiment did what it had learned to do best...disappear. Camouflage and concealment, honed through years of desert warfare, came into its own as the lighthorsemen melted into the hollows and gullies around the monument, lying low for two days, silent and unseen. No fires. No movement. Just waiting.

Then, at last, they moved to Makhadet Hajla, where the AN-ZAC Mounted Divisional Engineers had achieved the impossible. A pontoon bridge now stretched across the Jordan - a fragile lifeline forged from timber and rope. It was the first British military bridge to span that ancient river, and though it swayed and groaned under the weight of men and horses, it held. The crossing had begun.

The 60th Infantry Division had done its work well. The bridgehead was secure, the enemy driven back across the valley in disarray. The crossing over the newly built pontoon bridge - fragile but functional - was executed with the kind of swift precision that only came from long months of hard campaigning. The men moved like water over stone, silent and efficient.

Once across, 'C' Squadron was held in reserve, their horses restless, and their eyes searching the horizon for trouble that never came. 'A' Squadron turned south, hugging the river's edge to secure Ain Sueime, while 'B' Squadron pushed east to take Salha. Both objectives were seized without resistance. The Turks, sensing that the tide had turned, withdrew rapidly into the mountains, vanishing into the folds of the terrain like smoke on the wind. Patrols from both squadrons were dispatched to intercept them, but the enemy was elusive, their retreat well rehearsed.

At 1800 hours, the troopers stumbled upon a line of Cossack posts - small fortified outposts manned by Ottoman aligned irregulars, likely remnants of Russian or Balkan auxiliaries. These posts marked the edge of the enemy's new line, hastily established and already occupied. The Cossacks, famed for their horsemanship and frontier warfare, had dug in, but they offered no challenge. They were watchers now, not fighters.

By 2100 hours, fresh orders arrived. The 2nd Light Horse was to rejoin the brigade, which had completed its river crossing earlier that day and was now several miles to the north. The men mounted up once more, weary but focussed, the night pressing in around them like a shroud.

On linking up with the brigade on the 24th the regiment relieved the 3rd Light Horse Regiment, who were holding outposts from the river to the foothills, about four miles north of the bridge, and connected with the 1st Light Horse Regiment. The next day the regiment advanced its lines about six miles in order to cover the track from Umm Es Shert to Es Salt, but during the advance the regiment found themselves on the receiving end of artillery fire as well as opposition from enemy infantry posts, but still managed to gain positions covering the road.

When the first shell came screaming in it was a high-pitched whine, rising like a banshee's cry from the distant ridgeline. The ground shuddered as it struck, throwing up a column of dirt and smoke that sent the horses into a frenzy.

"Scatter!" Percy bellowed, already wheeling his horse. "Johnno...take the horses!"

Johnno didn't hesitate. He spurred his gelding and began rounding up the section's mounts, his voice cutting through the chaos as he led them at a gallop toward a shallow gully behind the ridge, closely followed by young Alfie on his donkey. The rest of the section dismounted in a rush, boots hitting the earth hard. They moved forward on foot, rifles at the ready, ducking low and sprinting between rocks and scrub as another shell landed behind them.

Then came the crack and thump of rifle fire.

Enemy infantry, dug into scattered outposts along the ridgeline, opened up with sharp, deliberate volleys. Bullets zipped past, slapping into rocks and dirt. The Australians dropped into cover, returning fire in bursts, holding their line.

Rachel was beside Chugger, crouched behind a twisted acacia. Her rifle was steady, her eyes narrowed. She fired, adjusted, fired again. One of the enemy rifles fell silent.

"Nice shot," Chugger muttered, not taking his eyes off the ridge.

Rachel didn't reply. She was already lining up her next target.

Boggy was swearing under his breath, Davo calm and methodical, Percy shouting short commands to keep the line in order. They weren't advancing - they didn't need to. Their job was to hold, to keep the enemy from pushing down toward the track, and they were succeeding.

Smoke drifted across the valley, mingling with the dust kicked up by the shelling. Somewhere behind them, Johnno and Alfie had gotten the horses to safety. The regiment was holding their ground.

Whilst this was all going on, the 3rd Light Horse had pressed on, scrambling up the precipitous goat tracks that clung to the hillsides like veins - narrow, crumbling paths carved into the rugged terrain of Moab. By evening, they had reached Es Salt, a stone-built village nestled twenty three kilometres west of Amman. Its steep streets and Ottoman-era buildings clung to the hills, surrounded by olive groves and terraced fields. The town, once a quiet administrative centre, now echoed with the sounds of boots and hooves, the clatter of kit, and the faint thump of artillery.

Back at Percy's position, the gunfire had tapered off. The enemy had gone quiet, perhaps regrouping, perhaps retreating. Percy moved along the line, checking each man. Boggy's shoulder was bloodied but intact having been grazed by a dangerously close enemy round. Davo calmly reloaded his magazine, whilst Chugger sat with his back to a rock, Rachel beside him, her hands steady as she checked her ammunition. The adrenaline was fading, replaced by the ache of tension and the creeping cold.

"Are you right mate?" Chugger asked.

Rachel nodded and laughed at the question.

"Yes...er...mate...I am well...you?"

He gave a half-smile.

"Still breathing..."

She leaned her head against his shoulder for a moment, just long enough to feel the warmth. Around them, the section settled into the rhythm of waiting - no fires, no chatter, just the quiet click of rounds being pushed into magazines and the occasional cough.

On the 27th, the 2nd Light Horse relieved the 1st, their disposition now being 'A' Squadron held in reserve, 'B' Squadron positioned north of Dadi Ralem - a rocky outcrop overlooking the Jordan Valley, its scrub-covered slopes offering limited concealment but vital elevation - and 'C' Squadron at Umm Es Shert. There, the River Jordan twisted through the valley floor, flanked by reeds and low embankments. The crossing at Umm Es Shert was shallow but treacherous, the kind of place where horses stumbled and hooves sank deep into the silt.

The order came at first light that 'C' Squadron was to secure the high ground north of Umm Es Shert. The terrain was rough - low ridges of limestone and flint, broken by thorny scrub and dry riverbeds. The Jordan twisted below, sluggish and brown. The high ground offered a commanding view of the valley, and the Turks meant to keep it.

The squadron dismounted under cover of a shallow wadi, their horses led back to a safe position, disappearing into the folds of the terrain like mist. The lighthorsemen moved forward on foot, rifles ready, eyes on the ground to their front.

Then the world erupted.

The Turks opened fire first - wild, panicked shots that cracked overhead and kicked dust from the rocks. 'C' Squadron didn't flinch, moving up the slope in extended line, bayonets fixed, firing volleys from the hip.

Rachel drew her scimitar.

The curved blade hissed from its scabbard, catching the morning light as she raised it high and roared, "Al-mawt lakum jamee'an!" - *Death to you all!* The words reverberated across the ridge like gunfire, freezing the Turks for a heartbeat. That was all she needed as she began her sprint towards the enemy.

Just as they had at Beersheba months before, the Turks hesitated. She was a woman - armed, charging, and to some of them, a death by her hand meant no paradise. That moment of doubt cost them.

She was among them in seconds, blade flashing, slicing through cloth, flesh and bone. One man screamed as she opened his throat, the sound gurgling into silence. Another dropped his rifle and tried to run - too slow. Her sword caught him across the back, severing spine and sinew, dropping him like a sack of grain.

Chugger and Davo were beside her, bayonets punching into bellies and chests. One Turk grabbed Davo's rifle, desperate, but Davo twisted and drove the blade up under his ribs, feeling it scrape bone. Chugger shoved a man to the ground and knelt on his chest, stabbing again and again until the body stopped moving.

Percy fired twice, the rounds cracking through skull and shoulder, then clubbed a man with the butt of his rifle, the crunch of bone loud in the stillness. It was over in minutes.

The ground was littered with bodies - some twitching, most still. Blood soaked the dust, pooling in the cracks between rocks. Flies buzzed already, drawn by the heat and the carnage. A severed hand lay near Rachel's boot, fingers curled as if still grasping for a weapon.

The Australians stood among the dead, breathing hard, rifles hot, and blades dripping.

No one spoke.

Percy stepped over a corpse his eyes still on the ridge. The fight had drained from the air, leaving only the stink of blood and cordite.

He saw Rachel standing over two bodies, sword still in hand, her sleeve soaked red to the elbow. The Turks had died fast - one with a look of shock frozen on his face, another half-turned as if trying to flee.

As she spat on her fallen enemies she met Percy's gaze, and just stared.

He gave a single nod. Not approval. Not surprise. Just recognition. This beautiful, kind young woman had turned in to a killing machine...but hadn't they all?

It was hoped - foolishly, perhaps - that the Light Horse might seize Mafid Jozele. The ridge was high, flat-topped, and untamed, a slab of rock that looked down on Umm Es Shert and the Jordan crossing like a watchful sentry. From its crest, a man could see everything - the flat country stretching east to the foothills, the winding river, and the long, exposed line of mounted troops strung out like thread across a hostile canvas.

More than that, Mafid Jozele overlooked the 3rd Light Horse Regiment's lifeline - their communications, their supply routes, and their chance of reinforcement. Hold the ridge, and you held the war in that corner of the valley.

But the Turks had moved faster. They had taken the high ground, dug in deep, and reinforced it with everything they had - guns, wire, trenches. Enough to make any assault a bloodbath before the first boot touched the slope.

So the plan was shelved. There was no glory to be had on Mafid Jozele. No charge, no heroics. Just the bitter truth of good ground lost and the quiet order to hold position.

Percy stood at the edge of the bivouac, looking up at the ridge through his binoculars. He could see the glint of metal, the movement of soldiers. They were there, watching...waiting.

He lowered the binoculars and cast a glance towards Chugger.

"Thank God someone saw sense for a change eh?"

Chugger, beside him, sighed.

"It's just a bloody shame we didn't get there first...would've been a fine place to dig in".

Percy nodded.

"Right now it would be a fine place to die".

There was, if truth be told, a quiet sigh of relief among the ranks. No bugle call, no orders to mount up, no mad gallop into the teeth of Turkish guns. Just the blessed silence of common sense; rare as snow in the Jordan Valley.

Percy said little, but the look he gave Chugger spoke volumes. They had both seen enough men thrown at positions like that - good men, brave men - cut down before they had even reached the wire. This time, someone up the chain of command had looked at the map, looked at the ridge, and decided not to feed the valley with more lives just for the hell of it.

"It's a bloody miracle it is though," Chugger remarked, chewing on a bit of date-stone, "someone's finally worked out that we're not just cannon fodder".

Percy gave a dry laugh.

"Yeah...well don't get too excited about it...you might tempt fate".

Even the officers seemed different...less eager. There was a weight behind their orders now, a caution that hadn't been there at Gallipoli. As if they had learned, slowly and painfully, that courage and winning the fight wasn't just about charging. Sometimes it was about not.

Later, as they sat beneath an olive tree, it's branches gnarled like old hands, offering shade that barely softened the heat, Percy scribbled in his diary, trying to make sense of the day, whilst Chugger peeled off his boots with the solemnity of a man unburdening himself of sin, letting his feet breathe foul vengeance on the breeze.

The smell hit first. A sour, ancient thing that seemed to rise from the earth itself.

"Good God," Davo muttered, recoiling, "what died in there? A flamin' camel?"

"Two camels I reckon," Boggy said, pinching his nose, "and all of their kids".

Chugger inspected his socks, which were less garments than loose collections of holes held together by stubborn will. One heel flapped like a wounded bird, whilst his big toes protruded like a rabbit peering out of its warren.

"What are you on about?" he asked, proudly wiggling his toes. "There's plenty of wear in these beauties yet".

"I don't think it's the wear we're worried about mate," Percy replied, not looking up.

Rachel arrived just in time to catch the full bouquet. At first she didn't flinch, but simply raised an eyebrow and muttered something in Arabic that Percy suspected wasn't complimentary. Then she stopped mid-step, blinked, and took a cautious breath through her mouth.

"Chugger!" she said, with the patience of a saint and the tone of a schoolmistress, "if you do not burn those socks, I will".

"They've got sentimental value," Chugger protested, "been with me since Gallipoli".

"Then I think that they have suffered enough," she replied, turning on her heel.

Boggy leaned over to Percy.

"You reckon we could use 'em to repel the Turks?"

"Not even *they* deserve that," Percy said, still writing.

Chugger shrugged and lay back, feet to the breeze, socks flapping like bunting. The olive tree groaned above them, as if even it had limits.

"*She's* settled in well," Davo said, watching Rachel stride off toward her tent, "and she even puts up with Chugger's feet. That's *real* courage".

"Real madness more like," Boggy added, "but yeah...she's one of us now".

It was hard to believe it had only been a year since they had pulled her from the murderous mob, one of whom being her own father. She hadn't said much at first. Just sat by the fire with her arms wrapped tight around her knees, watching everything, missing nothing. But now she moved through the camp like she had always belonged. She stitched torn uniforms, rationed tea like a quartermaster, and could silence a tent full of troopers with a single look. Most importantly she had won the heart of Chugger, and he hers.

Percy glanced up from his diary as she disappeared behind the tents.

"She's a bloody good soldier too don't forget...tougher than half the regiment," he said quietly.

Chugger nodded, still inspecting his socks.

"And smarter than the other half."

Boggy grinned.

"Which half are we?"

"The fragrant half," Davo said, nudging Chugger's foot away.

"We could have done with Rachel at Gallipoli," Percy added.

"Gallipoli?!" exclaimed Boggy, "I wouldn't wish that place on my worst enemy...the Turks can bloody keep it as far as I'm concerned".

Chugger pondered for a moment.

"Quinn's Post...now that was a bastard of a place".

Davo gave a grunt.

"Yeah, you couldn't cough without someone shooting at you".

"Couldn't sleep either," Boggy added, "not with old Abdul whispering through the sandbags. Bloody close, they were. Close enough to smell their tobacco".

Percy nodded.

"I remember the dead...ours...theirs...all tangled in the wire...I hope the Turks gave them a decent burial after we left".

There was silence, then Chugger spat into the dust.

"Don't forget the orders...hold the post...no real plan...just hold it till you couldn't".

They fell quiet again, the memory thick between them.

"Difference is," Chugger said, nudging a stone with his heel, "back then, no one blinked before sending us in".

Boggy tapped his tin of bully.

"Now they're hesitating, deciding not to just throw us at the Turks without thinking".

Percy gave a dry smile.

"Well, thankfully it means someone's learning. Maybe not fast, but they're learning".

Davo looked up at the ridge.

"Yeah mate, they're seeing us as men now. Not just pieces on a chess board".

"About bloody time," Chugger muttered.

Percy leaned back, eyes half-closed.

"Quinn's Post taught *us* what it costs. Maybe Mafid Jozele is teaching *them*".

On the 28th of March, the 1st Light Horse Regiment took over the forward positions. They relieved 'C' Squadron at Umm Es Shert and assumed control of the remaining 2nd Regiment positions strung out along Wadi Ralem and the Es Salt road. It was a quiet handover, just the usual exchange of maps, whispered warnings, and the weary nods of men who had spent too long watching the same horizon.

Umm Es Shert was little more than a cluster of trenches and canvas, perched above the river crossing like a stubborn blister. Wadi Ralem twisted through the valley like a scar, dry and treacherous, while the Es Salt road climbed eastward into the hills - narrow, exposed, and always under threat.

The men of the 1st settled in quickly. They knew the drill - dig in, stay low, and keep your eyes open. The Turks wouldn't come in daylight, but they would probe at dusk, test the wire, and look for weakness. Percy watched the changeover from a rise above their newly vacated positions, noting the way the new arrivals moved - quiet, deliberate, no wasted motion. After years of warfare they were experts in soldiering and knew exactly what was required of them. Their lives depended on it.

At 1000 hours on the 28th, a sizeable Turkish column was spotted advancing across the brigade's front - marching in disciplined formation from the Jisr ed Damie crossing, eight miles upstream along the Jordan, angling eastward toward Es Salt. Their flank brushed against Wadi Ishkarara, a dry, twisting gully that offered cover and concealment. Dust rose behind them in long, deliberate plumes. It was no feint. They were coming.

The 2nd Light Horse Regiment, exposed and outpaced, was forced to fall back roughly a quarter of a mile south. The Turks had seized the high ground east of their position - an unforgiving ridge that turned the valley below into a shooting gallery. The withdrawal was orderly, but tense. Every man knew the cost of ceding elevation.

Simultaneously, 'A' Squadron was ordered forward, scrambling up the high ground to secure the head of the Es Salt road and the plateau beyond. They dug in fast, forming a second defensive line behind them. The signs were clear - the main Turkish force was swinging east, but they had left a strong rear guard, and the Australians were about to be hit...hard.

On the 29th the ANZACs attempted to retake the ground lost the day before. It was a bold push, but they were outflanked by superior numbers. The Turks had the terrain, the momentum, and the advantage. The Australians held, but only just.

Sniping continued throughout the day - sporadic, sharp, and constant. The men learned to move low and speak little. Then, at midday on the 30th the silence broke. An enemy battery opened fire from Mafid Jozele, its shells thudding into the dry earth with a sound like distant thunder. Four hours later, it fired again. The damage was minimal, but the message was clear...the Turks weren't done yet.

The plan had been to cross the Jordan, climb into the Moab hills, and take Es Salt. Not to hold Amman - just to reach it, cripple the railway, and withdraw before the Turks could regroup. Es Salt was the hinge. Perched high above the valley, it offered control of the roads and passes, and a chance to threaten the Hejaz railway - the Ottoman Empire's lifeline through Transjordan and Arabia.

General Allenby's strategy was bold. By striking east, he aimed to disrupt Turkish logistics, support the Arab Revolt, and draw enemy forces away from the coastal front. If Es Salt could be held, it would anchor future operations and shield the right flank of the British advance.

The force assembled for the task was a patchwork of grit and experience. It was known as Shea's Force. The ANZAC Mounted Division, including the 1st and 2nd Light Horse Regiments, rode alongside the Imperial Camel Corps Brigade and the British 60th (London) Infantry Division. Together, they would climb the wadis, face the guns, and try to carve a foothold in the hills.

But the Turks were waiting. They held the high ground, reinforced their ridges, and counterattacked with precision. The Australians were forced to fall back, regroup, and dig in. Es Salt was taken briefly - but the cost was steep, and the position couldn't be held.

Still, the raid had done its work. The Turks watched the east. They didn't see what was coming.

The situation was deteriorating rapidly. The main assault on Amman had stalled, with little ground gained despite repeated efforts. Turkish forces were reinforcing their positions, and pressure was mounting across the front.

In the Jordan Valley to the north, the only British unit still holding ground was the 1st Brigade, now reduced by the absence of the 3rd Light Horse Regiment, which had been detached elsewhere. This left barely five hundred men to defend a critical stretch of terrain. The 1st and 2nd Light Horse Regiments were spread thinly across a four mile front, tasked with holding a position vital to the overall campaign.

If the line were breached, it would sever communications with three divisions operating east of the Jordan River, isolating them and potentially leading to a collapse of the offensive. The strategic risk was clear to all ranks.

Veterans of Gallipoli recognised the signs. Many compared the exposed and precarious position to Quinn's Post - where thin lines, steep terrain, and constant enemy pressure had once defined survival. The parallels were unmistakable.

"We've been in this position before boys, but we must hold," said Percy.

Quinn's Post had always been a knife-edge. Perched on the steep slopes of Gallipoli, it was barely a position at all - more a scar carved into the rock, held together by sandbags, prayer, and stubbornness. A breakthrough there wouldn't have just bent the ANZAC line - it would have split it clean through, unravelled the defence, and handed the Turks a path straight to the beachhead. Defeat would have followed, swift and merciless.

But now, even the staff officers had begun to learn. The war had taught them - sometimes slowly, sometimes brutally - that maps and orders weren't enough. They saw the danger. The 1st Brigade was stretched thin, exposed, and holding by determination alone. So they acted. A battalion of infantry was sent forward, in quiet reinforcement. They took up position in the second line, about a mile and a half to the rear - where the 2nd Light Horse had already begun scraping trenches into the dry earth, preparing for the worst.

For the next twenty four hours, the front held. The Turks shelled intermittently and sniped from the ridges - but the line didn't break. It didn't bend. It simply endured.

As other NCOs and officers were doing, Percy moved along the trench where 'C' Squadron was dug in, offering reassurance and a quiet joke here and there. The men looked up as he passed - tired eyes, dust-streaked faces, hands wrapped around rifles, fingers along the trigger guard.

Carrying a battered billy, he stopped beside his section and crouched.

"Tea's up," he said, as he poured the steaming brew into any mug which was offered.

Boggy took a sip, paused, smiled and winced.

"Did you boil this in a boot or something?"

"Chugger's boot," Percy replied, "adds character".

The men chuckled, just enough to break the tension. Percy took a brief look at the horizon, then the faces. There was no panic, no bravado, just the quiet readiness of men who knew what was coming.

He moved on, offering a word here, a nod there. Reassurance didn't need speeches. It needed presence.

Behind him, the second line was filling with fresh boots and quiet orders. The defence was layered now, thin, but thoughtful, and for once, it felt like someone up the chain understood the *cost* of holding ground.

Water was scarce, so all horses had been ordered back to the watering area, roughly four miles behind the front line. Their absence was felt - not in the trenches themselves, but in the knowledge that mobility had been stripped away. If the enemy broke through now, the men would have no mounts to fall back on. Their only escape was on foot, and with Turkish cavalry known to be operating in the area, that was a terrifying prospect. No one spoke of it aloud, but the thought hung in the air like cordite - unseen, but impossible to ignore.

That evening, Percy sat with his back to the trench wall, pencil in hand, writing slowly. Around him, others did the same. Not dramatic farewells, not declarations of heroism - just quiet letters to mothers, wives, brothers. Just in case. Folded carefully, tucked into tunics, they were written not out of fear, but love. A final act of steadiness, in case the line didn't hold.

CHAPTER 3

The Ground Gave
Nothing Back

On the Western Front the first few days of March consisted of the occasional artillery barrage, but at 1600 hours on the 6th, the enemy artillery became increasingly vociferous and belligerent, with a heavy four hour bombardment of gas shells dropping around Battalion HQ and 'D' Company, in the reserve line. Clouds of poison gas filled the air, unleashing a hellish nightmare on the men trapped in the trenches, as they rolled across the battlefield - thick with the acrid sting of "Yellow Cross" (mustard gas) and the suffocating burn of "Green Cross" (chloropicrin) - the soldiers had no choice but to endure its brutal effects, as cries of "Gas! Gas! Gas!" echoed along the front line and men quickly donned their respirators. For three brutal hours, the gas lingered thick over the trenches and valley, seeping into every crevice, filling the trenches with its lethal fumes. Those who were caught without their respirators paid the price immediately. The first signs of exposure were subtle - an itching in the throat, a dry, raspy voice. But these symptoms quickly escalated.

The men began to cough violently, each hacking breath an ordeal, as their lungs fought against the poison invading them. For those unlucky enough to breathe deeply, the pain was excruciating - a burning sensation in the chest, as though their very lungs were being scorched. The mustard gas, with its blinding yellow vapour, caused skin blisters that erupted painfully in seconds, while the chloropicrin attacked their eyes, leaving them streaming and burning, unable to see through the blur of agony. The battalion headquarters and 'D' Company were hit hard, and this is where an error in the siting of HQ and the reserves became apparent. With no wind the poisonous fumes hovered around in the low lying dead ground, so that when the shelling ceased, and the Aussies were given the all clear to remove their respirators, most of them were gassed. Men staggered, unable to escape its clutches, their eyes red and swollen, and their breath coming in strangled gasps. The most horrific effect was the sense of suffocation that followed. The phosgene and diphenyl chlorarsine worked quickly, causing swelling in the airways, suffocating men slowly as they gasped for air that became more and more toxic with each passing second. Their once strong bodies trembled from the strain, and the sound of their desperate coughing filled the trench. One hundred and fifty men, almost all of 'D' Company, the Commanding Officer and eleven officers had to be evacuated, with Lieutenants Bryson and Warneminde, and Private Spratt, dying a few days later. All who were gassed were also burned by splashes of the toxic liquid. HQ had to relocate to a deep tunnel in Railway Trench, while 'D' Company of the 9th Battalion was quickly replaced by 'D' Company from the 11th.

The Division Gas Officers quickly cleared the dugouts and pill boxes of gas and placed the area out of bounds, but the next day at around 1100 hours the enemy resumed their chemical attack but their effort was wasted, falling on the abandoned ground.

Further evacuations followed over the next few days as more men succumbed to the effects of gas poisoning. On the 8th of March, the 9th Battalion, or what remained of them, was finally relieved by the 11th, withdrawing to Tournai Camp a few miles south of Dickebusch, where they remained for the next two weeks.

There being only so much military training that could be carried out, the men *really* did have a proper rest period for a change.

"Bloody hell, what's going on?" asked Clancy.

"What's up now?" replied an inquisitive Roo.

"Well...there's quiet...and there's flamin' quiet mate," said Clancy.

Pip, who had been having a doze, slowly raised the brim of his hat.

"After all these years I reckon we deserve *some* time off".

"You're right mate," replied Archie, "I don't think we've ever had a *real* break...you know...apart from sports days and such like".

A look of satisfaction suddenly appeared on Clancy's face.

"Perhaps old Fritz really has given up the ghost eh?"

Clancy's hopes were wishful thinking, for on the 21st of March the Germans unleashed a huge artillery bombardment along the French occupied front in Picardy, as well as on the front lines of the British 3rd and 5th Armies. This was followed in less than a week by Ludendorf's mighty offensive. Infantry in their thousands launched a huge onslaught, resulting in almost all of the territory captured over the previous eighteen months, since the Somme offensive in the summer of 1916, being retaken. Indeed, on the first day of the attack over sixteen thousand allied soldiers had been taken prisoner. Their aim was to drive a wedge between the British and French forces, intending to crush the British first before turning their full might on the French. With Russia now out of the war, German commanders saw an opportunity. Divisions freed from the Eastern Front were redirected west, but time was against them. The rapid arrival of American troops in Europe threatened to tip the balance of power decisively in the Allies' favour. The Germans knew they had to act swiftly.

The anticipated German Spring Offensive had begun.

"Here we go again!" said Clancy.

The thunderous artillery explosions could be heard for miles around.

The boys from the 9th, now knowing that the enemy had not packed up and gone home, were again despatched to Hollebeke, where they relieved the 11th Battalion. They quickly established their positions and began improving defences where they could.

As Pip filled sandbags, he sang a quiet tune, just loud enough for those nearby to catch a few words.

"Old soldiers never die," then he paused, a wide grin stretching over his faced, as he winked at Roo, "...the young ones wish they would".

Roo, glancing over at him, gave a wry smile.

"Well, I'm glad I'm not old, then, eh?"

Pip laughed to himself and went back to his task. Then, as if to change the subject, he muttered, "When do you reckon the Yanks will show up? They declared war on the Germans back in April last year, but not a sign of them yet".

Roo shrugged, his expression a mix of impatience and disbelief.

"Bloody politicians I reckon. Hopefully they are using the time to train their blokes up before they come".

Pip glanced over at him, taking a drink from his water bottle.

"I hope so mate, but you'd have thought they'd have sent instructors over to learn our new tactics wouldn't yer lar?"

"Like I said...bloody politicians mate," replied Roo.

The Americans had indeed finally entered the war back in 1917, landing their first troops in France around June. But it wasn't until late October that they actually saw any action, and even then, it was only a small effort by a few regular soldiers near Nancy. For the most part, they hadn't done much yet - but their presence was growing.

The boys continued their digging and filling of sandbags, but no sooner had they taken over the 11th's positions that the CSM arrived with Lieutenant Dearden.

Clancy proudly eyed his mates up and down.

"These are the blokes I was telling you about sir. Salt of the earth the lot of 'em," Clancy announced.

Archie looked over to Roo.

"Sounds like trouble is coming".

"G'day fellas," said the officer, "the CSM here tells me that you blokes might want to accompany me on a patrol...apparently you're bored".

"Bored? No mate, I think the Sergeant Major is mixing us up with someone else...himself! But yeah, we might be interested," said Stowie as he cast a glance at his mates, "what do you blokes reckon?"

The group nodded more or less in unison.

"Yeah we're up for it sir," replied Roo, "anything to break the monotony".

"Good man!" said a relieved Lieutenant Dearden as he eyed the group up and down, "I see some of you are original 9th Battalion men...Gallipoli veterans".

Archie smiled.

"That we are sir. We *do* have a few bloody new chums, but they'll do".

It transpired that the Lieutenant was to lead a small patrol out into no man's land in a few days, so the boys had ample time to be briefed, stock up on ammo and bombs, and have a sleep or two.

At approximately 0216 hours on the morning of the 26th, under a sky as black as a gun barrel, and just as cold, a small six man patrol clambered out over the parapet of an outpost known as 'Potsdam Group' and vanished into the night. Lieutenant Dearden led the way, followed closely by Roo, Archie, Stowie, Ten Bob, and Pip - each man bent low, footsteps muffled in the churned up mud, breath steaming in the bitter air.

The night had been chosen carefully - moonless and thick with cloud - perfect for creeping unseen across no man's land, though it offered no comfort to the men. They moved by feel and instinct, threading through the ruin of war, twisted coils of rusting barbed wire, duckboards splintered by shellfire, and the husks of dead men and shattered equipment frozen into the mud like macabre signposts.

Not a word was spoken. They knew the routine, each man watching the ground ahead while listening for the faintest sound - an enemy cough, a click of a bolt, the whisper of movement in the dark. A careless step could mean a flare, or worse, a burst of machine gun fire. But these men were veterans and they moved like shadows - ghosts amid the graveyard of war.

After around fifteen minutes the Lieutenant signalled the group to halt and temporarily shelter in a shell crater, where he quickly briefed his men.

"Righto men, I need Sergeant Taylor, Corporal Stowe and Private Bartholomew to act as a covering group and remain here. Myself, Kropp and Sergeant Taylor will carry on towards the 'Wet Pond' just over yonder".

Archie and Roo looked at each other for a moment before Roo asked the obvious question.

"Er...sir?" Which Sergeant Taylor is coming with you...the black fella or the white fella?"

The officer laughed quietly, realising his mistake.

"Sorry Roo, you come with me, and Archie commands the rear defensive party".

"Roo's the best scout anyway sir," Stowie added, with quiet groans of agreement coming from the other men.

Both groups checked their weapons before quietly wishing each other good luck.

"See ya later mate," Archie whispered, as he shook Roo's hand.

"You will if I smile...its bloody dark you know," Replied Roo.

"Who said that?" remarked Stowie as he pretended to search in the dark for his mate.

"Bugger off you bludger," Roo laughed quietly as he, Ten Bob and the officer climbed out of the hole.

As the scouting party moved off into the darkness, Archie arranged himself and his two mates in to an all round defence formation on the crater's edge. They moved without a word, settling into their positions like the old hands that they were, eyes searching the blackness, rifles held loosely in their shoulders, but ready. Again they had decided on the password *Waltzing Matilda* just in case any Germans made an attempt to infiltrate their line.

Being only the first month of spring, the night was chilly and the air still bit with winter's teeth. But at least there was no snow - Mother Nature had, for once, been kind this year.

"We could do with some fog or mist," Roo thought to himself as he led the small group in the direction of 'Wet Pond".

The patrol moved with great stealth, almost ghost like, hardly making a sound, the mud swallowing the noise of their feet. They were phantoms in the night, slipping between shell holes and broken wire with the silence of seasoned soldiers; which is more than could be said for the Germans this night.

Up ahead, a crunch, then another. Roo suddenly halted, raised his right hand and, as one, the three men sank slowly to their knees, motionless.

"What is it sarge?" the Lieutenant whispered.

"About a hundred yards to our front sir...can you hear it? About twenty or so pairs of boots...I think they're coming this way," Roo replied.

Ten Bob fumbled silently in his satchel and pulled free his battered binoculars, pressing them to his face. As he squinted to see in the blackness of the night, he could just make out at least twenty silhouettes moving slowly towards them.

"You're right mate," he whispered, "a platoon I think...*and* they're definitely coming this way".

Lieutenant Dearden was quick to react.

"Right boys, quick smartish; let's bugger off back to the others".

Slowly the three men crept back along what seemed an endless expanse, towards the crater where Archie and their mates waited, retracing their path with agonising caution, every nerve as taut as a bowstring. As they moved, Ten Bob kept an eye to their rear, monitoring the Germans' direction of travel. But the enemy soldiers were still following; whether intentional or not they were on a collision course with six determined Aussie veterans.

Roo, like a homing pigeon, brought the three men to within five yards of the shell crater, where he halted the group and raised his rifle above his head - a dark silhouette against a darker sky.

"Waltzing Matilda," he whispered as loudly as tactically possible.

In reply came a cheeky whisper from Stowie.

"Alright...alright...no need to shout...how many in your party?"

"Three," came the response.

"Advance one and be recognised," said Stowie.

As the three men moved individually towards the crater they were counted in, and welcomed with silent appreciation as they dropped one by one into the hole.

Archie immediately turned to the Lieutenant.

"So...what's the news skip?"

Lieutenant Dearden informed the men about the enemy platoon, and quickly organised them in to a defensive line along the top of the hole.

That was all the men needed to hear. Instinct took over as they quickly shifted into their defensive positions along the crater's edge, rifles braced, and eyes watching the black horizon. No panic. Just quiet, steady preparation; the calm of men who had been here before and knew exactly what they had to do.

"Ten Bob, Pip and Stowie, get ready with your bombs, Taylors...ready your weapons, we'll let them get about ten yards in...what do you reckon?" whispered Dearden.

"Fine by me sir," Archie answered.

As the German boots continued to trudge noisily towards them, Stowie was becoming impatient and began slowly easing the pin from his Mills Bomb, as he tightly gripped its handle.

Roo glanced across.

"Mate you'd better hold that firm or we're *all* for it".

Realising his predicament, not even the cold wind could prevent a bead of sweat from rolling off Stowie's forehead.

"Hurry up you bastards," Stowie thought to himself, resisting the urge to scream the words out loud.

The enemy kept coming...closer...closer...then the challenge from Lieutenant Dearden.

"HALT! WHO GOES THERE?"

The enemy soldiers, momentarily surprised, paused but said nothing.

"That'll do for me...eat this yer bastards!" Stowie shouted as he launched his impatient grenade in their direction, the handle making a pinging sound as it sprang left, bouncing off Roo's helmet.

Roo flinched at the handle, as Stowie shouted "GRENADE!"

The Aussies then sent death, in the form of .303 rounds, into the night.

Cries of pain echoed in the darkness as two enemy stick grenades landed a few feet to the front of the shell hole.

"DUCK!" Archie shouted, as the six Aussies instinctively dropped down into the hole and pulled the rim of their steel helmets down over their eyes.

Two pathetic sounding explosions rocked the ground above them, followed by silence.

Roo quickly peered over the top of the crater, and then dropped back out of sight just as fast.

"What's happening mate?" asked Archie.

"I think they've legged it Arch," replied Roo.

The six men clambered to the rim of the hole and strained their eyes to see into the night.

"You're right sergeant," said a relieved Lieutenant Dearden.

The men were stunned. One grenade and they retreated? This wasn't like the German soldier that they knew and respected.

"What the?!" Stowie whispered.

"Ssssh!" Lieutenant Dearden interrupted, "can you blokes hear that?"

The men listened intently and eventually heard it too; groans and whimpering a few yards to the front of their position.

"Who wants to check it out?" the officer asked.

Ten Bob immediately spoke up.

"I'll go sir".

"Me too," said Pip.

"Good men," replied a grateful Lieutenant Dearden, "the rest of us will cover you".

As Ten Bob and Pip dragged themselves out of the crater, Pip turned to Stowie then glanced at his own backside and winked.

"Yeah, yeah...don't shoot you in the ass, I know," Stowie whispered.

"Ass?" laughed Pip, "have you got a donkey there or something mate?"

The sounds of pain became louder as the two men crawled forward. Eventually they came upon a wounded German officer. He had been peppered by Stowie's grenade and had shrapnel wounds over most of his front, although not apparently life threatening. The officer was alone, lying on his back and was grateful to see the two men.

"Englander?" he asked.

"No mate...Aussies...Australia," replied Ten Bob, "where are your men, sir?"

The officer rolled his eyes and turned his head slowly to the direction in which his soldiers had fled. They were inexperienced troops being taught the ropes. Fear had gotten the better of them and they had run off, forgetting their wounded comrade.

"Come on sir, let's get you to the doc," said Pip, as he and Ten Bob dragged him to his feet, and linked their hands and arms to form a seat on which to carry the wounded man.

Upon reaching the crater they gently passed the officer down to their mates.

"His mates scarpered and left their officer," said Pip.

The Aussies couldn't believe it. Neither they, nor the enemy that they thought they knew, would ever do such a thing; at least not intentionally.

"The bastards!" exclaimed Archie.

As he searched the German's pockets for any intelligence paperwork and maps, Lieutenant Dearden cast a glance on Ten Bob and Pip.

"Can you blokes take him back to 'Potsdam Group' and then come back here?"

"Yeah...no worries sir," replied Ten Bob.

The two men returned forty five minutes later, re-appearing out of the darkness, covered in mud and breathing hard. No words were exchanged - just a nod from Roo, and the patrol moved off again, this time cutting through the shallow, stinking stretch known as 'Wet Pond', their feet squelching in mud and slime that reeked of rot and old blood, and on to 'Hessian Wood', a twisted patch of splintered trees and shadowed menace.

On reaching the wood the silence was shattered when a sudden burst of machine gun fire, a stuttering roar of death, preceded an assault from their rear by a party of thirty enemy soldiers. The 9th Battalion men quickly turned and engaged their attackers. Muzzle flashes lit up the trees in harsh white bursts, and for a moment, the wood became a battlefield illuminated by gunfire and stoked by the fires of hell. Grenades came next - half a dozen of them arcing through the dark like spinning fire-flies, hitting the ground with hollow thuds. Despite immediately dropping to the ground, all six Aussies were hit by shrapnel from the bombs, which had landed just close enough to inflict minor wounds.

Ten Bob, however, did not get off so lightly, being knocked flat on his face by at least four enemy rounds which had hit him squarely in the chest, erupting in a spray of blood and bone. Poor Ten Bob, Private Jeremy Kropp, from Toogoolawah, was dead before he hit the ground, his arms splayed like a broken doll, a dark pool already spreading beneath him.

Although wounded and bloodied, the remaining Aussies held their ground and returned fire, rifles cracking in reply as they spat curses through gritted teeth. Somewhere amid the smoke and chaos, the Germans began to falter - why, no one could say. Perhaps they thought the Australians had reserves tucked in behind the tree line, or maybe the weight of return fire made them second guess the strength of the patrol. Either way, the enemy began to melt back, slipping into a line of shell craters a dozen yards off, dark figures ducking low and vanishing into the pockmarked earth.

Observing this, Lieutenant Dearden quickly seized the moment and ordered his men to pull back to their own lines. The men didn't need telling twice. At this point Ten Bob's fate was not apparent, but as Roo turned to scramble, he paused just long enough to thump Ten Bob on the shoulder.

"Come on, mate...we're off!"

But Ten Bob didn't move.

Roo frowned. The lad was lying prone, just as he had been during the fire fight, one hand still clutching his rifle. Roo leaned down and gave him a rough shake...nothing.

Then he grabbed hold of Ten Bob's webbing straps and lifted him off the ground, but the body came easily; far too easily. He was lifeless, like a rag doll. Arms flopped loose. Head lolled to one side. The warmth had already begun to slip from him.

Roo stared into the young face of his mate, the knockabout kid with the slow grin and a heart as big as Queensland. His tunic was soaked through across the chest, the wool dark and shiny where the enemy rounds had punched through. No cry, no warning. He had died silently, still facing the enemy.

Roo's voice cracked as he bellowed, "Ten Bob's dead! Ten Bob's gone!"

Even as the words left his mouth, the air lit up again - bright, angry flashes tearing open the night as German rounds began to search for them in the darkness, sweeping the woods, stitching the earth with angry hisses and whines. Dirt kicked up all around them.

"Move!" someone shouted.

"Roo...get his pay book...we'll have to leave him," Lieutenant Dearden shouted.

The enemy rounds were now bursting and flying over their heads like a swarm of blow flies.

Roo quickly reached into his young mate's breast pocket and retrieved the document, also managing to take one of his identity discs.

He then placed his hand on Ten Bob's cold forehead, and his eyes welled up.

"God bless you mate," he whispered, as he stood up and joined the others as they made their perilous dash across no man's land, each man casting a rearward glance towards their mate's lifeless body.

All in all the six men had been attacked by fifty or so Germans, proving that they *were* still there and, for the most part, willing to engage. As for their wounds, they were minor, but enough to send them to the Regimental Aid Post (RAP) in the rear.

In the mean time a twenty man patrol, led by Lieutenant Sargent, was sent out at 0530 hours, this time with a Lewis Gun. The morning was damp and grey, the air heavy with smoke and the smell of wet earth. The men moved cautiously, spread out in short bounds, bayonets fixed. Pretty soon they *also* made contact with the enemy who again fled when fired upon. Sargent, unwilling to let them go that easily, pushed forward in a fire and move advance, leapfrogging forward, laying down covering fire as they went. Their fire was accurate and cut down several of the retreating figures, driving the rest through the wire. Pressing on through broken ground and shattered timber, they found themselves facing a strongpoint - low, squat pillboxes set deep in the embankment ahead. The enemy survivors darted into the openings, slamming shut the iron doors. Realising the position was far stronger than first thought, and not willing to sacrifice his patrol on a futile charge, Sargent gave the order to withdraw.

This move obviously injected a new feeling of bravery into the Germans, as they flooded out of the pill boxes and poured fire on the Aussies, courtesy of two machine guns. The chatter of the guns was instant and savage. Bullets tore through the mist and the brittle stumps around them. Four of the ANZACs dropped where they stood, lifeless in the mud. Two more were hit, crawling to cover with blood running from their legs and sides.

The patrol was pinned down, daylight creeping higher by the minute. To add to their woes, their own machine gun was brought to bear but had jammed almost immediately, the drum magazine slipping awkwardly as the gunner tried to clear it. It was inoperable and there was no time to fix it. The men pressed themselves into shell holes, trying to disappear into the earth.

The sun was rising now, spilling pale light over the muddy wasteland. The enemy gunners adjusted their sights and swept the craters with methodical precision.

By now, part of the patrol had managed to escape, retiring to the Aussie lines at around 0900 hours, crawling from crater to crater until they reached the safety of their own wire. Lieutenant Sargent, still out among the dead and wounded, took his chances later, through a combination of rolling and crawling, a slow, painful path back through the shell swept ground. He reached the line after midday, exhausted, bloodied, his uniform ripped, the side of his helmet dented. He flopped into the trench without a word and just sat there for a while, breathing hard. Clancy appeared beside him with a canteen.

He handed it over in silence and sat with him for a moment, both of them staring at nothing.

That evening, under the cover of artillery fire, a rescue party was sent out to recover the wounded. They found both men alive and got them onto stretchers, but the rescue came at a cost. Two of the party were shot and killed in the effort.

When they returned, one of the younger diggers sat heavily against the parapet, pulling off his helmet.

"Well," he muttered, lighting a bent cigarette with shaking hands, "that went bloody well. Next time, maybe we should bring a tank".

No one laughed. But no one argued either.

It had been a bad day for the 9th Battalion and for 'B' Company in particular - a patrol gone wrong, seven good men lost and little gained.

The battalion spent a further eleven days in the line, and when Archie, Roo, Stowie and Pip returned from the RAP, 'B' Company were resting in the reserve trench. Clancy and Freddy, trying to hide their sadness for the loss of Ten Bob, welcomed the four men with the usual smiles and humour.

"G'day yer bastards and...oh...alright Pip?" laughed Clancy.

The light heartedness was momentarily lost on the men.

"Yeah mate, we're good. They didn't get all the shrapnel out but they did their best," said Archie.

"Crikey! You blokes will be clanking like loose change then won't yer..." Clancy joked.

Captain Ponsonby coughed and cleared his throat.

"It was a shame about Ten Bob boys. I'm so sorry".

Roo looked towards the captain and smiled a reassuring smile.

"It's not your fault Freddy. It's just this bloody war".

"I liked Ten Bob," Pip added, "was he with you from the start?"

"No mate... he joined as a Fair Dinkum after Gallipoli," replied Archie.

Roo laughed.

"Remember how keen he was to get stuck in to the Turks?"

"Ha! Yeah mate. He saved us ten shillings I recall," added Clancy.

"Ten shillings? How?" asked Pip.

"Well mate, he was so up himself with how he was going to do this and that to the enemy...you know...anyway, Roo and me we made a bet see...ten shillings if he either pissed or shit himself in his first battle," Clancy explained.

"Yeah? Who won?" asked Pip.

"Neither of us mate," replied Roo.

"What, so he did well then?" asked Pip.

"Yeah...I suppose he did...eventually anyway," said Clancy, "but he reacted in both ways...if you know what I mean, so he sort of cancelled out the bet".

"But he got a good nick name out of it eh?" said Archie.

The men had a brief chuckle and smile as they thought about their fallen mate.

"He turned out to be a bloody good soldier though eh?" Ponsonby added, "As have all of you".

Clancy's eyes and ears pricked up.

"You almost sounded Aussie then skip..."

"Yes...I suppose I did," replied Ponsonby, "I shall be writing to Kropp's family later if any of you have anything to write and put in the envelope".

"Thanks sir, I'll definitely do that," said Stowie.

"I wish we could have brought him back in with us though," said Roo.

"Yeah, I hate to say it but that barrage later on has probably seen him lost forever now," said Archie.

The small band of mates nodded in unison, thoughts of lost mates over the years, and the sadness for their loved ones at home.

Heavy fighting continued. It was almost as if the Germans were reminding them that they hadn't gone anywhere, and were still a force to be reckoned with.

The entire 3rd Brigade was replaced by British troops on the 3rd of April. Relief for the battalion finally arriving in the guise of the Royal Scots and Cameron Highlanders. The Aussies were happy to see the jocks who had been fighting further south and had only just been relieved themselves.

Despite the exhaustion on both sides, the handover was marked with the usual dry humour and mutual respect that passed between seasoned men of different regiments and nations.

"About time you showed up," Roo joked, squinting at a kilted figure trudging through the mud.

"Aye," the Scotsman replied, eyeing Roo's mud splattered tunic, "an' by the smell o' ye, we should've come yesterday".

One of the Highlanders gave a cheeky whistle as he looked over the battered trench line.

"Is this what passes for luxury up here then? We were told the Aussies lived like kings".

"Kings of the bloody shit heap," Stowie replied, tossing a biscuit tin to one of the Scots.

The Scot caught it, pried it open, sniffed, and recoiled theatrically.

"Is this food or a new form o' trench gas?"

"I'd say enjoy, but I'd be lying," Stowie grinned.

Another pair - one young digger and a wiry redheaded Highlander - were exchanging smokes and stories already, swapping tales of rations, rat infestations, and unreliable staff officers.

As Roo and the others gathered up their equipment, one of the Scotsmen slapped Roo on the shoulder.

"Left a bit o' Fritz for us, eh?"

Roo grinned and nodded.

"Wouldn't dream of hoggin' him. All yours mate," Roo replied as he shook the soldier's hand.

The handover complete, the weary Australians shouldered their rifles and began the long, slow crawl to the rear. The trenches were clogged with movement - Royal Scots and Cameron Highlanders filing in, fresh faced replacements nodding nervously to the sunken eyed diggers squeezing past them. Pipes and rifles clattered against trench walls, hob nailed boots slipped in the ankle deep mud, and whispered orders echoed uselessly in the confusion.

"Keep to the left lads!" someone called out up ahead, as a train of stretcher bearers tried to force their way through.

"Left, he says. There's barely room to scratch my backside, let alone march," muttered Clancy, who had somehow wedged himself between a bundle of duckboards and a Highlander with a moustache like a handle bar.

Pip stumbled over a discarded helmet and caught himself on Roo's shoulder.

"Bloody trench is narrower than a nun's confession," he joked.

As they shuffled forward, a pungent waft of stagnant water and pipe smoke drifted back through the line.

"Smells like someone's boiled a goat," Stowie said, wrinkling his nose.

The men laughed - quiet, tired laughs - but it eased the tension as they squeezed through a narrow sap choked with broken duckboards and coils of rusted wire.

At last, they emerged into a communication trench that widened slightly and wound like a snake toward the rear. The sounds of artillery were more distant now, though still ever present; a dull rumble, like the growl of an angry god just over the horizon.

Once clear of the trenches the battalion formed up in companies and began the long march back to 'Spoil Bank', where they hitched a ride on a narrow gauge light railway - rattling open wagons that shunted and squealed their way south toward Murrumbidgee Camp, just outside the village of Clytte.

Clytte itself was a quiet rear area settlement, its low, red-brick cottages and timber barns crouched under the pale Belgian sky. Though the thump of faraway guns still rolled across the horizon, the farmland here remained patchy but green - fields lined with leafless trees and hedgerows, with the odd shell crater scarring the pastures like a forgotten wound.

From there, on the afternoon of the 4th, they were bundled into open-topped buses and sent further back to Caestre.

"I've never been on a bus before, let alone seen one," said Archie.

"Really?" said a surprised Pip, "there were loads in Liverpool, mind you I could never afford the bus fare, so this is my first go on one as well".

"Yeah mate its pretty remote where we come from, though we do have a train line," Roo added.

"A bloke could settle here," said Clancy, gazing out across the fields, "bit of land, couple of chooks, peace and quiet".

"You settling down, are you?" Roo grinned, "Should we send word to all the broken hearted women back home?"

The road south passed through a gently undulating landscape, dotted with broken farmsteads, half-ploughed fields, and the silhouettes of other battalions marching in long columns. Caestre itself, though brushed by the war, still clung to its rural soul - stone farmhouses, crumbling walls, and neat rows of poplars whispering in the breeze. For the weary diggers, it was the first real breath of peace they'd had in a while.

The 5th of April was another long day of travelling, this time by train. An early reveille saw the battalion on parade at 0530 hours, where they were informed that they were off to the Somme. An almost solid groan rippled through the ranks of veterans, to whom the Somme Valley held memories most would rather forget. The train departed at 0630 hours and arrived at St Roche Station at 1600 hours. St Roche was the station at Amiens.

On arrival the Battalion formed up again and marched the five miles to Argoueves, reaching their destination two hours later. There was no camp so the soldiers were billeted in the village whilst the officers were housed in an unoccupied chateau.

For some reason Battalion HQ had concluded that following the Battalion's stay in the northern trenches, the men had become "soft". News of this travelled fast.

"Soft?!" Stowie growled, "Tell that to Ten Bob!"

Clancy nodded.

"I'm with you mate...the bastards!"

"More like stupid, no good, ungrateful bastards," Roo added.

Captain Ponsonby decided to hold an impromptu OC's briefing, but the CSM and NCOs were so lost in their anger that they almost forget where they were.

The captain coughed a few times in order to bring them back to the matters at hand.

"Chaps...chaps. Whilst I agree entirely with you, the fact is that it has *been* said and that is that. For now, we shall spend our time here training...starting today".

All went quiet, for training meant only one thing...something big was coming and they were going to be in it.

CHAPTER 4

The Justice of Our Cause

In the Jordan Valley, on the 2nd of April, the word came down that the column was withdrawing. The attack on Amman had failed - ambitious in design, but undone by terrain, resistance, and the sheer weight of the Ottoman defence. Now the priority was clear...get the men out, intact, and fast.

The most obvious move for the Turks would be to strike at the Allied communications - cut the lines, sever the retreat, and trap the column in the hills. But if that *was* their plan, they were too slow. The brigade's withdrawal was swift, disciplined, and well co-ordinated. By 1400 hours, the bulk of the force had reached the valley floor, dust trailing behind them like smoke from a fire that hadn't quite caught.

At 1430, the 2nd Light Horse Regiment began its move south. They had been selected to act as rear guard - a thankless job, but one they knew well. Their task was simple; hold the line long enough for the rest to get clear, and make damn sure the Turks didn't get bold.

Enemy cavalry shadowed them from a distance, keeping pace but never closing the gap. They were cautious, respectful even. The Australians had earned that reputation the hard way.

Percy rode near the centre of the line, his eyes constantly on the horizon. Chugger was just ahead, his horse flicking its ears at the dust. Rachel had drawn up beside him, her posture calm, eyes alert beneath the brim of her hat.

"They're still watching us," Davo muttered, nodding toward the distant shapes on the rise.

"Let 'em," Boggy said, "they know better than to try anything stupid".

The officer ahead raised a hand. The column slowed, and then wheeled into an extended line across the valley floor - horses shoulder to shoulder, facing the distant enemy. Dust settled. Silence held.

"Volley fire," the officer called, "one round only...put the wind up the bastards...show them we're still here".

The men raised their rifles, aimed high toward the enemy cavalry - well out of range, but close enough to see the gesture. Rachel did the same, her fingers steady on the trigger. Chugger gave her a glance – not of surprise but more of admiration - but said nothing.

The volley cracked across the valley, rifles firing in near-perfect unison, echoing off the hills. But the Turks didn't flinch, didn't retreat. They simply stood, watching.

Percy lowered his rifle, watching them stand their ground.

"Clever bastard, Abdul," he muttered, "he knows when not to push his luck".

Chugger grinned. "So do we".

The Aussies turned their horses south and rode on, the line reforming, the silence behind them holding firm.

For the Turks, it had been a day of hesitation and missed chances. Their cavalry had shadowed the retreat but never pressed, and even their artillery - usually quick to harass a withdrawal - remained silent. Whether it was confusion, caution, or sheer fatigue, the opportunity to strike had passed them by.

By late afternoon, the entire ANZAC force had reached the Ghoraniyeh bridgehead, where the 180th Infantry Brigade held the crossing. The pontoon bridge stretched across the Jordan like a lifeline - narrow, swaying, and precious.

The lighthorsemen filed across in silence, horses stepping carefully on the timber planks, hooves thudding in rhythm. The river below was sluggish, brown and flecked with reed. On either bank, infantrymen stood watch - dusty, sunburnt, rifles at the ready, eyes alert. They had held this ground for days, repelling probes, guarding the way home.

As Percy passed, he gave a nod to a young Londoner posted at the bridgehead - barely more than a boy, helmet too large, eyes rimmed with exhaustion. The lad returned the gesture with a faint smile and a nod.

Chugger leaned sideways in his saddle, calling out just loud enough to be heard.

"Good on yer boys...thanks for keeping the door open".

One of the infantrymen gave a short laugh.

"Just don't slam it behind you..."

Rachel rode close behind, her gaze sweeping the far bank. She caught the eye of a Sikh soldier from the Indian brigade, standing tall beside a Lewis gun. He nodded once, solemnly. She returned it.

The line moved on, one squadron after another, dust rising in soft clouds. No cheering, no fuss - just the quiet satisfaction of a withdrawal made good. Behind them, the hills still held danger, but ahead lay the valley, and the promise of rest.

Sadly though, the only rest they were to have was a few hours of uninterrupted sleep - rare, precious, and gone too soon. By dawn, the 2nd Regiment, now reinforced by the 5th Light Horse, was ordered to take control of the bridgehead. The position had been divided into four equal sectors, each assigned to a regiment and its supporting units.

To Percy's quiet astonishment, the 2nd, although the smallest in number, was tasked with holding two of the four sectors. It was either an error by the brigade staff, a vote of confidence, or perhaps an act of desperation.

"They must think we're the best blokes in the brigade, eh?" Chugger muttered.

Percy gave a dry snort.

"We might be the best," he said, "but we're sure becoming less".

Their sectors, on the enemy side of the river, were flanked by the 1st Regiment on the right and the 5th on the left, with the 3rd held in reserve behind the line. The stretch was long, exposed, and perilous. With no other option, all three squadrons of the 2nd were committed to the line - no rotation, no relief.

They compensated for their thin ranks by working their hardest to improve and consolidate the position. The heat of the sun was oppressive and merciless by day, and the Turkish guns had a habit of waking at first light, so the troops worked under moonlight, shovels muffled, tools scraping against dry earth, sweat soaking through tunics.

Rachel arrived at the line like a Florence Nightingale of food, with the field kitchen mule and two steaming tins strapped to its sides...plus young Alfie in tow. The men paused as she passed - some offering nods, others too tired to speak.

"Hot stew...very good...eat," she said simply, handing a tin to Chugger, who blinked at her like she had descended from heaven.

"You're a bloody miracle mate," he murmured.

She smiled, and then moved down the trench, ladling food into mess tins, her presence a balm against the dark.

By the 10th of April, the regiment had completed its wire defences and laid a single apron - an angled stretch of barbed wire designed to catch crawling attackers before they reached the main line. It wasn't much, but it was enough, and in the days to come that apron would prove decisive.

Patrols continued to push out from the Australian lines - quiet, deliberate movements through the scrub and gullies, always under threat. Contact with enemy patrols was frequent. Sometimes it was a brief exchange of fire in the dark. Sometimes it was a glimpse of movement on a ridge, a flash of steel, a hoof print in the dust. The Turks were probing too - infantry and cavalry both - testing the edges, watching the roads.

Percy's patrol moved at first light, hugging the folds of the terrain as they crept eastward. The air was still, heavy with the scent of dry grass and dust. They were only four miles from their own lines, but it felt like another world.

Ahead lay Shunet Nimrin - a natural fortress where the Es Salt road entered the mountains. The position was formidable - steep ridges, layered trenches, and dug in artillery. The Turks had reinforced it heavily since the failed raid on Amman. Now it stood like a gate, barring any advance toward the interior.

Percy lay prone behind a low rise, checking out the defences through his binoculars. Sandbags, wire, and stone, machine gun nests tucked into the folds. A few figures moved along the parapets – disciplined and alert. He passed the binoculars to Davo, who whistled softly.

"Wouldn't want to knock on that door," he whispered.

"No," Percy replied, "but it's good to know what's behind it".

They stayed low, sketching the layout, marking gun emplacements, noting the positions of sentries. As they pulled back, they passed a pair of Turkish deserters - thin, hollow-eyed, their hands raised. The men were now their prisoners. One spoke broken Arabic, asking for water. Another simply sat down, too exhausted to stand.

Later that afternoon, another patrol brought in two more prisoners - young infantrymen, barely shaving age, captured in a dry wadi while scouting too far forward. They were quiet, resigned, and didn't resist.

The intelligence was patchy, but it was enough. Shunet Nimrin was no bluff. It was a wall, and if the Australians were to move east again, they would have to find a way around it - or through it.

The sky was still as dark as ink when Percy's section edged forward through the rocky terrain near Hut, hugging the left bank of Wadi Nimrin. It was just past 0430 hours on the morning of the 11th of April, and the air carried that brittle stillness that comes before first light. They were fourteen hundred yards ahead of the safety of the brigade's main line - too far for comfort. The silence was broken only by the soft clink of stirrups and the occasional snort from a restless horse.

Percy raised a gloved hand, halting the patrol. He had sensed something behind them and, upon turning his horse, saw the movement of far off shapes - too many for a routine scouting party. A large enemy patrol, cavalry by the looks of it, was cresting the rise to their rear, silhouetted against the faintest blush of dawn.

"Look at these cheeky buggers," Percy muttered, squinting through the haze.

Rachel, who as usual had attached herself to the patrol, instinctively drew her scimitar and pointed it menacingly in the direction of the Turks.

"We kill the bastards...yes?"

Percy turned his gaze to Rachel. Her eyes showed nothing but hatred for the enemy to their front, who were now galloping at speed towards them.

"Hold your horses...let's get a few rounds into them first before we go charging anywhere eh?" he said as he turned his attention to the advancing Turks. "Right boys...and lady...let's give them one volley, then we leg it...make it count ".

He turned back to the section, his voice rising just enough to cut through the tension.

The group raised their rifles and, as one, and sent a small hail of bullets towards the enemy, dropping three troopers in the front rank, whilst the rest spurred forward, shouting, sabres raised.

"Come on...let's get the hell out of here," Percy shouted, wheeling his horse hard, "back to the wire...now!"

The patrol turned and began galloping full tilt toward their own lines. Hooves pounded the earth, kicking up dust and stones. Turkish bullets snapped past them, some close enough to feel the air shift. One round clipped Percy's stirrup, another tore through the tail of Rachel's tunic. She didn't flinch.

The sounds of the skirmish alerted the entire Aussie front line who watched as the patrol galloped towards them. The designated entrance in the barbed wire loomed ahead - two sentries already scrambling to pull it open.

Percy's section thundered through the gap, horses dripping with sweat, lungs heaving. The wire slammed shut behind them.

They dismounted fast.

"Johnno," Percy called, his breath ragged, "you and Rachel take the horses to the rear...then get back here, quick smart".

Rachel hesitated. She was disappointed as she wanted desperately to be in the trenches killing Turks.

"Cheer up Rach," said Johnno, "the quicker we get the horses to safety the quicker we can join the others".

She gave a reluctant nod, and then turned with him toward the rear lines.

Meanwhile, word was already racing up the chain. Runners were dispatched to Brigade HQ. Something was stirring out there - something bigger than a routine patrol, and Percy's section had just lit the fuse.

The trench was quiet, but it wasn't calm. Percy crouched behind the parapet, his eyes fixed on the ground to the front. The light was beginning to shift - still grey, still soft - but enough to see movement.

"They're coming," he said.

Chugger leaned over the sandbags, squinting.

"How many do you reckon?"

Percy didn't answer.

All along the line rifles were brought to bear and murmurs passed between men like static. The 2nd Regiment was stretched thin, holding two sectors of the line, every man committed. The trenches were shallow, the wire newly laid, and the ground dry and rutted.

Rachel and Johnno came tearing back from the rear, Rachel vaulting into the trench with her rifle already in hand.

"Where?" she asked, her breath sharp.

Percy pointed toward the Wadi.

A few minutes later, shapes began to emerge - first a hundred or so, scattered along both banks of Wadi Nimrin. At first it looked like a reconnaissance in force. But as the light improved, the truth became clear.

"Stone the crows," Chugger exclaimed, "there's thousands of the bastards".

Two thousand, to be exact, spread across a frontage of six hundred yards, their centre anchored on the Wadi. They moved in waves, extended formation, using the semi-darkness and natural cover to their advantage. Near road number 5, they reached to within a hundred yards of the brigade wire.

Percy's section held their fire. Their orders were clear - don't give away the regiment's strength too early. The Turks didn't know the wire was complete. They didn't know the Australians were fully dug in.

Then the order came.

The trench erupted. Aussie machine guns and Hotchkiss rifles opened up along the whole front, stitching the valley with fire. The first wave staggered, broke, fell. The second hesitated. The third tried to press forward and was shredded.

At 0550 hours, artillery joined the chorus. The 60 pounders and field batteries found their range quickly - shells arcing overhead, landing with brutal precision. The fall of shot was devastating - geysers of earth, bodies flung skyward, the sound rolling back like thunder through the hills. Now it was the turn of the lighthorsemen, finally being given permission to join in the fight. There was no reason not to now. All types of hell were breaking loose.

"About bloody time!" shouted Chugger as he let rip with his first round, his mates following suit.

On the right flank, the 5th Light Horse brought their guns to bear, raking the enemy's exposed edge. Percy saw it happen - Turkish formations folding inward, men scattering, the line buckling. The men of the 2nd cheered, brief and loud, before ducking back down to reload.

"Bloody beautiful," Boggy said as he recharged his magazine.

But the fight wasn't done. At around 0600 hours, the enemy moved nine machine guns into position, raking the trenches, roads, and rear areas with vicious accuracy. Sandbags burst. Dust flew. A round snapped past Percy's ear and buried itself in the earth behind him.

"Bastards!" he exclaimed as he momentarily ducked before regaining his composure.

Sniper fire followed. The Turks had dug in before dawn, and now their marksmen were working the line. One round punched through the top of the trench, scattering dirt across Chugger's boots.

Boggy raised his rifle, sighted, and fired. A pause. Then another shot. He ducked, swore, and fired again.

"Got one," he shouted.

The enemy began shelling with 4.2 inch and 77 millimetre guns. The blasts were erratic, most falling short or wide. But the horses behind the line took the worst of it - cries from the rear, the thud of hooves, the sharp report of mercy shots.

With the 2nd stretched across two sectors, every man was in the line. One squadron from the 3rd Light Horse was sent forward to reinforce them. The two regimental machine guns were rushed into the threatened sector, their crews already looking for targets.

"I reckon they waited too long," said Chugger, "they should have attacked when it was dark".

Percy nodded.

"Well more fool them eh, because they're bloody paying for it now".

The Australians held. Their small arms fire was ferocious and accurate. The artillery continued to hammer the enemy's supports, whilst the regiment's snipers, dug in and patient, began to silence their counterparts one by one.

By full light, the Turkish advance had stalled. The wire held. The trenches held, and the men of the 2nd, exhausted and dirt covered, were still standing.

By early afternoon, the dust hadn't settled. At 1245 hours, the 3rd Light Horse launched a mounted sortie from the regiment's left, while a squadron of the 1st Light Horse swept forward from the right. Their horses moved fast as they probed the flanks. At the same time, the artillery intensified - shells thudding into the valley with increasing rhythm, the fall of shot walking across the ridges like a drumbeat.

Percy watched from the trench, crouched beside Rachel and Chugger. The 2nd had made ready to advance on foot, just in case the enemy broke. Bayonets had been fixed and magazines charged. But the Turks didn't flinch. They had dug deep, layered their machine guns, and held their ground with deadly resolve. No rearward movement, no panic, just the steady, stubborn defence of men who knew the terrain and had no intention of giving it up.

As dusk fell, the tension shifted. The enemy grew restless. Lights flickered in the Wadi, voices carried on the wind - shouted orders, laughter, and the clatter of equipment. It felt like something was building. From the trench, Percy could see the glow of lanterns bobbing like fireflies in the dark. The men stayed low but at the ready, listening.

The noise continued until about 0300 hours, then fell away. Silence returned, heavy and expectant.

At 0400 hours, the 2nd Light Horse struck first.

Percy's section moved fast, slipping through the wire and into the scrub. The raid was sharp and clean - no shouting, no hesitation. They hit the nearest enemy posts with bayonets and rifle butts, clearing trenches in minutes. The Turks were caught off guard, some still half asleep, others scrambling for weapons they never got to fire. As one Turk tried to shout, Percy silenced him with the butt of his Lee-Enfield, the crack of bone louder than the gunfire that followed.

Rachel was amongst them too slashing in all directions with her terrifying scimitar. When the first man lunged she didn't flinch - just stepped aside and drove the blade home, quick and final.

Johnno came behind, panting hard. He fired once, then again, then didn't bother, instead just swinging his rifle like a club, teeth bared, eyes wild and angry. There was no room for fear, only speed...and steel.

The trench was cleared in minutes.

Follow up patrols pushed deeper and found the truth - the main body had withdrawn under cover of darkness, leaving behind a thin rear guard. Most of them were captured without a fight - exhausted, resigned, some wounded, some simply lost.

By dawn, the scale of the battle was becoming clear. The attack had been launched solely against the two sectors held by the 2nd Light Horse. During the battle the 2nd had fired over thirty eight thousand rounds of small arms ammunition. Eight men were dead. Fifteen wounded. The cost was real, and it hung heavy in the trench.

But the enemy had paid dearly. One hundred and fifty Turks lay dead across the valley. Twenty five wounded were taken prisoner. It was estimated that five hundred more had been carried or dragged from the field by the Turks under cover of night.

Among the unwounded prisoners were sixty six Turks, eleven Arabs, and eight Armenians - silent, watchful, their faces marked by fatigue and the long unravelling of hope.

Percy stood at the edge of the trench, watching the sun rise over Wadi Nimrin. The light was soft, almost kind. Behind him, the men were quiet, cleaning rifles, bandaging wounds, boiling tea.

The line had held. The enemy had broken. But the fight didn't end with the last shot. Now came the work no one spoke about - the slow, methodical task of burying the dead.

The ground was torn and uneven, littered with bodies in twisted positions, some half covered by dust, others sprawled where they had fallen. The smell was already rising, thick and sour.

Shovels were passed out. Men who had fought all night now dug in silence, sleeves rolled, faces blank. There was no religious service. No time for it. The Turks were buried in shallow mass graves, marked with stones or not at all. Their own dead were handled with more care - names checked, pockets emptied, pay books collected. A few were wrapped in blankets. Most weren't.

The sun was high and hot. Flies gathered. Somewhere behind them, a chaplain muttered a prayer over a stretcher. No one paused to listen.

By midday, the valley was quieter, the wounded had been moved, the dead were in the ground and the men who remained were too tired to feel much of anything.

As in the Middle Eastern campaign, on the western front constant training was an important part of life when occupying supposed rest areas. Apart from the usual weapons and tactics, new forms of what they now referred to as field craft were emerging. The days of head long mad frontal attacks were gone, not that the Aussies did any of that after their time fighting the Turks, and smaller assaults were now the flavour of the month. Camouflage and concealment were also an important part of daily routine, as not being seen by the enemy was both a tactical and life saving requirement. As part of this, the Battalion had the men dig small two man trenches with overhead and frontal cover. An officer, who had not been briefed on the positions, was then tasked to locate them...unsuccessfully as it turned out. In fact the Aussies were so studious with their camouflage that during the evening Clancy managed to crash through Stowie and Pip's overhead cover.

Whispers of laughter were heard from the men as Clancy climbed out of the trench, brushed himself off and congratulated his mates on their "good camouflage", before strolling off as if nothing had happened.

There now seemed to be a huge concentration of British and ANZAC troops in the area, as the Battalion discovered on the 9th of April, upon moving to Flesselles, five miles away. Here they found limited accommodation due to the presence of the 12th Battalion, HQ 3rd Brigade and the Headquarters of the British 17th Division.

On that same day the Germans had broken through in the north, attacking a sector held by two exhausted Portuguese divisions. The line collapsed under the weight of the assault, with the Portuguese retreating in disarray and offering little resistance. Laventie, Estaires, Sally-Sur-La-Lys, Bac St Maur, and Steenwerck all fell in quick succession. Messines Ridge, however, was still in the hands of the British. On the 11th of April, the 1st, being the only Australian Division not yet engaged on the Amiens front, was ordered back to Flanders to defend the strategically important railway junction at Hazebrouck.

This phase of the offensive would later be called the Battle of Hazebrouck - part of the larger Battle of the Lys - centred in the Lys River region of northern France. Though only a modest town of thirteen thousand inhabitants, Hazebrouck was critical to the Allies, as its rail network delivered nearly half of all daily food and munitions to the front.

By the 10th of April, the German Army's Operations George I and George II had opened alarming gaps in the British line, bringing them within a day's march of Hazebrouck. With the British running low on reserves and the French commander General Ferdinand Foch holding his troops back for future counter-attacks, the outlook was grim.

The orders came down from Brigade just after noon, delivered by a mud-smeared runner who looked like he hadn't slept in a week. Captain Ponsonby unfolded the paper slowly, his gloved fingers cracking with cold despite the April sun. The men of 'B' Company were scattered along a sunken road outside Flesselles, taking what rest they could - smoking, cleaning rifles, or dozing with their backs against sand bags.

Ponsonby cleared his throat.

"All right, eyes front, you lot," he called, and the murmurs faded.

He held the order high and tapped the page.

"This comes straight from Field Marshal Haig himself. I am to read it to every man".

Clancy nudged Archie.

"This oughta be cheerful," he muttered.

Ponsonby ignored the comment and began to read.

"Three weeks ago today the enemy began his terrific attacks against us on a fifty-mile front. His objects are to separate us from the French, to take the Channel ports and destroy the British Army..."

A few men shifted uneasily. Archie crossed his arms and stared straight ahead.

"There is no other course open to us but to fight it out! Every position must be held to the last man - there must be no retirement..."

Ponsonby's voice, though steady, grew firmer.

"With our backs to the wall, and believing in the justice of our cause, each one of us must fight to the end".

He let the words hang a moment before folding the message and tucking it into his coat. The silence lingered.

"That sounds a bit like the message from Hamilton at ANZAC...do you remember?" Clancy said.

"Yeah...dig, dig, dig...until you are safe," replied Roo.

"Well, *I'm* up for it...I've got nothing better to do...how about the rest of you?" said Archie.

Groans of agreement sounded down the line and the men felt a new vigour to get the job done.

Ponsonby smiled and gave a nod.

"Righto, let's get moving boys".

At 1100 hours the next day the Battalion was on the move to Amiens.

As they marched many of the soldiers cast their minds back to their previous visit to the area, and here they were again.

"This is getting a bit like that Grand Old Duke of York bloke," Clancy remarked.

"What *are* you going on about Clance?" Roo asked, as he winked at Archie.

"Huh...I thought you Taylor boys were supposed to be well read mate," replied Clancy, "I'm just saying that we keep fighting the same battles over and over, so it's like marching up to the top of the hill and marching back down again".

"Yeah mate," said Stowie, "*I* know what you're talking about".

Clancy smiled.

"Good on yer Stowie. With any luck we'll keep the top of the bloody hill this time eh?"

"Too right we will," replied a confident Stowie.

On arrival the Battalion, along with the rest of the brigade, set up camp near the citadel on the edge of the town. Spring sunlight glinted off the brickwork and moss-flecked stone as the men gazed up at the vast pentagonal fortress, its moats dry but still formidable, its bastions looming over the field like the shoulders of some sleeping beast.

Built at the turn of the 17th century - so the locals said - it was a relic of old wars, of halberds and arquebuses, not howitzers and Lewis guns. Yet it still held an air of menace. Five great bastions jutted out from its core, surrounded by broad earthworks and the faint remains of a covered way. The southern entrance - the so-called "Royal Gate" - had been walled up long ago, replaced by the older city gate nearby, the Montrescu Gate, with its pointed sandstone arch; all that remained of the medieval original. Over it loomed the old residence of the King's Lieutenant, its weathered walls looking down over the new arrivals with something like disdain.

"Bloody fortress looks like it's waiting for Napoleon to show up," Archie said, easing off his pack and eyeing the stonework.

"I wouldn't fancy storming that," Roo said as he admired the structure

The field in which they pitched their tents was cut by the ghost of the old Roman road, the one that had once run from Senlis to Boulogne. Now it ended at a tangled fence and a cluster of barbed wire, blocked by the Citadel's shadow.

Pip looked up at the walls, then back across the sprawling camp, where cooking fires were being lit and letters from home were already being read aloud.

"Perhaps we should all nip in there for a bit of safety".

"I don't think we'd last long against modern weaponry in there old boy," said Ponsonby as he strolled past with a roll of orders in one hand and a mug of tea in the other, "but let's be grateful it's on our side this time".

Still, there was something comforting about the ancient fortress. It had seen invaders come and go over the centuries, and now it watched over them too - tired, bloodied, but still standing.

Owing to the dire situation due to the lightning enemy advance, Amiens was placed out of bounds to the troops, but there was a common saying that if the powers that be really wanted to end the war, the simplest thing to do would be to place Berlin out of bounds to the Aussies. This was because, like naughty school boys, tell an Aussie *not* to do something and he'll go ahead and do it anyway. So, as it was, the town *did* in fact receive a number of visits from many unruly "school boys" who would return with such souvenirs as wine and other delights.

That evening, as dusk settled over the camp near the old citadel walls, the men sprawled around a low fire, boots off, steaming socks stretched toward the flames. The smoke from a brazier mixed with the faint scent of stew, tobacco, and the earth itself - damp and heavy with spring.

Clancy, warming his hands on a dented mug of tea, leaned back against a pack and cleared his throat.

"You know that estaminet we passed back in Flesselles?" he began, looking around at the group, "the one with the crooked sign and the three-legged dog out the front?"

"Yeah...what about it?" replied Archie.

Pip's eyes lit up.

"I do too. The dog gave me a filthy look...I thought he was gonna bite me like".

"Well," Clancy went on, "I walked in and asked the old woman behind the counter for a beer. Used me best French too...even said it slow...you know...une bière, madame...she looked at me like I'd asked for her boots or something".

"Ladies don't wear boots!" said Stowie.

Roo slapped him on the shoulder and snorted.

"So...what did she give you?"

Clancy grinned.

"A glass of something brown...flat as a duck pond, and twice as warm. Tasted like it'd come straight from the horse. Still, I drank it".

"You'd drink gun oil if it came in a glass," said Pip, taking a drag on his cigarette.

There were chuckles from the group. The laughter wasn't loud - just enough to warm the air around them, like the fire itself. For a moment, the war seemed far off, as though they'd slipped back to a country pub on a Sunday afternoon.

"Did she charge you for it?" Roo asked.

"Bloody oath!" said Clancy, "and then tried to flog me a boiled egg and some bread that'd been sitting out since bloody Christmas...said it was 'fresh'... fresh from the pig sty most like".

Even Archie laughed at that, rubbing a hand through his hair.

The Citadel loomed quietly above them, its old red brick glowing dully in the firelight. Beyond the walls, the road to Haze-brouck beckoned. But for now, the men just sat, boots off, hearts quiet, sharing warmth, fire, and the sort of talk that kept them human.

The Australians were good soldiers and, like the rest of the Empire troops, had endured much, so their leaders tended to look the other way. Yet even now they were still enduring with the train station being sporadically shelled throughout the day, and a three hour bombing raid by enemy aircraft on the neigh-bourhood which housed the bivouac area. The troops had been lit up by enemy flares whilst dozens of search lights illuminated the sky, revealing the offending aircraft, which soon became the attention of machine guns and rifles hoping to down one of them, with Roo testing his theory, but to no avail.

"I'll get one of those bastards one day, you mark my words," he growled.

Thankfully there were few casualties that night, and none from the 9th.

Yet another early start, at 0200 hours to be precise, on the 13th of April preceded a march to the train station at St Roche. On route they past an egg store, which they raided of all its stock. This resulted in each man carrying a basket, or helmet, full of eggs. The enemy bombing had damaged the track so the battalions' departures were delayed whilst hasty repairs were made. Enemy aircraft were also still carrying out attacks, which left civilian staff scurrying for shelter, whilst the soldiers just got on with it...as usual. After all, what are a few bombs and bullets between "friends" anyway?

The battalion rested until late morning in the boulevard and park near the station. The tree-lined avenue offered rare shade and a moment of calm while the small park - trimmed hedges, wrought-iron benches, and neat gravel paths - seemed oddly untouched by war. A few ducks pottered along the edge of a shallow pond, and children's laughter drifted faintly from a nearby street. It was a peaceful setting, made strange by the presence of hundreds of weary, khaki clad soldiers sprawled across the grass or perched on benches, dozing, smoking, or scribbling in battered notebooks.

Roo watched a leaf spiral slowly to the ground and murmured, "Almost feels like peace, this".

Clancy, lying on his back with a rolled up greatcoat for a pillow, snorted.

"Yeah, right...wake me up when the war starts again".

As they rested, many slept, others wrote letters home, whilst some pondered the fate of their liberated eggs.

Pip and Stowie had been off for a bit of a stroll and returned feeling quite proud of themselves.

"You two look like you've been up to mischief," said Roo.

Pip smiled and shrugged his shoulders.

"Well, it depends on what you might call mischief".

"Bloody hell boys!" Clancy exclaimed impatiently, "come on...out with it!"

"We've had a word with the train driver," replied Stowie.

"That's nice...taking you for a choo choo ride is he?" Clancy replied sarcastically.

"Better than that mate," Pip replied, "he says he can give us hot water from the engine to boil our eggs".

"You bloody beauty boys!" exclaimed Archie, as they gathered their haul and headed over to the train.

But, like anything, good news travelled fast and, before long, the entire battalion was queuing up for hot water. There was, however, a negative side to a hearty egg breakfast in that the loss of water from the engine had reduced its steam pressure, which only added to their delayed departure time. But depart they did at around mid day, ten hours after marching out of their bivouac area.

Fifteen hours later, at 0300 hours, the train arrived at Hondeghem, following a long and laborious journey. From the station they marched to a position about a mile east of Hazebrouck, where they became Divisional Reserve. Prior to their arrival the German attack had been brought to a standstill by the 1st and 2nd Brigades, just after the enemy had taken Merris and Meteren.

The first major attack on the Australian positions had begun shortly after midnight on the 13th of April. A small force held firm against a German company, killing over twenty attackers and capturing several machine guns. With that initial thrust repelled, the main German effort resumed in earnest the following morning.

At first light on the 14th, the enemy brought down a thunderous artillery barrage upon the Australian line, the bombardment intensifying around 0630 hours. Soon after, masses of German infantry began advancing across open ground in disciplined ranks - grey-coated columns moving in waves, officers on horseback riding up and down to urge them forward.

British field artillery supporting the Australians raked the massing troops, disrupting their lines but not halting the assault entirely. The Germans pressed on in six densely packed waves. The enemy was so numerous it was impossible to miss.

"It's like firing into a haystack," one soldier remarked as he pushed the bolt forward on his rifle and fired again.

The first German effort broke off at around 1030 hours. Isolated enemy pockets that had managed to cling to ground near the Australian line were swiftly cleared in counter attacks. But at 1400 hours the second wave of German assaults began, with four more lines thrown at the defenders.

In many places, the Australians held their fire until the enemy were within thirty yards, then unleashed devastating bursts of rifle and machine gun fire. In the thick of it, even the attacking officers displayed fierce resolve - some refusing to fall until struck multiple times.

Though some of the forward Australian posts were briefly overrun, the German advance ultimately failed to breach the main line. When the 1st Division arrived, they did so knowing the cost already paid - but their presence helped anchor a vital position just as the fate of Hazebrouck and the railway behind it hung in the balance.

By the 14th of April the 133rd Division of the French Army also began to arrive in the sector as the first of the reinforcing units, while the 1st Australian Division's artillery also arrived and went into positions between Hazebrouck and the Nieppe Forest. Furious work was now taken on, preparing defensive works with the 3rd Australian Tunnelling Company and a mix of other units including the 78th Chinese labour battalion.

CHAPTER 5

It Seemed Like a Good Idea at the Time

As part of the 1st Division the 9th Battalion was back with the 2nd Army, forming part of the XV British Corps. It would remain with the Corps for the next four months. The troops were very happy during this period as they were billeted in comfortable farmhouses, some with feather mattresses, sheets and blankets. On arrival it was obvious that the occupants had made a hasty departure, with Clancy and the boys finding a cooked meal laid out on the kitchen table, which they eagerly consumed.

"It would be rude not too eh?" said Archie.

There was ample milk and poultry available, and much of the livestock became a welcome addition to the men's rations.

The Estaminets, or grog shops, as the troops called them, were fully stocked and followed the large numbers of soldiers from location to location.

The availability of alcohol became an occasional worry. On inspecting 'B' Company on the front line, Captain Ponsonby and the CSM noticed that their numbers appeared to be stretched a little too thin for their liking. A quick visit to a nearby wine cellar revealed many company men enjoying themselves on the local tipple. As the Captain and CSM entered the cellar the boisterous party suddenly became quiet, the men springing to their feet.

"What the bloody hell boys?!" the CSM shouted.

No one dared speak for fear of Clancy's personal justice, which he had learned from Sergeant MacDonald.

"Come on you chaps. I don't mind you having some enjoyment, but you've left your mates to hold the line. What if the Germans attacked? Could you live with yourselves if something bad happened to them?" said the Captain.

There were murmurs of agreement throughout the men as they, bottles in hand, marched back to the front line trenches.

"Good work mate," said Clancy as he slapped Captain Ponsonby on the back.

The Captain was aghast.

"Truly dear boy, I didn't think it would be *that* easy".

"Well, what you said must have been just the ticket eh? Mind you we've been lucky," said Clancy.

"Really? How?" asked a surprised Ponsonby.

"I heard a furphy that old Fritz has been in the boozers a bit much too. That's why they haven't attacked for a bit," replied Clancy.

The 9th Battalion relieved the 12th on the 16th of April on the front line at Borre, a mile further forward. The area in which they were situated was reasonably flat, lush farmland with a tree lined ridge just on the edge of the village.

The next day, as the 'B' Company boys admired the land to their front, Pip became suddenly curious.

"Does Kilcoy look like this?" he enquired.

Archie managed a sly laugh to himself.

"No mate, Kilcoy is up in the ranges. It's not flat and lush like this...quite hilly really. That's why it is cattle country I suppose".

"So, no crops then?" Pip asked.

"No mate, not unless you count Mum's veggie patch," replied Archie.

"Yeah," Roo added, "Aunty Doris certainly loves her garden...flowers too mind you".

"So, what do you do on the farm then?" asked Pip.

"Station mate...not farm. Anyways, we check the fences, make sure the cattle are moved around the different paddocks...you know...all sorts of stuff," Archie replied.

Roo pondered for a moment.

"That reminds me Pip, I've arranged with the cooks for us to use one of their horses so you can learn to ride".

"Great...cheers mate," replied Pip, a worried look on his face.

"Cheer up mate, we'll get you there," said Archie, noticing Pip's expression.

"Yeah mate," announced Clancy as he turned his gaze towards Stowie, "old Stowie here can ride...and he's a *fat* bastard".

Clancy's remark caused a ripple of laughter amongst the men, as did Stowie's two fingered salute.

Pip looked towards Stowie.

"What do you mean fat? Stowie looks normal to me".

"Don't worry about it Pip...but thanks...it's just a bit of a joke from Gallipoli that's all," said Stowie.

Pip nodded, still none the wiser.

The chatter of the troops was soon interrupted by a familiar sound; a low thump and crack in the distance, followed by the whining and screeching of shells flying overhead. Moments later, dull concussions rolled across the landscape, accompanied by the sharp, splintering crack of bursting shrapnel. The men did the best that they could, instinctively ducking their heads, whilst their eyes searched the skies as the next salvo followed, but there was no running for cover as an artillery barrage was usually the pre-cursor to an infantry attack. So they braced themselves, crouching low behind the earthen walls and sandbags of their defences, rifles at the ready.

The bombardment continued for five long hours, its tempo rising and falling like a fevered drumbeat. Most of the shells slammed into the village nearby, the Germans clearly hoping to catch resting troops unprepared. Roof tiles soared into the air like birds, chimneys collapsed in clouds of red dust, and timber beams snapped as houses were reduced to ruins.

It was dinner time for the reserve troops, and the Aussies, meals in hand, scattered quickly to the surrounding fields where they sat low in folds of ground observing the fall of shot on the village with grim composure. Some wolfed down spoonfuls of stew between shell bursts, others simply stared, the clatter of cutlery replaced by the thunder of war.

Then the shellfire lifted. Silence hung for a moment - too long, too expectant. In the forward trenches, heads rose. Eyes narrowed.

There was no shortage of excitement as a sea of grey began advancing across no man's land; German infantry, lines of them, shoulder to shoulder, moving forward with slow precision beneath the rising smoke. But the Aussies were quickly on to them, no shouted orders, no panic, just the sharp report of rifles, the hammering of Lewis guns, and the flat crack of Vickers machine guns in rhythm, sending a hail of rifle and machine gun rounds in their direction.

Lieutenant Sargent moved along the line of men calm and steady.

"Keep your aim steady boys," he called out, "don't waste your rounds - make them all count".

A pause, then: "They're not getting past us...not to bloody day".

Clancy's ears pricked up.

"To bloody day? Are you making up new words mate?"

The officer smiled.

"But of course...I'm full of them you know".

Clancy laughed.

"You're definitely full of something that's for sure," he replied, before ducking into a firing bay and crouching beside a pair of privates working the Lewis Gun.

"Just like roo shooting back home...except these bastards shoot back eh? Steady now, nice bursts and give them shit!"

He gave one of the soldiers a pat on the shoulder.

"Make your mum proud, mate...oh...and drop a few of the bastards for me".

The wall of lead met the advancing enemy with shattering force. Men fell, tripped, scattered, and those behind them hesitated, and then faltered. Within minutes the grey ranks had dissolved, withdrawing in disarray, leaving the ground littered with the fallen.

At 1000 hours and again at half 1730 hours, the Germans renewed their efforts, throwing fresh waves of men against the line. But each time, they were met with withering fire and immovable resolve. Over seven hundred enemy dead would be counted in front of the Australian positions that day alone. Nearby, British and French troops had likewise shattered German assaults on Meteren.

By nightfall, it was clear. The Germans had failed to break through. Their once vaunted offensive had run aground on the stubborn, bloody determination of the Australian 1st Division and their British allies. The price for pushing further was now too steep, the defenders too strong.

The battlefield was strewn with wreckage and silence again crept in - not peace, but the uneasy quiet between storms. Once the artillery had ceased, the resulting casualty list for the Battalion was four dead and eleven wounded.

The line was quiet now, whispered conversations replaced by the occasional cough or the soft scrape of a bayonet being sharpened. Most of the men sat low, still gripping rifles, eyes fixed on the empty stretch of no man's land.

A few muttered comments passed between them.

"I didn't think they'd pull back that quick," someone said.

"Yeah...neither did they, by the looks of it," came the reply.

A little way down the line, Archie stood beside Stowie at the trench bend. Both were quiet, straining to see in the dark ahead. The smell of powder still hung in the air.

Captain Ponsonby appeared without fanfare, his tunic muddy, his face set.

He nodded to Lieutenant Sargent, who stepped forward.

"We'll need to remain vigilant through the night," Ponsonby said in a low voice, "have the lads rotate in half sections, but keep them alert. We don't want a second show while we're half asleep".

Sargent gave a short nod.

"Understood, sir".

Ponsonby turned to go, and then paused.

"Good work today, Tommy. Please let the chaps know...and Archie..."

Archie glanced over.

"Sir?"

Ponsonby looked at him.

"You and Stowie man the OP, I need some good eyes out there...good luck".

"Yes, sir," Archie said simply.

Ponsonby moved on, his boots squelching and sliding in the mud.

Archie turned to Stowie.

"Let's get moving. It'll be as dark as coal out there soon".

Stowie gave a nod, slinging his rifle over his shoulder.

The trench was damp and quiet under a low, moonless sky, the only sound the occasional whistle of the breeze and the far off explosions of artillery. Archie and Stowie were tucked into the forward observation post - a narrow, cramped, sandbagged dugout set just ahead of the main line. There was barely enough room for two men, a periscope, *and* a field telephone, and it stank of sweat, damp wood, and the lingering tang of old cordite.

Archie, squinting into the dark with his Lee-Enfield rifle balanced across his knees, suddenly tensed.

"Hey mate," he whispered, "did you hear that?"

Stowie froze mid-yawn.

"Hear what?"

Archie held a finger to his mouth signalling Stowie to remain silent.

A faint clinking sound floated through the night. Then another.

"Sounds like bloody wire cutters," Archie whispered.

Stowie strained his eyes through the gloomy darkness. Shadows moved beyond the tangle of barbed wire - not just one or two, but a whole platoon.

"Bloody hell...twenty, maybe more," he breathed.

Both men instinctively dropped to a crouch. Archie groped for the field telephone, gave the crank a quick wind, and held the earpiece close.

"Anything?" Stowie whispered.

"Nothing...it's bloody dead," Archie replied as he set the handset down, "the line's probably cut somewhere".

"Now there's a pleasant surprise," whispered Stowie sarcastically.

"Looks like the bastards are coming through the wire," said Archie as he yanked open the battered ammo box beside him and pulled out a couple of Mills bombs, "right...get to Battalion HQ. Tell them we've got a raid on...and stand-to across the whole line. Go!"

Stowie cast a look of concern to his mate.

"Are you gonna be alright on your own?"

Archie smiled and nodded at his rifle and box of bombs.

"Yeah mate, don't worry about me I've got my mates Enfield and Millsy to keep me company...now bugger off...quick smartish".

Stowie didn't argue. He scrambled up the duckboards and took off at a run, his boots sloshing in the wet earth as he bolted to alert the nearest section.

Archie lobbed his first grenade toward the enemy soldiers. It soared into the darkness and burst with a hard, cracking explosion, lighting up the wire for a split second. In that flash he counted at least two sections of Germans bundled at the breach, ready and waiting for the wire cutters to do their work. The enemy had been caught by surprise. Shouts followed - screams, curses, startled German voices, the clatter of men hitting the mud - then more movement, faster now. He pulled the pin on a second Mills bomb, counted to three, and then hurled it a few yards short of the first blast to stagger the next wave, following up rapidly with a third. But the Germans were still coming.

"Persistent bastards..." Archie thought to himself.

As the grenades went off, Archie brought his Lee-Enfield to his shoulder, sighted on the brightest splash of movement, and fired. He pulled back the bolt to eject the spent cartridge, which pinged against the sandbags, then pushed the bolt forward ramming another round home. He settled his sights on another shape. Bang! Crack! Thump! Each shot was slow and deliberate; he could almost feel his pulse settle into the rifle's rhythm.

Shadows ducked and scattered as Archie tossed another grenade, before firing more controlled shots into the night, dropping shadowy figures as they closed in.

German voices shouted in the dark - orders, curses, panic. A stick grenade sailed overhead, exploding behind the parapet in a cloud of earth and rocks. Archie dropped, waited, and then came up again. He leaned forward into the corner of the OP, firing as fast as he could work the bolt, dropping Germans all over the place.

A burst of machine gun fire tore through the air in reply, ripping into the sandbags and spraying dust and dirt inches from his head. Archie ducked low, then popped up and fired twice, quick and accurate. One figure collapsed in a heap. He quickly pulled back the bolt and pushed a fresh ammunition clip into the magazine, then rammed the bolt forward and fired again, taking the machine gunner high in the chest. The weapon fell silent, barrel drooping like a dead limb.

Gunfire snapped back, bullets slicing overhead. Archie ducked and kept firing, holding the position alone. Another enemy grenade landed just short of the post and exploded with a jarring crack. Archie threw himself to the floor, ears ringing.

Then a dull, close thump - a German stick grenade landed just beyond the trench corner, right where Stowie had passed moments before. It went off with a savage bang, and the ground shook.

Archie's heart dropped. He peered through the darkness and spotted two German shapes dragging someone - someone tall and limp - back through the wire.

"Stowie," Archie growled.

Instinctively he slung his rifle over his shoulder, grabbed the last two Mills bombs, and vaulted over the parapet of the post. He splashed into shell pocked mud and sprinted low and fast, the wheat scraping at his sleeves, hurling a grenade ahead of him. It exploded with a blinding flash and concussive blast, showering earth and metal. One of the Germans hauling Stowie dropped instantly. The other tried to run, dragging Stowie with him.

Archie lobbed the second grenade. Shrapnel whined, and the surviving kidnapper, half stunned, swung his rifle up - too late. Archie was on him in seconds, crashing into him shoulder first. Rifle muzzles tangled; they grappled, slipping in the mud as they fought. Archie slammed the butt of his Lee-Enfield into the man's jaw with a loud splitting sound, and then punched his bayonet into the man's ribs. He felt the blade grate along bone - then jerked it back and kicked the German free, the man collapsing as he groaned in pain. Blood darkened the mud as his guts spilled out onto the ground.

Another German appeared from the smoke, bayonet fixed, roaring as he lunged. Archie parried with his rifle, felt wood splinter under the impact, and then swung the butt in a brutal arc that broke the attacker's cheekbone. The man crumpled.

Stowie was lying face down, half conscious. Archie knelt beside his friend and shook him hard.

"Come on, mate, wake up".

Stowie groaned, eyes fluttering open.

"Did someone hit me with a bloody horse?"

Archie grinned with relief.

"Something like that. Are you alright?"

"Yeah...I must have got outed by a grenade or something, but I'll live...probably".

More German voices rose - frantic now, unsure if they were being overrun. A hoarse whistle signalled their withdrawal. Archie didn't wait to celebrate. With one arm over Archie's shoulder, Stowie half-stumbled, half-walked back toward the post, with Archie turning occasionally to fire a shot towards the enemy. Small arms fire crackled sporadically behind him - warning shots now, not aimed. The raiding party dissolved into chaos and was falling back, leaving behind their dead and wounded.

By the time Captain Ponsonby and the CSM, with a section of diggers in tow, arrived from the main line, the worst had passed. The wire was littered with enemy bodies, no Australians had been hurt and the line had held.

Stowie groaned as Archie lowered him onto the duckboards.

"Bloody hell boys," said Clancy, looking over the scattered bodies, "what the flamin' blazes happened here?"

Archie helped Stowie settle on a crate.

"The Germans dropped in for a visit and a yarn. They tried to take Stowie here for a souvenir. I said no".

Clancy was impressed as he offered his hand to both men.

"I reckon *you* earned a brew".

Stowie gave a weak grin.

"Maybe something stronger than that..."

They sat in the rising dawn light, caked in dirt, ears ringing, but alive. The trench held, no one was taken, and every man in the area was now alert and ready, thanks to Archie's quick thinking and one hell of a sprint from Stowie - even if it did land him on the receiving end of a stick grenade on his return journey.

Stowie turned to Archie as he wiped mud from his face.

"Not bad for a quiet night eh?"

Archie just laughed.

"Next time," Archie said, reloading his magazine with shaking fingers, "we swap jobs. You throw the bombs, and I'll get knocked out".

Stowie snorted, as the first hints of dawn lit the trench that still belonged to the 9th.

"Deal..."

The previous day's shelling had resulted in an abundance of pork, due to the deaths of several pigs. Roo stood in the trench mesmerised as he watched one wounded pig hobble out into no man's land before succumbing to its injuries. Clancy saw it too, his stomach heavily influencing his next decision. Ensuring that the area to their front was relatively safe he shouted "STRETCHER BEARERS!" before accompanying the medical staff to retrieve the poor, unfortunate porker. Laying the stretcher beside the pig, the three men rolled it on to the canvass, and then covered the animal with a blanket.

"Righto," said Clancy, winking at the stretcher bearers, "it's off to the cookhouse with *you* mate".

As the three men and their cargo clambered back into the trench they were met by a solemn faced Lieutenant Sargent who, on seeing the unfortunate casualty, quickly threw up a smart salute, much to the amusement of all.

"What *are* you doing Tomo?" asked Clancy.

"Saluting a dead hero Sergeant Major," replied the officer.

"Silly bugger," replied Clancy, as he pulled back the blanket, "it's our bloody dinner mate".

As laughter echoed along the trench, Tomo saw the funny side and joined in.

"Well, that's something to write home about eh boys?"

Unfortunately, the enemy shelling was far from over. Two days later, just after first light, a sudden barrage came crashing down on the outskirts of the village, targeting the billets occupied by 'A', 'B', and 'D' Companies. The morning had begun with an eerie calm - low mist clung to the broken fences and muddy lanes, and a few of the lads had even stepped outside for a quiet smoke or to stretch stiff joints.

Then the first shells hit - sharp, brutal impacts that tore through the roofs and churned up the cobbled laneways. One landed squarely on the barn where a section of 'B' Company had been billeted, throwing slates and splinters into the air like shrapnel from a giant's hammer. Men burst from doorways and windows, half-dressed, packs and weapons clutched to their chests, some with nothing but their rifle, boots and a blanket.

Clancy was already bellowing like a fog horn.

"Out! Get out! Into the paddocks...don't wait for the next one to tuck you in!"

Lieutenant Sargent was fast on the scene, calm and collected, issuing quick orders to keep the panic down.

"Spacing! Keep low! Move fast but don't bunch...go!"

Roo and Archie had been sleeping in the hayloft when the first shell landed. They bolted down the ladder and made it out just before a second round smashed through the far wall.

"Bloody hell," Roo gasped as they hit the ground running, ducking between fence posts and broken wagons, the air thick with dust and smoke.

Out in the open fields, the men spread out and dropped flat, the worst of the barrage landing behind them now. For a while, they just lay there in silence, listening to the thunder and watching smoke spiral into the sky above the battered village.

When the shelling finally tapered off, the men emerged cautiously from cover. Orders came down to retrieve what they could, but to move quickly and stay alert. With the barrage lifting, the danger wasn't over - it could start up again any minute.

Roo and Archie made their way back toward what remained of the barn, stepping over charred timber and smashed crockery. Part of the roof had collapsed, and a wagon wheel had been thrown clear across the yard.

They found their kit in a corner still somewhat protected by a stone wall - blackened and scattered, but mostly intact.

Roo knelt, brushing ash from his pack.

"Got it," he muttered with relief, pulling out a small cloth wrapped bundle.

Archie reached for his own kit, undoing the buckles and digging through the contents.

"Still here," he said quietly, pulling out a bundle of letters from home, "Mum and Dad's last one...and Percy's. I thought they were gone for good".

Roo opened his bundle to check inside. Nestled between a pair of socks was his rock from Lemnos.

"Still got my rock," he announced, proudly holding it up in the air for all to see.

Archie smiled.

"Yep...me too".

They stood for a moment, side by side, clutching pieces of their past, silent amidst the wreckage.

Clancy's voice rang out again from down the lane.

"Right, back to it! If you've found your boots and rifle, you've found enough!"

As the sun began to set, the battalion was once more on the move, this time to the support trenches at Phincboom on the Meteren Becque front, travelling via Rouge Croix. Here they experienced something new, when they relieved the 321st Regiment of the French Army.

They were met by an extremely jovial, yet organised, Captain Cyril Mateus who, along with his fellow officers, ensured a meticulously detailed handover. In a few cases the handover briefings took longer than expected with Roo, when taking over a hill crested out post, having the location of every enemy machine gun post pointed out to him, plus a complete description of the intricacies of no man's land. Despite the lengthy briefing Roo was both grateful and impressed, and said as much as he wished the departing French well.

The front line consisted of outposts, with troops occupying trenches, as well as barns and farmhouses, around two hundred yards to the rear. If the buildings became subject to shell fire the occupants would quickly evacuate to some small trenches. The ANZACs were very impressed with the earth works and wire entanglements, which were very well constructed. Their latrines, however, left a lot to be desired, but that was soon rectified by the very picky Aussies.

The new position, being under constant and direct observation by the Germans, made it difficult for any daytime movement, resulting in any sleep periods being undertaken *then*, thus allowing for the dark nights to be used to improve their defences. It was almost as if they were on Australian time, especially when hot meals were served at 2030 hours and 0330 hours respectively, with tea being provided at midnight.

The line itself ran near to the village of Meteren, two miles west of Bailleul, situated along the road to Cassel. It held strategic importance due to its location near the front lines. In October 1914, the British Expeditionary Force had engaged in its first formal attack in the area during the "Race to the Sea," aiming to outflank German forces. The village changed hands multiple times and suffered extensive damage from artillery bombardments. The town had been captured by the enemy on the 13th of April and now it was up to the 3rd Brigade to retake it.

The plan appeared relatively simple with the Aussie lines advancing on either side of the village and effectively surrounding it in a pincer movement. Once held in this tight vice, parties of the Brigade would be sent in to mop up any resistance.

It was to be a two phase operation over two nights, minus any artillery preparation. The first phase would see the 11th and 12th Battalions advancing on either side of the village and halting once in line with its centre. On the following evening the 9th and 10th would attack with three companies each, the 9th to the south west and the 10th to the north east, in order to out flank the village. One hundred soldiers from the 11th and 12th would then be dispatched to the town to capture or drive off any remaining enemy troops. Once complete the 9th and 10th would then send out their reserve companies in order to link up the four battalions by forming a line just beyond the southern edges of Meteren.

It was five days before ANZAC Day and although it was spring, the air was still chilly.

"Right. I need two volunteers," said Captain Ponsonby, scanning the trench.

As one, the entire platoon suddenly discovered their boots, clouds, and dirt under their fingernails terribly interesting. Then his eyes fixed on Roo and Pip.

"Well, well...Roo and Pip...congratulations chaps".

Roo didn't even look up.

"I thought you said volunteers mate".

"I did...and I just volunteered you. The Adjutant has a job for you two blokes. Get to the Command Post...he'll fill you in".

They two men trudged off without a word with a chorus of laughter and mock sympathy trailing behind them.

Inside the dugout, the Adjutant looked up from his map table, a battered cigarette drooping from the corner of his mouth.

"Perfect timing, lads. That last barrage ripped out half our lines between Hazebrouck and Amiens. We've lost all contact with 11th Brigade up on Morlancourt Ridge. They're holding a forward salient on the flank - damned exposed, and cut off. This..." he tapped the envelope with a stained finger, "needs to get to them fast".

Roo frowned.

"Morlancourt? That's over fifty miles away, sir."

"Eighty four to be exact. I've arranged space on a munitions truck heading toward Amiens. From there you're on foot, or what passes for foot in this bloody country. Stay off roads, watch for patrols, and keep your heads down. The sky's crawling with enemy aircraft lately".

Roo was concerned.

"But what about the big attack, sir?"

"I'm sure it will be able to go ahead without the pair of you. Besides, this is more important," replied the Adjutant.

Pip could see the disappointment in Roo's face, so tried to change the subject.

"Why two of us, sir?" he asked, already knowing the answer.

"To double the chances it gets through," the Adjutant said flatly.

"That's a bit of a worry, sir," Roo said as he scratched his chin, "how about the whole platoon go, then you have over thirty chances to ensure it gets there?"

"You're a cheeky bugger Sergeant Taylor," the Adjutant responded with a smile, whilst clouting him on the head with the document, "now on your way fellas...and good luck".

"Cheers sir," said Pip, with a half-hearted salute.

They slipped out and began the long, grey slog - weaving through collapsed trenches and shell-scarred earth, where blasted trees rose like burnt matchsticks and wire twisted across the mud like spilled entrails. The stench was the usual cocktail of wet dirt, old blood, and the acrid tang of cordite that never quite faded.

The morning after being "volunteered," Roo and Pip stood in the back of a battered Army lorry that lurched and shuddered southward out of Hazebrouck. The sky was a pale sheet of steel, low and heavy, and though it was spring, the wind still had teeth.

The countryside, once tidy with fences and ploughed fields, was now churned and cratered. Each village they passed through bore the black scabs of shellfire. Tall poplars stood shattered along the roads like snapped matchsticks. Roo squinted at a rusting sign half hidden behind a scorched tree trunk.

"Bailleul," he said, "bloody hell, it's been flattened".

"Like someone dropped a big brick on it," Pip agreed, watching a group of refugees shuffle by.

They were mostly old men and women, children clinging to coats, faces grey with exhaustion. A donkey cart carried what little they could salvage - a cracked mirror, a mattress soaked with rain, and what might have been a cradle.

The roads were chaos. Ambulances howled past, mules brayed, dispatch riders cursed as they weaved between the columns of trudging infantry. Somewhere ahead, near Armentieres, a military policeman in a trench coat tried to direct the chaos with a whistle and a waving arm - as useless as a broom in a cyclone.

Beyond Lille, the lorry was forced to halt near a small village where a bridge had been shelled into a mess of scorched timber and twisted iron. Engineers were shouting at one another, laying down planks across the remaining struts. The driver leaned out and shook his head.

"You're on foot from here, lads".

"Cheers," Roo muttered, unslinging his rifle.

"I suppose it's a walking holiday now," Pip said, slipping on his pack.

They set off along the road, climbing down the bank of the stream that the damaged bridge traversed, hopping across protruding rocks to the other side, then back up the neighbouring bank on to the roadway, which was also congested with vehicles, marching soldiers and fleeing locals. They passed the tail end of a column of Australian soldiers - weary Diggers in greatcoats with fixed bayonets, sweat-streaked faces beneath their slouch hats. Men nodded as Roo and Pip passed, some too tired to bother. A padre sat on a box by the roadside offering cigarettes and quiet words. A dead donkey, stiff and blackened, lay half-buried near a ruined barn, its load of shells scattered like spilled dice.

The two men plodded on, weaving between the last hedgerows of what had once been farmland. The trees were little more than matchwood, their tops shredded by months of artillery. Fences had long since been blasted flat, and every field was a patchwork of shell holes and rusting wire.

Overhead, the sky, which had been dull all morning, began to whine. Two specks in the sky, dipping in formation, banked sharply and began to descend.

"Shit! German planes...get down!" Roo shouted.

A flicker of canvas wings - then the spitting chatter of twin Spandau machine guns. The road erupted in clods of dirt and shards of iron as the twin German aircraft swept in, low and fast, screaming along the road, guns flashing, stitching the verge with bullets. A wagon up ahead burst apart, horses screaming, men scattering into the ditches.

"Christ almighty!" Pip yelled.

Both men threw themselves off the track, sliding headlong into a muddy drainage ditch, the bullets chopping up the road beside them as the aircraft passed overhead. The engine noise roared above them, and then faded.

A truck full of supplies exploded behind them, sending a wheel spinning into the air. Shouts rang out - some in English, others in pain.

The two aircraft climbed and turned, disappearing eastward into the clouds.

Roo and Pip lay still for a few minutes, their hearts hammering.

"So that's the famous Flying Circus?" Roo spat, wiping mud from his face. "Von Richthofen's mob...the bastards love showing off".

Pip groaned as he surveyed the scene of carnage along the road.

"And killing people...lucky it wasn't the whole column".

Roo gave a grunt.

"Right...stuff this...we'll take the safer route in".

They moved off into the countryside across fields, away from the roads now choked with smoke and broken wagons, through a maze of shallow valleys and hills littered with wreckage - a burnt out tank half buried in the mud, a dead horse swollen stiff in a ditch. The birdsong was gone, replaced by the boom of faraway guns.

As they passed Arras, in the distance they could see the spire of a ruined church jutting like a jagged tooth from the wreckage. Beyond that, fields once green now lay crusted in shell holes and tangled wire, the ghosts of old trenches still visible beneath moss and mud.

Nightfall found them outside Albert, crouched near a low ridge. The broken silhouette of the Golden Virgin atop the basilica loomed eerily against the darkening sky, leaning at an unnatural angle as if bowing to some unseen horror.

"We're close now," Roo said, "Morlancourt is just over there on the other side of the river".

Pip glanced upward, but the sky was empty.

"No more planes at least. The sooner we drop this message off and get back to the lads the better".

They pressed on under cover of dusk, the rattle of machine guns, miles away, rising again like a steel storm ahead, finding an old barn to shelter in overnight.

The dull rumble of artillery never stopped; a background growl to the chaos ahead. The land around them resembled the inside of a meat grinder and the smoke and mist clung to the churned ground like ghosts. As they crested the last rise, Morlancourt Ridge came into view - a low line of broken trees, scarred earth, and scattered dugouts clinging to the slope like lice.

Roo pointed.

"There she is. Brigade HQ should be dug in just past that knoll".

"And with any luck," Pip muttered, "a brew and a bloke waiting to take this flamin' message".

As they neared the rise of Morlancourt Ridge, a sudden heavy clatter of machine gun fire rose up ahead, followed by the whirring noise of a low-flying rotary engine; drawing their eyes skyward. Both men dropped instinctively.

"There!" Pip pointed. "Bloody hell, he's low!"

A Sopwith Camel buzzed overhead, banking hard and wobbling slightly. It was piloted by a novice Canadian pilot Lieutenant Wilfrid "Wop" May of 209 Squadron, Royal Air Force.

Unbeknownst to May, he had just fired on the Red Baron's cousin Lieutenant Wolfram von Richthofen.

"What the hell...?!" exclaimed Pip.

Roo pointed skyward.

"Ave a go at that!"

The Sopwith Camel twisted in a desperate turn, its engine coughing. Behind it, like a red comet, came the unmistakable Fokker Dr.I triplane - all scarlet and fire. The Red Baron. On seeing his cousin being attacked, the Red Baron, Manfred von Richthofen had flown to his rescue and opened fire on May, causing him to pull away. In his thirst for vengeance, Richthofen then relentlessly pursued May across the Somme. His Fokker dipped low, its triple wings flashing crimson in the sunlight as he dropped in again behind the Camel. Bullets punctured the air. The Camel jerked wildly, barely staying aloft. Roo and Pip scrambled into a shell crater for cover, their heads tilted skyward. A second Sopwith Camel, piloted by Captain Roy Brown, also a Canadian, streaked in, diving hard at an impossible angle. He fired a burst, just enough to distract the Baron. The Fokker flinched, peeled away, then swooped in back on May's tail like a bloodhound, its twin Spandaus spitting lead at the fleeing aircraft.

"Bloody hell...look at that red bastard on his tail!" Pip said, "that's *him*...that's the bloody Red Baron!"

Down below, every digger within cooee opened up - rifles, Lewis guns, even a couple of Vickers from the support trenches. A line of tracers reached skyward like angry wasps.

"We've got to be in this, mate," said Roo, bringing his rifle into the aim, "and besides...I've still got a theory to test".

Pip scratched his head.

"A theory? What do you mean?"

Roo smiled.

"I reckon it's just like shooting rabbits, Pip. Aim ahead of his nose, and let him fly into the bullet".

"You reckon we can hit the pilot?" asked a surprised, yet intrigued Pip.

Roo winked.

"Watch and learn mate. Watch and learn".

Pip hesitated, then followed suit. Dozens of rifles cracked around them as ground troops added their fire to the sky. The plane looped down, following its prey. But Roo focused - timing it. Waiting. He braced his rifle against the rim of a crater, and followed the red aircraft through its arc. The sun caught the blood-coloured fuselage. For a moment, it gleamed like fire. The Baron banked again, engine roaring, closing in on May. Roo exhaled, and steadied himself. He squeezed the trigger gently to the first pressure, continually tracking the crimson killer. May's aircraft swayed desperately from left to right, and then dived. The red tri-plane turned to follow - low and fast, almost grazing the trees.

Then Roo breathed in and held it - second pressure on the trigger. Crack. The rifle jerked back in Roo's shoulder. A single shot rang out amidst the chaos. Roo didn't even flinch.

"Got him!"

Pip blinked.

"You reckon? There must be a hundred blokes shooting right now".

He felt it in his chest. Like something old and angry had been set right.

"*Oh, I know*," replied Roo, "I can feel it...in my bones...and in the silence from our fallen mates watching from somewhere up there".

The red tri-plane shuddered midair - a slight wobble, then a nose-dip, before it began a steep, uncontrollable dive. It didn't spiral, didn't explode, but just glided down in a long, slow arc, like a dead bird carried on a breeze.

It clipped a ridge, bounced hard, skidded, and smashed into the earth a few hundred yards ahead in no man's land, flames already licking at the broken frame.

Diggers from all directions poured over the parapets. Roo and Pip were among them.

By the time they reached it, the wreckage was already surrounded. Smoke curled from the twisted fuselage. The tail was splintered. The undercarriage was gone. One wing had folded like wet paper.

A few soldiers had already pulled the pilot's body from the flames.

"That's him," someone said. "That's bloody Richthofen".

Richthofen lay sprawled in the grass. His lower body was badly burnt, but his top half remained untouched - save for the blood from a single neat bullet wound in the left side of his torso. His face was cold, expressionless. Blood stained his tunic, and one glove had been torn away.

Roo crouched beside the body and stared intently at it.

Manfred von Richthofen.

His face, young, pale and elegant, seemed frozen in mid-thought. A trickle of blood ran from one corner of his mouth. His eyes were half open, staring at nothing. Roo leaned closer.

"So this is the bloke who killed eighty of our mates?"

He expected to feel triumph.

Instead, he just felt...tired.

The Baron looked like any other dead soldier. No different from the mates they had buried a dozen times over.

Roo scanned Richthofen from head to foot then smiled to himself as he turned his gaze to Pip.

"Nice boots...what do you reckon?"

"They're yours if you can get 'em off, mate," replied Pip, "he doesn't need them where he is going, does he?"

Roo didn't need telling twice. They were fine leather, perfectly polished even now. The Baron certainly wouldn't be walking anywhere. With care, Roo worked the boots free, tugging them from the dead ace's feet, and stuffed them into his pack.

Both men then eyed the downed aircraft which was rapidly being pulled apart by souvenir hunters. Then they stepped around the shattered tail of the Fokker and peeled off one of the black crosses.

"Tail would never fit in my pack anyway," Roo muttered.

When Roo and Pip finally made it back to the battalion lines late the following evening, muddy and grinning like thieves, the boys swarmed around them.

"What took you so long?" Stowie asked. "Fall in a shell hole?"

"Nah," Roo said casually. "Had to stop and shoot down the Red Baron".

They laughed - until Roo reached into his pack and yanked out a pair of fine leather boots and the tail insignia.

"No way..."

"Yep...dead set," replied Roo.

The men gathered around, their jaws wide in awe.

"Bloody hell. Roo downed the Red Baron".

Someone laughed, and then they all did.

Later, a cross was nailed to the trench wall which simply read:

Roo: 1. Red Baron: 0.

The laughter soon changed back to the serious job of soldiering and winning this war. The advance on Meteren was about to begin, the first phase commencing at 0100 hours on the 23rd of April. It was a success, with little or no opposition.

A hot meal arrived for the 9th at 2030 hours, carried forward in steaming dixies by the quartermaster's crew, who looked nearly as haggard as the men they served. There were whispered thanks as the stew was ladled out - chunks of beef and vegetables thick with gravy, enough to warm the belly and settle nerves.

"Not bad," muttered Roo, wiping his mess tin clean with a crust of bread, "you cooks are bloody legends".

"Too bloody right," added Archie, "we could almost be home...if you shut your eyes and ignore the shelling".

But not all comments were so generous.

"Might be the last meal we ever get," someone muttered grimly in the shadows, to which Clancy shot back with his usual charm.

"Well you'd better make the most of it then you miserable bastard!"

A few chuckles followed, but the tension was thick as the men readied themselves. Weapons were loaded, bayonets fixed, voices dropped to whispers.

At 2200 hours, 'B', 'C', and 'D' Companies began moving forward under orders to relieve the 12th Battalion. The front line was under constant harassment from German guns - shells bursting with monotonous regularity, their concussion lighting up the sky in brief orange flashes. The ground shuddered with each impact, and by the time the relief was completed at 2355 hours, eleven of their number had fallen.

Then, on the stroke of midnight, with the sky washed in ghostly silver from a bright, unrelenting moon, 'B' and 'D' Companies went over the top.

The countryside before them unfurled like a dream - hedgerows casting long shadows, open fields glimmering with dew, shattered trees like skeletal sentries. Somewhere in the distance, a cow lowed mournfully. The line advanced in silence, every man acutely aware that the moonlight, so helpful to them, could just as easily betray them.

"If *we* can see this well," hissed one man, "so can the square heads".

But the German line gave no cry, no warning shot. It seemed they had caught the enemy napping, for both 'B' and 'D' Companies reached their objectives with little more than startled resistance - a few stray shots and shouted commands from the enemy line, quickly silenced by rifle fire.

Five minutes later, as 'C' Company began *their* advance, the silence was shattered.

From behind a thick hedgerow and a ruined manor house at the edge of the village - nicknamed "The Chateau" by the diggers - came a sudden eruption of German machine gun fire. Bullets tore through the night, slapping into the dirt and whizzing overhead in furious arcs. Men dropped to their bellies, crawling for cover. The advance halted almost instantly.

Pinned down and exposed, 'C' Company sent back urgent word. Artillery was requested but denied - friendly lines were too close, the risk too great. Mortar crews adjusted quickly, loosing projectiles toward the muzzle flashes, but the fire from the Chateau did not falter. German gunners were dug in, well-shielded and precise.

An attempt was made to flank the machine guns, but it was beaten back with more losses. Every movement drew fire. They were well and truly stuck, and above them, the moon still shone...bright, indifferent, and cold.

The next stage of the operation was now on. At 0130 hours the 11th and 12th Battalions advanced in what was meant to be a mopping up phase. However, they found instead that what was meant to be a basically unopposed manoeuvre was now a frontal attack on an entrenched German position, which up until this moment in time had still not been captured. Despite the line having advanced on two flanks, not one enemy post had been taken.

Not surprisingly, as the 11th and 12th Battalions pushed forward, they were met with a hail of murderous machine gun fire raking from the edge of the village. The ground ahead was a checkerboard of churned fields, cratered lanes, and shattered fences, littered with torn uniforms, twisted wire, and the broken remnants of earlier attacks. Shell holes brimmed with muddy water and the stench of death, while the low, cracked stone walls offered little cover against the deadly scythe of bullets sweeping across open ground.

The Germans had dug in deep, their guns perfectly positioned among the forward buildings and behind collapsed barns, firing through prepared loopholes and from cellar windows. As the Australians reached the outskirts of the village, the air was filled with smoke and dust. House by house, yard by yard, brutal close-quarters fighting erupted. The sharp bangs and cracks of rifles were soon drowned by the deafening clatter and drilling of machine guns and the muffled booms of grenades echoing between walls.

Several times, small groups attempted to crawl or dash to within bombing range of the gun positions - some making it as far as a shattered orchard or the corner of a burnt-out café. But each time they were spotted, and each time they were cut down, their bodies sprawled across the torn verge, their grenades unused. The Germans held the advantage - fields of fire were clear, their arcs overlapping, and the attackers had precious little to shield them.

Yet amid the fury and confusion, the 9th Battalion finally had its moment.

'D' Company, moving in coordination with the larger assault but holding slightly further to the right, found a gap. A sudden lull in fire - a reloading gun, a moment of hesitation - and they surged forward across a shallow gully lined with brambles and broken poplars. Bayonets fixed, voices low, they advanced under cover of a stone wall and the smoke curling up from a burning haystack.

With ruthless determination, they rushed a German outpost nestled in a partially collapsed farmhouse, surprising the defenders as they scrambled to bring their weapon to bear. A short, savage struggle followed - sharp, brutal, and over in moments. When it was done, the post was theirs; a small foothold in a wider maelstrom. The remaining Germans lay dead or wounded, and the gun was silenced. Amid the blood and chaos, the 9th had struck true.

At 0200 hours, under a pallid moon and drifting smoke, A' Company arrived on the extreme right, their objective being to move past Meteren from the south west. The ground here too was broken and black with shell holes, hedgerows and fences reduced to splinters, every tree a charred stump. The Officer Commanding (OC), Major Ross, located a length of trench that angled forward from the battalion's line in the direction of the enemy. Though narrow and only partially intact, it offered the only usable cover in the immediate area, and he resolved to launch the assault from there. The men waited in silence, pressed close in the narrow cut of earth, their breath clouding faintly in the cool night air. The only sounds were the occasional pop of rifles in the night and the low moan of the wind as it swept through the shattered remnants of Meteren. Orders were given quietly. Bayonets were attached. Faces stern. Then, with a whispered signal, the leading section of one of the platoons climbed the parapet. With echoes of The Nek at Gallipoli, they were cut down almost immediately as a sudden, terrible burst of German machine gun fire tore through them - short, savage, and deadly. Muzzle flashes lit up the dark for a heartbeat, and then bodies slumped and fell, some backwards into the trench, others toppling forward into the wire-strewn mud. Many men were killed instantly. The thud of collapsing men was followed by the high, agonised cries of the wounded. One man groaned continuously, his voice rising and falling like a wounded animal's, while another sobbed softly, and curled around his belly where the bullets had torn through.

Those still in the trench froze, their faces pale in the flickering light. Years of war had taught them bitter truths - about when to charge, and when not to, and thus the other sections hesitated and remained in the trench, in turn blocking any further movement for the other platoons waiting to move forward. What might once have been called cowardice became, in that moment, a lifesaving decision. No further orders were given. None were needed. As it turned out, it was the best thing that could have happened as it prevented any further senseless loss of life.

All forward movement stalled. The men waited in silence, the trench rank with the stink of sweat, gun powder, and blood. Out ahead, the lifeless forms of their mates lay strewn across the rise, limbs tangled, rifles fallen, eyes staring sightless into the night. Occasionally, a faint cry would rise from the dark - pleas for water, for help, or for mothers long gone.

'A' Company remained pinned there, half in the trench and half lying belly-down in the open earth ahead of the new front line. No glory, no gain - just another bitter lesson carved into the cold ground of France. They awaited new orders, but none could undo what had already been done.

Various attempts were made by brave souls from 'C' and 'D' Companies to silence the chattering machine guns. Time and again, men crept forward through the shell-churned mud, clutching Mills bombs or rifle grenades, darting from crater to crater in the faint hope of getting close enough to throw. But each effort ended the same way - with a burst of gunfire and a limp figure collapsing into the dirt. One after another, these lone charges were cut short before they could draw breath for a final yell. The guns didn't falter, didn't waver - just kept sweeping back and forth, cutting down anyone who dared to move. The courage was real, the sacrifice absolute, but the outcome always deadly.

The plan had not been a good one, and each man knew it. After the initial advance, without a preliminary bombardment, it had become obvious to the enemy what the ANZAC intentions were, and he had thus re-enforced the outskirts of the village with machine guns, making it impossible to take it. Even the battalion officers, working in unknown territory and moving at short notice, had no chance of getting their bearings.

The losses in the battalion, for a relatively small engagement, were twelve dead and thirty two wounded. The battalion strength was now seven hundred and sixty one.

CHAPTER 6

Neither Up Nor Down

Early on the 25th of April 1918, 'B' and 'C' Companies withdrew their forward posts slightly so as to make a continuous line. An attempt was made to recover the fallen, but heavy enemy fire put paid to that.

It was a misty morning, only to be complicated further by a gas and heavy high explosive bombardment at around 0900 hours, on 'B' and 'C' Companies' front line posts. Three men were wounded and the mist dispersed two hours later to reveal a clear day.

Today was also the third anniversary of the Gallipoli landings, a message of greetings to all comrades of the peninsula days being sent by Headquarters 1st Division. The veterans were both grateful and moved, remembering all who had fallen there, and since.

As Stowie read the message he felt worried, sad and cynical.

"We'd better get this thing over with soon or there'll be none of us left".

"Too right mate," said Clancy as he patted Stowie on the back.

'B' Company's HQ had taken up residence in a battered old farmhouse on the outskirts of Meteren. The place was little more than a skeleton of its former self - slate tiles missing from the roof, shutters torn from windows, and walls dotted with shrapnel holes. Inside, the air was damp and cold, breath fogging in the early morning chill. Draughts crept under doors and through broken panes, and the wooden floors groaned under every step. But, albeit temporary, it was home, a place of warmth compared to the freezing and damp trenches a few yards to the front.

Up in the attic, where a narrow window faced north over the rear of the company's lines, Captain Ponsonby stood hunched in his greatcoat, peering through a pair of field glasses. The lens was smeared with condensation, and he wiped it with a gloved thumb as he scanned the mist-veiled landscape. A grey fog clung low to the ground, swallowing up detail, but there - just visible - a lone figure emerged through the haze.

"Bloody hell," Ponsonby exclaimed, lowering the binoculars.

The sudden outburst broke the chilly silence and stirred Clancy, who was curled in a blanket against the attic wall, beside a pile of sandbags.

"What is it, skip?" Clancy asked, groggily pulling himself upright.

But Ponsonby didn't answer. He was already picking up his rifle and striding toward the stairs. Clancy, sensing urgency, grabbed his own weapon and followed.

Down the narrow staircase they went, their steel toe and heel caps clumping on the warped timber, then out through the shattered front room and across the cobbled courtyard. The morning mist hung densely around the trees and outbuildings, their breaths coming in quick puffs as they pushed through the gate and onto the rutted road beyond.

There, just up the track, walked a solitary man in field grey, his greatcoat buttoned tight, hands tucked in his pockets. He was strolling - not skulking - just walking calmly behind the Australian lines as if he belonged there.

"Stop right there, mate!" Clancy shouted, rifle raised.

As they pointed their weapons at the man, the German seemed very familiar to them. But it was the German who first recognised his two captors. Startled at first, he froze, then turned slowly, his eyes widening; then he spoke, his voice soft but clear.

"Ah...Captain Ponsonby," he said in lightly accented English, "we meet again...it is good to see you".

Ponsonby's expression lightened as he lowered his rifle.

"Werner...is that you?"

It was the officer they had met when they first saw Pip.

"Ja...it appears the fog has got me lost," he replied.

He had crossed the battalion front line whilst conducting a reconnaissance of no man's land, having lost his way with the limited visibility.

As the three men ambled back slowly towards the farmhouse they were laughing and joking like old friends. The OC of 'A' Company, Major Ross, who had been sleeping in the cellar, was awoken by the commotion, and had to look twice when he saw Werner walking down the steps in deep conversation with Captain Ponsonby and the CSM. Werner sat down and warmed his hands by the fire, and felt quite relieved at being captured by the Australians.

"I am so happy. I thought those mad Highlanders were located here".

"No. It's just us Aussies," replied Ponsonby, "mind you *we* are a little mad too".

"Well," said Werner, "I am safe now and will be going home after the war".

Ponsonby smiled and patted Werner on the back, feeling a slight pang of jealousy.

The fog seemed ever present and danced over the countryside like a woollen blanket until almost mid day, every day. An abundance of gas also lay around, and affected the soldiers on the front line, many of whom had either lost their voices or found it difficult to speak in anything other than hoarse tones.

Despite the fog, on ANZAC Day the French had been driven back from Kemmel Hill, seven miles north east of Meteren. As a result, part of the allied line in that sector was also withdrawn. This in turn put paid to plans to take Meteren on the 26th of April.

As 'B' Company stood watch along the lines the next day, a lone enemy aircraft flew very low over the 9th Battalion trenches for well over thirty minutes. Small arms fire erupted, cracking skywards like a stockman's whip.

"Hey Roo, you should do a Red Baron on this bloke...what do you reckon?" said Archie.

Roo shook his head.

"Not today. This one keeps circling overhead so I can't really get him from this angle".

"You could shoot him up the arse," added Clancy.

Eventually the aircraft was driven off by the Lewis gunners, but not before it managed to drop a single bomb, which exploded ten yards from a German outpost, much to the laughter and applause of the Aussies.

"I reckon he was bloody lost," said Clancy.

"More like he forgot his glasses mate," replied Roo.

"Well, I reckon he'll be for it when he gets back to his own lines eh?" said Archie.

Once the commotion had died down Lieutenant Sargent arrived from Company HQ.

"If you liked *that* show you're going to enjoy what's coming next".

Ever the pessimist, Clancy rolled his eyes.

"Let me guess, we're attacking Meteren?"

"Better then that Clance," replied an excited Tomo, looking at his watch, "the gunners are going to try to silence the machine guns at the chateau, so you'd better get your heads down because it's coming now".

A special 4.5 inch Howitzer was detailed to do the deed and, as it turned out, it's shooting was deadly accurate, demolishing the chateau and dropping shells on the building's former occupants who were fleeing, taking refuge in the neighbourhood and behind hedgerows. Simultaneously the battalion snipers were also downing all opportune targets. Once the onslaught was over, the allied troops in the vicinity had a rare, but welcome, quiet night.

The battalion were relieved the next day, the 28th, by the 3rd Battalion, who were settled in at midnight. The 9th then marched out to a railway camp at South Borre, but had to alter their route due to the town of Courte Croix being set alight by enemy incendiary shells, and the fear of the illuminated battalion becoming a prime target for artillery. Here they remained for five days, in comfortable billets and only taking part in working parties.

Then next morning, over two thousand miles away, the Jordan Valley was already stirring with quiet purpose. The second series of operations against Es Salt and Amman was about to begin. Orders had been passed down the line the night before, and now the brigades were shifting into position - each man aware that the day ahead would be long, and likely costly.

The 60th Infantry Division, supported by a brigade of mounted troops, was tasked with a frontal assault on the Turkish positions at Shunet Nimrin and El Haud. These ridgelines loomed tall over the valley, their rocky faces carved by centuries of wind and war. The objective was to force a path up the main Es Salt road. But the enemy held the heights in strength, and El Haud in particular was known to be a brilliant artillery observation post - its elevation offering a commanding view of the British advance.

To the north, the Australian Mounted Division and the 1st Light Horse Brigade were threading their way up the Jordan Valley, aiming to strike the enemy's right flank via the Nablus to Es Salt track and the rough-cut trail from Umm Es Shert. The Turks had dismissed these routes as impassable for large mounted formations - a misjudgement the Australians were quietly hoping to exploit.

The terrain was rough. The tracks twisted through dry wadis and over jagged ridges, littered with shale and thorny scrub. The dust from the hundreds of horses hung in the air like a bad smell, and the heat pressed down with a quiet cruelty. As the column moved, Davo glanced back at Alfie, who was perched awkwardly on his donkey as he followed the column.

"So what have you decided about young Alfie, Perce?" Davo asked.

Percy, riding just ahead, didn't turn.

"I'm taking him back home with me," he said, after a pause, "Lil's up for it, so once we're out of the line I'll speak to the squadron commander. See what needs doing".

Davo raised an eyebrow.

"Back to Australia eh?"

Percy nodded.

"He's got no one...well...except us...and I reckon he's earned more than just a pat on the back and a wave goodbye when we leave".

Davo didn't reply straight away. He looked at Alfie again - his small frame hunched as he spurred Bow on like he always had done.

"That boy is a real trooper," Davo thought to himself, before turning to Percy.

"He's a lucky chap," he said finally, "and so are you".

Meanwhile, the 4th Light Horse Brigade had been tasked with securing the Jsir Ed Damieh crossing over the Jordan River. Their job was to hold it against any Turkish attempt to swing around and strike the Allied columns from the flank or rear. It was a vital position, and the men knew it.

The King of the Hedjaz had pledged seven thousand men to support the offensive, promising to move in concert with the British advance. But the Arabs were full of broken promises, and whether they would arrive in time - or arrive at all - remained to be seen.

Before dawn, under intermittent fire from Turkish guns at Mifad Jozele, the 3rd and 4th Brigades moved swiftly up the valley. The darkness cloaked their movement, and by first light they had reached their objectives with minimal delay.

The 5th Cavalry Brigade took to the goat track known as Number 7 Road, leading their horses in single file up the steep incline. The climb was brutal - two thousand feet of zig zagging turns and bends, and silence - but the horses, hardened by months of campaigning, took it in their stride. The men, too, had learned not to waste their breath on complaint.

With the 4th Brigade now in position, command deemed that only one squadron was needed to monitor Mafid Jozele. Therefore, at 1500 hours, the 1st Light Horse Brigade - less a squadron from the 1st Regiment - was ordered to follow the 5th Cavalry up the track.

Once atop the crest, the regiment had a clear view of the battlefield below. The 60th Division had failed to break the Turkish line at Shunet Nimrin and El Haud, and the Turkish positions held firm. El Haud, in particular, proved to be a devastating artillery observation post. From its heights, Turkish gunners rained fire with precision, inflicting severe casualties on the British infantry.

The Allied guns, by contrast, were blind. With no observation posts of their own, they could offer no meaningful support. The imbalance was striking - and costly.

The Turkish grip on Shunet Nimrin and El Haud remained solid, and with the heights still in enemy hands, a new dilemma emerged for the Australians. Their rear - once considered secure - was now exposed. The tracks they had laboured up, the same narrow arteries that had carried them toward Es Salt could just as easily become a route for enemy counter movement. Vulnerability had crept in, quiet and insidious.

'A' Squadron, under Major Brown, was dispatched to guard the road they had just travelled, tasked with holding the line and watching for signs of Turkish infiltration. The rest of the regiment pressed forward, halting within a mile of Es Salt. The town lay ahead, quiet for now; its stone buildings crouched against the hills like wary observers.

By first light on the 1st of May, Major Brown sent word that two enemy posts had been spotted to the south of his position. They were moving deliberately, not probing but positioning - an unmistakable sign that they intended to cut the line of communications.

The regiment responded swiftly and the men turned back, retracing their steps like men who had learned not to waste time or breath. Their new task was clear - keep the mountain track open at all costs. If the Turks severed that lifeline, the entire forward movement could collapse into isolation.

The men dismounted as they took up defensive positions. The regiment's horses - dusty, restless, and still bearing the sweat of the trek - were tethered in a sheltered hollow just off the track, where the terrain offered some protection from stray fire. A small guard was posted over them, quiet and watchful, knowing full well that without these mounts, retreat would be a distant hope.

Percy was checking the line when he spotted Alfie sitting near a low stone wall, his leather boot black pouch clutched tight against his chest. The boy looked up, a worried expression on his face.

"Mister Percy," he said quietly, "where shall I go now?"

Percy crouched beside him, and whispered calmly.

"I bet you're frightened, mate".

Alfie shook his head.

"No...I am a soldier...just like you".

Percy paused, studying the boy's face - earnest, defiant, too young by half. Then he nodded.

"Yes mate...you are, aren't you...but do you know what...*I'm* scared and so are all these blokes?"

"Really?" replied a surprised Alfie. "Then I am too...scared shitless I am".

Chugger's use of the English language had obviously struck again, but Percy just smiled and ruffled the boy's hair.

"Good on yer Alf".

He stood and glanced around, spotting Rachel nearby, who was already watching them, concern written plainly across her face.

"Rachel," Percy called gently, "can you keep an eye on him?"

She stepped closer, her voice soft.

"Yes...come," she replied as she beckoned to the boy.

Percy gave a quiet nod.

"He's got a good head. Just needs someone steady near him".

"Come, Alfie," she said, touching his shoulder gently, "you sit with me, yes? I have place near Chugger...come".

Alfie looked up at her, uncertain for a moment, and then nodded, before following her across the uneven ground, weaving between tethered horses and crouched troopers. Chugger, already settled behind a low rise with his rifle resting across his knees, gave a sideways glance as they approached.

"G'day Alfie, keeping us company are yer mate?"

Rachel smiled, settling Alfie beside her.

"He is good, brave boy. I look after him, like he once look after me".

Chugger gave a small nod, and then turned his eyes back to the ridgeline.

Alfie sat cross-legged, close to Rachel's side, watching the men around him. She handed him a piece of dried fruit from her satchel and whispered something in Arabic - just a few words, soft and familiar. He relaxed a little, chewing slowly, the tension easing from his shoulders.

Rachel then glanced at Percy, who was now searching the ground through his binoculars. She caught his eye and gave a small nod - nothing dramatic, just enough to say *he's alright now*.

Percy returned the nod, and then turned back to the line. The track was quiet for the moment, but the silence felt temporary. The men were ready, the horses guarded, and the boy - though not a soldier - was as safe as could be.

The regiment settled into its new role, watching the track like sentries at a gate. The enemy was close now, and the margin for error had narrowed to a breath.

Plans to dislodge the enemy from their vantage points were made without delay. The Turks, dug in along the high ground, had the advantage of height and cover - positions that allowed them to harass the Allied movement with impunity. Something had to give.

Under a veil of machine gun fire, two troops under Lieutenants Joyner and Henderson began the push. The climb was steep and exposed and the ground was loose underfoot. Men scrambled upward in bursts, ducking low behind rocks and scrub as bullets whistled overhead. The enemy resisted fiercely, but the Australians pressed on, inch by inch, until the crest was taken. By mid-morning, the position was theirs - henceforth known, with quiet pride, as Joyner's Hill.

But the fight was far from over. Two enemy posts on the regiment's left flank sat uncomfortably close - too near for comfort, too well placed to ignore. Lieutenant King was tasked with leading a night raid to clear them out. Twenty men were selected, including Percy's section. Rachel, though technically a non-combatant, insisted on accompanying them.

Before they moved out, Percy crouched beside Alfie, who was tucked behind a large boulder.

"Stay here, mate," Percy said gently, "we'll be back soon...promise".

Alfie looked up, uncertain

Rachel knelt beside Alfie, brushing dust from his sleeve.

"You stay quiet, yes? I go with Chugger and Mister Percy. I come back when sky is light".

Alfie nodded, swallowing hard.

The raiding party moved out just after dusk. The ground was treacherous - uneven, rocky, and riddled with thornbush. They advanced in silence, their boots muffled by cloth wraps, or by wearing socks over them. The night was still, save for the occasional rustle of wind through scrub.

Lieutenant King raised a hand, signalling a halt. The men froze, crouched low. A moment passed. Then, from the enemy position ahead, came a sound - unexpected, unmistakable.

A long, wheezing fart.

Rachel, crouched beside Percy, clapped a hand over her mouth. Her shoulders shook with suppressed laughter. Percy gave her a sideways glance, half amused, half incredulous.

King's eyes narrowed. He motioned again - this time forward.

The Australians crept closer, using the terrain to mask their approach. The enemy, lulled by the quiet and their own bodily functions, never saw them coming. The trench line was barely visible until they were on top of it - just a jagged seam in the earth, half-shadowed by scrub and moonlight. Then the silence snapped. A startled shout...a flash...then the Australians were in.

The attack was swift and brutal, and the night erupted into mayhem. Percy dropped into the trench and drove forward, his bayonet charged. The man ahead of him buckled, clutching his side, and went down hard. Someone screamed - short, loud, then cut off. A rifle fired from the far end of the trench, but the angle was wrong, the shot went wide.

Rachel moved through the chaos like a demon. Her scimitar caught a Turk mid-turn, sliced through shoulder and chest, and left him folded over the sandbags. Then she pivoted, ducked, and struck again - clean, fast, final.

Davo was already in the trench, elbowing a Turk aside and slamming him into the wall. No finesse - just brute force. Boggy followed, his rifle raised, but he didn't fire, using the rifle butt instead, swinging it once, twice, and dropping any Turk in his path.

A Turkish soldier lunged at Percy with a shovel, but Percy managed to sidestep before grabbing the man's arm, kicking his feet from under him, and then driving his bayonet into the soft gap below the ribs. The man gasped then went still. Percy stepped over him and kept moving.

Chugger was somewhere to the left, swearing between breaths, dragging a Turk by the collar, then punching him to the ground. Johnno vaulted the trench lip and landed hard, knocking a man flat. He didn't bother with his weapon - just fists and knees until the Turk stopped moving.

The trench was narrow, the fight tighter than expected. Men collided, slipped, grappled. One of the Turks tried to climb out - Rachel caught him with a downward stroke that split his back open. He twitched once, then stilled.

Five Turks were killed outright, four more taken prisoner. A supporting Turkish squadron, caught off guard and rattled by the sudden violence, fled in disorder, leaving behind packs, rifles, and a half-cooked pot of lentils.

Thankfully there were no casualties amongst the lighthorsemen.

Despite the success of the raids, the broader operation faltered. The King of the Hedjaz, having consulted his oracle, declared the day unfit for battle. He withheld his promised support, leaving the British and ANZAC columns exposed and over extended. The consequences were immediate.

The Hedjaz, a stretch of Red Sea coast anchored by the holy cities of Mecca and Medina, had become a kingdom in name only - born of revolt, sustained by British gold, and ruled by Sharif Hussein with one eye on prophecy and the other on imperial promises. His alliance with the British was never simple. Though he had declared the Arab Revolt against the Ottomans in 1916, the Hedjaz campaign was shaped as much by mysticism and tribal politics as by military strategy.

Rumours had already circulated among the ranks that the Arabs under the command of T.E. Lawrence came only when there was murder to be done and riches to be had. Once their greed was quenched, they vanished into the desert until called again. They weren't always reliable, and no one was ever quite sure what they were really fighting for. Some rode for faith, some for vengeance, and some for the spoils of war. But none stayed long once the blood had dried.

For Percy and his mates, the delay was more than a tactical inconvenience. It was a fracture in the illusion of unity. The Hedjaz had their own war, their own gods, and their own reasons for turning back, and now, with the oracle's verdict hanging in the air like smoke, the Empire's columns stood alone - stranded between prophecy and pragmatism, waiting for the next move in a game they no longer understood.

Chugger had never been shy about his opinion of the Arabs - their reluctance to fight, their vanishing acts when the bullets started flying, their outdated and sometimes hateful beliefs. But with Rachel nearby, he held his tongue. She wasn't one for sentiment, but she was still Arab, and Chugger, for once, chose silence over insult.

Rachel, however, had no such reservations. She called Hussein a coward, a man of robes and riddles, not of blood and honour. He was not of her people, and *not* her King.

Chugger felt a flicker of relief. Not joy, not agreement - just the easing of a tension he hadn't known he'd been holding. For all their cultural differences, Rachel had said what he hadn't dared; the lines between loyalty and lineage blurring just enough to make sense.

It soon became clear that the 60th Division had been handed a task far beyond its capacity at Shunet Nimrin. The terrain was merciless, offering no cover and no kindness, whilst their persistent enemy, pressed forward with the certainty of men who knew the land better than those defending it. From the north, a formidable Turkish column advancing out of Nablus had struck hard at Jisr Ed Damieh, driving the 4th Brigade from their positions and capturing nine guns in the process. The brigade, already stretched to its limit, fought desperately to prevent the enemy from sweeping down the Jordan Valley and severing the only tenuous link to the plateau above.

This marked the regiment's second bitter setback in the region - a district that seemed to offer nothing but dust, dead ends, and disappointment. With the threat of encirclement growing by the hour, the Commander-in-Chief issued the order to withdraw. The retreat began under cover of darkness on the night of the 3rd of May. Any delay would have risked the entire column, which now clung to the plateau with only a single route of escape - a narrow, winding track hemmed in by cliffs and scrub, impossible to manoeuvre through with any speed or cohesion.

The commanding officer of the 2nd Light Horse was appointed Officer Commanding Rear Guard, with the Sherwood Rangers and Canterbury Mounted Rifles placed under his command. But the 2nd itself was already fully committed to a critical task, that of keeping Number 7 Road open. It was the only track in the valley not yet overrun by the enemy - a lifeline, fragile and exposed.

For nearly three miles, the regiment was forced to fan out along both sides of the track, facing outward into the scrub and ravines. Each man took up position with the knowledge that if the line broke, the entire column - men, animals, guns, and refugees - would be trapped. The manoeuvre was carried out in silence and haste. Troopers slid from their saddles and took cover behind boulders and thorny brush, their horses tethered out of harm's way, whilst orders were passed in whispers. There was anticipation in the air.

At 1900 hours, the withdrawal began. The narrow passageway held by the 2nd Light Horse became a funnel for the retreating force. Christian refugees moved in clusters, clutching bundles and children. Camel convoys groaned under the weight of supplies. Donkey carts rattled over the uneven ground, whilst mountain batteries rolled past, their gunners pale and silent. The column stretched for miles, winding through the valley like a wound that refused to close, inching forward with every heartbeat of retreat.

The CO of the 2nd Light Horse sat motionless in the saddle, listening to the dark. The valley was hushed now, no hoof beats, no rattling carts, no whispered orders, just the occasional creak of leather or a snort from a horse. As the last unit passed down the track, dawn began to break. He turned to his second in command, his voice a steady whisper.

"That's it. Pass the word. Time for us to go".

There was no bugle or shouted command, just silent hand signals. The CO rode ahead, passing through his own men where they lay prone on both sides of the track. He gave a silent nod of acknowledgement as he went, and a few troopers returned it, just as quietly - no salute, no words, just the shared knowledge that the line had held, and the last man was through. As the column reached them, men began to rise from the dust, swinging into the saddle without fuss. The soft clink of stirrups and the rustle of horses marked their joining. The rear guard wheeled quietly onto the track, slipping into the half light like a shadow folding in on itself.

The withdrawal of the regiment was carried out sector by sector. B' Squadron passed through the lines of 'A' Squadron, each taking its turn as rear guard before falling back through 'C' Squadron, which held firm on the crest of the plateau. The manoeuvre was orderly and deliberate, whilst the terrain itself - steep, broken, and narrow - worked in their favour preventing the enemy from pursuing rapidly or deploying on a broad front. They shelled the track, but missed their chance to cut it.

By 0800 hours the following morning, the last of the troops had passed through. The 2nd Light Horse remained in position until the final man was clear, and then fell back in disciplined silence, leaving behind only hoof prints, spent cartridges, and the echo of a battle narrowly escaped, following the withdrawing soldiers and civilians slowly down the narrow track.

A section of the regimental staff, under Saddler Sergeant Jorgensen, was the last to leave the high ground east of Road Number 7. They had remained to cover the withdrawal of two troops of Sherwood Rangers, exposed and vulnerable in the early light.

During the action, Jorgensen and Private Brennan were both wounded - Brennan seriously. Under fire, the regiment's Medical Officer, Captain Trinca, had dressed their wounds and saw them safely removed.

Enemy aircraft harassed the retreat, bombing and strafing both the rear guard and the column, but by 1400 hours, the 2nd Light Horse had rejoined the brigade near Umm Es Shert. The sun was high, casting hard light across the valley floor. Dust filled the air like smoke, and the track behind them shimmered with heat and silence. They remained in support of the 4th Brigade, waiting, and when midnight came, it was the 2nd that covered its final withdrawal - quietly and competently.

By 0320 hours, the regiment reached its bivouac near Jericho. Horses were unsaddled in silence. Men lay down without speaking. The valley behind them was empty now - held for as long as it needed to be, and no longer.

On the 3rd of May Captain Ponsonby had requested volunteers for a raid. Twelve men, including Stowie and Pip were chosen and placed under Ponsonby and Lieutenant Sargent for special training. In the mean time, on the 4th, the rest of the battalion went in to reserve on the right of Pradelles, and were billeted in farm houses. However, this was short lived as on the next day 12 inch shells began to fall, forcing the battalion into the surrounding open fields. It then moved out and relieved the 11th Battalion in the front line between Meteren and Strazeele.

There was some welcome rest from the front line, however, for some of the troops.

"Roo, Archie...you're a couple of Queensland drovers eh?" asked Clancy.

Archie was confused by the question.

"You know we are mate...but so are you, *and* half the blokes here".

"Yeah mate, but I've got an easy job for a couple of boys with your talents," Clancy replied, "now grab a couple of helpers and come with me".

Something strange was going on, but at least it was a break from the forward trenches. Archie rounded up four soldiers and Clancy walked the five men down the saps, past the reserve trench and out into open fields. It was a dark night and, for once, a quiet one, the only sound being the distant mooing of cattle.

"Can you hear that?" asked Clancy.

The men stood for a moment straining to hear, but there was nothing obvious.

"No mate...what are we listening for?" asked Archie.

"Stone the crows boys...I thought you blokes were stock-men...*cows*...can't you hear them?"

Obviously the men *had* heard the animals, but they had dismissed them for the more obvious sounds of war.

"Yeah Clance, we can, but what's that got to do with anything?" said Roo.

Clancy explained that the company had been tasked to round up some stray cows that had been walking on to the front line, and drive them back towards St Sylvestre Cappel, where they would be taken into custody by the MPs.

Archie was aghast at such an order.

"You're bloody kidding!"

"No mate...find 'em and round 'em up," said Clancy.

"With no bloody horses...*and* we can't *see* the bastards," replied Archie.

Cows were hard enough to round up during the daylight, let alone in the pitch black of night, with mud up to the ankles and nerves frayed from the ever present thunder of guns. The Taylor boys and their team stumbled and slipped through fields and ditches, their feet squelching in the sloppy mud, and tempers boiling over. There was certainly no shortage of profane language flying through the night - half directed at the cows, the other half at each other.

After a few maddening hours of stubborn refusals, false starts, and one unfortunate incident involving a collapsed fence and a furious bull, they finally managed to round up a small herd of ten scruffy looking cows and coax them onto the road. The animals lowed and shuffled, herded along by a chorus of curses and waving arms.

But just as they began to make headway, the enemy decided it was a good time to liven things up. A low thump echoed in the distance, followed by the rising whine of incoming shells. Within moments, explosions began creeping closer, the gunners clearly adjusting their aim. Earth and shrapnel erupted in the fields beside them, sending dirt clods, cow pats and curses flying.

The cattle didn't wait for instructions. With a terrified bawl, the whole herd bolted - horns flailing, hooves hammering the road like thunder - and disappeared into the dark with the speed of a cavalry charge. The stampede was met with a renewed storm of foul language, some of it inventive enough to earn a medal.

Covered in mud, thoroughly soaked, and with their pride in tatters, the team regrouped behind a stone wall to wait out the barrage. But the Taylor boys weren't ones to give up easily. As dawn slowly crept over the countryside, casting a pale glow across the broken fields, they set off again, muttering threats and promises to the wind.

By mid morning, after much scrambling and more than one undignified tumble into a ditch, they had managed to track down the scattered cattle - still jittery, but none the worse for wear - and drive them at last to the waiting MPs.

Archie gave a theatrical bow as he handed over the small herd.

"Your cows, gentlemen...delivered under fire. They might be the only livestock in France with battle experience".

The MPs said little, but the smirks on their faces suggested they had heard the story already. The Taylor boys and their mates just shook their heads and trudged off in search of a cup of tea and something hot to eat, muttering darkly about cows, Germans, and the general injustice of war.

To the front of the 9th Battalion's line loomed the shattered remnants of the Meteren Baths - a squat cluster of buildings the British had thrown up three years earlier, when this sector had been a quiet backwater, well behind the lines. Some of the older hands remembered steaming water and clean towels there, long before the front had lurched backwards over the countryside like a drunkard. But now, the ruins housed less welcome company. A German machine gun was positioned near the baths and Captain Ponsonby's raiding party's mission was to capture it.

In the cold, moonless early hours of the 12th of May, the raiding party crouched in the forward sap, their breath misting in the still air. They were ready. Faces were blackened, bayonets fixed. All eyes on the looming silhouette of the Baths.

Then came the signal.

For eight thunderous minutes, trench mortars whizzed silently overhead, their dull thumps followed by jarring explosions as the bombs landed amidst the ruins, flinging bricks and timbers skyward. Flames licked at shattered beams, and smoke clung low to the ground. When the barrage lifted, the raiders surged forward swiftly, one section moving in from the north, the other sweeping in from the south west. They advanced at the crouch, weaving through shell holes and barbed wire until they reached the trench beside the Baths.

But when they reached the trench, it was empty.

Vacant firing bays, abandoned scraps of kit, and the acrid tang of high explosives were all that remained. The men scanned the night, half expecting an ambush. But nothing moved except the smoke curling from the shattered wall. Disappointment welled in every chest. Frustrated, the raiders turned back to the lines, casting wary glances behind.

"Bloody Fritz," Stowie whispered, "off for some sour kraut I suppose".

The fifteen strong Number 9 platoon of 'C' Company was then dispatched to dig in near the empty trench. The wind was still and the battlefield was enveloped in a mist which curled around the twisted wire and broken bricks like smoke from a dying fire. Dawn crept in slowly. The eastern sky turned the colour of dirty pewter as the light bled across the battered landscape. It was then they saw them. A handful of German soldiers - careless, unhurried - picking their way across the open ground, likely unaware that the Baths had changed hands. They walked as though heading back to their old post, rifles slung over their shoulders, their heads down.

The Aussies held their breath. Fingers curled around triggers. The silence was broken by a short burst from the Lewis Gun - sharp, stuttering, brutal. The enemy party scattered.

Two dropped their rifles and raised their hands without hesitation. They stumbled forward, pale-faced and shaking, and were quickly searched and hauled back across no man's land.

No cheers, no bravado - just grim nods and quick glances toward the German lines. The business was done. The trenches held and Number 9 Platoon had marked the early hours with a quiet victory.

As the dawn mist lifted along 'B' Company's position, it revealed a quiet stretch of torn earth between the lines - quieter than expected. Archie, crouched beside Roo and Stowie in the trench, peered through his periscope at the vague outlines taking shape in the distance. The churned mud and half-dried craters had a pale sheen under the early light, and every now and then, movement flickered near the horizon.

"Something's crawling about out there," he whispered, nudging Roo with his elbow, "between those two blasted stumps. See it?"

Roo cupped his hands around his eyes and squinted.

"Yeah...can't tell if it's friend or foe though".

"Yep," Stowie grunted, fixing his bayonet to his rifle, "I saw it too. Could be a recce party".

A few figures darted from one shell crater to another, bent over low. They appeared disorganised. Every time one tried to move, a sharp crack from the 9th's rifles would send them scrambling back down into the dirt.

"Whoever they are they don't know their arse from elbow," Roo replied, "they're all over the flamin' shop".

Just then, Lieutenant Sargent appeared, moving briskly along the duckboard. He crouched down beside Archie.

"So what's happenin' Arch?"

"There's some mob stranded out there, sir. Couldn't say how many, but they're hugging shell holes and making a dog's breakfast of any escape attempt".

Sargent raised his field glasses, studied the figures for a moment, recognising the enemy uniforms, and then nodded.

"Bloody Germans...they're cut off, that's for certain. Probably slipped forward in the dark and lost their bearings. If they were serious, they'd have called in artillery by now".

"If they move again, shall we drop 'em?" Archie asked quietly.

Sargent shook his head.

He turned and gave a quiet order to a runner, who dashed back down the trench.

"Not unless they make a serious go of it. Maybe just keep their heads down for now eh? They could be inexperienced troops or even bait to lure us out, so let's not get too hasty".

"Yeah mate, I agree," Roo added.

The officer quickly addressed the troops.

"Keep your heads down and your rifles ready men. If they try a proper breakout, let them have it. But don't waste ammo".

The soldiers nodded, eyes on the field, fingers resting on triggers.

The morning light strengthened, burning away the mist. Now the enemy party was fully visible - about twenty of them, scattered and dug in, clearly reluctant to make a run for it.

From time to time, one of the enemy figures would lift their head or try to crawl toward the German lines, but the Aussies had the field covered. A few .303 rounds unleashed in their direction saw to it that they stayed put.

"*Those* poor bastards are in a bit of a pickle," Clancy said, strolling up with a tin of bully beef and his usual half-grin.

"I don't know mate..." Archie replied, "they might surprise us yet".

But the enemy didn't try anything bold. They just sat there, stuck between two armies, motionless and waiting.

By mid-morning, Lieutenant Sargent ordered a small flanking party to move up through some dead ground on the right, cutting off any hope of retreat. Roo, Archie, and a handful of others crept forward, using shattered trees and folds of mud for cover. The wind carried the scent of damp soil, cordite, and something sour - like fear.

When the Aussies reached a section of high ground that gave them a clear view of the stranded party's rear, Sargent signalled from the trench.

Archie, slightly hunched, stood slowly, rifle raised but not aimed, and called out in his best schoolboy German, rough and loud across the torn up landscape.

"Hands up...hände hoch...hände hoch!"

Their leader, a young corporal barely out of school, looked from man to man, realised the hopelessness of it all, then slowly nodded and raised his hands. The effect was immediate. Startled faces looked up, tense and grey with fear. Helmets were pulled off and rifles thrown down. One by one, the enemy soldiers clambered to their feet, hands raised, awkward and stiff. The youngest looked barely seventeen, and one lad was visibly trembling, his knuckles white where he gripped the air. There were eighteen of them. Not a one over twenty.

As Roo and Archie approached with caution, the reality settled over them.

"Bloody hell..." Stowie whispered, "kids".

Their faces were pale, eyes full of terror, chins trembling despite their efforts to look composed. One soldier still had a shaving rash. Another clutched a rosary in his hand. Most hadn't even managed to fire a shot during their short time in the war.

"They're soldiers all the same mate," Archie replied.

Roo stepped forward and relieved the corporal of a pistol, nodding to him respectfully.

"You'll live to see your home, mate...not a bad trade, eh?"

The corporal didn't understand the words, but something in the tone must have struck him, because he gave a faint, grateful nod.

Lieutenant Sargent approached from the rear.

"Looks like they've had enough; get them moving, lads".

Archie nodded and motioned the prisoners forward, forming them into a line. They began their slow march back across the cratered ground, flanked by silent Australians.

"Green as spring grass," Roo said. "no wonder they didn't make a run for it".

As they marched, a few of the young Germans sniffled quietly, and Archie found himself thinking of his young nephew

Frank back home, praying to himself that the war would be over long before he could have his turn.

But as they passed along the trench line, other diggers leaned on their rifles, watching. Some sneered, others simply stared. There was no cheering, no gloating. Just a long silence as the war's brutal symmetry played out once more - only this time, the enemy wore the faces of frightened boys.

Later that evening, under the fading twilight, a section from 'C' Company began digging a new Observation Post just forward of the old village bathhouse ruins - the eerily skeletal structure still a risk of being re-occupied by the Germans. The work was quiet and careful, spades biting into the damp soil with soggy thuds. Then, just after stand-to the next night, word came down that the baths had to go. Orders were clear - they were to deny the enemy any chance of reoccupying the structure.

The plan was to torch it with incendiary rifle grenades. The men fired half a dozen, one after the other, the thump of each launch echoing off the shattered walls.

Nothing.

Each grenade landed with a wet splat or a dull thud, but not a single one ignited. Many a whispered curse swept down the trench line.

"That's bloody right," someone muttered from behind, "bloody things were made by the lowest bidder".

So it came to the old fashioned way.

With a grin that didn't quite reach his eyes, Corporal Holm grabbed two petrol cans, whilst Private Allen snatched up a box of matches.

"Bugger this for a game of soldiers," growled the corporal.

They waited for a pause in the gunfire, then vaulted the parapet like it was a schoolyard fence and sprinted across no man's land.

From the trenches behind them, dozens of heads popped up to watch, silent at first, then erupting into whispered encouragement and clenched fists.

The two figures zig zagged across the muddy ground, dodging shell holes and twisted wire, reaching the bathhouse in under a minute. Holm sloshed petrol onto the shell blasted timber while Allen worked his matchbox furiously in the breeze.

Then - a flash of flame. The dry boards caught instantly, and fire licked up the remains of the walls like it had been waiting all day to be born.

"Go, boys!" someone shouted from the trench.

Just as they turned to run, the sharp rattle of a German machine gun opened up, tracers whipping past them like angry wasps. Allen stumbled but didn't fall. Holm grabbed his sleeve, and the two tore back across the open ground, silhouetted by the growing inferno behind them.

From the trenches came a loud and defiant cheer.

"You bloody beauties!" Clancy roared, pounding the trench wall.

The whole battalion had seen it. It was a mad, foolish, and utterly Australian act of bravado - and the men loved every second of it.

Back in the line, Allen and Holm tumbled into the trench, breathless but grinning.

"Didn't fancy a bath anyway," Allen puffed.

"Too bloody cold," Holm added.

The fire behind them rose higher into the night, crackling like applause, as the lads slapped the two on the back and passed around whatever was left of the rum ration.

CHAPTER 7

Pack Up Your Troubles

The 5th Battalion took over the line from the 9th on the 13th of May, and at last, the men were able to shoulder their rifles and make their way from the stinking ruins of Meteren. The withdrawal was done with the businesslike movement of war-worn men heading to a brief reprieve. They trudged through South Borre, where they became Divisional Reserve, thankful for the lull in the action and a chance to scrape the dirt and grime from their skin.

Five days later, the 9th struck out again, this time farther to the rear, marching under a baking sun through Hazebrouck and Sercus. It was only May, but the day bore down like mid-summer. Dust rose in clouds from the roadside, coating everything in a film of chalky grey.

Pip, red-faced and dripping with sweat, wiped his face and adjusted his slouch hat for the hundredth time.

"Blimey, I'm melting. I reckon I've lost two stone since breakfast," he said, "and you could fry a bloody egg on my boots".

"If we had an egg..." Roo replied.

Archie chuckled beside him, barely breaking a sweat despite the load on his back.

"You call this hot?" he said. "Mate, back home we'd call this a cool change. Wait till you're digging post holes in January with the blowflies trying to cart you off".

Pip rolled his eyes.

"Cheers mate. Certainly sounds like something worth waiting for".

Archie laughed and slapped him on the back.

"Yeah...right".

To pass the time, the men even managed a song or two. First it was *Click Goes the Shears*, and before long, someone launched into *Botany Bay*, the rest of the column joining in with gusto. The old songs drifted ahead of them like a banner, a reminder of the life they had left behind and the mates who still sang with them.

As they marched, they passed wave after wave of traffic heading back toward the fighting - lorries groaning beneath the weight of supplies, guns drawn by weary draught horses, ambulance wagons bouncing over ruts with wounded men inside staring grimly from beneath their bandages. Dispatch riders roared by in a blur of dust and oil, their faces set with urgency.

Fields on either side of the road were dotted with civilians. Refugees from the overrun towns sat in clutches beneath canvas sheets and scavenged awnings. Some stirred salvaged cooking pots over tiny fires; others simply sat on kitchen chairs and watched the column pass. Children, smudged with dirt, waved at the soldiers, and a few of the men - Roo among them - tossed them a packet of biscuits or a spare tin of bully beef.

"Here you go, young fella," Roo muttered, handing over a biscuit to a boy no older than eight. The child blinked up at him, then offered a hesitant smile.

"Breaks your bloody heart," said Clancy quietly as he watched a mother cradle her baby beneath a tree, her face worn and blank.

They carried on, and as the sun sank low behind them, the countryside began to change. The air cooled, hedgerows thickened, and the landscape softened into a picture of rolling pastures and quiet lanes. By the time the men arrived that evening, they were greeted by a patchwork of green fields and copses of trees that offered shade and, for once, a sense of peace. Tents were pitched near a stand of oaks, the ground dry and firm beneath them.

The war wasn't far off - not really - but for the moment, the front was behind them, and the stillness of the French countryside settled gently over the battalion like a long-overdue blessing.

The blessing got even better when, on the 20th of May, three days of sporting competitions began, taking the place of battle for just a brief moment. Rifles were laid aside, and for a short while, the men swapped bayonets for cricket bats, sprinting spikes, and tug-of-war ropes. It was as if someone had turned the war off for a moment - just long enough to let them breathe.

Each company fielded teams, and the contests were fierce but full of laughter. Bare-chested men with sunburnt shoulders charged through makeshift obstacle courses, hurled javelins fashioned from old tent poles, and cheered themselves hoarse. The prize wasn't much - maybe a tin of peaches or the last drop of rum - but pride was more than enough.

On the 22nd they were even treated to an inspection by the Division Commander, Major General Walker, another Gallipoli veteran. Although a career British Army officer, Walker was well respected by the ANZACs for his directness and tactical ability. 'Walkers Ridge' at Gallipoli had been named for him, and he had commanded the Division since the Dardanelles campaign.

So, late in the morning, the battalion fell in on the flat grass near their encampment. The sun was warm overhead, the breeze light, and the ranks stood straight, uniforms brushed down, boots as clean as could be expected after weeks in the line. The CSM moved down the line like a sheepdog, straightening slouch hats, adjusting belts, and muttering reminders about chin straps and buttons.

Then the unmistakable bark of the Garrison Sergeant Major, a hush falling over the assembled ranks as they came to attention. As the staff car pulled up the General took his place on the make shift podium.

"General salute...present...arms," came the order.

A quick chorus of *God Save The King* sounded out from the massed bands of the battalions, whilst Walker saluted smartly to his men.

Following the order to shoulder arms, Major General Walker, his face lined by experience rather than age, stepped briskly along the line, moving steadily along the ranks, occasionally stopping to speak with a man or glance over a rifle. He carried himself with the easy confidence of someone who had seen it all - and been through most of it himself.

As he neared the centre, his gaze lingered on one weathered, broad shouldered figure. He came to a halt.

Walker's brow furrowed, and then his face broke into a small, knowing smile.

"Sergeant Major...er...Clancy, isn't it?" he said, tilting his head.

Clancy straightened; his expression one of surprise.

"McBride sir...Clancy is my first name".

"Ah yes...I thought so. I remember you from Gallipoli. You were the fellow who told Field Marshal Kitchener that the AN-ZACs had reached their objectives on the first day, but couldn't push on for want of manpower".

"I did, sir. It was the truth...I was there".

"A rare thing, telling it so plainly," Walker replied, "the Field Marshal thanked you at the time, but I didn't...but...I do now".

Some of the men nearby, trying their best to remain composed, let the corners of their mouths twitch into small grins.

Walker moved on, pausing to exchange a few brief words with a young private from Toowoomba about the cricket scores. At the end of the line, he addressed the assembled battalion.

"You have all done well - held firm when it mattered, and I have no doubt you will do so again. Enjoy these days while you can. You have earned them".

Then he was gone, striding back toward his staff car with the crisp step of a man who knew full well that calm days like these were rare and precious.

And just like that, the war faded again - for an hour, for a day - and was replaced with cricket balls, laughter, and the scent of grass.

But, all good things must come to an end, and after only eight days at Sercus the battalion began its move back to the front line, marching along the St Omer-Hazebrouck Road. The spring sunshine glinted on bayonets and belt buckles, and the mood was light enough, but there was also a sense of purpose in the ranks.

General Walker had positioned himself at a point near Hazebrouck in order to watch the 3rd Brigade go by. The men were happy to see their commander, with some spontaneous outbursts of cheering from the ranks. The cheering, however, soon changed to shouts of "SCATTER" when the Germans unleashed an artillery barrage on the column, with two shells bursting in the ranks of the 9th, black smoke and shrapnel tearing through the morning calm, wounding two men. The battalion barely missed a step and calmly formed itself into artillery formation - a wide, staggered spread designed to reduce casualties from incoming shellfire - and continued their march. Each company moved to its assigned sector, platoons breaking into columns of four, spacing themselves out across a frontage no more than four hundred yards. It wasn't elegant, but it was effective. The formation evolved as they marched – an almost controlled disorder, learned through bitter experience. Officers called out brief orders, whilst section commanders guided their men with hand signals. The column snaked through fields and alongside the road, adjusting to the terrain while maintaining direction. It was the perfect balance between cohesion and survival. Spread too wide, and the men became unmanageable. Too tight, and one well placed shell could fell half a company. But like so many times before, the 9th had drilled this into instinct. Under fire, their discipline held, and so they pressed on – calm and unshakable.

Meanwhile, unperturbed, the General had repositioned himself further along the road to continue his review undisturbed. Clancy smiled to himself when he saw him.

"That bloke is sure made of the strong stuff eh?"

The battalion marched around Hazebrouck to Rouge Croix, and the following day relieved the 1st Battalion in the front line at Klite-Hil, half a mile north of Strazeele. Here they remained for nine days.

The countryside they now occupied was familiar and grimly changed; open and undulating, a patchwork of farmland stitched together by narrow lanes, low hedgerows, and occasional thickets of trees. The land sloped gently down towards the railway that ran from Hazebrouck to Bailleul, a long, easy fall that offered little concealment and no real sanctuary from watchful eyes or enemy guns. The shallow rise on which Strazeele stood was barely worthy of the name "hill," but out here, any height mattered. The town itself was little more than a crossroads of cracked stone and scorched timber - its brewery, blacksmith's shop, and windmill now charred silhouettes against the sky. The church, once a quiet sanctuary, was roofless and broken, its bell long silenced.

Just weeks earlier, the battalion had fought bitterly to hold this very ground during the enemy's push through Borre. The Germans had crept up ditches and hedges, advanced along farm tracks in small parties at first, then in broad waves, hoping to overrun the railway line and take the rise at Strazeele. But the Australians had been ready. In trenches dug into the folds of farmland, among hop-piles and shattered fences, they had lain in wait, and when the moment came, they had let the enemy come close - close enough to see the strain on their faces - and then they opened fire. The result had been devastating. Whole enemy files disappearing in the withering storm of rifle and machine gun fire. Furrows were shredded, hedges torn to ribbons, and men had fallen like sheaves of wheat. At first they withdrew, then they had come again, in greater numbers, pushing forward from Merris and Vieux-Berquin, trying to overrun the thin line of defenders stretched from Strazeele to the edge of Nieppe Forest. But still the line had held...and here they were again.

From the trench line at Klite-Hil, the men could see the sprawl of flat farmland stretching in all directions, dotted with wrecked carts, abandoned fields, and the hollow frames of homes caught in the tide of war. The ground sloped gently down toward the railway to the south, and beyond that the woods of Nieppe loomed in soft greens and spring bloom - a cruel contrast to the battered soil beneath their feet. A few sturdy farmhouses clustered around the roads, while others were scattered across the fields beyond, tucked behind tangled hedges and narrow ditches.

As they settled in, Archie leaned against the parapet, chewing a biscuit and shaking his head at the smoke curling from a far off farmhouse.

"Poor buggers," he muttered, "they just start patching things up and then get turfed out again. Same bloody paddocks, same bloody war".

Stowie grunted beside him.

"Yeah, it's like that mob we saw camped in that field the other day. Kids wrapped in blankets, trying to keep warm...when will it all end?"

Archie sighed.

"Soon I hope...soon".

Further along the trench, Clancy walked the line, checking on the men and trading quiet words with small groups.

"Keep your heads down, lads," he called cheerfully, "you can still see the windmill from here, which means Fritz can see you just as well".

From their shallow positions dug into the very hedgerows and fence lines where they had once played football or helped locals herd cattle, the battalion took stock of their surroundings. They weren't just returning to the front - they were returning to something half remembered and half ruined. Trenches ran through old fields they had drilled in, and gun pits now marked the spots where they had once dozed in the sun during training months ago. The outbuildings they had used for kit inspections or Sunday naps were now firing positions. Hedgerows that had concealed courting couples now housed machine gun nests. The girls, the cows and the laughter had gone or fled. Only the war remained.

To the left front, about a mile off, Merris lay crouched among trees, smoke from occasional shellfire curling above its rooftops. Further right, the dark silhouette of the Nieppe Forest framed the horizon, once a place of springtime walks and picnics during brief reprieves from the front, now scarred and echoing with the violence of war.

The men knew why they were here. They had fought to hold this ground once before, and now they were back to make sure the Germans didn't punch through again.

It was the last day of spring. The centre post of the battalion's sector was quiet - for now. Pip quickly removed his steel helmet to scratch an annoying itch, and then leaned against the rough timber of the firing step, peering through the gaps in the sand-bags. The sun was low and angry, shadows darkening the ground over no man's land. He yawned and glanced at the man beside him.

Private Knight stood motionless, his eyes fixed as he watched the horizon. He barely blinked. A wiry fellow from western Queensland, Knight was a quiet bushman with a keen eye and a steady nerve. He spoke little, but when he did, the others listened - there was something about the way he carried himself - like he belonged out there in the open, more scout than soldier. Pip had heard the others say he could spot a goanna in a gumtree from a mile off, and could smell a trap and pick out movement that others had missed.

"See that trench line out there?" Knight said, nodding toward a jagged lip in the churned earth some sixty yards ahead.

Pip squinted.

"Yeah, what of it?"

"Haven't seen movement in hours. Reckon it might be empty".

Pip hesitated.

"Or full of Huns playing dead".

Knight didn't smile, but the corner of his mouth twitched.

"Could be. But if it *is* empty, that's worth knowing, eh? Might be useful to the captain".

Pip raised a brow.

"You're not saying we should go take a squiz?"

"I am".

Pip looked again, then back at Knight. The man's calmness made it all sound simple. Not brave. Not stupid. Just necessary.

"Bugger it," Pip muttered, giving a nod to a soldier to his right, "lead on McDuff".

They two men slipped over the parapet like shadows, staying low. The mud sucked at their knees as they crawled, elbows digging into the cold earth. Shell holes dotted the landscape, many still filled with stagnant water. Insects buzzed lazily around them, indifferent to the war.

They paused halfway, flattening into a dip as a gust stirred the dead grass. Pip could feel his heart thudding in his chest, but Knight seemed unaffected, searching ahead like a man tracking Kangaroos back home.

A few more yards and they halted again, just short of the edge of the enemy trench.

Knight raised a hand for silence, then pointed. The trench was still. No helmets. No periscopes. No voices.

"What do you reckon mate?" whispered Pip.

He leaned close to Pip and whispered, "Looks empty...let's wait a minute...just to be sure".

And so they lay still, rifles at the ready, watching the ghost trench for signs of life. Minutes ticked by in silence, broken only by the occasional breath or the feint boom of artillery. Then, slowly, cautiously, they crept forward once more and eased themselves over the edge and into the enemy trench.

It was narrow and crudely built; the duckboards splintered and slippery underfoot. A brief wander around confirmed that it was empty, apart from a single Mauser rifle propped against the wall, and a few stick grenades scattered on the trench floor.

"Nobody home mate...wanna have a quick look for souvenirs?" asked Knight, his tone dry and unhurried.

Pip shrugged.

"Aye lar...why not?"

They moved along the trench at a steady pace, eyes darting over the walls and duckboards. Ahead, a cloth bag hung suspended in front of a shelter dug into the trench wall, swaying slightly in the breeze.

Knight reached for it.

"Hey...soft lad...what are you doing? It might be a booby trap," Pip warned, grabbing his arm.

Knight stepped back. Pip scanned the ground and spotted a long, broken plank. He hefted it and, like a spear, hurled it at the bag. It struck true, knocking the bundle to the floor with a loud, meaty thud.

Both men edged forward, wary. But just as they reached it, there was a sudden shout - a startled cry in German - and a soldier, roused from sleep in the dugout, scrambled half upright in confusion.

Without hesitation, Knight raised the Luger he had been carrying and fired once. The shot echoed through the trench. Blood sprayed from the man's chest, and the German dropped lifelessly back into the shadows.

The silence was shattered. From further along the trench came the unmistakable sound of boots on duck boards and shouted orders. Within seconds, around twenty five Germans were pounding toward them.

"SHIT!" Pip yelled, firing off quick shots down the trench, as Knight snatched up the grenades and hurled them towards the soldiers.

One burst mid-air, showering the approaching figures with shrapnel, then a German, bomb in hand, raised his arm to throw - but Knight dropped him with a single, well aimed shot.

"Right...time to leg it," said Pip.

The two men vaulted out of the trench, sprinting hard for the safety of their own lines. Behind them, chaos erupted. But by this time the Lewis gunner in the Aussie trench had been alerted by the mêlée and now fired at the helmets of the advancing Germans, the rounds stitching across the top of the enemy parapet, thus preventing them from leaving the trench.

Knight and Pip, hearts hammering, zig zagged across no man's land, ducking and weaving until the familiar voices of their mates called out from the safety of their own lines.

The two men breathed a sigh of relief as they dropped back into their post.

"Yep...it's definitely occupied boys," said Pip as he pulled out his canteen and took a sip.

But this wasn't to be the only excitement for the Aussies.

At 0200 hours the next morning Captain Ponsonby and the CSM were conducting their rounds of the line when there was a muffled shout from no man's land.

"Bloody hell, it's like Piccadilly Circus here at the moment," whispered Ponsonby.

A cry of "Stand to" reverberated along the line as three figures, hands raised, emerged from the darkness. They were unarmed and dressed in British style tunics, but they were a bluish grey colour.

"Portoogarl," one of the men called out.

"Portoogarl...what's that?" asked Clancy.

"Portoogarl...?" Ponsonby thought for a moment, "Portugal...they're Portuguese...stand down!"

Clancy was none the wiser.

"Is that a country mate?"

"Oh Clancy we are *definitely* going to have to teach you more about geography, " replied the captain, " yes it is...and they are our allies".

"Well, bugger me, you learn something new every day," said Clancy.

As the men were helped own into the trench the Aussies discovered that they had been captured at Lille but had escaped two days earlier, having successfully made their way through enemy lines. One of the men could speak a little English so was able to convey their adventure to the Australians.

That evening, the night of the 1st of June, there was more excitement as the dark fields behind the front line were momentarily split by the sudden rumble of German guns. Moments later, shells began falling with a deliberate, methodical rhythm. Battalion Headquarters, housed in an old weathered barn just off the main communication trench, took a near-direct hit. Slates from the roof came down like shrapnel, and the walls shook with the impact.

Worse still, one shell struck the Regimental Aid Post - set up under canvas and in the adjoining stable - igniting a fire that spread quickly. The flames roared up through the straw and old timber beams, lighting the night sky with a sickly orange glow. Men scrambled to drag out the wounded, shielding their faces from the heat as carts, stretchers, and a few crates of precious medical supplies were consumed in minutes. The Red Cross flags, one nailed to the barn door, fluttered defiantly in the heat before catching fire and disintegrating.

The groans of the injured and wounded mingled with shouted orders and curses, whilst smoke billowed out across the field, lighting it up against the moonlight. From nearby trenches, men watched angrily as the fire raged unchecked until midday the next day.

"Bloody hell - they're shelling the bloody RAP!" someone yelled.

"That's a hospital, for God's sake!"

"Bastards knew what it was," muttered Roo, shaking his head, "that was no bloody accident".

"Old Johnny Turk would never have done that," said Stowie, spitting in the mud. "Back on Gallipoli, they saw a Red Cross and gave it a wide berth".

"Different kind of enemy now mate," Archie added darkly. "The Turks had honour. These blokes will shell anything that moves...or doesn't".

"Yeah...I'm starting to see that more and more...they really are a vicious bunch these Huns," replied Stowie.

The fire continued to burn through the night and well into the next day. Smoke rose in a tall black column, visible for miles, prompting bitter jokes that the enemy didn't need spotters - he could follow his own handiwork.

Just two days later, in the early hours of the 3rd of June, the shelling resumed. This time, another direct hit smashed into Battalion HQ, which had changed location following the earlier attack, tearing a corner off the dugout and sending splinters of timber and clods of dirt flying through the air. Men dived for cover as the ground shook beneath them. Within minutes, another round came screeching in. This time, it was the turn of 'A' Company's Headquarters, which was housed in a crumbling stone farmhouse not far from the main trench line. A shell slammed into the upper floor, blowing out windows and part of the front wall, collapsing part of the roof and sending the men inside scrambling out into the open, swearing and gasping.

"Good morning to you too...you Hun bastards!" one shouted as he scrambled into a nearby trench.

Inside what was left of the farmhouse, the signaller's station had been wrecked, maps torn from the walls and kit flung across the room.

Down the road, at Battalion HQ, an officer surveyed the damage through a crack in the stable door.

"They're getting bloody bold," he said, "shelling the aid post, then Company HQs. They want us rattled".

But the men weren't rattled. Angry, yes - disgusted, certainly - but not broken. They patched what they could, shifted the wounded, and got back to their duties, grumbling to one another as they worked.

"Gallipoli was hell," someone said quietly, "but at least you knew where you stood".

"Yeah...about a hundred foot up, perched on the side of a bloody cliff," laughed another.

As the dust settled, the men crouched back in their positions, bitter and silent. Some casting uneasy glances toward the still smoking ruin of the Aid Post.

On the evening of the 4th and 5th of June, the 9th was relieved by the 5th Battalion and went to Hondeghem then on to Sercus on the 7th. The move offered a brief respite, though the men marched with slumped shoulders and heavy feet, their faces drawn from months of continuous strain. The countryside blurred past them in a haze of fatigue, the same hedges and farm-houses they had seen a dozen times before, now just markers on a road they were too tired to care about. For a lot of the men, four years in uniform, and the strain showed in every step - bent backs, hollow eyes, and a silence that lingered even when no orders were being given.

General Plumer even managed an inspection after church parade, his presence polite but distant, like a shadow passing through their midst, and on the 12th the men were treated to yet more Brigade Sports, but the cheers were quieter now, the laughter more forced.

"I reckon the big wigs are planning a footy match between us and Fritz," said Archie, "the loser goes home".

"I'm up for that mate," said a weary Clancy, "four bloody years of this...it's got to end sometime".

Around them, others nodded in agreement, too tired to speak. Even the promise of rest now came laced with doubt - how long would it last, and where would they be sent next?

The answer came sooner than hoped for. Yet another German attack was expected, so, on the 15th the Battalion moved forward to La Kreule.

"La Kruele? That sounds a bit *cruel* to me...what do you reckon lads?" joked Pip.

Clancy slapped him on the back of the head and laughed.

"Stupid pommy bastard!"

The men didn't say it out loud, but they remembered the place well having passed through it many times over the previous months. Just north of Hazebrouck, La Kreule was little more than a cluster of farm buildings perched on the flatlands where two main roads met. The fields were lined with old hedgerows and dotted with barns and stone houses that had seen better days. A railway line sliced through the countryside nearby, and somewhere along it - Ana Jana Siding - they knew the field hospitals had once stood.

Now, the only sign of those frantic days in April was the neat cemetery behind a hedgerow, where row upon row of makeshift wooden crosses stood in silent formation. They passed it without a word, but each man gave it a glance.

As they passed a small farmhouse, an elderly man in a long coat and battered cap waved them down from the gate.

"You are les Australiens?" he asked, eyes scanning their slouch hats.

"Too right, mate," said Roo with a wink, "we've come to kick Fritz up the arse".

The man smiled and gave a firm nod.

"Bon. We have heard you stopped them at Meteren. You fight hard. Maybe now, it is safe again, oui?"

"We'll do our best mate," said Clancy with a grin, "we don't like sharing our campsites with the Huns".

The old man chuckled and gave a half salute as they continued on. His quiet confidence, drawn from their reputation alone, lifted the mood just a little.

Where they were headed was a quiet place - but not peaceful - and with the Boche pressing again, there would be no rest at La Kreule.

The weather was pleasant enough as they set up their bivvie area in open fields. Movement was restricted however, as the troops were under observation from seven enemy balloons.

"Can't the flyboys just shoot the buggers down?" asked Pip.

"No mate. They are usually protected by machine gun groups so it aint worth the risk for the pilots," replied Stowie.

For the next two days, a strange hush fell over the lines. Barely a shell was fired, and rifle shots were few and far between. It was a lull, rare and uneasy, as if both sides had momentarily agreed to draw breath.

Then, under a sky heavy with cloud, the 9th Battalion once again moved into the front line at Merris, relieving the weary men of the 5th Battalion. The relief was carried out under cover of darkness, with whispered passwords exchanged at the junctions. The right sector was taken over by 'A' Company, the left by 'B', with 'C' in support and 'D' held in reserve in trenches just short of a ruined barn marked by a shattered windmill. The right flank of the Battalion now stretched as far as the Hazebrouck-Armentieres railway line, barely distinguishable in the dark but still a vital boundary.

The ground was sodden and cratered, strewn with old wire and the broken timbers of long-abandoned dugouts. Dead wheat stalks brushed the knees of the men as they moved into position, their outlines only just visible in the pale glow of the crescent moon, filtered now and then through streaks of cloud.

Captain Biggs of 'C' Company had devised a minor operation to push the line forward by two hundred yards - just enough to secure a better view of the terrain and deny the enemy a concealed approach. It was a small step on paper, but every foot of Flanders soil came at a price.

Just before midnight on the 20th of June, 'C' Company filed silently into place along a taped white line behind 'B' Company's observation posts. The line was little more than a faint thread stretched across the broken earth, but to the waiting men, it was a launch pad into who knows what...

At 0030 hours, for five minutes only, a lightning bombardment by artillery, trench mortars and rifle grenades was unleashed on the enemy positions to their immediate front. The bombardment lit up the darkness in violent flashes - brief glimpses of wire dancing in the wind, of shattered trees trembling, of rats fleeing blindly. The shells burst just ahead of the Australian lines, then rolled forward one hundred yards in a carefully timed sequence, with 'C' Company hot on its heels.

After a minute it crept forward another one hundred yards. The men surged from their line like shadows unleashed, bent low, bayonets fixed, their feet sloshing in mud, and their breath rasping in their throats. The first hundred yards passed quickly, the ground uneven but familiar. Barely eight minutes after the commencement of the barrage, leaping forward another hundred yards, the centre and left platoons had reached their objective and each fired a green Very Light - brief emerald arcs cutting through the night - as a signal to Battalion Headquarters of a successful operation. The smoke hung low and thick, curling around the tree stumps and barbed wire like a living thing. The digging began at once. Spades struck earth. Lewis guns were set, fields of fire established, and new orders whispered along the line.

These platoons had met with little resistance, the Germans, stunned by the intensity and suddenness of the barrage; however, it was a different story for Number 12 Platoon on the right, who could advance no further due to heavy machine gun fire erupting from a hidden post near the railway embankment. Bullets sliced through the dark like angry wasps. Within moments, their platoon sergeant was dead, and their platoon commander seriously wounded, along with eight of the men. Pinned and exposed, the survivors launched rifle grenades toward the source of fire, but the enemy could not be dislodged and held firm. The Sections from the Company were held up at between forty and fifty yards from the railway and were forced to dig, dirt flying in hurried scoops as they scratched out shallow scrapes in the mud. The crack and thump of German rifles cut through the night, answered by the defiant rat tat tat of an Australian Lewis gun, its section hastily summoned forward in a desperate bid to relieve the pressure. Still, the enemy refused to budge.

Behind them, in the main line, the rest of the battalion watched anxiously - murmured prayers, clenched fists, and quiet curses. Green flares had gone up, but they knew something had gone wrong on the right; the groans of the wounded and the sudden chatter of gunfire telling the tale.

In the smoky hush of the fire-step, Archie craned his neck, eyes fixed on the flashes up by the railway.

"Come on boys!" he whispered to himself.

Seeing how dire the situation was becoming, Captain Biggs requested assistance form 'B' Company

"About bloody time..." said Clancy.

Lieutenant Sargent and his platoon advanced along the right of the railway at 0230 hours, gradually working their way, inch by inch, up the railway to a position in line with the platoons to the left of the railway line.

"This is as good a place as any," the officer thought to himself, as he signalled for his men to settle in a large shell hole.

As the light of the new day slowly crept in, the Queenslanders could just make out the shape of a German soldier as he emerged from a shelter in a hedge about fifteen yards to the front of Lieutenant Sargent's platoon.

Roo was on to it straight away.

"Look at this cheeky bugger Tomo".

Lieutenant Sargent could not believe his eyes.

"Drop him boys!"

Roo squeezed his trigger and let one round fly towards the soldier. This was followed by shots from other men, eager to have a go at the Hun. The German's body jerked back, obviously hit, but not downed. He then suddenly broke into a sprint and vanished from view.

"Look at him go!" shouted Clancy, unable to contain himself, "good on yer mate".

Tomo peered through his binoculars.

"It's *got* to be occupied," he said, turning to Clancy, "I reckon we should fire a few rifle grenades their way".

For half an hour or so the 'B' Company boys scored a few direct hits on the shelter; but there was nothing for it, they needed to ascertain if the shelter was clear or not.

"Bugger this Tomo, we need to get up there," said Clancy.

The Lieutenant agreed and called for volunteers, Privates Cauchan and Ward immediately putting up their hands. After a snap briefing by the officer the two men left the relative safety of the shell hole, sliding over the edge of the crater and disappeared into the damp grass. As they crawled, the sloppy mud sucked at their arms and legs, whilst the vegetation snagged their tunics. The hedge loomed ahead, dark and tangled, the entrance to the German shelter no more than a jagged hole under the roots. Close enough now to smell stale tobacco drifting from within, Cauchan pulled the pin of a Mills Bomb, counted under his breath, and lobbed the grenade through the opening.

They didn't wait. Both men wheeled about and began the tense, belly down scramble back toward the platoon. Behind them the Mills Bomb went off with a flat, heavy thump - timbers splintering, dust blooming in the pale dawn light. In that same instant a single rifle cracked from the right flank - sharp, precise. Cauchan jerked, the breath punched from him, and slumped face first into the earth, motionless. Ward froze, stared for a heartbeat, then shook Cauchan's shoulder, but his mate was gone. A sniper hidden in the low brush had done his work.

Ward forced himself onward, his heart racing, each yard an eternity until eager hands hauled him back into the shell hole.

Sargent's voice cut through the shock as he looked at Ward.

"Well?"

"I think it's occupied but I can't say for sure," replied the soldier.

"Corporal Stowe..." said Lieutenant Sargent.

"Sir?"

"Fancy another look?"

"Yes sir, I'll take Private Vance and Lance Corporal Miller, but you'll need to deal with that sniper first," replied Stowie.

As Stowie and his band crawled towards the shelter, the Platoon's Lewis Gunner laid down suppressive fire in the direction of the sniper's post...but he was long gone; his deed done. Surprisingly they met no resistance and went to ground just short of the objective.

"Want me to take a quick look?" Miller asked Stowie.

"That's why we came here bud...so fill yer boots," Stowie replied.

Miller gingerly inched his way forward as Stowie and Vance kept watch for any Germans. He reached the post unhindered and stuck his head inside to find three enemy soldiers; one alive, but wounded, and two dead. Miller beckoned to the wounded man, and in his best German, called out "come and zee here". The soldier hesitated for a moment, until he had deciphered what Miller had just said to him, and then crawled slowly out of the post. The man could hardly walk and, seeing this, Stowie and Vance moved quickly forward, followed by the Lewis Gun team who would now dig in on the position.

"Looks like we'll have to carry him," said Stowie, eyeing up the German prisoner, "anything useful in that hole?"

"Just a machine gun mate," replied Miller.

"Grab it and let's get the hell out of here before Fritz spots us".

Vance hoisted the German over his shoulder and the three men ran back towards the platoon, whilst being repeatedly fired upon from the right front, bullets whipping past, kicking up little geysers of dirt at their heels.

Ahead, Lieutenant Sargent shouted to his men.

"Give it to them, boys…keep those Hun heads down!"

Rifles along the crater's rim answered at once, a fierce, rolling volley that raked the enemy positions, sending German helmets ducking.

Miller slipped once, recovered, and pushed on, whilst Vance, staggering under his human cargo, refused to slow. Another burst snapped overhead; a round tore through the sleeve of his tunic, but he kept his feet. With a final dive they tumbled back into the shell hole, men yanking them down just as fresh rounds whined through the air above.

Once back in the shell hole Lieutenant Sargent knelt beside the prisoner, tugging at the tunic collar to inspect the insignia. A dark green patch with silver numerals glinted in the half light revealing that he was from the 4th Bavarian Division. The officer looked around at his men.

"Boys, Battalion HQ need to know who we're facing, so I need a couple of volunteers to take the prisoner back down the line".

It was still night time, but soon the summer sun would begin to rise revealing the landscape for all to see, so it was a risky task for anyone to undertake; sure enough though, Pip was quick to put his hand up.

"Are you sure mate?" asked a concerned Lieutenant Sargent.

"Yeah…not a problem lar, and I'll be fine on my own like. Now give us a hand sticking him over my shoulder will yer?" replied Pip.

Once loaded up, all present wished him well.

"Run like buggery mate," said Roo.

As soon as Pip climbed out of the crater the Germans opened up on him, but adrenalin sent him flying along the line, zig zagging like some demented ancient heavenly messenger, and he was soon out of range.

"Can you believe that?!" exclaimed Archie, "Those Germans didn't even care that he was carrying one of their own...the bastards!"

Roo thought for a moment then laughed.

"Your Mum will be washing your mouth out with soap with your bad language mate".

Archie considered the irony of the statement for a brief moment.

"Hah! You can talk mate..."

During this action the battalion lost six men killed and eighteen wounded, with another five being wounded due to intense sniper action on the right.

CHAPTER 8

New Mates and Family

The 7th of May for the lighthorsemen broke not with bird-song, but with a roar from above.

Percy jolted awake as the snarl of engines tore through the early light, followed by the thud of bombs slamming into the camp. Tents were ripped apart by the concussion of the explosions, leaving the occupants exposed to the elements, whilst the earth almost buckled and spat skyward, horses rearing against their tethers in blind panic. Seven German aircraft streaked overhead, dropping their payloads in uneven lines across the bivouac like a child scattering stones.

Rachel had thrown herself over Alfie, shielding the boy with her body as the ground shook under another blast. Men scrambled from their tents, some still half asleep, drawn by instinct to the chaos unfolding around them.

They moved quickly. Troopers rushed to the lines, grabbing at reins, looping them around ropes and posts, calming the animals with firm hands and soothing voices. Others darted through the smoke, calling out for mates, checking shelters, dragging equipment and stores clear of the danger. The air was choked with dust and the sharp tang of explosives, but the men worked with the kind of urgency that came not from panic, but from experience.

Then, just as suddenly as it had begun, it was over.

The last of the aircraft dwindled into the horizon, leaving behind a camp stunned into stillness. Men rose from the dirt, coughing through the haze, brushing off shirts and muttering dark jokes. A few horses lay still, but most had been saved - thanks to the regiment's habit of spreading their lines wide. Relief came not in cheers, but in that brittle, half laughing chatter that always followed a close call.

Three days later, the regiment marched into the stony hills between Jericho and Jerusalem, halting near Talaat Ed Dumm. The Inn of the Good Samaritan stood nearby, its pale walls catching the sun like something out of a Bible story that Percy's mother used to read. For six days they rested - drawing water from deep wells, sleeping against cool stone, and savouring the rare quiet.

Then came Solomon's Pools.

Nestled between Hebron and Bethlehem, the place felt almost civilised. Compared to the dusty bivouacs of the Jordan Valley, it was a gift. The AIF Canteen and YMCA rolled in with their wagons, spilling out tins of peaches, chocolate, cigarettes and all manner of goodies. Mornings were for training - rifle drills, practice assaults on rocky slopes, endless formation work – but afternoons belonged to the men, with day passes sending them wandering through Jerusalem and Bethlehem, where chapels, mosques, and ancient stones stood shoulder to shoulder.

Percy had other plans, having visited these areas only weeks ago.

He watched Alfie dart between Johnno and Davo like a sparrow chasing crumbs, the boy as much a part of their section now as any recruit. Percy knew he wanted more than just to feed and clothe him. He wanted Alfie to have a family, a home...a place he belonged.

That would take paper. Not the kind the regiment handed out, but city documents - stamped, signed, and sealed in ledgers. But in order to adopt Alfie, he needed a birth certificate. Jerusalem had no shortage of clerks willing to look the other way for a handful of shillings, and Percy reckoned he would find one soon enough.

"Alfie!" he called across the camp.

The boy skidded to a halt, grinning, knees streaked with dust from whatever mischief he had been in.

Percy beckoned him over.

"We're off to Jerusalem mate. It's time we got you sorted so you can come *home* with me".

Alfie blinked, caught between confusion and pride.

"Will I be your son?"

"That's the idea, we can't have you running about forever as no one's lad, can we?" Percy gave him a wink. "You'll have a new Mum in Lil too, and a younger brother".

Alfie scratched his head and thought for a moment.

"So you will be my papa Mister Percy and my mama will be...er...Lil?"

Percy nodded.

"And my brother? What is he called?"

"He's called Frank mate, and he and your Mum are looking forward to meeting you," replied Percy, "and you have grandparents too don't forget".

"Mum...and brother Frank," he whispered proudly to himself.

Chugger, cleaning his rifle nearby, looked up.

"Well, that's gonna be a job and a half to sort Perce. You'll need a big wallet to get that done with *these* local pen pushers".

"Yeah, I know mate".

Rachel placed a hand on Percy's arm and spoke softly, her English broken but clear.

"We come with you...I help speak...yes? Better...together".

Percy scratched at his jaw.

"You little ripper Rach...that's good of you...but it might be a long day".

Rachel smiled.

"No worries...er...she will be right mate," she replied, casting a quick glance towards Chugger, "yes?"

Chugger nodded his approval.

"Close...good on yer mate".

Within the hour, Percy, Chugger, Rachel, and Alfie were making their way down the dusty road toward Jerusalem. The city shimmered on the horizon, domes and minarets rising above the stone walls. They passed through the crowded gates into streets alive with vendors calling out in Arabic and Hebrew, the air smelling of a mix of spice and sweat.

Chugger nudged Percy.

"Where's this place you've got in mind?"

Percy pointed toward a narrow alley branching off the main bazaar.

"The Adjutant gave me some directions...says there's an old Ottoman records hall round here. The British run it now, but most of the clerks are the same as before - paid in Turkish lira one day and English shillings the next. A few coins and a little bluff, and Alfie will be legally mine and Lil's on paper".

They pushed through the alley, past shuttered shops and hanging laundry. At the far end stood a carved stone doorway, half hidden, its heavy timber marked by a fading crescent moon. Inside, the air smelled of ink and old parchment. Men hunched over ledgers in the dim light, robes flecked with ink stains, eyes sharp with calculation. Behind a heavy desk sat a clerk - a thin Arab man with a neat moustache and an oily smile that never reached his eyes.

Percy stepped forward, Alfie at his side.

"Righto," he whispered, "time to make it official".

As the man with the moustache looked up, Percy spoke.

"I require a birth certificate for the boy," he said, "and I want to adopt him...you know make him my son".

The clerk tapped his pen against the blotter, eyes flicking over Percy's uniform, then to Chugger's frame and Rachel's quiet stance.

"Such things," he said slowly, rubbing his fingers with his thumb, "require...considerations".

"Considerations?" asked Percy.

"I give you birth certificate for one pound and adoption for four pounds," replied the clerk.

"Five quid! You robbing bastard!" Chugger blurted out.

The man, indignant to Chugger's profane language returned to his work.

Percy elbowed Chugger.

"You're not helping mate..."

Chugger shrugged as Percy reached into his tunic pocket and pulled out his wallet, placing five one pound notes on the counter top.

"Alright...you have a deal. Here is the money".

The clerk nodded, gathered up some paperwork and sauntered over to the counter. He gave Alfie a cursory glance, then spoke to Percy.

"What is the boy called?"

"My name is Alfie...Alfie McGuire," said Alfie.

The man looked towards Percy, obviously not wanting to talk to a child.

"Talk to Alfie mate...he has all the answers, not me," said Percy.

"Very well," replied the clerk, "where were you born?"

"Cairo," replied the boy.

"Cairo? This is Bethlehem. If you want to register the boy you must go to Cairo".

Percy was becoming frustrated.

"Hold your horses mate, we can't just up sticks and go to Egypt, just register him here or I'll take my business, and money elsewhere".

The clerk eyed the money on the counter.

"Very well...what is your date of birth?"

Alfie shrugged as an idea came to Chugger's head.

"He's what...nine now...so what about the 25th of December 1908...it sort of fits with where we are eh?"

"Yeah, why not?" replied Percy as he pointed to the certificate. "Write that mate".

The rest of the information was sketchy to say the least. Alfie knew his mother's name was Hala, but his father's first name was a mystery. So Fred it became, scribbled in with the kind of shrug that passed for officialdom in back rooms like this.

The clerk dipped his pen, scratched out the boy's particulars in a looping hand, and then pressed the seal down with a grunt. He slid the certificate across the desk and held out his palm, expectant.

Once the payment was in hand, he pushed a notepad and pencil toward Percy.

"Write down your information here and the document will be ready in one hour," he said, already reaching for the rest of the banknotes.

Rachel's hand landed on the money before he could touch it. She spoke sharply in Arabic, her voice quiet but firm. The clerk froze, and then nodded reluctantly, his eyes filled with fear.

"What did you say Rach?" asked Percy.

"I tell him he get paid when we have papers," she replied.

She had likely said a good deal more than that, but no one asked or even cared. The message had landed and that was all that was required.

They returned just after midday, the city humming with heat and voices. Inside the records hall, the clerk was waiting - papers stacked, seal pressed, the ink still faintly damp. He slid the adoption certificate across the desk without a word.

Percy picked it up and read it slowly. Alfie's name was there, printed in careful script. Beneath it, his own - Percy Taylor, father, and beside that, Lil's, Lilian Taylor, mother. It was a fiction, but a kind one. A name to carry. A story to stand behind.

He held the paperwork open for the boy to see.

"That's you," he said quietly. "Alfie Taylor. Son of Lil and Percy".

Alfie stared at the page then looked up at Percy and grinned.

"Father," he said, testing the word like it was new, "I am Alfie Taylor now...from Australia...thank you".

"No need to thank me mate...you're a good boy...oh...and it is Dad, not father," Percy replied.

"Dad..." Alfie whispered to himself, almost trying to get used to the new word.

Percy folded the certificate and tucked it into his tunic pocket. He turned to the clerk and placed the remaining four pounds on the desk.

"You know," he said, "I'd have paid you twenty".

The clerk blinked, unsure whether to smile or scowl. He settled for silence.

Rachel gave a quiet nod. Chugger smirked. Percy rested a hand on Alfie's shoulder.

"Come on, Alfie Taylor," he said, "let's get you back to camp".

As they walked, Rachel whispered to Alfie.

"You very lucky boy...I am very happy...you go to Australia, have new life".

Overhearing this Percy turned to both Rachel and Chugger.

"We just need to get you two married so you can both go home too".

This brought a smile to Rachel and a bit of a blush from Chugger. But Percy was right and this is what they both wanted.

By early June, the Americans were slowly trickling into the front line in France, arriving at a rate of ten thousand a day. Most were attached in small drafts to seasoned British, Canadian, and Australian formations. The arrangement served a dual purpose: the inexperienced Americans gained their first taste of real trench life under veteran eyes, while the Empire battalions - thinned by over four years of hard fighting - received a short term boost in manpower. For at least six weeks the newcomers trained under experienced British, Canadian, and Australian officers and senior NCOs before they were considered ready for independent action.

The 9th Battalion naturally received its batch of new American mates with the platoon being joined by a small group of soldiers of the 131st Infantry Regiment who had been attached to the battalion for a few weeks.

The trench was quiet, but there was still the stench of wet sandbags mixed in with cooking smells hanging in the air. Roo crouched over a small fire tucked into a corner of the bay, the dull glow only just visible under a scrap of tin meant to shield the flame. His hands were blackened with dirt, but his face was calm, eyes fixed as he poked at the scraps of wood which fuelled the fire. The billy was almost boiled, steam curling in the stagnant air. Nearby, Archie and Clancy sat on overturned crates, watching the lines, rifles propped beside them.

Footsteps squelched along the duckboards, boots and uniforms too clean for anyone who had been here long. A small group of American doughboys shuffled into view, their helmets crooked and their eyes wary. One of them, a barrel chested Private with a cocky strut and too much mouth, stopped at the bay and eyed Roo with a sneer.

"You makin' coffee, boy?" he said loud enough to turn heads. "Pour me one".

The trench fell still.

Roo didn't react - just calmly removed the billy from the fire.

Clancy slowly stood up.

"What did you just call him?"

The American glanced up, not bothering to hide the curl of his lip.

"I told the nigger to pour me a coffee".

Clancy felt the anger inside him light up like a bush fire as he immediately stepped forward and smashed a hard right into the American's face, dropping him like a sack of potatoes, his helmet skittering into the mud. The American staggered but fell on his backside, rage in his eyes, and blood pouring from his nose - but before he could open his mouth again Captain Ponsonby rounded the corner, having heard the scuffle from the saphead.

"What the hell's going on here?"

Clancy pointed at the blood stained American.

"It is too disgusting, and I am embarrassed to say mate," said Clancy as he leaned towards the captain and whispered in his ear.

The expression on their officer's face changed to one the men had never seen before...one of absolute anger.

"What?!"

Ponsonby didn't blink. He stepped over, looked down, and without a word, drove his fist straight into the man's face as he tried to rise. The crack of knuckle on bone echoed down the trench louder than a rifle shot, and the man fell backwards into the mud again.

Roo stood slowly, rolled his shoulders, and then stepped forward. His voice was calm, but his eyes were hard as he looked down at the groaning American.

"I can fight my own battles thanks fellas".

Before Ponsonby could reply, Roo hauled the man up by the collar and buried his own fist into his gut, then laid him flat with a punch square in the jaw that thudded like a boot on wet timber, dropping him again.

The other Americans stood frozen, not saying a word - ashamed, silent.

Ponsonby straightened his tunic.

"He's not welcome in this sector. Get him out of my trench".

Clancy nodded and stepped in, teeth clenched, brushing mud from his sleeve.

"You...you bastard...you're not wanted here. Empty your pouches and weapon of ammo. Fix your bayonet and bugger off back to whatever shithole you crawled out of".

The American groaned, spitting blood.

"I'll have no bullets...what if I'm ambushed on the way back?"

Clancy just grinned, wiping his knuckles on his trousers.

"My boys will come and rescue you".

Archie leaned forward, chuckling darkly.

"Or maybe we won't".

There was a low murmur from the other Aussies watching - not laughter exactly, but something rougher. Approval. The American looked at his own mates, but none met his eye.

Ponsonby turned to the others.

"You men can stay or go. It makes no difference to me. But you will respect *every* man in this trench - or you can bloody well piss off".

One of the Americans - a young kid with freckles and a wide jaw - nodded.

"No trouble here captain," he said, finally, "the man's a fool".

Roo sat back by the fire, unfazed, gave the billy a stir, and poured himself a mug of tea. Archie handed him a slice of bully beef on a biscuit.

Clancy sat beside him and smirked.

"Best bloody cuppa in France, eh?"

Roo shrugged.

"Shame about the company though eh?"

The silence lingered a moment longer after the offending American had slunk off down the trench, his equipment rattling as he limped out of sight.

Then one of the remaining Americans - a lean, clean shaven sergeant with a Chicago twang - stepped forward, removing his helmet and nodding toward Roo.

"Name's Sergeant Daniels," he said, "these fellas are O'Malley, DeWitt, and Russo. We just wanna say...we're sorry for what that bastard said. That ain't us".

The others nodded, one of them even holding out a tin of cigarettes toward Roo, who gave a small nod of thanks but didn't reach for one. He just sat drinking his tea and stirring the billy with his spoon, staring into the little flame licking at the blackened tin.

Clancy gave Roo a glance, before speaking.

"I said some rotten things to Roo when we were kids".

He looked at Daniels.

"Schoolyard stuff...stupid words that came from a stupid kid...but that doesn't excuse it...no way. But Roo's my mate now...my best mate...and I wouldn't want anyone else beside me when the bullets start flying...well...except *these* lot I suppose".

Daniels nodded slowly, visibly moved by Clancy's honesty.

Stowie, standing at the fire with a mug in hand, added, "I'm from Texas. Seen that sort of hate most of my life. That's why I left America and moved to Australia...to get away from it. The place ain't perfect, but people like Roo made it worth staying".

Daniels sighed.

"The truth is...our army is segregated. Black soldiers get stuck unloading ships or diggin' roads while white outfits fight. Draft boards even mark their papers so nobody mixes 'em up. Only a couple of coloured divisions have seen real action - Harlem Hell fighters, the 93rd – in fact they've seen more of this war than any white soldier. The rest? Labour".

Archie shook his head in disgust.

"That's bloody ridiculous. If a bloke's got the guts to wear khaki, he's earned the right to fight".

Daniels met Roo's eyes.

"Couldn't agree more".

Roo rose, dusted his palms on his trousers, and extended a hand.

"I don't hold grudges," he said quietly, his voice calm but firm, "not unless someone earns one".

Daniels smiled and shook it firmly.

"Fair enough. We've heard stories about the Aussies. Tough bastards. You fight hard and you look out for each other. That's the kind of unit we want to learn from. It's a hell of an honour to be here".

Clancy gave them a long look, and then finally cracked a crooked smile.

"Well...you'll fit in just fine then fellas...you're in the 9th now...well...sort of".

He leaned in a little.

"So long as you do what you're bloody told".

The trench erupted in a few chuckles. Even Roo gave a quiet snort of laughter.

Archie grinned, slapping one of the Americans on the back.

"Welcome to the circus, fellas. Now grab a shovel. We've got rats to chase and a war to win".

The war, this day, wasn't just about the rats however. The next morning, at 1000 hours, two parties were sent out to assault and capture another enemy post to the right of the railway. Each party consisted of an NCO and four men. Sergeant Sutton led one, whilst Archie led the other. They slipped over the parapet in pairs, hugging the damp ground. Wind rattled the loose strands of wire that laced no man's land like a spider's web. Sutton's party worked left, Archie's swung right, both aiming to storm the post from opposite ends, with fire support from a Lewis gun team. Both parties came across barbed wire entanglements and were fired upon whilst trying to find a good place to cross it.

Sergeant Sutton's party on the left flank managed to find a gap through the wire and were able to move forward to engage the post.

"Through here, lads...quick as you can," he whispered.

His men darted in after him, but they were met by fierce small arms fire from all directions. Muzzle flashes blinked from a sunken dugout, from the railway verge, and from a half collapsed shed on the flank. Sutton went down hard - one round through the chest, another through his helmet. Another Aussie cried out, clutching a thigh that pumped blood into the chalky dirt.

Archie heard the shots and saw the men crumple. He swore, for he could see that the attack was doomed to fail, and flung a Mills Bomb to keep enemy heads down; then he and his team quickly rushed to meet up with the survivors of Sergeant Sutton's band, bullets buzzing like angry bees around their ears. They reached the wounded digger - Paddy McGaghey - dragging him by his webbing while another man kept firing off covering shots. Archie knelt beside Sutton long enough to know it was over - eyes open, staring past the morning clouds. No time to linger. He gripped the dead sergeant's shoulder once, and then signalled the withdrawal.

The Lewis gun hammered from behind them in short stutters, cutting a curtain of dust as the little party heaved McGaghey across the mud. A final burst of German fire shredded the air above them, but the Aussies tumbled into their own trench in one piece, bloodied yet alive.

Clancy hauled McGaghey down onto a stretcher, cursing softly. Archie wiped mud from his face, his chest still heaving.

"It's a flamin' wasp's nest out there," he said, before making a quick count of the two parties.

"Hang on...where's Robbo?"

Private Robertson was nowhere to be seen, so was presumed dead.

Lieutenant Sargent was there to meet his men and was saddened at the losses.

"It's not your fault mate," said Archie, "take a look out there. No one knows what obstacles there are until you actually get there".

In the early hours of the next morning the 9th Battalion established a new post, which was slightly forward of the right hand post. A former enemy position, they had obviously foreseen their fate should they have chosen to stay.

At 1330 hours on the 24th of June there was a silent commotion out in no man's land. A soldier from one of the platoons called stand to and yelled out a challenge to a figure crouched low in the cratered ground to his front.

"HALT! WHO GOES THERE?"

The figure called out in reply.

"Robertson...from the 9th Battalion".

Now listed as missing in action for three days, he had taken cover but could not move due being under observation by the enemy. When the Germans finally gave up launching flares, or just lost interest, he had decided to crawl through a field of tall crops, but lost his bearings, thus taking three days to find his way back to the Battalion line.

At 0100 hours on the 25th of June, Roo led a reconnaissance patrol out from the front line. Alongside Pip and Stowie were two of their new American mates - Privates O'Malley and De-Witt. Both looked keen, and eager to do their part.

Before they left the trench, Roo paused at the Americans, giving their equipment a once over.

"Hold still," he muttered, fingers probing webbing and belts.

He gave O'Malley a stern look and pulled out a mess tin swinging loose from his belt.

"This'll have the whole German line looking our way," he snapped, yanking it off, "if it rattles or you don't need it, leave it here".

O'Malley looked sheepish. DeWitt fumbled with his webbing silently.

Pip gave them a wink.

"Don't worry lads, if we get lost, Roo's got a sixth sense. Like a fox sniffing for a chicken coup".

Stowie grunted.

"Just keep your heads down and your traps shut".

Neither O'Malley nor DeWitt spoke. They just nodded stiffly, clearly nervous. Roo saw it. He had seen it a hundred times.

"Stick with us fellas, do what we say, and you'll be fine".

The patrol stepped into no man's land, bent low to make themselves a smaller target, moving through thigh-high wheat swaying in the night breeze, under the dim glow of a half-moon. It was quiet - eerily so. A mist hovered inches above the ground, dampening their boots and muffling sound. Somewhere to their front a shell thumped lazily, but no flares came up. No machine guns stuttered.

They crept for a good twenty minutes before Roo motioned for them to halt. They had reached a slight rise overlooking a section of German line. Stowie crouched beside Roo, peering through a slit in the crop. Through the wheat, they could see enemy troops working under the cover of darkness - laying out coils of barbed wire, hammering in pickets, quietly reinforcing their trench.

Roo knelt and pulled a small notebook from his breast pocket, writing down positions and strength, careful to note bearings and distances, and then marking the area on his crumpled map.

"Looks like these fellas aint going anywhere," Stowie whispered.

Roo nodded and whispered a reply.

"Unfortunately".

Then, through the corner of his eye Roo saw movement from the two Americans. He immediately elbowed Stowie.

It appeared that the inexperienced Americans did not seem to understand the difference between a fighting and recce patrol, and were about to fire on the Germans.

"Shit!"

Stowie spun round. O'Malley had raised his Springfield and was staring down his sights, trigger finger already tightening.

Before he had a chance to shoot, Stowie launched himself forward, smashing into the American with a snarl. The rifle was knocked sideways as both men thudded into the wheat.

"What the bloody hell are you doing?!" he hissed, pinning the American down.

DeWitt had lifted his weapon too, but Roo was on him in an instant - ripping it from his hands and grabbing the man by the collar.

"Are you trying to get us all killed?" said Roo in a whispered growl. "This is a recce not a bloody fighting patrol!"

O'Malley squirmed beneath Stowie.

"I...I saw 'em! We could've..."

"You *saw* them?" Stowie spat. "You'll see your own guts next time you raise a rifle without a good reason!"

DeWitt stammered, "We thought...back home, we'd..."

"This isn't bloody back home," Roo whispered angrily, jabbing a finger in his face, "out here you fire without orders on a recce and you're as good as dead...and you'll take us with you!"

O'Malley looked up at Stowie, shocked.

"We didn't know..."

Stowie hauled him up roughly, but quietly.

"Yeah...right. Now you do".

The Aussies were fuming. Even Pip, who had hung back, looked ready to belt one of them.

Both Americans nodded quickly, ashamed and silent.

Roo checked his map again, and then growled a whisper, "Let's move."

The patrol withdrew, slower this time, tenser. No one spoke until they were safely back in their trench. Then Roo laid into the Americans.

"You want to shoot Germans? Good. So do we. But you do it *our* way - or not at all," said Roo, still visibly angry, "next time, you keep your bloody fingers off the trigger until you're told. *Understand*?"

Neither American replied.

Archie who had been listening to Roo's rebuke muttered under his breath as he lit a cigarette.

"Bloody Yanks...like handing matches to a child in a haystack".

He then looked over to Stowie.

"No offence to you of course mate".

Stowie just shook his head.

"None taken...let's just hope they learn quicker than they shoot".

That evening the 9th was relieved by the 12th Battalion and were sent back to Borre, as Brigade Reserve. The battalion remained there for ten days, rotating through training and supplying work parties up to the front line. The Germans had gone unusually quiet - too quiet for anyone's liking.

"Something aint right," said Stowie, eyeing the blue, cloudless sky like it had wronged him. He tipped the last dregs of tea from his mug and swatted away a persistent fly.

"Maybe Fritz has finally had enough," Roo offered.

Archie gave a short laugh.

"Or he's planning something big".

Stowie's instincts were correct for on the 4th of July, while the 9th was filling sandbags and cursing their way through work party duties, a historical series of events was unfolding in the area of Le Hamel that would go down as a textbook case of modern warfare done right.

The attack had been a complete surprise, even though there had been many clues, with tanks moving in the dark, long convoys of artillery limbering forward under cover of night, aircraft circling lower than usual. But to the soldiers who had been fighting for years this was nothing new...and that was part of the plan.

By late afternoon that day, news had filtered through and the rumours had reached full boil.

"Have you blokes heard what Monash pulled off this morning?" asked Clancy, flicking through a crumpled copy of Routine Orders.

"Yeah mate," said Roo, "by the sounds of it the whole thing was over in about an hour and a half".

Clancy looked up.

"That's what they reckon...tanks, planes, artillery, even some Yanks thrown in. Monash ran the whole show like a bloody orchestra".

It was true. Just past dawn that day, the Australian Corps, under the newly-promoted Lieutenant General John Monash, had executed a near-flawless assault on the German lines around Le Hamel. Monash's long promised "all arms" blow had come off like clockwork. The plan had been written down to the minute with Tanks lumbering forward, with ammunition panniers strapped to their hulls for battle field supply, whilst cutting the wire and providing support and a shield for the advancing troops, aircraft dropping supplies by parachute and spotting for artillery, and the infantry advancing under the rolling curtain of a precisely timed barrage.

The whole engagement took ninety three minutes from first whistle to final objective.

It had been, in every sense, a masterpiece of planning, organisation and execution.

But along with the cheers came the other story: General Pershing had ordered most American companies withdrawn on the eve of the assault, insisting U.S. troops fight only under U.S. command. Some detachments were yanked out at the last moment; others, already placed among the forward Australian battalions, stayed put - too late to move without wrecking the timetable. A handful of Yanks ignored the recall altogether, slipping back into the ranks rather than sit out the show.

Archie folded his arms and gave a half smile.

"Good on *them*...I'm bloody proud of 'em, even if *we* weren't there".

"Proud?" Stowie growled. "I'm bloody spewin'. We're slogging sacks of sand back and forth while the rest of the Aussie Corps gets to make history!"

That night, the men of the 9th gathered in a quiet bay of the trench. No jokes or moans this time - just hushed voices in the dark.

"Three months planning so they say, perfect to the minute," Archie said, finishing off a letter to home, "tanks, planes, creeping barrage...the lot...and it worked".

"Do you reckon it changes things?" asked Pip, a bit more quietly. "If we can do that to the Boche line in under two hours..."

Clancy nodded.

"It does, mate. Monash is showing 'em how it's done. This ain't no more slog-through-the-mud madness. It's the beginning of the end...just wait and see".

Stowie rubbed at his jaw.

"It's a shame for those Yanks who were marched out hours before jumping off time. I can't imagine what that felt like...watchin' the fellas you've trained with go over without you".

Roo poured tea into tin mugs, the steam drifting between them.

"What the hell their General was thinking is beyond me, but I'm glad that some decided to stay no matter what," he said quietly, "that takes guts, and it must have been a weight for them...obey orders or do something honourable".

Archie stared into his mug.

"Good on them for making a good choice I say".

Clancy set his cup down on a crate, the tin ringing softly.

"Aye...but next time there's a break through to be made, I want the 9th to be in it...start to finish".

No one argued. The firelight caught their faces - tired, hard, but quietly determined. They listened to the sounds of the guns in the distance, thinking of Le Hamel, of orders obeyed and dis-obeyed, and of whatever came next.

Somewhere beyond the dark fields a new kind of war was taking shape, and the 9th meant to be ready when the call came again.

CHAPTER 9

Never Give Up

The 6th of June saw the entire 1st Light Horse Brigade return to the Jordan Valley - a place as unforgiving as it was familiar. Summer had settled in with a vengeance. The valley, sunk twelve hundred feet below sea level, baked under a sun that drove temperatures to a blistering one hundred and twenty eight degrees Fahrenheit. The men knew the terrain well; the regiment had been stationed there almost continuously since February, and the prospect of spending the summer in this spot was a daunting one. But others now required relief, and the unit, having been recently rested, was deemed fit to resume the burden.

The brigade assumed control of the Auja Sector from the 4th Brigade.

This included the Masallabah Salient, a stretch of ground already carved into memory for the Camel Corps' gallant stand, only two months earlier, when they ran out of hand grenades and resorted to heaving boulders down upon the attacking Turks - an area destined to host one of the 2nd Light Horse Regiment's most pivotal confrontations. The 1st and 3rd Regiments were deployed to the right and left flanks respectively, their horses sent four miles to the rear to spare them the worst of the heat and shelling.

The 2nd Regiment remained in reserve, its horses kept close. Command had judged that any counterattack would demand swift reinforcement, and mobility was paramount. Each night, one squadron from the 2nd was dispatched to assist the flanking regiments with wiring and entrenchment - work done under cover of darkness, in silence, with the distant sounds of artillery as a constant punctuation.

The 2nd's bivouac came under daily shellfire. Though every effort was made to conceal the horses, through strict movement discipline, the enemy seemed to know their location. The men grew accustomed to the routine - the whistle of incoming rounds, the scramble for cover, the grim tally afterward. Casualties were light, but nerves frayed. Flies swarmed unceasingly, drawn to sweat, blood, and the latrine pits. The heat shimmered across the valley floor, warping the horizon into a wavering mirage that made even distant movement hard to trust.

"You reckon the horses know what's coming?" asked Boggy.

"They flinch before we do. Smell it, maybe," replied Davo.

"I'd trade boots for hooves if it meant getting out of this oven," said Boggy as he took a sip from his canteen.

On the 30th of June, the 2nd Regiment relieved the 1st on the right sector of the brigade line. The handover was brisk and businesslike, a nod, a few muttered warnings about exposed ground, and the quiet footsteps of men taking up positions where others had just stood.

The horses were withdrawn to the rear under the supervision of Major Franklin, newly returned from Australia and now serving as second-in-command. His arrival brought a measure of steadiness to the ranks - he was known for his calm under pressure and his quiet way of reading a situation before speaking. The men respected that. He rode at the head of the column, reins loose, eyes constantly on the horizon where the heat shimmered like water. The animals moved slowly, their heads bowed, their flanks already darkened with sweat though the sun had barely cleared the ridgeline.

Beside him rode Lieutenant Harwood, one of the younger officers, his uniform sun-bleached and stiff with dust. They spoke little at first. The valley had a way of quieting men.

"They'll be glad of the shade," Harwood said eventually, nodding toward the horses.

Franklin didn't look over.

"I doubt there will be any of that".

A pause. Then Harwood added, "Two hundred and thirty rifles. It's not much".

Franklin gave a slow nod.

"It's not. But we've held with less. We had to".

The lieutenant didn't reply. The sound of hooves on dry earth filled the silence. Flies buzzed around the horses' heads, and the horizon rippled ahead, distorted by heat and dust.

Franklin watched the horizon for a moment, as if waiting for it to settle into something solid, then turned to Harwood.

"We manage. That's the job."

In the preceding two months, the regiment had been steadily thinned by malaria. The valley's stagnant heat and swarming insects had taken their toll, and evacuation became a daily routine. Stretchers moved not just the wounded, but the fevered - men too weak to stand, their uniforms soaked more with sweat than blood. Reinforcements were scarce, trickling in with no rhythm, and often already worn down by the journey.

By the time the 2nd Light Horse moved into position, its fighting strength had dwindled to just two hundred and thirty men. It was a quiet admission of the cost. No speeches, no complaints - just fewer backsides on saddles and more space between men in the line.

To compensate, a section from the 1st Machine Gun Squadron was attached.

Their arrival was practical, nothing more. The extra firepower was welcome, but it did little to mask the fact that the regiment was stretched thin. The machine gunners set up quickly, their weapons covered against dust and heat, their routines already honed by months of similar deployments. They spoke little, worked fast, and kept their heads down.

Masallabah sat at the tip of a narrow salient in the northern defensive line held by the 1st Light Horse Brigade. Its base stretched roughly five hundred yards along the Auja River - a sluggish, reed-choked watercourse that offered little in the way of comfort or concealment. The position was exposed, awkward, and difficult to reinforce.

Three miles to the east, the 2nd Brigade occupied a similar salient in the Wadi Mallaha, a dry gully that twisted through the valley floor like a scar. To the west, the land rose sharply - three to four miles of harsh incline culminating in the mountains that formed the eastern rim of the Jordan Gorge. These heights marked the beginning of the broken country between Jerusalem and Nablus, a region of steep ravines, jagged ridgelines, and narrow goat tracks that defied easy passage.

The Turks held those hills.

From their elevated vantage point, they could observe nearly every movement in the valley below. Patrols, supply runs, even the shifting of sentries - nothing escaped their notice. Their long range artillery, emplaced high in the mountains, had clear lines of fire. Closer in, field guns were dug in along Bakr Ridge and scattered across the northern and north eastern approaches to the brigade's sector.

Each day, the Australians received what the men grimly referred to as their "ration of shells." It came without fail - morning, midday, and often again at dusk. The shelling was rarely concentrated enough to break the line, but it was persistent, methodical; a form of pressure. The ground shook, dust rose, and the men learned to read the whistle of incoming rounds like a second language, as they had done so many times before. Some flinched. Others didn't bother anymore.

Pretty soon it became a kind of routine, marking the time more reliably than watches. Morning shells meant breakfast was over. Midday rounds signalled the heat's peak. Dusk bombardments came just as the flies began to settle and the light turned copper across the valley floor.

The men adapted. They learned to eat quickly, to sleep lightly, to dig deeper. Major Franklin kept a small notebook in his breast pocket. He didn't write in it often - just co-ordinates, timings, and the occasional name. But he checked it after each barrage, noting patterns. He never called it a diary. Diaries were for private thoughts. This was for survival.

One afternoon, a shell landed short, striking the edge of the 'C' Squadron's position. No casualties, just a billy of tea flung into the dust. Boggy retrieved the billy, wiped it with his sleeve, and poured what was left into a tin mug.

"Still hot," he said, handing it to the Percy beside him.

Percy took it without comment. They drank in silence as the horizon still trembled in the heat.

The ground held by the 2nd Light Horse Regiment was inhospitable to say the least - bare rock, fractured limestone, and sunbleached rubble that resisted every attempt at digging. In most places, digging was not just difficult but futile. Instead, the men built sangars - low, dry-stone breastworks assembled by hand, stone by stone, under cover of darkness.

Every movement - drawing rations, evacuating the sick or wounded, laying wire, reinforcing sangars - had to be done at night. The enemy's vantage was too commanding, their observation too precise. By day, the valley was exposed, and even the smallest change in position risked drawing fire. The men learned to move silently, to work by feel, and to trust the moonlight.

From experience, sangars proved their worth when the attack came. Against rifle and machine gun fire, they held firm, but as shelter from high explosives, they offered little, with shrapnel finding the gaps and blast pressure rolling over the stones. Even so, the men would crouch behind them during bombardments, knowing full well they were better than nothing - but not by much.

The regiment's position could be shelled from three sides. Turkish spotters in the hills had clear lines of sight, and their guns had the range and accuracy to make life in the sangars a daily gamble. Dust often hung in the air long after the shelling had stopped, and the sound of falling rock became part of the landscape.

Yet the position held value. It was the most accessible high ground on the northern line, offering clear observation over the valley and the right bank of the Jordan. From here, the Australians could monitor enemy movements, co-ordinate patrols, and prepare for operations further north. The Auja River ran nearby, its waters slow but reliable - vital in a place where heat and dehydration were constant threats.

But the same ground, if taken by the enemy, would have been a serious liability. In Turkish or German hands, the position would have dominated the valley floor, placing the entire British force in jeopardy. Every movement, every supply run, every bivouac would have been under threat. The men understood this. They didn't speak of it often, but they knew why they were there.

The key to the northern defence was Abu Tellul Ridge, divided for operational clarity into right and left sectors. Its shape was awkward, its slopes exposed, but its position was vital. From its crest, the Australians could observe the Jordan Valley's eastern approaches and the movement along the right bank with rare precision. It was understood across the brigade that, at the first sign of enemy attack, the reserve regiment - currently the 1st Light Horse- would immediately garrison Abu Tellul. General Chauvel would make this point unmistakably clear during his inspection on the 13th of July.

Each night, the men worked to strengthen the defences. The digging was slow, the ground brittle and stony. Picks struck rock more often than soil, and progress came in inches. One squadron from the reserve joined the effort nightly, their movements timed to avoid Turkish observation.

By day, the shelling resumed, but the men had built with purpose. The sangars and shallow scrapes, though crude, offered just enough cover. When the first shells came, usually mid morning, the men dropped into their positions with practiced speed, there was no panic, and casualties remained light, not by luck, but by instinct.

At 2215 hours on the night of the 4th of July, a Turkish raiding party made an attempt on Masallabah. They managed only to push back the forward listening post, and even that was brief. The would-be attackers met a stiff reception - rifle fire from sangars, and a swift counter attack by half a squadron. Within minutes, the listening post was reoccupied, and two prisoners had been taken.

They tried again in the early hours of the 6th of July. This time, they were driven off before reaching the wire. The men were alert, the ground familiar, and the response immediate. No ground was lost.

From the 7th of July onward, the shelling intensified. Roughly three hundred shells fell daily across the brigade's positions - some timed to catch ration runs, others aimed at sangars and water points. The pattern was deliberate. The men suspected it was the prelude to something larger.

"You can set your watch by those bastard shells," one trooper muttered, crouched behind a sangar as the midday barrage began.

Water was a constant concern. Each post kept a reserve ration in empty petrol tins - functional, but vulnerable. One lucky shell could rupture the entire supply. In response, the commanding officer ordered an emergency measure - two beer bottles per man, filled and distributed across the positions. They were replenished nightly, carried in under cover of darkness, tucked into sangar crevices or buried shallow for easy reach.

When the guns fell silent, a few men from each squadron were permitted to slip down to the Wadi Aujah. There, in the brief quiet, they washed their clothes, scrubbed the dust from their skin, and filled their bottles with the warm water whilst the flies buzzed around their faces.

On the 13th of July, signs of enemy movement became impossible to ignore. From the forward posts near Masallabah, large bodies of Turkish and German infantry were observed moving through the vicinity of Wadi Bakr - columns on the march, dust clouds rising behind them, officers gesturing from ridgelines. It wasn't subtle.

Divisional Headquarters issued a report which stated that intelligence suggested the enemy intended to retire. The 2nd Light Horse was tasked with verifying this claim. But the shelling told a different story. That morning alone, the barrage was heavier than anything seen in weeks. If the enemy were pulling out, they seemed oddly determined to leave their ammunition behind one shell at a time.

By mid-afternoon, fresh tents had appeared in the enemy's field hospital. Canvas went up quickly and orderly. It certainly didn't look like a withdrawal. It looked like preparation.

The information was passed up the chain, and the regiment readied itself. The men didn't speak of it much – they had seen enough to know what was coming.

Chugger, watching the tents go up through a gap in the stonework, gave his usual verdict.

"Retiring, are they?" he said. "Looks more like they're setting up a bloody picnic...and we are lunch".

Percy, crouched beside him, gave a dry laugh.

"Division reckons they're pulling out".

"Division talks out of their arse," Chugger muttered.

The light was beginning to shift, and the flies were swarming. Somewhere behind them, a billy rattled on a small fire. The men waited.

It seemed that Brigade Headquarters had taken its cue from Division, favouring distant speculation over ground level insight. The commanding officer of the 2nd Light Horse had recommended that one squadron from the reserve regiment be moved into position at Abu Tellul - quietly, pre-emptively. The ridge was the key to the sector, and its occupation would have strengthened the rear of the 2nd in the event of an attack.

But the suggestion was brushed aside. Division's view - that the enemy was preparing to withdraw - had filtered down and taken root. Brigade HQ, influenced more by reports than by the dust and shellfire on the ground, chose not to act.

The men in the line didn't need maps or stupid decisions to read the situation. They had seen the tents go up, heard the shelling intensify, and watched the Turkish infantry shift like a tide gathering force. Abu Tellul remained unoccupied, and the

2nd Light Horse prepared to hold without the support they had asked for.

Chugger was dismayed as he glanced back at Abu Tellul.

"Must be a new tactic...leaving the back door swinging in the breeze".

The shelling had picked up again just after midday - short bursts, scattered across the line, close enough to keep heads down and nerves tight. Dust from the explosions hung in the air like fog, and the flies were relentless.

Boggy waved a horde of the annoying insects away as he attempted to bite into a hard tack biscuit.

"Bloody hell, its bad enough breaking your teeth on these things, but these flies are getting just as bad as at Gallipoli".

Percy stood behind the sangar, watching the ridge. The Turkish guns were probing again, and the tents in the hospital sector hadn't gone anywhere. If anything, there were more.

He turned to Alfie, who was sitting cross-legged nearby, drawing shapes in the dust with a stick.

"Alfie," Percy said gently, "I need you to go down to where the cooks are. Ask Sergeant Muir if he's got any more bully beef. Tell him we're starving up here".

Alfie looked up, blinking.

"Is it far?"

"Not too far. Take the low track. Stay close to the rocks".

Alfie nodded, brushing his hands on his shorts.

"All good papa...Dad".

Percy smiled at that, and then crouched beside him for a moment.

"Don't stop on the way...and if you hear anything loud, just lie flat and wait...and take your time".

Alfie didn't ask why. He stood, took hold of the pack Percy handed to him, and started off with quick, careful steps.

Behind them, Chugger watched him go.

"Now that excuse was a pack of "bully" if ever I heard one".

Percy nodded.

"Yeah, me and Rach arranged it as a sort of code with Bob Muir. It's to keep Alfie safe when a big stunt is on".

"Good call Perce...he's better off down there than up here".

Rachel was nearby, recharging her magazine.

"It is good that Alfie is sent away," she said, "he not safe here...not now".

Percy glanced at her.

"I'd send you too, but I know you want to be here killing Turks".

Rachel nodded and smiled at Chugger.

"Yes...I stay...stay with my Chugger".

"Isn't love wonderful?" Boggy added with a quiet laugh.

The 2nd Light Horse held three forward posts, each built for all round defence and mutual support. It was understood, quietly, but without doubt, that if the Turks came during darkness, they would push between them.

Maskerah was held by 'B' Squadron, minus two troops but reinforced with two machine guns, whilst Masallabah was manned by 'C' Squadron, with an extra troop from 'B' attached. Vyse Post was under 'A' Squadron, short two troops, but also supported by two machine guns.

Out in front of Vyse Post sat the advance bombing post. Its orders were clear - fall back to Vyse if pressed, or as soon as daylight broke. It wasn't expected to hold - just to warn.

Two troops from 'A' Squadron and one from 'B' remained in regimental reserve. The 'A' troops bivouacked at Vyse Post, ready to reinforce if needed, whilst the 'B' troop was positioned at the Bluff. It was assumed - quietly again - that if the Turks made a serious move, and the reserve regiment, who were under Brigade orders, was held up, these three troops would be the ones standing between the enemy and the key position.

No one said it outright, but the men knew the layout was sparse. They had seen the ground and walked the gaps, and they knew that if the attack came fast, it would come through the dark.

The shelling had eased, but no one believed it. The ridge was quiet in the wrong way.

Percy moved through the section, saying little. The men were already doing what needed doing.

Chugger looked up.

"I could do with a few more Mills bombs," he said, "if they come through quick we might as well be throwing rocks".

Percy nodded.

"I sent Davo and Johnno down to the Q stores. They should be back soon".

Chugger gave a grunt.

"As long as they didn't stop for a brew...you know what those two bludgers are like".

Rachel sat close beside him, her hand resting on his, rifle beside her.

"They come," she said. "I shoot".

"And slash and stab eh mate?" Chugger added.

Percy didn't reply. He looked out toward the ridge, where the light was thinning and the wind had dropped.

"If you're coming...just come yer bastards," he thought to himself.

Regimental Headquarters was located in Wadi Dhib, just behind Vale Post, which was held by one troop from the 3rd Regiment. It wasn't far enough to be safe. The shelling didn't let up, and by night, enemy patrols were reported moving close to the post. Not in numbers, but near enough. The kind of movement that made men speak quietly and keep their rifles at the ready.

HQ stayed put. There was nowhere better, and too much risk in shifting. Messages came in, orders went out, and everyone knew they were being watched.

At 0100 hours, Percy saw them.

Dark shapes moving beyond the scrub line - slow, deliberate, too many for a patrol. He watched for a moment longer, and then turned to Chugger.

"Pass it down the line to make ready, it looks like they're coming".

Chugger didn't ask how many. He just nodded and moved off.

Percy called over one of the younger troopers and scribbled down a note.

"Take this to HQ. Tell them they're coming. I can't tell their strength, but it's too big to be a bluff".

The runner took off without a word.

By 0245 hours, Vale Post reported the same - enemy in strength outside their wire. Artillery fire had picked up again, a murderous way to drown out the sound of movement.

Between 0200 and 0300 hours, the phones went dead. No line to Brigade. No line to RHQ...nothing.

The CO didn't wait. He sent the Signal Sergeant with a field telephone to an alternative battle station at Abu Tellul - Number 3 Right. His orders were clear - get a line to Brigade HQ and the 3rd Regiment before *he* got there.

At the same time, one troop from the regimental reserve was ordered forward to Tellul Right Number 1. Their job was to hold the line with the Bluff Posts and delay the Turks until the brigade reserve arrived.

The attack had begun. Not with a charge, but with silence, movement, and the sudden absence of communication.

At 0310 hours, Vale Post reported they were under heavy risk of being overrun. In response, the CO of the 2nd ordered the garrison - one troop from the 3rd Light Horse Regiment - to withdraw to their secondary position at Abu Tellul Left Number 1, where they reverted to the command of their own CO.

Ten minutes later, at 0320 hours, the enemy broke through Vale Post. The CO of the 2nd withdrew with the regimental staff and details to Abu Tellul Right Number 3. By this time, Masallabah was also under heavy attack. The Turks succeeded in cutting the wire opposite Number 4 Post and temporarily bombed the defenders out.

Sergeant Carlyon was already moving along the line, gathering men for the counterattack.

"Rifles and bayonets," he said, "those bastards can get stuffed if they think they're keeping our post".

Percy and his group joined without hesitation.

Carlyon gave Rachel a quick glance. He knew her reputation well.

"Is *she* coming?"

Rachel didn't blink, and certainly didn't need anyone to answer for her.

"I come".

Carlyon nodded once.

"Right...good on yer".

They moved fast. The Turks were inside Number 4, regrouping, when Carlyon's party came in hard, bayonets fixed. No shouting. No warning.

Rachel didn't wait for the line to close.

She broke left and went in with the scimitar. The blade moved fast and without mercy. One Turk dropped, then another. She didn't speak. She didn't stop. Chugger was with her stabbing and clubbing any Turk who had escaped Rachel's fury.

The rest followed through. Percy drove forward with Davo and Boggy beside him; Johnno just behind. The clash was close and brutal - bayonets used with deadly efficiency. The post was retaken in minutes. Blood in the wire. Bodies in the dust.

Carlyon didn't pause to admire it. He pointed to the parapet.

"Get up. Fire into them. Anything moving".

The lighthorsemen leaned into the parapets and gave the enemy hell, firing into the retreating Turks, dropping anyone still visible in the darkness. Spent cartridges clinked against stone and cordite from the rifles blackened the faces of the troopers. No one spoke. They just kept firing.

Throughout the night, Posts 1, 2, and 3 held firm. The enemy made repeated attempts to break through, but none gained ground. As daylight broke, the defenders at these positions reversed their fire, bringing rifles and machine guns to bear on the exposed flanks of Turkish forces occupying the Bluff and Abu Tellul Right. The effect was immediate and punishing - casualties mounted, and the pressure they applied materially supported the 1st Regiment's counterattack that followed.

Vyse Post, reinforced earlier by the withdrawal of the Vane Post garrison at around 0230 hours, managed to stall the enemy's direct advance. But it didn't last. Within the hour, Vyse was completely surrounded. The men inside held their fire until first light, then turned their weapons outward - targeting enemy concentrations in Wadi Dhib and across Abu Tellul. The volume and accuracy of fire broke the momentum of the assault, and when the counterattack was launched, the enemy began to fall back in disorder.

Maskerah, meanwhile, came under threat from the rear. Its layout made defence from that direction near impossible. Captain Evans, anticipating such a move, withdrew the garrison to a fallback position already prepared for the contingency. From there, they were able to bring effective fire onto the Bluff, providing critical support to the small party still holding out there.

At 0600 hours, the enemy attempted to push down the flat north of Maskerah. They were met with concentrated fire from the repositioned post and scattered before they could form up. The line held.

Earlier, by 0330 hours, the situation on the Bluff and Abu Tellul Right had become critical. These positions were plainly the key to the whole defence - if they went, the rest would follow. To hold them, the last of the regimental reserve was committed - one troop from 'B' Squadron took up position on the Bluff, while one troop from 'A' Squadron occupied Number 1 Abu Tellul.

That left Numbers 2 and 3 Abu Tellul manned by regimental staff and a handful of details - clerks, cooks, signallers, anyone who could carry a rifle. It wasn't ideal, but it was what was left.

The importance of these posts couldn't be overstated. Even a brief loss would have exposed the three artillery batteries positioned just south of Abu Tellul - either knocking them out or handing them over. Worse still, if the ridge had fallen, it was doubtful the 1st Regiment could have taken it back in time, and the right flank of the 3rd Regiment would have been wide open.

The CO of the 2nd Light Horse Regiment gave clear instructions to the men holding those positions. They were to hold at all costs. No fallback. No surrender. Help was coming, but until the 1st Regiment arrived, they were it.

The men at Number 2 and 3 may not have been front line troops in the same sense as their mounted infantry mates, but they weren't new to it either, having endured at Gallipoli and in the desert patrols and battles like the rest of the troops. Clerks, signallers, a cook, a corporal from the quartermaster stores – they had all fired their weapons in anger before, and they knew what it meant to hold ground. The post was thin, but it mattered. Everyone understood that.

A signaller scanned the dark.

"Movement near the rocks".

The corporal shifted beside him.

"Keep your eyes on it. If they come close, we'll sort it".

No one panicked. They had heard the fighting at Number 4, seen the flashes, and felt the ground shake when the Bluff lit up. They knew what was coming.

A clerk passed a bandolier to the cook.

"You right?"

The cook nodded.

"Yeah mate, it's nice to get out of the cook house for a bit...*and* I used to enjoy a bit of rabbit hunting back home...paradise eh?"

The corporal checked his watch, and then looked to the east.

"Here comes the morning...watch and shoot boys...watch and shoot".

At first light, they opened up - steady, deliberate volleys into the scrub. The Turks were pulling back in patches, some crawling, some running. The men at Number 2 didn't waste rounds. They fired with purpose, aimed shots only, keeping the pressure on.

The corporal called down the line.

"Good work boys...send them to hell".

The enemy came in force - over a thousand men - striking all three posts under cover of heavy, well-placed shell fire, masking the advance until the Turks were almost on top of the positions.

Lieutenant King and his troop from 'A' Squadron held their ground at one of the forward posts. They fought hard, but the numbers were against them from the start. King was killed in the fighting. Every man in his troop was either killed or wounded.

There were no stragglers. No one fell back. They held until they couldn't.

At the Bluff, Lieutenant Henderson's 'B' Squadron troop faced similar odds. He was wounded early, but stayed in command. His troop was reduced to three men. With those three, he held the post - scavenging ammunition from the dead and wounded, passing it along, keeping the rifles firing.

"Still got rounds?" he asked one of the men.

"Found a few on Mick," came the reply.

"Good. Keep firing".

They held until the counterattack reached them. By then, the Bluff was littered with bodies, but the post was still in their hands.

Abu Tellul Numbers 2 and 3 were also hit hard. The men of the 2nd Light Horse held as long as they could, but Number 2 was lost under sheer weight of numbers. The defenders were forced out, falling back to regroup and rejoin the fight elsewhere.

There was no panic. They moved where they had to, fired when they could. The posts held because the men did.

The crest of the ridge and Number 3 Post were held through the worst of it - thinly manned, but not abandoned. For nearly two hours, the handful of men there were the only barrier between the Turks and Germans, the batteries, watering points, and rear lines. They held without reinforcement, without relief, and without complaint.

Shortly after 0500 hours, two squadrons from the 1st Light Horse Regiment arrived under Major Weir. Thanks to the defence already in place, they were able to reach the ridge without taking casualties and immediately began preparing their counter-attack from a strong position.

The CO of the 2nd Light Horse Regiment gave the order without delay. Major Weir was to counterattack at once. Covering fire was arranged from the garrison at Abu Tellul - the mixed group of troopers and support staff, already blooded and dug in. Their fire kept the enemy's head down and gave Weir's men room to move.

The counterattack was well timed. Weir's squadrons pushed forward under concentrated support from the posts at Vyse, Masallabah and Maskerah. The enemy, already stretched and exposed, began to fall back under pressure.

Lieutenant Henderson's continued hold on part of the Bluff was a key factor. His position allowed enfilading fire and disrupted the enemy's cohesion during the push. By 0900 hours, the entire position was back in the hands of the 2nd Light Horse Regiment.

Enemy casualties were heavy. Artillery, machine gun, and rifle fire inflicted serious losses outside the wire. Though many of their dead and wounded were removed during the withdrawal, the known count stood at fifty five dead, forty five wounded, and three hundred and thirty taken prisoner. The regiment also recovered fifteen automatic rifles, one machine gun, and one hundred and thirty rifles from the ground around the posts.

It was one of the regiment's strongest showings. Every man did his job under extreme pressure, and the success of the operation hinged on one critical fact - the key ground was never given up. The enemy never got the ridge.

Casualties for the 2nd Light Horse were serious, but light in context. Given the scale and intensity of the fighting, the regiment came through battered but standing. Every man did what was asked of him, and the ground was held because they didn't let go.

CHAPTER 10

For Valour

On the 5th of July the 9th Battalion moved back to La Kruele, as the 3rd Brigade was now in reserve...again. Grumbles circled as usual - feet dragging, backs aching, men muttering about the war lasting forever - but this return to reserve lines had a different air. There was something stirring in the camp. Rumour had it a royal visitor was on the way.

That rumour became fact when the orders came down - His Majesty King George V would be presenting medals in person to a handful of men from the 3rd Brigade. One name, when whispered through the dugouts and tents, lit a spark among the battalion...Sergeant Archie Taylor...their mate.

Word of his actions for single handedly fighting off an attempted German break through back in April had already done the rounds. Everyone remembered it, the frantic hours, the confusion, the noise, and now, the King himself would pin the Victoria Cross to his tunic.

The parade ground had been laid out beside a battered barn. It wasn't much, but the lads did what they could with lengths of bunting and a few fresh flags. When the King's car arrived, flanked by senior officers, the battalion stood straight and still as fence posts, the line bristling with pride despite the aching legs and sunburnt faces.

His Majesty walked the line, pausing briefly to speak to the officers before stepping up to present the medals. Then came the moment. The King's voice, firm yet affable, rang out as he spoke of gallantry and duty. As he pinned the Victoria Cross to Archie's chest, he gave the young Queenslander a measured look. There was a beat of silence, the kind that stretches deep into a man's bones. Archie saluted crisply, holding the King's eye for a second longer than protocol might allow.

"For Valour and conspicuous bravery. Well done, Sergeant," the King said quietly, a faint smile beneath his moustache, as he pinned the medal just above Archie's breast pocket, "you are a credit to Australia and the Empire".

Archie gave a nod and a firm salute.

"Thank you sir...er...your majesty...I just did what needed doing...what every man here has done at one point or another".

The King smiled before stepping aside.

"You did more than that Sergeant".

After the formalities, the King lingered for a few minutes, shaking hands with several of the men, before being steered towards the Officers' Mess for a light meal.

After the King departed, the tension broke like a shell burst. Cheering erupted, handshakes, slaps on the back. Someone handed Archie a cigarette. Another handed him a tin of bully beef with "VC" scratched into the lid.

Stowie grinned.

"You're still makin' the tea tonight, mate."

Archie just laughed, embarrassed by the fuss.

It wasn't until later that evening, when the noise had died down and the lads were settling into their usual mix of cards, tea and banter, that Roo sat beside his cousin, the firelight catching the gun metal surface of the medal.

"You've done us proud, Arch," Roo said quietly, watching the flame flicker, "Aunty Doris and Uncle Ray...they'll be over the moon".

Archie looked over, a little lost for words, but he gave a slow nod.

"I just did what had to be done," he said as he cast a gaze towards Stowie, "*we* did what had to be done".

Stowie smiled.

"Nothing to do with me mate...I was unconscious...remember".

"Nothing new there eh?" joked Clancy.

La Kruele still bore the scars of the war that had torn through it only weeks before. Shattered rooftops, blackened window frames, and collapsed walls stood like broken teeth against the soft morning light. The village was quiet but for the occasional clang of tools and the murmur of soldiers going about their duties. A few locals moved cautiously through the wreckage, eyes hollow with the weight of occupation and liberation.

Clancy, Roo, Stowie and Archie - his tunic freshly pressed, the ribbon for his Victoria Cross sewn neatly along the top of his left breast pocket - ambled down the rutted main road, the fog of last night's small celebrations still lingering in their limbs. The battalion had been given the morning off. The mood was subdued, a strange calm settling in after so much chaos.

Stowie gave a sharp whistle.

"Well, if this ain't the bloody end of the world".

Roo raised an eyebrow.

"Aye, aye, what's this?"

From the far end of the village came the low purr of engines. Two staff cars, both muddy, rounded the corner slowly. Soldiers looked up from what they were doing, curiosity tugging at their faces. The second vehicle carried the Royal Standard.

Clancy squinted through the smoke curling from his cigarette.

"That's not who I think it is…"

The car slowed. A few men straightened to attention, though half-heartedly, unsure of the protocol. The windows were down. And then they saw him.

King George.

"Bloody hell," Clancy muttered.

A soldier from another platoon shouted, startled but smiling, "Well, I'll be…it's Georgie!"

Even though the men had seen him the previous day, the name passed through the ranks like lightning, melting hesitation. Laughter bubbled up, followed by a ragged but spirited cheer from the men lining the street.

"G'day Georgie!"

The chant grew, more playful than reverent, but full of genuine affection. The King, perhaps startled himself, gestured for the driver to stop. The car pulled up just near the old chapel ruins, and after a moment's pause, King George V stepped down onto the muddy lane.

He was smaller in stature than many had imagined, his bearing neat but unpretentious. His uniform was immaculate, but not ostentatious. He wore a long greatcoat and gloves, and his eyes - intelligent, watchful - met theirs without flinching.

The soldiers, their boots covered with dried mud, and greatcoats hanging loose, instinctively shuffled into something orderly, but no one called them to attention.

King George approached a small knot of men - Clancy, Roo, Archie and Stowie among them.

"Are you men from Queensland?" he asked, his voice clipped but not unfriendly.

"Yes, Your Majesty," Archie answered, standing straight despite the dull ache from yesterday's parade and ceremony.

"I see...and you..." the King turned to him, noting the medal ribbon on Archie's tunic, "Sergeant Taylor, I presented you with the Victoria Cross yesterday".

Archie nodded.

"Yes, sir".

The King smiled slightly.

"A proud day. Well deserved".

"Thank you, Your Majesty," Archie said, then added, awkward but sincere, "good of you to come out here. Most wouldn't".

King George's expression softened.

"It's the least I can do".

He shook Roo's hand next, then Stowie's, then Clancy's realising that he was *indeed* in the company of brave heroes, spying a variety of medal ribbons on each man's uniforms; including the Distinguished Conduct Medal and Military Medal. Clancy, who tried not to smirk but failed, gave a mockingly subtle bow as the King moved on.

"Look at us," Clancy murmured to the others once the King was out of earshot, "shaking hands with the bloody King...never thought I'd see the day".

Roo chuckled.

"I don't think he expected to be called 'Georgie' by a mob of Diggers, either".

The King moved from group to group, speaking briefly, nodding, and shaking hands. There were no speeches, no pomp. Just a few quiet words exchanged between a monarch and the men who had borne the weight of empire and come to fight on his behalf.

When he climbed back into the car, the soldiers gave a final cheer - not out of duty, but genuine appreciation. The engines coughed, gears ground into motion, and the royal motorcade rolled slowly down the ruined street and out of sight.

The men stood silently for a moment, watching the dust settle.

"Well," Stowie said eventually, "guess we'll be tellin' the grandkids about *that* one".

Archie looked down the road, his voice quiet.

"Funny, isn't it? After all that...he seemed just like a normal bloke".

"Maybe that's what makes it mean something," Roo added.

They turned and made their way back through the village, smoke curling from chimneys, birds beginning to return to the rafters. War still lingered in the rubble - but for that one brief moment, something lighter had stirred among them. They had met their King and spoken to him as a man, a moment which truly would stay with them forever.

Eight days later the 9th was on the move again, this time heading for the front line at Le Waton, two miles east of Strazeele, where they relieved the 5th Battalion just after midnight. The Battalion was now the left battalion on the Division front with the 11th on the right. Patrols were immediately sent out, but sightings of the enemy over the next few days were rare.

Lieutenant Sargent was always keen to take out patrols, especially with Roo having a reputation of being like a bloodhound when it came to locating the enemy. Right now, with all that was going on further south, the high command was keen to know who they were facing. Accordingly, Sargent, and his small patrol, was dispatched at dusk with orders to capture a prisoner or two. There were a couple of hedgerows in no man's land and they were considered a prime spot for a possible enemy OP.

"Why don't we just knock 'em out with the big guns sir?" enquired Pip.

"Well, usually we would, but today we want to find out what units are to our front," replied the officer.

Behind the hedges they discovered a very well dug, and concealed, OP. However, it showed no signs of recent occupation. Inside were a number of German stick grenades, as well as a crate full of captured Mills Bombs.

Lieutenant Sargent carefully examined the explosives and decided to distribute the Mills Bombs amongst his men, whilst removing the detonators from the enemy grenades.

"These things are about as much use as a light house in a desert anyway," said Stowie, as he unscrewed the detonator from one of the German bombs.

Roo, who was guarding the entrance to the OP, turned to Tomo.

"Is that it then mate? There's nothing here to see is there?"

Tomo shook his head.

"No sarge. I reckon we should lay up outside and see if anyone turns up".

Even though it was summer and the days were long, the nights were still cold, and the small patrol shivered in semi darkness for a few hours until, at 2230 hours, Lieutenant Sargent decided it was time to return to their own lines.

As the six man patrol slowly rose, a party of about a dozen soldiers appeared from the right, to their rear. Roo saw them first and quickly held up his hand indicating for the group to freeze. Tomo called out a challenge which was answered in German, and he reacted immediately by shooting the leading man. The Germans fired off a few rounds in their direction but then took shelter in the OP, before appearing again.

There was a silent thud as a stick grenade landed in the middle of the patrol. The weapon was lost in the night but the Aussies reacted by instinct, throwing themselves to the ground whilst shouting out "GRENADE!" The men lay there for what seemed like an eternity...but nothing.

"It's a dud," whispered Stowie, "they've chucked one of the disarmed grenades".

Roo straight away was up on his knees, and there was a metal pinging noise as the arming handle of a Mills Bomb let fly, along with the bomb, which exploded amongst the enemy soldiers.

"Take that you Hun bastards!" Roo shouted.

"Right boys...run for it!" Tomo called out to his men, who began their sprinting withdrawal to their trenches. No casualties occurred in the patrol, though some of the Germans had paid the ultimate price.

The Germans made yet another effort to advance the next day, the 14th of July, targeting the French in what was to become known as the Second Battle of the Marne. Fighting erupted along the Marne River, east of Paris, and near Rheims. Expecting the attack, the French deliberately kept their front line lightly manned so that as the German forces advanced, they were met by strong French reserves and forced to retreat.

On the 18th of July, the Allies counterattacked. Reinforced by fresh American divisions, the French launched a powerful assault that caught the Germans off guard. The advance pushed the enemy back toward their main supply railhead, forcing the Germans into a hasty retreat. The German High Command, desperate to stabilize their lines, cancelled a planned offensive in Flanders to divert reinforcements south.

On the same day the 9th took over a post from the 11th Battalion. Orders were now given for an offensive along the front in this area. At the same time as the 9th (Scottish) Division advanced on Meteren, the 3rd Australian Brigade were to capture the small hamlet of Le Waton, which lay a mile to the south west. Once a quiet farming cluster nestled amid gently sloping fields and hawthorn hedgerows, Le Waton had become little more than a scar on the landscape - flattened walls, cratered orchards, and the burnt-out frames of cottages now marking its position. The surrounding farmland, once golden with wheat, was just a churned mess caused by months of shellfire and spring rain.

The attack on Le Waton formed part of a broader push in early July of 1918, as the Allies sought to straighten the line west of Hazebrouck and ease pressure on this vital logistical hub. For the Australians of the 3rd Brigade, this was familiar territory - many had trained in the area before the German spring offensive, and now they returned to reclaim what had once been friendly ground. The assault was co-ordinated to align with the larger operations conducted by British and Dominion forces along the Flanders front, including the methodical retaking of Meteren by the 9th (Scottish) Division.

Though smaller in scale than some later offensives, the capture of Le Waton was strategically important as it provided improved observation toward the Lys Valley and tightened the line before the planned Allied breakout operations. For the men of the 9th Battalion, it was another day of pushing forward under fire - step by bloody step - toward the promise of final victory.

To the relief of many in 'B' Company, they were to sit this one out, acting as reserve, whilst 'A', 'C' and 'D' Companies carried out the attack, with the 11th Battalion on their right.

Not all of the men were happy at their reprieve.

"This isn't on mate," said Clancy to Tomo.

Tomo scratched his head.

"Nothing I can do about it CSM. Orders are orders".

"Well, what they don't know won't hurt them eh?" replied Clancy.

"Bloody hell Clance," said Tomo, knowing there was no stopping the CSM now, "let me guess...the usual blokes are going with you?"

"Roo, Archie, Stowie, Pip and ten of the other lads".

Tomo looked worried.

"Cheer up mate. We'll be back soon enough...and fifteen less blokes resting won't make any difference," said Clancy.

Tomo smiled and shook Clancy's hand.

"You blokes will be the death of me".

The advance on Meteren was accompanied by an artillery bombardment; whilst the attack on Le Waton received no support...no artillery, no mortars.

The attackers were on their jumping off points at 0300 hours on the 19th of July, the 'B' Company contingent attaching themselves to Number 3 Platoon. The Platoon Commander, Lieutenant Wrench, gave Clancy and his mates a suspicious look, but was happy to see a few extra men.

Clancy noticed the look and re-assured the officer.

"G'day sir, us 'B' Company blokes thought we'd drop by and give you fellas a hand".

Lieutenant Wrench smiled.

"Do I have a choice Sergeant Major?"

Clancy laughed.

"We could always help one of the other platoons mate..."

The officer smiled again and directed them to where his men were laying up.

Laying up was indeed the word, for the attack did not commence for another five hours. The officers, however, were on to it, realising the danger which a daylight attack would incur.

Whilst 'C' and 'D' Companies occupied the left and right outpost lines, with 'A' Company located just to their rear, 'D' Company advanced forward one hundred and fifty yards before dawn broke.

The Meteren barrage commenced at 0755 hours then, five minutes later, Numbers 1 and 3 Platoons jumped off at 'Ewe Farm'. Their orders were for one of the platoons to clear the ground around Le Waton, whilst the other attacked from the left to mop up and resistance in the houses of the village. This would be a house by house operation with a section laying down fire on the building, whilst another tossed in grenades before entering and working their way room by room through the house, before moving on to the next building once it was clear.

Simultaneously the other two 'A' and 'D' Company platoons were to support the attackers with rifle grenade and machine gun fire.

Before the assault began, the Lewis gunners crawled out through the tall crops ahead of the Battalion's position, establishing themselves in a forward arc that stretched from the centre to about one hundred and fifty yards along the left flank, with positions staggered between fifty and one hundred yards deep. It was a good position with plenty of cover. Once the other platoons began their advance, the fire from these guns kept the heads down of several enemy machine gun groups. One enemy post, caught under enfilading fire, waved a white flag before the attackers had even closed to within fifty yards.

Lieutenant Myers's Number 1 Platoon split into four sections and moved cautiously through the tall wheat that swayed above helmet height in no man's land, the stalks whispering over shoulders and rifle barrels. Close behind, Number 3 Platoon mirrored their movements in staggered formation. Both concealment and personal field craft came in to play on this day, with each man camouflaging himself with green wheat stalks, which were attached to their helmets, webbing straps and their uniforms, helping them to vanish into the green; each soldier looking more like a moving shock of grain than a man. The advance was deliberate, every heartbeat loud in the hush.

Suddenly a burst of machine gun fire from a hidden German post shredded the wheat, and Number 1 Platoon went to ground. Keeping low, they wormed forward by inches, using small folds in the earth for cover, whilst still being continually harassed by the enemy guns. Spotting a cluster of crumbling ruins nearby - that had once been a farmhouse or outbuilding - they crept between the shattered walls, slipping from shadow to shadow, working their way slowly through the buildings. From there, they circled to the rear of the machine gun post.

At the same moment, bullets slashed into the tall stalks around Number 3 Platoon, ripping through the wheat with a vicious scything noise, pinning them flat for a few minutes.

"Keep your bloody heads down!" Clancy shouted.

"Did anyone see where those shots came from?" Archie shouted, scanning ahead through the swaying stalks.

The platoon waited, lying tense and silent, each man's heart hammering in their ears, as the enemy gun spat bullets in regular bursts - until, finally, the firing stuttered and stopped.

"They're reloading...go!" came the order.

Without hesitation, the platoon took their chance, springing forward in short, bounding rushes - leap frogging through the wheat field.

Archie led his little knot of mates, calling out brief directions between strides, Roo running beside him, while Stowie and Clancy covered the flanks, ducking and weaving between tufts of wheat and scorched patches of shell-churned earth.

"Come on boys!" Lieutenant Wrench called out as another burst tore through the stalks behind them.

They eventually broke through the edge of the crop onto slightly higher, open ground with an unobstructed field of fire. From here they were able to locate the enemy positions and, with rifles cracking and Lewis guns chattering, they poured suppressive fire into the German positions, pinning the gunners and giving Number 1 Platoon the opening they needed to finish the job.

"Enemy platoon, one hundred yards, two o'clock!" Archie shouted.

"Seen!" Pip replied, already swinging the Lewis gun into position.

The Aussie rifles cracked like stock whips. Stowie, lying prone, let fly with rapid, deliberate shots. The Lewis gun roared into life in Pip's capable hands, chattering and juddering against his shoulder as empty cartridge cases piled up on the ground.

The effect was immediate. The German gunners ducked low under the storm of suppressive fire, pinned hard. Their return fire grew wild and scattered, giving the lads of Number 1 Platoon the opportunity they needed to surge forward and strike.

In the lull between bursts, Clancy risked a glance up and grinned as he spotted the silhouettes of their mates in Number 1 pouring into the enemy position.

"Bloody beautiful!" he yelled.

"Not bad for a bunch of tourists eh?" Pip muttered, grinning through gritted teeth as he reloaded.

Archie didn't reply - his rifle was in his shoulder, another round chambered, eyes waiting for any movement. They held their ground on the rise, steel nerves behind hot barrels, until the last German gun fell silent and the enemy post was overrun.

At around 0815 hours 'C' Company surged forward in support of 'A' Company. The ground trembled as over a hundred pairs of boots thundered along, the wheat parting in waves as the men advanced. Up ahead, the German defenders, realising they were about to be outflanked and cut off, broke into a panicked retreat, scrambling to gather what equipment they could.

"Look at 'em bolt!" someone shouted, bayonet levelled.

Sensing the moment, Captain Biggs didn't hesitate.

"Up and at 'em boys!" he bellowed.

With barely a round coming their way, the men of 'C' Company rose from the cover of the crop and charged, their war cries tearing through the air. As they neared the enemy post, a few Germans tried to stand and fight - but it was too late. The Aussies were on them like a pack of dingos, rifles jabbing and swinging, bayonets glinting with wicked promise.

In the chaos of the melee, a German NCO raised his hands too slow and was driven to the ground with a rifle butt to the ribs. Another lunged with a bayonet, only to be tackled into the mud and disarmed with brutal expertise. Two more scrambled out of a shallow dugout only to find themselves face to face with a Lewis gun barrel. They dropped their weapons without a word.

Within minutes the post was in Australian hands, along with several German prisoners and five machine guns, which were now silent, their crews captured or dead.

But the fight wasn't over.

Number 1 Platoon, spotted a cluster of thirty to forty enemy soldiers making their escape, legging it across open ground, trying to reach the safety of their secondary trenches. There was no hesitation.

"After the bastards!" yelled Sergeant Fallon, waving his men forward.

The platoon broke into a sprint, bayonets fixed, leaping over wire and ducking through shell holes. But the fleeing Germans, driven by pure fear and adrenaline, were flying - arms pumping, helmets bouncing, a chaotic retreat toward their lines.

"They're like a flock of bloody Emus, the bastards!" panted one soldier.

Not giving up, and realising they wouldn't catch them, the Aussies dropped to one knee and opened fire on their prey, letting loose a disciplined and murderous volley dropping many. German figures crumpled mid run, some tumbling into the grass, others crawling for cover. Still the rest escaped, diving into their reserve trench and out of sight. The echoes of rifle fire faded, leaving only the wind and the heavy breaths of the men of Number 1 Platoon, now standing tall and flushed with the rush of the charge.

Smaller enemy posts in the vicinity were also cleared, and then 3 Platoon swung right and began attacking the enemy front line from the flank. The German front line lay on a road running from south to west in to Merris. Number 1 Platoon became involved too, by going round the back and advancing from the rear of the German positions.

Heavy machine gun and rifle fire from a strong German OP at the head of the road soon slowed the advance.

Clancy and Lieutenant Wrench guided the platoons in slowly with support from their Lewis guns. There was no immediate cover available, so the men improvised, firing the machine guns from the hip as they moved, whilst others rested them on another soldier's shoulders. Roo and Archie rallied a few more men equipped with rifle grenades, which were soon raining down on the enemy positions. Snipers also played a part, picking off anyone who looked to be organising the troops. The platoons were soon within bombing distance and began hurling their Mills Bombs towards the Germans. Some made attempts to surrender, but other die-hards threw badly aimed stick bombs at the Aussies, missing their targets.

Clancy was becoming annoyed now and directed the platoon to take down those unwilling to surrender.

"That bloke over there..." he shouted, as he pointed towards a belligerent, "drop him!"

BANG!

Down he went...and another...and another.

Eventually, being left with only would-be prisoners of war, the post was captured. Number 2 Platoon, sent to re-enforce the attackers, arrived just in time and was directed by Lieutenant Wrench to occupy the captured post. 'D' Company arrived shortly after and, whilst it became the new garrison of the post,

2 and 3 Platoons moved forward along the road and managed to capture a number of smaller posts. Despite being equipped with machine guns, the posts offered no resistance.

Stowie looked at the captured Germans, barely out of school.

"I think these fellas have given up the ghost".

Archie nodded.

"Yeah…I thought that. I reckon the fight has gone out of them…if these young lads ever had it in them in the first place".

"That's fine by me mate," added Clancy as he trotted past waving the platoons forward, "but there's a bunch up ahead who aint giving nothing up…so come on!"

A strong enemy post ahead offered a stubborn resistance with machine guns, rifles and grenades. But the Aussie platoons were organised, co-ordinated and well led, moving through the tall wheat under covering fire from their Lewis Guns and rifle grenades, which were exploding with deadly effect on the enemy. As 'A' Company, and it's 'B' Company intruders, began to circle the post, 1 Platoon to the enemy's rear and 2 and 3 from the front and flank, the Germans began lobbing stick grenades. This was much to the annoyance of the ANZACs.

"Right lads…when I say *now*, everyone lob a bomb at Fritz, then, while they're all in a tizzy we'll run in and kill the bastards," said Clancy, "ready…NOW!"

Over thirty bombs flew through the air at once; a daunting and terrifying sight for anyone to behold, exploding amongst the Germans like penny bangers on bonfire night.

"CHARGE!" shouted Clancy.

The Germans didn't see them coming as they exploded out of the wheat field and, bayonets fixed, launched themselves into the enemy trench.

What followed was madness - a storm of screaming men and clashing steel. The first ANZACs dropped into the trench like thunderbolts, slamming onto duckboards. Clancy was in the lead, bayonet glinting as he drove it hard into the chest of a German soldier, who barely had time to turn. The blade jammed on a rib - Clancy snarled, yanked it free with a grunt, then turned and brought the butt of his rifle down on another helmeted head.

All around him the trench erupted into a frenzy of close-quarters slaughter. Roo shouldered a huge German into the trench wall, fists flying, knocking the man's helmet clean off before pummelling him with one massive hand and burying a bayonet deep into his gut with the other. A shriek rose and choked as the man slumped, blood pouring down the corrugated iron wall like spilled wine.

Stowie fought like a demon, jabbing low, slashing high - rifle lost somewhere in the melee. He grabbed a heavy plank from a shattered duckboard and swung it like a cricket bat, cracking it across a German's skull with such force that fragments of wood and bone exploded outward. The man collapsed like a sack of wheat, twitching violently.

Archie fired point-blank into a German reloading his pistol, the round tearing through the man's jaw and sending a spray of teeth and gore into the trench wall. He turned, ducked a bayonet thrust, and retaliated with a savage downward stab that caught his attacker in the collarbone, the point crunching through and into his lungs.

Men screamed - in German, in English, in no language at all - blood spurting, boots slipping, hands clawing at throats. Helmets flew. Someone fell into the trench with his intestines spilling out like sausages from a split bag. Another tried to surrender, only to be bowled over and trampled as the wave of Aussies pressed on, all red-eyed and roaring, caught in the madness of the charge.

A German machine gun crew tried to swing their weapon around, but Roo was on them before they could fire - he grabbed the barrel, screaming with rage as it scorched his palms, and wrenched it aside while Archie shot one and Clancy drove his bayonet into the other's ribs.

The trench was a slaughter house now - smoke, cordite, the reek of blood, excrement and sweat thick in the air. Grenades exploded behind them. One man - nobody could tell whose side he was on - staggered forward without a face.

The post fell in less than three minutes, a flurry of German hands shooting up.

Then it was over.

The Aussies stood panting, soaked in blood and dirt, weapons hanging from tired hands. The post, and what was left of the garrison, was theirs. Flies already buzzed around the carnage. A German moaned softly from beneath a mound of corpses.

Clancy spat and wiped a smear of blood from his cheek with a torn sleeve.

"Well," he uttered grimly, "that shut the bastards up".

Straight away the platoons took on their new defensive positions, for the battle was still on. As 'D' Company moved through the new front line they encountered and attacked another enemy post a short distance away. Again the Germans put up a short, half-hearted, resistance until 'D' Company rushed and captured the position.

Meanwhile, 'B' Company, in reserve, had moved forward, gathering up the wounded and the prisoners.

As Clancy's mob rested on their rifles, Captain Ponsonby and Lieutenant Sargent appeared.

"Ah...CSM...chaps," Ponsonby nodded, "finished your jollies have you?"

Roo looked towards the Captain.

"Not just yet Fred. Give us an hour or two and we'll be done".

"Alright...but not too long...your brekkie is going cold," Ponsonby replied with a wink.

"Bloody hell mate you sound just like my Mum," laughed Archie.

It was now 0900 hours and the battle had been raging for sixty five minutes, with quite a gain in territory.

"Sergeant Major..." Lieutenant Wrench called to Clancy.

"Yes sir?"

"Your help has been much appreciated, but I think your OC would like you back now".

"But sir..."

"No buts CSM. 'A' Company is holding here whilst 'C' and 'D' consolidate the position; so time to bugger off I'm afraid".

Lieutenant Wrench held out a hand in thanks, which Clancy happily shook.

"Thanks for a fun morning...good luck sir," Clancy replied as he nodded to the 'B' Company men, "come on boys, home time".

Unlike Clancy's mob, the Germans weren't going quietly, laying down inaccurate machine gun fire on the new front line and later dropping an artillery barrage on the roads and tracks leading to the rear.

Although one of the most successful operations carried out by the 9th Battalion, it came as usual at a cost, with nine dead and thirty nine wounded, whilst ninety eight prisoners were taken, along with sixteen machine guns and two Minenwerfers.

The attack by the 9th Division had been a success too with the capture of Meteren. Ironically this battle had been fought on the anniversary of the first Australian battle in France, Fromelles, two years earlier on the 19th of July 1916, in which the 5th Division had taken part.

The next day the Germans attempted two counter attacks, which were driven off by Lewis gun fire, and eventually routed by accurate artillery fire. For several days after the capture of Le Waton the Battalion was extremely active, taking part in daylight patrols in the wheat fields, hunting and harassing the enemy.

CHAPTER 11

Love, Hope and Buses

For the men of the 2nd Light Horse the morning of the 15th of July was spent clearing the battlefield, burying enemy dead where they lay and collecting rifles, grenades, and any kit which had been left behind. It was slow work - quiet, methodical, and necessary.

Enemy parties came out under Red Cross flags, collecting their own dead and wounded beyond the regimental wire. They kept their heads down and didn't speak. But it was clear they were doing more than just retrieval, for the following day, the 2nds's positions - especially the horse lines - were shelled continuously for two hours. Five men were killed. No one doubted the enemy had taken notes while under the flag.

The rest of the day was spent repairing wire entanglements and trench damage. The ground was torn, the posts battered, and the men worked without complaint.

Late in the day, the Padre came through the lines. He stopped here and there, speaking to the men as they worked - offering a word, a prayer, a bit of scripture if anyone wanted it. Most didn't.

Chugger spotted him near the horse lines and wiped his hands on his tunic.

"Padre," he called, "got a minute?"

The priest turned, squinting.

"What is it, son?"

Chugger stepped closer, speaking in a low voice.

"I was wondering if you'd marry me and Rachel...after all this...if we get through?"

The Padre's smile vanished and he stared at him for a moment, before letting out a short, dry laugh. He was well aware of Rachel, her having been with the regiment for nearly a year now, but more than that she was an Arab, and a Muslim. Rachel was sat with Alfie, just out of earshot, laughing as they both drew pictures in the sand with twigs.

"You're serious?"

Chugger nodded.

"Dead set sir..."

The Padre shook his head and jabbed his finger into the air in Rachel's direction.

"*That* woman? She's a heathen. Filthy, godless. You want a wedding; you'll need a proper bride..."

Chugger didn't flinch.

"She's proper enough for me".

"Well, not for me," the Padre said, "and not for the Church. I won't be part of it".

He turned and walked off without another word.

Chugger stood there for a moment, in shock, then went back to where the others were working and picked up the coil of wire he had left behind. He started threading it through the stakes. The others were quiet - the only sound the clink of tools.

After a minute, he said, "Whatever happened to that bit from the Bible...you know...*You shall love your neighbour as yourself*?"

Boggy paused and wiped his brow with his sleeve.

"What do you mean?"

Chugger kept threading.

"That bastard Padre says Rachel's a heathen and he won't marry us".

Boggy snorted.

"I've told you before, mate...religion's run by a pack of bastards. That's why I keep clear of it".

No one argued. The wire kept going up, and the sun kept climbing.

Once their work was done the boys returned to the bivvie area. Chugger found Rachel sitting by a small cooking fire stirring a pot of something aromatic.

He sat beside her and scratched at the dust on his sleeve.

"That smells good mate," he said hesitantly, "I spoke to the Padre before".

Rachel didn't look at him but continued stirring.

"I saw".

"He won't marry us," Chugger said, "he says you're a heathen".

This was a new word for her.

"Heathen...what is this heathen?"

Chugger paused and contemplated the word for a moment.

"Er...I think it's a nasty word for saying you are not good enough for the Christian church...but that is just a load of bull".

Rachel gave a small nod.

"Yes...my...er faith would say same...call you infidel...but I do not care...I am yours and you mine...yes?"

"Too right we are".

Chugger hesitated.

"Can one of us change religions?"

She turned to him then, her eyes steady.

"If I do that, my people will kill me".

Chugger didn't speak.

Rachel looked back to the horizon.

"It is not just words...not for them".

They sat in silence a while. The wind picked up, carrying the scent of Rachel's stew across the camp. Somewhere behind them, a horse stamped and snorted.

"Religion is an arse!" Chugger suddenly said.

Rachel nodded.

"Yes...but we find way to be together".

The regiment was relieved at 2350 hours by the 8th Light Horse Regiment and departed the Jordan Valley for a rest. Apart from a brief inspection by Lieutenant General Chauvel, the Corps Commander, the regiment continued through Jerusalem and reached Arrub on the 20th.

Arrub sat along the Hebron-Jerusalem road; a small village surrounded by rocky hills and terraced fields. The area had long been used as a staging point - first by the Ottomans, now by the British. Water was available from nearby springs, and the terrain offered enough cover for bivouacs. The men settled in, tending to horses, sorting kit, and taking stock.

On the 21ˢᵗ, thirty men were selected for leave in Port Said. Percy and his section were among the lucky ones, with Rachel and Alfie tagging along.

The café was quiet, tucked off a side street near the docks. Percy's section sat around a table, nursing lukewarm tea and watching the traffic roll past - porters, sailors, and stray dogs cutting through the heat.

Chugger, still concerned about the Padre's comments, leaned forward.

"We've got to sort this. If we don't get married, Rachel can't come back to Australia with me".

Johnno tapped his spoon against the rim of his cup.

"I heard sea captains can do weddings".

Chugger looked around.

"Yeah? Well I don't see any sea captains around here...or ships for that matter...do you?"

Boggy gestured toward the harbour.

"Mate, we're in a bloody port. They're floating all over the place".

That was enough. They paid the bill and headed down to the docks where they scanned the ships moored along the wharf. After a few false starts and one confused Greek steward, they found a British merchant vessel – the SS Calder - tied up and prepping for departure.

She sat low in the water, hull streaked with coal dust and salt, paint dulled by years of hard use. Not a warship, not a passenger liner, just a merchant freighter built for hauling cargo and surviving rough seas. The kind of ship that didn't need to look pretty, because it had nothing to prove.

The ship's hull was in need of some paint and there was rust around the anchor housing. The funnel was squat and blackened, the bridge tucked in behind it like a boxer keeping his head down in a fight.

They walked up to the gangplank, where a sailor stood leaning on the rail, cap pushed back, sleeves rolled up.

He looked them over.

"You lot after something?"

Percy stepped forward.

"We'd like to speak to the captain".

The sailor raised an eyebrow.

"What for?"

Chugger cleared his throat.

"We're hoping he'll marry us...me and Rachel".

The sailor blinked, looked at Rachel, then back at Chugger.

"Right...well, that's a new one".

He paused, then nodded toward the bridge.

"Wait here. I'll see if he's in the mood".

They were eventually shown to the bridge. The captain stood near the chart table, pipe in hand, his uniform neat. He was a Yorkshire man, middle-aged, with a kind face and a quiet way about him.

He looked at Rachel in her slouch hat and poorly fitted uniform. His eyes lingered for a moment, taking in the rough fit of her clothes, then settled on her face. Whatever else he saw, it was her eyes that held him.

"Well," he said, "I can see who the bride is. So who's the lucky man?"

Chugger raised his hand.

"That'd be me".

The captain tapped his pipe against the edge of the chart table.

"Well," he said, "I've done it once before. Shipboard ceremony...legal enough if the paperwork's signed. The only trouble is...we sail tonight".

"We're all here, so why not do it now?" Percy suggested.

The captain nodded and thought for a moment.

"Right...I don't see why not...let's get it done then".

He led them down to his cabin - tight quarters, brass fittings, a desk cleared of charts. He fetched a small leather bound book and a lockbox from the drawer.

"Rings?" he asked.

Chugger hesitated.

"We haven't got any, what with the suddenness of things eh?"

The captain unlocked the box and flipped the lid. Inside was a jumble of rings, necklaces, brooches, and odd bits of jewellery.

"Lost property from the odd passenger that we carry," he said, "here...try these on for size".

Rachel picked out a plain silver band. Chugger found one that fit, slightly bent but solid.

The ceremony went ahead without a hitch. The paperwork was signed, stamped, and handed over - official and binding.

Percy shook Chugger's hand and gave Rachel a gentle hug.

"Congratulations to you both".

Johnno nodded.

"Well done".

Boggy gave Rachel a quiet smile.

"About bloody time..."

They stepped off the ship as the crew prepared to cast off. Chugger tucked the paperwork into his pocket as he walked beside his bride.

"Aussie here we come," he said, "just got to finish this bloody war first".

The 20th of July, and the following few days, were sad ones indeed for the 9th Battalion. It began with Lieutenant Henzell being blown up by a whiz bang which hit the parados of his post. After a long fight for life he eventually recovered. It was not as good an outcome for Lieutenant Russell who was killed on the same day.

To add to things a gas attack on Moolenacker went terribly wrong when some of the projectiles veered off course, with five of them falling on the 9th Battalion's right hand post, half a mile west of Le Waton. One dropped on the edge of a trench occupied by Number 1 Platoon, drenching many in the poisonous liquid. Despite immediately donning respirators, it was too late and the whole platoon had to be evacuated; two men sadly dying.

The unfortunate friendly attack halted the intended advance of the outpost line that night. But the next night two of the forward posts *were* slightly advanced and, at 2230 hours, the relief by the 12th Battalion commenced.

Over the three days since the capture of Le Waton artillery strikes on the Battalion lines had been constant, causing a number of casualties.

Following their relief the 9th returned to the area of 'Mango Farm', five hundred yards north west of Pradelle, a small hamlet nestled among gently rolling farmland and hedgerows. The surrounding countryside, once peaceful pasture, now bore the scars of war - shell-blasted fields, shattered trees, and hastily repaired farm buildings.

The trucks rolled to a halt in a churned up paddock bordered by shattered hedgerows and the leaning skeletons of apple trees. Beyond them, the battered farmhouse once known as Mango Farm stood crooked but still upright, its stone walls marked by shrapnel, and its barn roof half caved in.

Archie jumped down from the tailboard and took in the scene with a tired sigh.

"Well, it isn't a warm hut that's for sure," he said.

Clancy dropped beside him, slinging his rifle over one shoulder.

"Still it beats getting shot at".

"Barely," Roo added, brushing dust from his coat and stretching his long arms, "it smells like something died in that barn".

Ponsonby came striding down the line.

"Alright boys, this is us for a spell. We're Brigade Support now - which means carrying parties, working parties, and anything else the front line units need to stay in the fight. Not glamorous, but vital".

A few groans echoed from the ranks, but most were just grateful for a break from the front line.

"Where exactly are we?" asked Stowie.

"North west of a place called Pradelle," Ponsonby answered, pointing with his thumb, "bit of a ghost village now. Used to be farmland all through here".

"It still is," said Clancy, kicking at a splintered plough half-buried in the dirt, "just farmed by artillery now".

As the men settled into their new camp - erecting tents, unloading rations, and digging fresh latrines - the peaceful countryside around them groaned with far off echoes of shellfire. Birds no longer sang in these fields, and the quiet was rarely true silence. Still, after the chaos of their last action, 'Mango Farm' felt almost restful.

Archie stood a moment longer at the edge of the field, gazing over the torn-up landscape.

"I'd give anything for a proper cup of tea and a week without hearing a single bloody explosion".

Roo slapped him on the back.

"One day, mate...one day".

Work done, the men lounged near the edge of the ruined orchard beside the old farm house, some smoking, others jotting into notepads or dozing with hats over their eyes. A runner from Battalion HQ approached, clutching a small sack - letters.

"Mail!" he called, and a ripple of excitement ran through the group.

Pip took his envelope gingerly, as if it might crumble. He tore it open with his index finger, grinning when he saw the familiar handwriting.

He read quietly for a few moments, and then looked up, his cheeks flushed with pride.

"Your Mum says she and your Dad are real impressed with me learning to ride, *and* that they're looking forward to meeting me...and Clancy too, when this is all over".

Clancy looked up from cleaning his rifle and snorted.

"I hope they know I ain't exactly civilised," he said, smirking.

"They'll be thrilled," said Archie, "everyone loves a stray mongrel".

The others chuckled, and Pip folded the letter and tucked it safely into his tunic.

"Still," he said quietly, "its nice...thinking there's people waiting. I've never had that before".

Roo nodded, poking the fire with a stick.

"You'll be right mate".

On the 22nd of July Captain Ponsonby read a message to the 1st Australian Division from the General Officer Commanding the 9th Division.

"The GOC has sent a very nice message to thank us for our support during the capture of Meteren. He says he admires our fighting capabilities and hopes that we are on his flank when operations resume".

Clancy laughed.

"I'd have just settled for a cold beer".

Whilst at 'Mango Farm', Merris was taken by the 10th Battalion on the night of the 29th, and the next day the 9th moved back to La Kreule.

The Commander in Chief, General Sir Edmund Allenby reviewed the 1st Light Horse Brigade on the 31st of July. It was the first time they had assembled for a full mounted ceremonial parade since 1915, when Sir Ian Hamilton had inspected them before the Gallipoli campaign.

The General took his time, moving along the ranks, speaking with officers, nodding to troopers. He had seen the reports - Masallabah, Abu Tellul - and now he saw the men behind them. His praise was direct and without flourish. He commended the brigade for its discipline, its endurance, and its performance under fire. The mention of Abu Tellul carried a lot of weight. Everyone there knew what it had cost, and what had been held. Allenby's recognition didn't change anything - but it mattered.

The next fortnight settled into a routine - classroom lectures, weapons drills, and the usual maintenance of saddlery and kit. There was no urgency, just the steady rhythm of instruction and repetition. The men patched their uniforms, darned their socks, cleaned rifles, and listened to officers explain things they mostly already knew. It was rest, of a kind.

To break the monotony, there were a couple of sports meetings - foot races, wrestling bouts, and a rough game of football played with a heavy sand bag. Now and then, they were marched down to the beach for a swim.

It was a far cry from ANZAC, where swimming meant dodging sniper fire. Here, the sea was calm, the sand soft underfoot, and the only danger was sunburn.

None of the men had swimming gear, so they stripped off and waded in bare-arsed, laughing and swearing like schoolboys. Rachel didn't bat an eyelid. She'd grown up with rules and modesty, but war had a way of rearranging priorities. She joined them without fuss, wearing army issue shorts and a vest - neither flattering nor comfortable, but it did the job.

No one stared. No one commented.

She swam out past the breakers, turned once to glance back at the shore, then kept going - steady, unbothered, alone in the water. Chugger watched from the shallows. He didn't say a word, but the thought settled in - how had he ended up with her - a woman so fearless, so bloody beautiful, and somehow his?

It didn't make sense. But he wasn't about to question it.

"You're a lucky man mate," said Percy, who was sitting on the edge of the shore, the waves gently bathing him with warm water as they rolled slowly in.

Chugger nodded.

"Yes I am Perce...I really am".

By the end of July, the tide of war on the western front had finally begun to turn. General Foch's counterstroke along the Marne had already sent the enemy reeling northward toward the Aisne, and now, with the momentum shifting, the Allies were ready to press their advantage. Plans were quickly laid for a broader offensive, one that would strike east of Soissons and bring fresh fury to the German lines.

The Australians and Canadians were given the post of honour - trusted spearheads for the coming assault. With the French on the right and the 3rd British Corps holding the left, the stage was set for what promised to be a critical push.

After nearly four months apart, the 1st Australian Division received orders to rejoin the Australian Corps. There was no time for ceremony. The German Spring Offensive, once so fearsome, had faltered, and now it was the Allies' turn to drive forward.

From August 1918, the Australian Corps - no longer a typical three division force - now comprised all five divisions of the Australian Imperial Force. To these, General Monash added a vast number of Corps Troops and attached personnel, many of them non-Australians. With over one hundred thousand Australian soldiers and an additional contingent of supporting troops, the Corps swelled to nearly two hundred thousand men in total - making it the largest single corps ever assembled in any war. The hammer blow soon to fall on the Germans would be carried, in no small part, by Monash's mighty command.

Meanwhile, the 9th Battalion, having just arrived at La Kruele were pleased to be back with the 1st Australian Corps. Though officially out of the front line, the men knew full well that something was brewing. The tempo of drills picked up. Officers met behind closed doors. Messages moved more urgently between companies.

"Something's up," Roo muttered one morning, watching a pair of runners disappear toward Brigade HQ.

Clancy rolled his eyes and tutted.

"Too bloody right. Last time I saw this many maps and chin scratching was before Gallipoli... and we all know how that turned out".

Pip, who had just returned from delivering a message, slid down beside them, dusted in sweat and road grime.

"It's not just us. I'm hearing all sorts of rumours. Something big is coming, boys".

"Big?" growled Clancy, "everything in this bloody war is big. I'm just glad we're back with the Aussie Corps".

Though the 9th wasn't yet in the thick of it, they could feel the shift - like a storm building over the ridgeline. After four years of grinding losses and bloody stalemates, hope - real hope - had begun to creep back into the ranks. The enemy was on the back foot at last, and the Australians, tired but unbeaten, were ready to push. It was time to go home.

Following reveille on the 1st of August, the battalion were lined up, their boots dusty and uniforms already damp in the early morning haze. Packs were worn, rifles shouldered, and groans rippled through the ranks as the word passed down the line.

"Right lads, fall in! We're on the move again!"

"What a bloody surprise. Another bloody shuffle across half of France," grumbled Stowie, "I reckon I've lost a foot in height since we left Australia".

Grumbling drifted up and down the ranks like smoke. The men muttered and shifted, fully expecting another endless trudge along rutted farm tracks and dusty village lanes. Archie glanced around at the faces beside him - hardened, sunburnt, and good humoured despite everything.

"Ten quid says we're headed for another mud hole with a fancy French name," someone said.

"Ten quid? Who the hell's still got ten quid?" another voice answered.

Just as the men resigned themselves to a day of footslogging, came the first sound of something unexpected - a distant chugging, growling hum that didn't belong to wagons or horses. Heads turned. Voices stilled. Over the crest of the road came a column of motorised omnibuses, rattling and wheezing and belching black smoke into the air. The buses, many of them re-purposed London double-deckers with the roofs stripped and bench seats bolted to the floor, wheezed to a halt. They were big and boxy - long since commandeered by the Army - still bearing faded civilian advertisements for soap, tea, and musicals on their flanks. Some even retained the words *"General"*, *"Vanguard"*, or *"London Transport"* in chipped paint, as if they'd simply taken a wrong turn at Piccadilly and ended up in Flanders. Each one groaned under the weight of dents, rust and patchy paint, but to the diggers, they might as well have been chariots.

"Bloody hell..." said Pip, his eyes full of anticipation, "flamin' buses!"

"Looks like we're going up in the world," Archie grinned.

The rear doors clattered open and the sergeants waved the men aboard.

Inside, the buses smelled of oil, old leather, and pipe smoke. Wooden benches ran along the walls, narrow and hard, the suspension was non-existent, and the engine noise loud enough to drown out a bombardment, but none of it mattered, for it was better than marching. The men jostled into place, placing their packs beneath their seats as they settled in.

"I never thought I'd see the day," said Roo, taking it all in, "a few years back, the only wheels in Kilcoy belonged to the local bullock dray".

"And now we're riding to war like a bloody royal parade," said Clancy, grinning.

"Do you reckon they'll get us all the way there without catching fire?" shouted Archie over the din.

"Doesn't matter," laughed Clancy, "it's not my feet doing the work for once".

As the convoy jolted into motion, bouncing along the narrow country roads, some of the men leaned out of the open sides and windows, whilst others dozed, heads lolling with every pothole. Others sang snatches of songs, joked, or smoked as the countryside slid past - fields dotted with haystacks and crumbling farmhouses – as they waved to passing French villagers who stared or cheered as they rattled by. Dust rose behind them in long brown plumes, and the growl of engines echoed across the open countryside.

For many of the diggers, their experience of motorised vehicles during their time overseas was something foreign to them. Horses and their own two feet had been their only means of transport until now. But as the countryside rolled by - fields, barns, stone cottages flashing past at twenty miles an hour - they realised this was something new. War was changing. Everything was faster now, bigger, louder, and in this war of mud and misery, a ride in something with wheels was a rare and welcome reprieve.

"Wonder how long till they've got tanks with bloody kitchens in 'em," someone joked.

The convoy rattled and groaned its way into La Sablon a couple of hours later, the battered buses kicking up long tails of exhaust smoke behind them, the men dusty but smiling - none the worse for wear, and still marvelling at being carried to war by machine. The small farming hamlet was nestled among gently rolling fields, the land green and peaceful beneath a wide blue sky. Whitewashed cottages with slate roofs stood quiet in the summer sun, and a small stone church kept watch over the narrow lanes and hedgerows.

As the buses hissed to a stop near the edge of the village, the men clambered down stiff-legged, their boots thumping onto the dry earth. They stretched sore backs and shook out numb legs, some rubbing aching shoulders after the bone-jarring ride.

"Not bad," Archie murmured, hopping down from the bus with a thud, "better than walking eh?"

"Well," said Clancy, taking in the fields, "at least this place isn't under water".

"It'll do," muttered Roo, eyeing a cluster of barns in the distance.

The village itself seemed barely touched by the war. Children peeked from behind fences, curious but cautious, while an old woman nodded at the passing diggers from the doorway of a tiny cottage. A few French soldiers lounged outside a wayside estaminet, nursing tin cups of wine and watching the Australians with mild interest.

The air smelled of hay and distant cooking, a welcome change from smoke, rot, and cordite. A dog barked from somewhere unseen, whilst birds chirped from the hedgerows.

"Quiet little place," said Pip, "I reckon we'll get a few nights' kip here like".

"I wouldn't get used to it," Archie replied, glancing up the road, "I doubt we'll be here long".

The battalion was billeted in barns and outbuildings on the edge of La Sablon, a patchwork of haylofts, sheds, and lean-tos. It was rough, but dry, and after the trenches, anything was better. Before long, there were fires going, boots being cleaned, and letters being written.

Here they would remain, resting, training, and preparing for whatever came next. The war, they knew, was far from over - but for the first time in a long while, it felt like the tide was turning in their favour.

St Omer, a fairly large town and important railway junction, was five miles away and became not only a place of normality for the men, but also a great place for the cooks to acquire fresh vegetables such as cauliflower, cabbage, beans, peas, tinned fruit, milk and many other goodies. The men certainly ate well, and for some whose stomachs had not contained proper food for a long time, the subsequent payback was a little unpleasant.

"Thanks for that mate," said Roo as he pinched his nose with his finger and thumb.

Clancy smiled.

"You know me...always happy to share with my mates".

Archie sat, fanning the odour away with his slouch hat.

"Well, this mate wishes you'd take your smelly arse somewhere else..."

After five days they were on the move again, with 'C' Company boarding a train at Wizernes and the other three companies entraining at St Omer. 'A', 'B' and 'D' Companies reached Longpre at 0615 hours the next day. After breakfast by the wayside they marched to Villers-Sous-Ailly, arriving at 1230 hours. Here they were joined by 'C' Company, whose train had taken them to Pont-Remy. In usual fashion the men of 'C' Company were met with shouts of "Got lost did you?" and other sarcastic jibes.

At 1830 hours, the now complete 9th Battalion resumed its march through Long to Catelet. From here they boarded yet more buses, which drove them through the night, reaching the area of Amiens at around 0130 hours, at a point between Cardonette and Coisy.

The men couldn't believe their eyes when they saw a road sign for Amiens.

"Amiens?!" growled Clancy, "I don't believe it. How many times have we been here now?'

The furphy net was buzzing like billio as to their next move. What *was* known was that the battalion was to be ready to move at short notice into the front line...wherever that may be. Despite this the battalion marched in to Coisy, and by 0215 hours was settled into billets. The 1st Division was again in the 4th Army under General Rawlinson.

The opening battle of the great offensive, the Battle of Amiens, began at 0420 hours on the 8th of August. The front extended on a sixteen mile line from Morlancourt to Moreuil. Led by a huge force of tanks, which replaced the usual artillery, the Aussies and Canadians swiftly penetrated the enemy defences. Seventeen thousand prisoners were taken and five hundred artillery pieces captured on the first day. On the Australian part of the operation the initial attack was made by the 2nd and 3rd Divisions, and the 4th and 5th leap frogged over them, fighting through to the final objective.

Meanwhile the 9th, feeling disappointed at being away from the Australian Corps at such a time, received orders to move, and departed at 1330 hours on a forced march through Allonville, Querrieu, Pont Noyelles and La Neuville-Corbie, to Hamel. To complicate things, the distance they had to march was over thirteen miles on very dusty roads, during unusually hot weather. The battalion reached Hamel at 2145 hours, over eight hours later, where they occupied trenches between Hamel and Accroche Wood.

The next day they were ordered to advance four miles to positions just south of Bayonvillers, setting off at mid-day, crossing open countryside in artillery formation. On arrival the troops were very pleased as they were able to partake of a meal whilst the Company Commanders attended a CO's Orders Group. Towards the end of the afternoon the battalion moved further forward to the south west of Harbonnieres where they occupied some German huts. There was notably much aerial activity over-head that day.

It seemed to be a day of musical chairs for the battalion, and with little rest, at 2030 hours they were ordered to take up defensive positions south east of Harbonnieres and towards Vauvillers. They set off on the two mile march and dug themselves in on arrival.

Earlier that day, at 1400 hours, the 2nd Brigade had attacked a point known as the 'Red Line', which ran from Vauvillers to Lihons. It had made good progress, but the enemy had forced it to halt four hundred yards from its objective. Therefore, at 0200 hours the following morning, the 9th and 11th Battalions were instructed to move over the 'Red Line' and capture the 'Blue Line' which lay on the eastern side of the road that ran from Lihu Wood to Lihons; the line itself being six hundred yards. The men, who had spent three and a half hours digging in, advanced in artillery formation at 0630 hours reaching the 'Red Line' with no casualties. Then they waited...

Ninety minutes later the 9th, along with the 11th, attacked over flat open ground towards Crepy Wood. To the centre of their front were a brick chimney and an old railway line. Directly in their path there were wire entanglements which led up to Crepy Wood on their right.

Almost immediately the two battalions were struck by intense machine gun fire. The 9th received heavy casualties but reached the western edge of Crepy Wood. Amongst the casualties were at least six of the company officers and, for the moment, leaders were few and far between. Captain Ponsonby, without hesitation, took command, for now, ordering three platoons to advance. The German machine gun fire was still heavy and their resistance strong. Despite this some platoons of the 9th managed to force their way through the wood and reach its eastern outskirts. One of the 'C' Company platoons managed this feat quite easily, *and* without a single casualty. Others met a different enemy, discovering that as they moved forward the enemy machine gun fire began to come from their rear. Headquarters now decided to temporarily withdraw the advance parties and to form a line in an old trench running north and south along the western edge of the wood.

During the confusion of the advance, elements of the 9th and 10th Battalions had become entangled in the smoke and shell-blasted terrain. Orders were shouted across cratered ground, runners lost, and five officers from the 9th had been hit and dragged to the rear, leaving gaps in the command chain. With no time to waste, Major Ross stepped forward and assumed control of the firing line, rallying the men into something resembling order.

Reinforcements arrived minutes later in the guise of 'A' Company of the 10th Battalion, moving up at the double. They had been detached earlier and now found themselves swept into the fight. At their head strode Captain McCann, a tall, broad-shouldered man with a soot-smeared face and a calm authority in his stride.

He spotted Ponsonby near a shattered tree stump, issuing orders to two corporals.

"Glad to see you, Freddy," McCann called, breathless but steady.

Ponsonby turned, face streaked with mud, helmet pushed back on his head.

"Good timing, Jack," he said briskly, gripping McCann's hand in a quick shake, "we're thinned out, command's scattered, and we've got machine gun nests flanking the ridge ahead".

McCann nodded once.

"What do you need?"

"Anchor our left. Push in tight behind Ross's centre line and keep your men low - the bastards have eyes on this whole sector. Once you're set, we'll sweep the right".

"Understood," McCann replied, already turning to shout orders to his NCOs.

Ponsonby watched them go, and then turned back to the map spread across the ground. The plan had changed, as do all plans in the first few minutes of battle, but the fight pressed on.

At 1300 hours the combined forces attacked.

A shrill whistle cut through the thick, still air and the battered remnants of the 9th surged forward alongside what was left of the 10th. Men scrambled over broken tree roots, their feet churning up leaf litter and shell-blasted undergrowth as they stormed into the wood under a curtain of rifle and machine gun fire.

Archie was at the front of his platoon, shouting above the noise.

"Keep moving! Spread out through the trees!"

To his right, Clancy, his face blackened with sweat and powder, drove the next wave forward with a fierce bellow.

"Let's go, boys! Push 'em back! No bloody stopping now!"

Enemy fire raked the tree trunks, branches exploded in splinters overhead, and the undergrowth writhed with the wounded. Still, the diggers advanced, ducking and weaving through the smoking ruins of what had once been forest.

Grenades burst ahead of them in blinding flashes, and Germans - dug into rough pits and behind shattered logs - fought bitterly to hold ground. The Australians met them with bayonet and bomb, shouting curses and war cries. One German machine gun crew was taken by surprise when Archie's section flanked them. He didn't hesitate - two short, brutal shots from his Webley dropped the gunners, and the platoon pushed past, reclaiming the shattered knoll that had exchanged hands so many times over the years.

Clancy's group, meanwhile, overran a shallow trench near the eastern edge of the wood. The defenders fought like demons - one lunged at Clancy with a spade - but was met with a crack to the jaw from Clancy's rifle butt and a sharp thrust of bayonet from the nearest Aussie. Another German tried to run but was dropped by a Lewis gun burst from behind.

By 1600 hours, the exhausted remnants of the battalion were holding firm. With the help of a platoon from the 5th Battalion - who arrived red-faced and panting but ready - the new line was hastily scratched out among the stumps and craters on the northern and eastern edges of the wood.

Then came the counterattack.

A thin grey line of Germans emerged through the trees like ghosts; rifles raised and bayonets fixed, shouting as they advanced. But the Australians were ready.

"Hold your fire!" Archie shouted as he crouched behind a fallen trunk, watching through the iron sights of his rifle.

"Wait for it...NOW!"

When the Germans closed to within forty yards, the Lewis guns opened up with a vicious growl, along with a chorus of rifle shots from the entire company. Bullets tore through the enemy ranks, cutting down the first wave in seconds. Clancy shouted over the hammering guns.

"Rip into 'em lads! Don't let the bastards through!"

The fire was withering. The Germans stumbled, faltered, and then broke, the survivors dragging themselves back into the smoke-choked trees, leaving the field littered with bodies.

Silence returned in fits and starts - broken only by the groans of the wounded and the hiss of cooling barrels.

Archie exhaled hard, resting back against the log.

"That'll teach 'em".

Clancy knelt beside a fallen corporal, checking for signs of life. He looked over at Archie and nodded grimly.

"Bloody close. But we held".

By 1630 hours, the new posts were dug in. The wood was theirs - though the price had been high. Of the 9th Battalion, barely three hundred men were still standing. Dirty, bloodied, and shaking with exhaustion, but standing.

They had driven the enemy out once more, and they weren't letting go.

As it turned out, this position was *not* the 'Blue Line', the battalion's objective. The 9th was now in front of Crepy Wood, whereas the actual objective was in front of Auger Wood, some five hundred yards further out.

But after hours of vicious fighting, no one had the strength to care.

They had fought tooth and nail to reach the edge of Crepy Wood - a shell torn patch of earth where the trees had been splintered to jagged spears and the only cover came in the form of shell scrapes, dug with entrenching tools by exhausted hands. There were no trenches here, no dugouts, and no safety - only shallow, muddy graves waiting to be filled.

Despite this the 9th had taken ninety prisoners and captured eight 4.2 inch Howitzers, thirty machine guns, two trench mortars and three complete telephone installations - pulled from the mud by signallers already planning to wire them into the line.

But the price had been brutal. Casualties littered the wood line, groaning or eerily still, faces white against the red-soaked dirt.

Then, at 1730 hours, the sky opened up with a howl as the enemy unleashed a heavy barrage, which fell like an iron curtain - high explosive and shrapnel screaming down in a rolling wall that chewed the earth to pieces. Trees were flung sideways, and branches were shattered, raining down like knives. Dirt, bark, and chunks of flesh burst into the air.

The men dropped flat into their shallow holes, covering their heads as hot fragments hissed past, slicing the air just inches above the ground. Some tried to press deeper into the dirt, whilst others simply clutched their rifles and waited for it to end, praying that the next shell would not fall on them.

The barrage suddenly halted after thirty minutes, then movement was spotted in the tree line – a counter attack.

Three hundred Germans surged forward out of the trees, grey coats flaring as they stormed the line with rifles, stick grenades, and fixed bayonets, slamming into the posts occupied by McCann's company. The men fought desperately to hold them back but the Germans managed to overrun some of the posts, killing and driving out some of the defenders, and gaining a foothold in the wood. But the support troops were already moving in. The counter attack by the reserve elements came like a hammer - led by grizzled sergeants and corporals. There was no subtlety in it - just raw fury. The Australians came roaring out of their holes, some with bayonets fixed, others with entrenching tools, and even bare fists. It was pure slaughter as men grappled in the broken undergrowth, screaming curses in English and German, blades flashing, rifles smashing against skulls. One digger was seen driving his bayonet into a German's chest, then firing point-blank through another who leapt at him. Others tackled machine gun crews, slamming them into tree trunks, using boots and rifle butts to finish the job.

The enemy faltered, then broke.

The struggle had lasted an hour, and by the time the last shot rang out, ninety dead Germans lay scattered through the splintered trees, their assault broken on the bloodied resolve of men who simply refused to yield.

Then, almost like a child having a tantrum, the Germans resorted to shelling the outposts, supports and Battalion HQ incessantly.

Ponsonby's HQ was barely more than a widened scrape on a shallow rise, camouflaged under a few branches and a battered groundsheet. The Captain crouched among his runners and signallers, maps rolled up in a satchel, revolver clenched in his hand.

Shells peppered the earth around them, kicking up great clods of soil. The concussions shook the air. Twice Ponsonby was forced to duck lower as splinters hissed over their heads like wasps. One man lost his helmet to a near miss - another was left stunned, nose bleeding, ears ringing.

The barrage seemed to go on forever, but eventually stopped as suddenly as it had begun- a punishment for daring to stand ground and take what wasn't theirs to begin with.

On the morning of the 11th of August, the 10th and 12th Battalions attacked the 'Blue Line'. A dense fog clung low to the earth concealing any movement and as the assault troops stepped off through the 9th Battalion's forward defences, they were quickly swallowed by the foggy darkness, their figures vanishing into a wall of shifting vapour and smoke.

The noise of the battle echoed unseen in the early hours, whilst the men of 'B' Company stood at the ready, straining to see, to hear, and to know what was happening beyond the veil.

The rattle of machine guns cracked somewhere ahead. Then the dull thump of grenades, muffled shouting, screams, and over it all, the deep, rhythmic boom of artillery that rolled like thunder across the fields.

Pip shifted nervously and whispered, "It sounds bad out there".

Roo, crouched beside him, peered into the mist and nodded grimly.

"Yeah...and it's worse not knowing if our blokes are winning...or if Fritz will come stumbling through that fog any second".

The men of the 9th waited, rifles at the aim, eyes flicking left and right along the ghostly tree line. But soon the tide of the battle became known as shapes began to move - at first indistinct, wavering like smoke.

"Movement," Clancy muttered, tightening his grip on his rifle, "could be ours...could be them".

Someone shouted a warning.

"Hold your fire!"

Roo stood slightly, hand raised.

"Wait...look!"

Out of the mist unescorted German soldiers began emerging. They were unarmed, their helmets gone, tunics unbuttoned. Each man had one hand raised high in surrender, the other clutching packets of cheap German cigarettes, which they held out like offerings.

A strange silence followed.

"Bloody hell," Stowie muttered, "looks like our boys have done it".

The tension broke. The diggers lowered their weapons but remained wary. The Germans passed through, trudging between the Australian lines - tired, defeated, many with hollow eyes and shaking hands. It was clear now; the objective, which included the village of Lihons, had been taken by 0515 hours.

When the fog finally lifted, it revealed something more troubling. A mile wide gap yawned open between the right flank of the 11th Battalion and the left of the 12th - stretching from the northern edge of Auger Wood toward the northwest...a gaping vulnerability.

There was no time to waste.

Orders came through quickly. The entire 9th Battalion was to move forward and plug the breach. Boots hit the ground as the men of 'B' Company fell into step, their previous tension replaced with a determined resolve.

The battle wasn't finished...not yet.

Unfortunately for the 9th the Germans were also heading for the gap, having seen the obvious opening in the middle of the Aussie line, and as the 9th progressed they eventually came into contact with them.

It began with movement ahead - at first a flicker, then the unmistakable sight of grey coated figures pushing forward in staggered groups, rifles at the ready, bayonets glinting in the early morning light. Both sides froze.

For a split second, neither the Australians nor the Germans fired. It was as if time paused - two tides of men suddenly staring one another down at close range in the haze of dust and smoke. Then chaos erupted.

"Enemy front!" someone shouted.

"Line forward...fire at will!" Lieutenant Sargent ordered; his voice loud and urgent over the rising noise of battle.

The Australians fanned out, dropping to one knee or going prone, returning fire as the Germans scrambled for cover in a shallow trench system that ran diagonally through the open ground. Rifle fire cracked like whips. A Lewis gun chattered to life somewhere to the left, its distinctive rattle answering the drilling sound of German machine guns.

Fierce fighting ensued and the enemy were forced out, and as 'B' Company advanced in extended line they noticed at least fifty Germans being pursued by the 10th. Immediately Lieutenant Sargent's platoon moved to cut off their retreat. The Germans took refuge in a trench, so Clancy did the only thing he could, shouting to a Lewis gun section.

"You blokes...come with me!"

"Right you are, sir!" one of the soldiers shouted back.

He sprinted toward the slight rise beside the trench, breath rasping. The Lewis gun crew followed, hauling their weapon and ammunition. Clancy placed the Lewis gun section near a gap in the trench through which the Germans would need to pass.

"Keep this gap covered boys while I round up some more blokes," he told the gunners, "and don't let anyone through unless they're bloody singing *Waltzing Matilda*!"

Then he turned, scanning the shattered landscape for more support. But the chaos of battle had scattered the platoon - men were pinned down, repositioning, or already engaged elsewhere.

Clancy spotted two nearby figures.

"You'll do...come on!"

Without hesitation, the three of them rushed around twenty yards towards the trench, with bayonets, pointing menacingly towards their foe. The Germans saw them coming - one stood to fire and was immediately cut down. Then shots rang out, the crack of a Mauser echoed, and the man beside Clancy pitched forward, shot clean through the chest.

Clancy didn't slow.

He glanced sideways at the other soldier, a Private Young, and smiled.

"Come on mate...you'll never get to heaven if you don't die".

Even though there were only two of them, they jumped into the trench, shouting like madmen, and started stabbing the enemy soldiers who, despite their numbers, turned and ran along the trench, hotly pursued by Clancy and Young. The trench wasn't very deep and Clancy noticed a bend up ahead, so he leapt out of the trench and ran along its edge, overtaking the fleeing Germans. He then turned and flung a Mills Bomb in to the mass of men, killing four of them, and resulting in the prompt surrender of the remainder, who quickly raised their hands, shouting, "Kamerad! Kamerad!"

Private Young stood in awe of what they had just done, his chest heaving.

"Christ," he whispered, "they've surrendered".

Clancy lowered his rifle slightly, eyes hard.

"Only because we scared the shit out of them...now keep your bloody rifle up just in case they change their minds".

He and Private Young then did their best to "surround" their prisoners but some *did* manage to escape. Once the rest of the Company arrived there were twenty eight prisoners in total.

"Not a bad haul eh Youngy," Clancy noted, winking at the young soldier.

By 0930 hours, the 9th Battalion had managed to close the dangerous mile long gap between the 10th and 12th Battalions. The men worked quickly under tense conditions, establishing a string of defensive posts roughly one hundred yards apart, each a shallow scrape in the dry earth, hastily reinforced with salvaged timber, sandbags, and bundles of wheat stalks. There was no time for proper trenches - just enough to get below ground level and pray it was enough.

Within minutes the Germans responded.

The first shells came screaming in with no warning. The sharp hiss of whizz-bangs tore through the humid air and exploded along the line in short, vicious bursts - shrapnel buzzing like angry wasps. Then came the heavier artillery; deeper, throatier explosions that pounded the earth, shaking helmets and spattering men with soil. The men ducked low in their shell scrapes, pressed flat against the ground, teeth gritted and knuckles white.

"Here we go again," muttered Clancy, wiping dust from his eyes as a near miss showered his post in dirt.

A few men were hit - one Private caught a shard of shrapnel in the thigh and was dragged out under fire, groaning through clenched teeth. Others weren't so lucky. A post to the left was suddenly silent after a direct hit collapsed its walls.

Despite the shelling, the men were forced to keep an eye to their front. Any moment now, they knew the Germans might test the line again.

Their instincts proved right.

At 1330 hours, the mist above Lihu Wood, northeast of Lihons, began to stir. Movement - dozens, then hundreds of grey figures pouring from the tree line in rough waves. They were shouting as they came, charging with a kind of reckless fervour the Australians hadn't seen since Gallipoli.

"Jesus," muttered Stowie as he looked down his sights, "they're bloody keen, I'll give 'em that".

"They're mad," said Roo, shaking his head as he cocked his rifle, "mad as the bloody Turks at ANZAC".

"Hold your fire," came the order along the line, "wait...wait..."

Again, only when the enemy had closed within two hundred yards did the guns open up. The Aussies let loose with everything they had - rifles cracked, Lewis guns clattered, and grenades sailed into the oncoming ranks. The German attack faltered as quickly as it had begun, men dropping in heaps across the churned earth.

Within minutes, the counterattack dissolved into chaos - scattered survivors diving for cover, wounded men crawling back toward the woods. The rest lay still in the field, caught in the storm of lead.

The sun was still high when silence returned to the line, broken only by the groans of the wounded and the cough of a jammed gun being cleared.

As he stared out at the scores of dead and dying Germans to his front, Roo shook his head.

"What a bloody waste...and for what?"

By the end of the battle at Crepy Wood, the 9th had lost one hundred and seventy eight men - killed, wounded, or missing. It was a bitter cost, but the line had held.

CHAPTER 12

And He Marched Them Up To the Top of the Hill

In the early hours of the 12th of August, the 9th Battalion was finally relieved from the front line after more than eight days of continuous fighting, advancing, and holding under fire. The men moved out under cover of darkness, their feet dragging with exhaustion as they trudged away from the battlegrounds of Crepy and Lihons. They made their way to a new bivouac area near the village of Vauvillers, a small farming hamlet nestled among gently rolling fields scarred by shellfire.

Though the village itself had been battered in the fighting just days earlier, its proximity to the recently captured front allowed it to serve as a staging and rest area. The remains of cottages and barns offered crude shelter, and the shade of the orchard trees gave a rare sense of calm. The men collapsed into sleep wherever they could find space, some beneath wagons, others rolled in their greatcoats along the hedgerows.

For two full days, the battalion remained there, taking what rest they could. Wounds were treated, kit was repaired, and the cooks managed to boil up some decent stews with salvaged rations. For the first time in over a week, no one was shooting at them. Still, the mood remained subdued - tired, sombre, but steady.

Then, on the afternoon of the 14th, a welcome distraction arrived. Thirty one fresh faced reinforcements marched in - clean uniforms and boots that hadn't yet seen mud. The old hands watched them with the quiet resignation of men who had already learned the cost of war.

The reinforcements stood in a nervous cluster near the old stone well, trying not to look too fresh-faced under the scrutiny of battle-hardened eyes. Their uniforms were still the right shade of khaki, their boots barely scuffed. One had even polished the brass buttons on his tunic. It was all too much for Roo who was usually the quiet and understanding one.

"Would you look at that?" he muttered to Clancy, nodding towards a young private fiddling with the chinstrap of his slouch hat, "poor bugger's still got creases in his trousers".

Clancy chuckled.

"Leave him alone mate. He'll be covered in mud and piss before the week's out".

One of the reinforcements looked their way nervously, and Roo gave him a wink.

"Welcome to the bloody 9th, sunshine. Hope you like loud noises and bully beef".

Archie, sitting nearby with his back to a mossy wall and his tin mug resting on his knee, chuckled.

"Be nice...some of them might be 'B' Company".

One of the newcomers, a freckled lad barely out of school by the look of him, raised a hesitant hand on hearing Archie's reply to Roo.

"Is this...is this 'B' Company?"

"You've found us, mate," Clancy said, getting to his feet and offering his hand, "welcome to the madness".

The young man shook it gratefully.

"What's your name?" Roo asked, already slapping a bit of dust off a nearby sandbag to give him a place to sit.

"Private McDermott, sir".

Roo raised an eyebrow.

"I'm not a 'sir' mate...just Roo. This here is Archie, Stowie, Clancy, and the one with the big ears hiding behind his tea is Pip".

"I heard that," Pip muttered.

The reinforcements settled in slowly, grateful for the friendly tone and not quite sure if they were being gently teased or warmly included...probably both.

But, even better than the reinforcements was the next arrival...letters from home.

Cries of delight rang out across the company lines as names were called and letters handed out. Archie, Roo, Pip, and Clancy each received envelopes smudged with dust, but the handwriting was instantly recognisable.

"Doris and Ray again," Clancy said, carefully tearing his letter open.

"Same here," said Pip, already grinning, "bless 'em...I can't wait to meet them both".

"Me too mate, and getting all these letters and sending one back is really helping with my reading and writing," Clancy added.

"Come on Clance, you're a natural, and besides your writing has been great ever since Gallipoli," said Roo.

The boys gathered beneath a half collapsed lean-to, reading by the slanting light of the afternoon. Roo chuckled at something his uncle Ray had written, and Archie, with a faint smile, read his letter twice over, folding it neatly and tucking it away like it was made of gold.

"Mum says that Dad is putting up some fencing near the dam again...says he's got young Frank helping now, but I reckon that he's just chasing frogs while Dad does all the work".

Roo nodded.

"Yeah...same here. Uncle Ray reckons the grass is up past his horse's belly and the creek's running clear again".

Archie leaned back with a thoughtful grin.

"I bet the old place will look bloody strange after all this".

Roo gave a soft nod.

"Strange...but it'll be good to be home again".

As the stew was passed around and the last of the letters were tucked into tunic pockets, the group settled into a comfortable silence. The new men watched the seasoned diggers carefully, as if trying to decode the unspoken rhythm of army life.

Private McDermott - still clutching his mess tin a bit too tightly - shifted closer to Clancy and lowered his voice.

"Sergeant Major...can I ask something?"

Clancy glanced sideways.

"Yeah mate...go for it".

The lad hesitated.

"What's it like...I mean, being in a real battle?"

The question hung in the air for a moment, like a shell that hadn't quite landed. Even Roo looked up, and Archie paused mid sip.

Clancy didn't rush his reply. He scraped the bottom of his tin with a spoon, and then looked at the younger man squarely.

"It's loud, it's fast and it's messy".

He paused.

"But it's not all chaos. You've trained for it, and the bloke next to you has too. You're always with mates and you watch each other's backs, keep your head down, and remember what you were taught".

McDermott gave a nervous nod.

Clancy softened.

"Look, it's natural to be scared. You wouldn't be normal if you weren't. But fear keeps you on your toes. The first time is the worst, I'll admit that...and everyone here will too...right boys? But after that, you'll be thinking more about where your mates are and where Fritz is, than worrying about anything else".

Archie added, "And when it's all done, the best thing is a brew, dry socks, and someone to say 'bloody hell, we made it'".

Roo gave McDermott a firm pat on the shoulder.

"Stick close to us Macca. You'll be fine".

The young soldier gave a small, grateful smile.

"Thanks. I just...didn't want to ask something stupid".

"No such thing out here mate," Clancy said, standing up and stretching, "the only stupid thing is not asking when you need to".

They sat quietly after that, the night deepening around them. In the distance, a flare went up; casting the distant landscape in a ghostly light, but it didn't reach them. For now, they were safe - old hands who had once asked the same questions, and new faces bound by shared ground, bad jokes, and letters from a world that still waited for them.

On that same evening they were back on the line just north of Crepy Wood, where they relieved the 10th Battalion. The trenches were shallow and barely formed, hastily scratched into the earth by those who had held them the night before. Shell holes still smoked in places, and the air hung heavy with the drifting haze.

Their stay was very brief - barely time to blink - before word came through at dawn that they were to be relieved again. The front line had shifted forward another two hundred yards during the night. Orders were issued and the weary diggers trudged out once more.

That evening they settled into a bivouac area between Lihons and Herleville, where the open fields bore the scars of recent shellfire but at least offered room to stretch out. The grass was flattened in parts, and the few remaining trees were blackened and twisted like broken fingers. Even so, the men welcomed the change in pace, knowing that worse could be just around the corner.

By the 16th, the Battalion was on the move again - this time in artillery formation, skirting the main roads and moving cautiously across open country. They were off to Vaire, for a well earned five day rest, a village battered but not levelled, nestled amid gently rising ground and winding tracks. Although still within the range of the big German guns, Vaire had the feel of somewhere momentarily forgotten by the war, its roofless buildings and crooked chimneys bore the usual marks of shellfire, but here and there wildflowers poked through the rubble, and birdsong returned timidly to the hedgerows.

"Five days' rest," someone murmured, almost in disbelief, as they were shown to the scattered bivvie sites. The area had been used before, and trenches nearby served as crude latrines and water points.

As the men dropped their equipment, one of the new men spoke up.

"Is this what it's always like?" he asked. "March in, hold the line a day or two, march out again?"

Clancy, who was resting on an upturned ammunition crate and rolling a cigarette with grimy fingers, gave a short laugh.

"If only, mate".

The diggers nearby glanced over, listening.

Clancy continued.

"You've just walked into a luxury we haven't had in years. A proper rest...even just a few days? That's like bloody Christmas. There've been times we've held the line for weeks on end without relief - no hot meals, no dry clothes, rats bigger than Roo's boots...and don't get me started on Passchendaele".

The soldier swallowed hard but nodded.

Clancy lit the smoke, blew out the match, and said, "So no, this isn't normal. This is bloody paradise".

At 0700 hours on the 17th of August, the 2nd Light Horse Regiment moved out with the rest of the brigade, heading back into the Jordan Valley. It was a long and hot ride, and they reached their destination four days later.

On the 22nd they relieved the 10th Light Horse, taking over six forward posts - Vale, View, Vaux, Zoo, Zeiss, and Zerum. Each post was manned by an NCO and nine troopers, working in conjunction with detachments from the British West Indian Regiment.

For the West Indians, this was their first time in a front line role. Since 1915, they had served as labourers, storemen, stretcher bearers, and general support - digging trenches, hauling supplies, and working under fire without recognition. Now, for the first time, they were posted alongside fighting units.

The men came from across the Caribbean - Jamaica, Trinidad, Barbados, Grenada, British Guiana, St Vincent, the Bahamas, and British Honduras. They were keen, disciplined, and intelligent. Many had volunteered early in the war, only to be sidelined by policy and prejudice - not from the ordinary soldier but by those who thought they knew better. Despite this their morale was high, and they were eager to prove themselves.

The Light Horse troopers took to them quickly. There was no fuss, just shared rations, shared posts, and the quiet understanding that every man on the line had earned his place.

One of their new mates from the West Indian contingent was Sergeant Gadwyn Jones - a muscular Jamaican with a calm voice and a dry wit. He stood about five foot ten, broad through the shoulders, with the kind of build that came from years of hard labour. His uniform sat well on him, boots worn but polished, and his eyes carried both warmth and sharpness.

"Gadwyn? What sort of name is that mate?" asked Chugger.

"Its da name given to me by my mudder...it don't have no meanin' dat I know of," replied the sergeant with a smile.

"You'll have to excuse old Chugger here, he's not exactly known for his tact," said Percy.

"No, no it's not that, it's just not a name I've heard before...have you got a middle name?" replied Chugger.

Gadwyn rolled his eyes mischievously.

"Fedlyn," he replied, "but it can't be any worse dan Chugger".

"Well, you've got me there, but *my* real name is Wilbert. I don't love it but it was what I was given. At home they used to call me Bert or even Will, but Chugger is fine," Chugger replied.

"Well, my friends call me Jonah," Gadwyn said, shaking hands all round, "and I tink you fellas qualify".

His accent was soft but unmistakable - Kingston lilt wrapped around clipped British phrasing. He spoke with precision, but there was music in it. Not for show, it was just how he was.

The work was shared without any bother - sandbags filled and stacked, sentry duties sorted, rifles cleaned side by side. Jonah had been in the war since 1915, but until now had spent his days hauling crates, digging latrines, and carrying stretchers under fire. He didn't complain. But he didn't hide his pride either.

Chugger, and the rest of the troops, were annoyed that these men, who had joined for the same reason as him, had been held back.

"I just don't see the flamin' sense of it boys. Any bloke who puts on a uniform is as good as anybody in my books".

"The thing is mate, it isn't fellas like us who decide these things, it's those who think they are our betters...even the church," said Davo.

Chugger laughed a cynical laugh.

"Yeah mate, I saw that all too well with the padre and Rachel. But surely they're not all like that?"

"No they're not, but can you believe that the AIF nearly didn't take Roo? Even Davo here had to change the spelling of his last name," added Percy.

Chugger cast a confused eye to Davo.

"It's true mate. My father is Chinese and my mum is English. I had to change the spelling of Li...L...I...to Lee...L double E...you know...just in case".

"Well bugger me. I didn't know that...sorry mate," replied Chugger.

Davo laughed and shook his head.

"You've nothing to be sorry about...you're my mate and I trust you with my life".

"And we've done that a few times haven't we mate?" said Chugger.

Jonah stood nearby, listening without interrupting. When the moment passed, he gave a quiet nod.

"Yuh men have seen plenty," he said, "but yuh still carry each other. Dat's what count".

He smiled, and then turned back to the post, his voice trailing off as he called out to one of his men.

"Keep yuh eyes alert, Lewis. Dusk coming soon".

By mid-afternoon on the 21st of August, the 9th Battalion had formed up on the track just south of Vaire. The Australian Corps had resumed hostilities. For once, the road ahead was quiet, though the distant boom of guns still rumbled across the Somme valley like far-off thunder, echoing faintly from behind the eastern ridge. The men marched in loose columns at first, but after barely half a mile, they peeled off the road and began winding across the countryside, the earth cracked and dry beneath their feet, the grass faded gold under a low, hazy sun.

A kite balloon hovered far to the north, rising with a reluctant sway above a distant wood, its tether ropes vanishing into a shimmer of heat. Crows flapped lazily from one bare tree to another. Even now, with the war roaring just miles ahead, the afternoon felt strangely calm - almost peaceful.

The column advanced quietly across fields and hollows, through hedgerows and around shell marked rises, until at last, by 1700 hours, they reached the rendezvous point - an open area south of Morcourt where cooking fires already smoked and Dixies of hot food were being ladled out by the quartermaster's staff.

The smell of tea and stew drifted up like a gift from heaven. The men dropped to the grass where they stood, helmets off, boots dusty, shoulders aching. Some sprawled out fully, staring at the pale blue sky. Others just knelt by their mess tins, eyes half-shut with exhaustion but still grateful for warmth and food.

"This is the life," someone muttered between mouthfuls, and a few nearby chuckled, not because it was funny, but because it was true - compared to what lay ahead, a hot meal in the open air was as close to comfort as one could get.

Far in the distance, smoke from the guns still twisted lazily into the sky. The battle was about to resume. But at this moment in time, the men of the battalion sat quietly and ate, their minds somewhere between the clatter of the previous weeks of fighting and the silence of whatever waited for them tomorrow.

Tomorrow arrived soon enough, and the battalion was placed on a moment's notice to go into action.

The objective for the 1st and 2nd Brigades was the 'Red Line', while the 'Blue Line' was assigned to the 10th and 11th Battalions. The 'Red Line' lay halfway between Chuignolles and Bray, and the 'Blue Line' ran along the valley stretching from Chuignolles to Chuignes, then northward toward the River Somme in the direction of Bray.

Dominating the far side of that valley was an imposing and steep ridgeline - a natural barrier that rose sharply from the low ground. At its northern crest stood Froissy Beacon, a commanding height nearly four hundred feet above the canal below. In peacetime it had served as a signal point and landmark, but now, in 1918, its strategic value made it a magnet for artillery observers and machine gun nests. The hillside sloped down toward the Somme Canal, its scrub and broken fields now gouged by trench scars, dotted with the blackened ribs of shattered trees and the occasional rusted chassis of a wrecked gun carriage. From its heights, an observer could look down across the entire valley, making it a vital and dangerous piece of ground.

After a hot meal, the 9th moved off at 0230 hours on the 23rd, marching in silence under a dark and cloud-streaked sky. They reached the rendezvous point on the western edge of Germain Wood at 0420 hours. The cover here was excellent - steep banks and old sunken roads, and the wooded terrain provided shelter from enemy eyes. The men took what rest they could among the roots and shadows, checking their rifles and bayonets, and casting wary glances toward the looming shape of Froissy Beacon above, where dawn would soon reveal the day's grim work.

The first artillery barrage began at 0445 hours, a sudden and savage thunder that rolled up from the Allied guns like the crack of doom. The ground trembled as hundreds of guns opened up in a perfectly timed symphony of destruction. Shells screamed overhead, whistling into enemy territory, crashing into dugouts, trenches, and suspected machine gun nests. The sky flickered with the blinding glow of bursting shrapnel, and the distant ridge line was soon obscured by smoke, fire, and dust. Beneath that steel curtain, the 1st and 2nd Brigades surged forward and captured the 'Red Line', the thunder of guns drowning out even their shouts of triumph.

By midday, the guns had shifted, but the lull was short lived.

At 1230 hours, the 9th Battalion was ordered forward toward the freshly captured 'Red Line'. Barely had they begun to move across the shattered ground when the enemy responded with a furious counter-barrage. Eight inch high explosive shells and poison gas bombs began falling without warning. The air was suddenly filled with the deafening roar of impacts, the scream of metal fragments whipping through the air, and the hissing of gas shells cracking open, releasing thick, oily green clouds that clung low to the earth.

Men stumbled blindly through the churned earth, clutching gas masks to their faces as confusion reigned. Shell bursts sent bodies tumbling through the air like rag dolls, and the screams of the wounded were almost lost in the noise. Officers and NCOs shouted orders, runners zig zagged through the inferno, and the staggered formations dissolved into a grim, instinctive scramble for survival.

Despite the chaos and the rising toll in casualties, the 9th pushed forward, coughing through their masks, eyes red from gas and smoke. There was no time to rest, no pause to regroup. Orders came fast - the next stage of the offensive was imminent. At 1400 hours, the second phase began. The 9th were to strike again, this time aiming for Luc Wood. The battalion was positioned on the left flank, with the 12th Battalion on their right and the 11th in support.

Only a smoke barrage was available to shield their advance now. The misty veil clung to the low ground, rising in ghostly tendrils from shell holes and ditches, but did little to deter the German gunners who had zeroed in on the slope. Artillery fire slammed into the rising ground, sowing confusion and cutting men down by the dozen. The steep incline toward Froissy Beacon was a nightmare - exposed, cratered, and slippery with ripped up soil and blood. The smoke gave brief concealment, but it could not halt the storm of fire.

Clancy, crawling up beside a shattered tree stump, paused long enough to look up the incline and mutter, "Bloody hell...it's almost as steep as Gallipoli".

Machine guns hammered from concealed bunkers along the ground ahead, their tracers stitching death across the slope. The 9th, battered and badly scattered, pressed forward in broken sections, re-forming on the move where they could. By sheer determination and courage, they reached the main road running beneath Froissy Beacon, bodies sagging from exhaustion, their feet slipping in the mud. But here, they were met with yet another wall of resistance.

The crest of Froissy Beacon exploded in muzzle flashes as German artillery crews, firing at point-blank range from hidden redoubts, unleashed volley after volley down the road. Machine gun fire raked the shoulders of the track, and the men of the 9th had no choice but to dive for cover wherever they could find it. The forward momentum had stalled, caught between the unforgiving slope, fierce resistance, and a storm of iron and lead.

But the attack pressed on.

Meanwhile the 12th Battalion had advanced between Froissy Beacon and the village of Chuignes to attack Garenne Wood, and 'B' and 'D' Companies of the 11th swung left and, with Lewis guns, enfiladed two enemy machine guns, posted on the slopes of the Beacon, that were holding up the 9th's advance.

As the enemy guns fell silent, hit by counter battery fire, the 9th recommenced their advance, but after a hundred yards or so yet another machine gun began to spit death towards them, causing the men to throw themselves flat on the ground.

The attack had stalled again.

Pinned down by withering machine gun fire from a fortified position dug into the slope just below Froissy Beacon, the men of the battalion were flat against the earth, unable to move without inviting certain death. The enemy held the high ground, and every attempt to advance was met with a deadly sweep of bullets that tore through the grass and shrubs and rattled the helmets of the crouching Australians.

Lieutenant Sargent glanced to his left and caught Pip's eye, as if to say *we're stuck*. But before he could speak, Pip had already made up his mind.

Without waiting for orders, he unclipped two Mills bombs from his belt, and began crawling forward through the scorched stubble and shell holes, his webbing clinking faintly as he moved. Using a shallow dip in the ground for cover, he inched his way toward the enemy post, heart thumping, breath shallow, every nerve on edge.

He reached a position just five yards from the German emplacement - a bristling nest of sandbags, its gun chattering relentlessly. With a practised motion, Pip pulled the pins on both grenades, waited two counts, and hurled them with all his strength.

The explosions lit up the sky, flinging smoke, dust, and shrapnel into the air. Before the echo had faded, Pip was on his feet, rifle at the ready, and charging through the blast.

He hit the position at a sprint, leaping over the edge of the trench and landing amidst the dazed enemy crew. His first shot dropped the gunner. The next he dispatched with the bayonet, driving the steel home with a cry of fury and fear. The others fought back, but Pip fought harder - ducking, lunging, his rifle swinging like a club, his boots slipping in blood and soil. One German tried to flee - he didn't get far.

When it was over, four enemy soldiers lay dead or dying around the wrecked gun. Pip, breath heaving and eyes wild, stood alone among them, the ridge now eerily silent but for the ticking of the cooling weapon.

The suddenness of his assault shocked the nearby enemy troops into confusion. Seizing the moment, Lieutenant Sargent's platoon rose and surged forward, pouring over the slope with bayonets fixed and rifles blazing. The machine gun position, once the anchor of the German line, was gone. Within minutes the men of the 'B' Company had taken the ridge and, now joined by 'A' Company of the 11th following their storming of the steep cliffs, began digging in before the enemy could regroup.

The rest of the companies soon joined them at the summit, where they found themselves on a plateau which stretched towards the village of Cappy. One of the diggers impressed with the all round view at the top suddenly blurted out, "Would ya look at that...you can see half of bloody France from up here".

That night, the high ground at Froissy Beacon belonged to them.

Pip's reckless courage had broken the deadlock and given the battalion the foothold it needed. The fighting in the surrounding area would grind on for days, but his charge became one of those whispered stories passed from man to man over bully beef and tea - a reminder that sometimes, the tide of battle turns on a single man with grit in his teeth and fire in his heart.

The ridge was eerily calm now.

Smoke drifted lazily over the battlefield in the early evening light. The bodies had been cleared from the immediate line, and the surviving men of the platoon now crouched in shallow shell scrapes, keeping watch, some cleaning rifles, checking bandoliers, and sharing whispered thoughts of home. Pip sat with his back to a shattered tree stump, arms folded, tunic streaked with blood and dirt that wasn't all his.

He stared ahead in silence, the tremble in his hands finally beginning to ease.

Clancy flopped down beside him, wincing as he adjusted a bandage on his arm.

"Well, I'll be buggered," he said, glancing sideways and offering his right hand to Pip "I reckon you were trying to win the war on your own mate...good on yer".

Pip didn't answer straight away. He rubbed his eyes with the heel of his hand.

"I don't remember most of it like...just...noise...fire...and then I was in the trench with them Geermans".

"Geermans?" laughed Clancy, "I still like the way you say that...makes them sound...well...I don't know...strange".

Roo crouched nearby, trying with all his might to break up a hard tack biscuit.

"You don't remember the part where you bayoneted half of Fritz's machine-gun crew?" he asked. "Because we do, and I don't think we'll ever forget it either".

"You bloody well saved our bacon," said Stowie, flicking a spent shell casing away.

Lieutenant Sargent appeared and knelt beside Pip, his expression serious but not unkind.

"You alright, Pip?"

Pip nodded slowly.

"You showed remarkable initiative back there," Sargent said, "reckless, maybe. But sometimes that's the kind of recklessness that wins a war. You did more than knock out that post - you opened the door for the whole line to move".

Clancy gave Pip a friendly shove.

"Told you the pommy bastard had guts".

Pip looked at Clancy and smiled a cheeky smile.

"Hey, less of the pommy please..."

Sargent rose to his feet.

"We've sent word to Battalion HQ. Don't be surprised if someone comes looking to pin a medal on your chest. Until then, get some rest. You...well...all of us deserve it".

As he walked off, Stowie leaned in.

"You reckon they'll send you to London for that medal? Maybe get a handshake from a General...or a nurse".

Pip gave a tired grin.

"I'd settle for a nice hot brew".

Roo chuckled.

"Don't worry, mate. When we get home, we'll tell every girl in Queensland how you took Froissy Beacon with your bare hands".

"I used grenades," Pip replied.

"Yeah but that's too easy," said Clancy, "we'll say you used your teeth".

They all laughed - quiet, relieved, grateful laughter.

Their stay on the summit was a brief one with the 9th and 11th now moving through the low ground to the north between the Somme Canal and the Beacon, whilst the 10th formed a protective flank along the Canal. The 11th, who were exhausted, remained in support whilst the 9th carried on forwards, establishing their HQ at the base of the Beacon.

The war was now moving at breakneck speed, the front line shifting almost daily as the Germans reeled from the unstoppable Allied advance. That night, under a moonless sky and with only the distant flash of artillery to guide them, the 9th Battalion once again received orders to move forward - this time advancing nearly eight hundred yards to occupy a new line that passed through a patch of twisted trees and undergrowth known as 'Square Wood'.

The going was slow and tense. The men crept through fields still pitted with shell holes, skirting wire and shattered trees, the weight of exhaustion pressing on every step. As they neared the edge of the wood, the silence erupted - the harsh, drilling bursts of enemy machine guns cracked through the dark like tearing canvas. Bullets hissed through the trees and slapped into the ground, forcing the men to fan out, diving for whatever cover they could find.

But the Australians didn't stop.

Section by section, under cover of fire and using the trees as shields, they pressed forward. Bayonets were fixed, and in the close confines of the undergrowth the fighting turned savage. Shadows collided at close quarters - rifle shots at ten paces, hand-to-hand scuffles where fists and boots did the work of blades. The Germans, caught off guard by the speed and aggression of the attack, began to break. A final volley sent them fleeing into the night.

By the time the wood was secure, the smell of cordite hung thick in the air. The diggers dropped to their knees, gulping air, drenched in sweat and dirt. Some laughed nervously, brushing leaves and dirt from their faces; others lit cigarettes with trembling hands.

At first light, the full picture came into view. The Germans had left in a hurry. Abandoned ammunition crates, half-eaten loaves of black bread, crates of pickled cabbage and helmets - all were scattered among the dead. One dugout still had a pot of coffee sitting over glowing embers, the steam still curling into the morning chill.

"Bloody hell," someone muttered, "they must've been halfway through supper".

'Square Wood' may have been theirs but at 1630 hours the advance continued, with 'A' and 'B' Companies moving on the left along the Somme Canal, whilst 'C' and 'D' headed off towards 'Olympia Wood'.

Despite a dense morning fog clinging low to the ground and turning the landscape into a ghostly blur, 'A' and 'B' Companies moved steadily forward, establishing a line of posts just south of the battered village of Cappy. The fog hampered vision, but it also provided some concealment, allowing the men to slip into position with relative cover. Meanwhile, the remaining companies pushed east and secured positions along the southern flank of 'Olympia Wood', an area now stripped of most of its foliage by months of shelling, with only skeletal trunks and turned earth to mark its former boundary.

Over the next several hours, the new line began to take shape - stretching from the south western edge of Cappy, skirting the eastern fringe of 'Olympia Wood', and tying into a loose, defensive cordon. It wasn't perfect. There were gaps, blind spots, and confusion over exact positions. But it held.

Patrols were quickly sent out to probe the enemy's movements and fill the voids in knowledge. One such patrol, led by Lieutenant Wrench of 'A' Company, cautiously advanced through the rubble-strewn streets of Cappy. The village, once picturesque with pretty houses and narrow lanes, was now a maze of broken walls and debris. As the patrol passed through,

Wrench spotted a group of German soldiers on the far side of the village - not advancing, but withdrawing.

Without hesitation, he gave the order to open fire. The sharp crack of rifles and the rat tat tat of the Lewis gun shattered the eerie silence. Bullets filled the air, and the enemy scattered in panic. The Australians held their fire only when the last figure vanished into the mist. One of the gunners swore softly as he checked the weapon's magazine; they had used up the last of their ammunition.

Later, another patrol sighted additional German troops moving on the far side of Cappy. It was unclear if they were retreating or preparing to regroup. Back at Battalion HQ, reports flooded in, creating a tangle of conflicting sightings, vague co-ordinates, and unclear company dispositions. To make sense of the chaos, the Adjutant personally moved forward under the cover of fog and shell holes, inspecting the front and speaking with section leaders. After consulting with company commanders, he adjusted the line to better reflect the ground situation - anchoring it at the canal on the edge of the village and extending it southeast, about three hundred yards beyond the corner of 'Olympia Wood'.

At 0400 hours on the 26th of August, the 9th Battalion was officially relieved. Exhausted and dirty, the men trudged from the line and descended into the Chuignolles-Chuignes Valley, where they lay down to rest on open ground. Their pause was short-lived. By 1430 hours, they were on the move again, heading forward once more, this time to a position at 'Earls Wood' to provide support for the 10th Battalion. That night, however, fresh troops arrived, and the 9th was relieved once more, pulling back through the ruined landscape to 'Germain Wood', where they finally arrived at 0230 hours. The men collapsed into shallow shelters and bomb craters, some too tired to even remove their helmets. They slept like the dead.

A few hours later, at 0930, the battalion was roused yet again and pushed further back to the Creisy Valley. Many of the men were running on little more than sheer willpower due to the constant exertion. The eleven days of rest that followed were not so much a luxury as a necessity. The battalion was exhausted.

Monash's planning had been meticulous, and as part of his logistics scheme during the battle, three supply tanks had been assigned to the 3rd Brigade. Clanking forward over broken ground, they had delivered ammunition, food, and medical supplies directly to the forward lines with remarkable efficiency. So effective were the tanks that the usual reliance on pack horses was suspended, sparing the animals a journey that would have killed many.

To further raise morale, a Comforts Fund stall was established at the rear - a makeshift stand offering tea, cocoa, and the occasional cigarette to the weary survivors. The line to the stall never seemed to shorten, and for many men, that first hot drink in days felt almost as vital as a clean dressing or a letter from home.

But the cost had been high. The battalion was now so depleted that it fielded under two hundred and fifty men for the attack, and suffered eighty casualties. Still, their sacrifice had not been in vain. The Australian Division, as a whole, captured more than three thousand prisoners in twenty four hours, alongside twenty field guns and scores of machine guns. The prisoner tally was the greatest number of men captured in a twenty four hour period by *any* British Division during the whole war.

This had been an important and significant victory. The 1st Division had seized all of the ground between the River Somme and Herleville, pushing forward to a depth of one and a half miles. In doing so, they had forced the Germans to retreat from a relatively habitable and secure position into terrain already ravaged by earlier battles. The advance had also cleared the way for the 3rd Division's capture of Bray, days earlier on the 23rd, which was achieved with minimal resistance and few casualties.

For *his* day on Froissy Beacon, Pip was awarded the Military Medal.

CHAPTER 13

Everything Was Pain and Heat and Then...Darkness

Following the evacuation of Lieutenant Colonel Bourne due to a severe bout of malaria, command of the 2nd Light Horse Regiment was temporarily transferred to Major Stodart on the 27th of August. The change in leadership occurred amidst a period of routine but largely ineffective enemy shelling - sporadic barrages that rarely found their mark but kept nerves taut and movement cautious.

A flicker of activity broke the monotony on the 30th when a reconnaissance patrol was ordered west of Vaux Post. Its objective was to locate viable tracks for wheeled transport, in preparation for a possible advance northward through the Jordan Valley. Lieutenant Joyner led the patrol, navigating terrain that quickly proved treacherous - deeply broken, uneven, and wholly unsuitable for wheels.

Throughout the mission, Joyner's men came under continuous artillery fire, but despite the sustained shelling, the patrol returned without casualties, a fortunate outcome given the exposure and vulnerability of their route. However, the frequency and intensity of the bombardment underscored a grim tactical reality that any attempt to push wheeled units through that corridor would be both impractical and perilously exposed to enemy guns.

The 30th of August brought changes to the 9th Battalion. The four companies it had had since the beginning now changed to a three company set up of 'X', 'Y' and 'Z' Companies.

"X, Y and Z?" exclaimed Clancy, "that's not very original is it?"

"It's not much different from A, B, C and D though is it?" said Roo.

"What company are we now then?" asked Archie.

"We are 'X' Company old chap," replied Ponsonby.

"X?!" exclaimed Pip, "I wanted to be Y".

"Why?" asked Stowie.

"Exactly..." replied Pip with a cheeky wink to the others.

"Huh?" said Stowie, who didn't quite understand Pip's attempt at humour.

Clancy slapped Pip across the back of the head.

"Silly sod".

Clancy suddenly remembered something and tapped the front of his tunic.

"I nearly forgot," he said, fishing into a deep pocket and tossing a pair of crumpled envelopes to Roo, "get your eye balls round these".

This brought a smile to the faces of both men. Roo caught them mid-air, flashing a grin.

"Cheers Clance...one from Mum and Dad and the other from Sam...and look...he's a corporal now too," said Archie.

Archie opened his Uncle Sam's letter, his eyes scanning the familiar hand writing.

"Bloody hell Sam has been around a bit this year, much like us. He has even been in some of the same battles...I wish we'd have known".

"Blimey," added Roo, "he probably passed us in the dark and never knew".

Over the past few days Sam had been fighting in the same push against the Germans, but eighty miles north at Arras with the 3rd Army.

At first light on the 26th of August, the men of the British 3rd Army had moved forward once more, pushing hard against German positions east of Arras in what would become a key phase of the Second Battle of the Scarpe. Rain and low cloud had turned the ground to soup, the fields churned up by shellfire and the passage of countless boots and wheels. In the mist and drizzle, infantry battalions pressed forward behind a precise creeping barrage, shells bursting rhythmically ahead of the line as they clawed their way toward the next objective.

Among them Corporal Sam Ford, advanced with his section through a landscape shattered by years of war. The terrain offered little cover - just shallow gullies, shell craters and the ruins of hedgerows. As they neared the German lines along the Scarpe River, resistance stiffened. Machine guns opened up from concealed pillboxes, cutting down attackers in swathes. Sam Ford led his men through one of the gullies, flanking a stubborn enemy position. A well placed grenade cleared the way, and the section stormed the trench with bayonets and rifles. Fighting was close and brutal, fought man-to-man in the wet and reeking confines of the trench.

Despite mounting casualties, the British line pushed forward. The German front began to give way under the combined pressure of artillery and infantry, and by mid-morning, the 7th Battalion of the South Staffordshire Regiment had seized their section of the trench system, repelling several brief counter attacks and holding fast.

The attack was part of a broader advance co-ordinated by the 3rd Army under General Byng. The aim was to force the Germans further back across the Scarpe and toward the Drocourt-Quéant Line, a key part of the formidable Hindenburg defences. The 26th of August marked another turning point - not a sweeping breakthrough, but a grinding, relentless push that continued to wear down German morale and stretch their reserves thin.

By nightfall, positions were consolidated. Runners were sent back, wounded carried out. The smell of powder and blood lingered as the rain eased off. With the Scarpe secured, preparations began for the next phase of the offensive - toward the Hindenburg Line beyond.

For men like Sam Ford, there was little time to ponder. One trench line had fallen, but many more still lay ahead.

By the end of August 1918, following the successful Allied offensives at Amiens, Albert, and the Scarpe, the German Army was retreating in disorder, falling back toward its most formidable defensive position - the Hindenburg Line. The Canadians and British had just stormed and broken through the Drocourt-Quéant Switch Line, cracking open the northern hinge of that vast trench system. The German front was buckling, and momentum now firmly rested with the Allies.

Farther south, the Australian Corps was preparing to strike again - pressing toward the Somme crossings and pushing the line closer to the very heart of the Hindenburg system. For the men of the 9th Battalion, weary but battle hardened, the war was far from over.

Despite this, rumours were now spreading that the war was almost won, and that preparations were already underway for the return of the AIF to Australia.

Rumours or not, the 3rd Brigade moved forward on the 7th of September to Mt St Quentin where they bivouacked for three days, before marching to Tincourt, three and a half miles further east. Here they were quartered in warm huts, which were a nice luxury, especially considering that it was now autumn.

An attack was now planned against the formidable Hindenburg Line - the last great German bastion on the Western Front. The operation was to be undertaken by the British 4th Army, with the 3rd Army operating on its left flank and the 1st French Army anchoring the right. It was intended that the Australian Corps would attack in the centre of the 4th Army front. So, with the 7th Battalion of the South Staffordshire Regiment being part of the 3rd Army, the Taylor boys would finally be fighting alongside their uncle.

The 3rd Brigade had been assigned a key objective, the village of Villeret, six miles east of Tincourt and just a couple of miles short of the Hindenburg Line itself. The attack was to be conducted in well defined stages. The first objective, the so called 'Brown Line', would be seized by the 11th and 12th Battalions. Once secured, the 9th and 10th Battalions were to push through their positions and strike towards the 'Red Line'. If that too fell into Allied hands, the final advance would target the 'Blue Line', nestled deeper into enemy held territory.

The next eight days were spent at Tincourt, where the 9th remained in support of the 1st Brigade, which held the front line. Defensive positions were hastily prepared in case of a German counterstroke, while training intensified. Drills were repeated, maps carefully marked, and equipment meticulously checked. The men knew they were preparing for something momentous - not just another raid, but a hammer blow aimed at the heart of the German defence, but in their hearts they knew that the Hindenburg Outpost Line would not fall easily.

On the 17th of September, just before midday, the battalion marched off once more, this time via Hamelet and Hervilly, toward the assembly area near Jeancourt, four and a half miles east of Tincourt. The weather was miserable - oppressive heat, followed by bursts of drenching rain that turned the roads into quagmires and soaked every man to the bone - and made for an unpleasant march. Enemy aircraft buzzed overhead, swooping low to drop bombs across the very ground the battalion would soon cross. One fell perilously close, its blast sending shockwaves across the column, but the men were sheltered in a sunken road and escaped injury.

By 0230 hours on the 18th the battalion reached its assembly position. 'X' and 'Y' Companies were located in a sunken road near Battalion HQ, with 'Z' Company in a trench to the north west. The terrain offered little in the way of real cover, but the troops were glad of a rest after fourteen hours on the move. The SNCOs quickly went about their work, deploying sentries and ensuring that every man get at least some rest.

At 0400 hours, after stand to, the pre-dawn stillness was broken by the welcome quiet rattle of mess tins and steaming Dixies as the battalion cooks made their rounds with a hot breakfast and a rum issue for all, lifting spirits in the half light.

"I don't know what we'd do without you blokes," Roo said to one of the cooks, "you always manage to bring us a meal no matter where we are".

"Just doing our job sarge," replied the cook, "besides, I reckon you blokes have got the bad end of the stick compared to us".

Then, at 0520 hours...Zero Hour.

The sky split open as the artillery barrage began - a rolling thunder of guns that lit the dark horizon in brilliant flashes. Shells tore into the German line with staggering force, tearing up earth, wire, and anything unfortunate enough to be caught in their path. The 11th and 12th Battalions advanced into the inferno, following the rolling barrage towards their objective, picking their way over ground that had once been gentle, green farmland - now nothing but a landscape of shattered roots and cratered soil.

As the 9th's objective was about three thousand yards away they departed at 0620 hours, passing through the 11th on the 'Brown Line'. They then formed up to the rear of the barrage and waited for it to lift, their hearts pounding with anticipation.

Two tanks had been detailed to assist the 3rd Brigade, mechanical beasts lurching through the mud. The one with the 11th had found it difficult to keep up with the advance but arrived at the 'Brown Line' just after it had been taken. Here it came into its own, rolling forward like a juggernaut and demolishing the wire entanglements which the 9th would have to cross.

The barrage lifted at 0830 hours and the 9th went on the offensive, 'X' Company on the right, 'Y' on the left and 'Z' acting as mopper uppers, ready to clear out bypassed strong points. Raised hands, along the Battalions lines, from the company officers were the signal as the 9th rose from the ground and surged forward.

A screen of riflemen formed a skirmish line, fanning out in loose formation to the front of each company, which in turn advanced in lines of sections in file, with fifty yards interval and distance. The rising sun burned away the lingering mist, revealing a bleak expanse of no man's land. Yet the movement of the troops was brisk and ordered, honed by years of training and battlefield experience.

The old hands recognised the signs - the well co-ordinated barrages, the tanks arriving on time, the solid rhythm of the advance. Everything was going like clockwork, which increased their determination to get the job done.

The Hindenburg Line was just ahead.

The advance across the sodden French landscape was nothing short of gruelling, hampered by the rain soaked ground which had turned to clinging mud, a foul bog that sucked greedily at every foot step. Men slipped, cursed, and pulled each other up, their legs already heavy with fatigue. The slimy earth stank of cordite and old rot - the by-product of years of war and fresh shelling. The going was slow, but the men pressed forward.

Enemy fire flared up from shattered hedgerows and the ruins of abandoned outposts, but leading the way was a tank - a lumbering, iron-plated beast belching smoke and roaring like a lion. Its caterpillar tracks ground relentlessly forward, indifferent to the bullets that ricocheted off its armoured hull. Any Germans caught in its path were met with the wrath of its Hotchkiss machine gun and the thundering roar of its six-pounder cannon - or worse, were crushed beneath its weight, limbs and torsos disappearing beneath the grinding steel like rag dolls under a millstone.

The troops, including Archie and Stowie, advanced as best as they could behind the iron monster, their figures half lost in the haze of smoke and churned mud. As they entered the edge of Villeret, gunfire rattled from shattered windows and doorways. The tank turned its gun to a crumbling stone house and blasted it apart in a single breath.

"Bloody beautiful," Stowie muttered, firing a few rounds into a half seen figure darting across the street ahead.

"We'd best keep up," said Archie, recharging his magazine as he walked, "that thing doesn't stop for anyone".

"Do you think it minds if I take cover behind it forever?" Stowie grinned, ducking as a shot zipped overhead, "this village ain't exactly rollin' out the welcome mat!"

They pressed on, moving with the other infantry as the tank rumbled into the heart of the village. It did not pause - instead, it punched its way through barricades and thin stone walls, forcing defenders to either flee or die in place. The men of the 9th followed in its wake, firing steadily, working through alleyways and courtyards, clearing house by house with bayonet and bomb.

It wasn't all plain sailing though, especially for the 1st Brigade who met with, and were held up by, determined enemy opposition from a post known as the 'Egg', a well defended nest of concrete and earthworks from which German machine guns poured murderous fire.

Lieutenant Meyers, now the OC of 'Y' Company, dispatched Lieutenant Maddock and his platoon to assist them. The young officer led his platoon in a sweeping manoeuvre through a shallow depression, flanking the German position under cover. They set up two Lewis guns on the ridge above and opened fire from the side, scything the defenders with enfilading bursts. Surprised and unable to return fire effectively, the Germans were swiftly overwhelmed, and the 'Egg' cracked under pressure. With the position subdued, the 1st Brigade resumed its advance.

The 'Red Line' was reached by the appointed time of 0900 hours. Muddy, breathless, and low on ammunition, the men wasted no time re-organising and regrouping. Shovels came out, wounded were helped back, a resupply of ammunition was carried out, and officers rechecked their maps and watches.

Then, at precisely 1000 hours, the barrage lifted again - a fresh thunderclap rolling overhead. Without hesitation, the 9th surged forward towards the final objective of the 'Blue Line'. The final part of the advance, however, was not so easy. As they cleared a small rise, German field guns came to life barely three hundred yards ahead - point-blank range. The barrels swung with terrifying speed, and the opening salvos tore through the advancing line, sending soil, shrapnel, and bodies flying. 'Y' Company reacted quickly and split into two groups, peeling off like wings. They looped around the German position, one to the left, one to the right, flanking the gunners. The Germans fought hard but were overwhelmed. In the brutal close quarters struggle, rifles gave way to fists, boots, and steel. Lieutenant Maddock led the charge on the left, taking a gun crew head on. He bayoneted one and shot another before he was struck down - a bullet to the chest dropping him instantly. His men carried on, securing the guns and finishing the fight. No further opposition was encountered.

By 1030 hours the 'Blue Line' was in Australian hands, the soldiers already digging in on the line, which was on high ground giving a clear view of enemy territory for miles.

Both the Brigade and Division Commanders were surprised but pleased that the 'Blue Line' had been reached so quickly.

The new line, approximately a mile from the Hindenburg Line was in a state of disrepair, but within five hours the troops had carried out the necessary actions and set up a series of posts.

During the final stage of the attack, the smoke from the creeping barrage still hung low over the ruined fields like a wet blanket, and air reeked of burnt powder and damp earth. A thousand yards east of the shattered remnants of Villeret, near a copse known as 'Quarry Wood', a patrol led by Sergeant Bentley moved quickly and silently through the misty grey, their boots sinking into the mud with each cautious step. Without warning, they encountered an enemy party attempting to make a stand. Shots rang out in short bursts, and the Germans scattered like startled deer. The Australians pushed forward, forcing the survivors to flee deeper into the trees.

Meanwhile, 'X' Company too encountered their own pocket of resistance. The sun had started to break through the mist now, laying dark streaks over the fractured earth. In a shallow trench beside a bomb blasted hedgerow, two German soldiers, a couple of die-hards, stood rigid, their eyes flicking back and forth, nerves fraying visibly, preparing to make a stand of their own. A battered machine gun was perched between them like a viper ready to strike.

Archie raised his rifle, though not to fire, and stepped forward cautiously; his voice clear and firm despite the lingering chaos.

"Kommen sie hier...schnell," he called out in his best German, trying to coax them in.

The enemy soldiers refused; hesitant, twitchy and white knuckled, their faces pale beneath their dusty helmets.

"I don't like this, Arch...they look a bit shifty to me," said Roo, his voice wary as he watched the men's movements.

Archie ignored the comment and looked around, scanning the area - scarred trees, overturned soil, and wisps of smoke trailing up from a nearby shell crater. Then he spotted Captain Ponsonby approaching through the mist.

"Freddy..."

"Sergeant T...how can I help?" came the crisp reply.

"You speak German, don't you mate?" Archie asked, not taking his eyes off the two enemy soldiers.

"You know I do Archie...well, enough to get by at least".

"These two Germans won't do what I say. I'm trying to get them to surrender...no use them dying for nothing," Archie explained, a note of quiet frustration in his voice.

Ponsonby shrugged; his face expressionless.

"If they won't come out, just shoot the buggers".

Archie blinked, visibly taken aback.

"I can't do that...that would be cold blooded murder".

Ponsonby let out a short, dry laugh, the sound oddly hollow against the distant thud of artillery, and thought to himself.

"Morals in soldiers?"

Then he spoke.

"It's a *war* Archie. We've been murdering each other *legally* for years".

With that, Ponsonby strode over, his boots sloshing through the mud, stopping just short of the Germans. His eyes immediately picked out the machine gun sitting between them, the telltale glint of metal still slick with dew.

"Bugger this," he muttered under his breath.

With the casual ease of a man who had seen far too much, he stepped forward, with Archie at his side, kicked the weapon over with his boot, and jumped into the shallow trench.

The two Germans, now tense and fidgeting, gestured anxiously toward a dugout behind them, mumbling about needing to retrieve something.

Ponsonby pulled out his revolver and told them in no uncertain terms to get to the battalion lines "or else". The Germans stiffened, but the message was understood. With no further protest, they clambered out and began the trudge toward the rear under watchful Australian eyes, and were duly taken prisoner.

Ponsonby stared after them, and then looked toward the dugout entrance. Dirt clung to the wooden support beams and the damp air from within smelled of cabbage and smoke.

Ponsonby then pondered for a moment and pointed towards the dugout.

"I wonder what they wanted from in there?" he said aloud.

"Let's have a look shall we?" said Archie.

They ducked through the low entrance. The gloom took a moment to adjust to, but it didn't take long to find what the Germans had been after - a stack of stick grenades piled in the corner, each one ready for use.

Archie's face turned to stone, his fists clenched. He was fuming with anger.

"The bastards! We know *exactly* what they were going to do".

Without another word, the two men stormed back out of the dugout and climbed out onto the parapet. Up ahead, Stowie and Pip were escorting the now sheepish prisoners toward the rear lines.

Archie held up one of the captured grenades like a trophy.

"Hey Stowie...kick them two bastards up the arse will you mate?"

Stowie grinned and nodded, happy to oblige.

"With pleasure boys..."

The two prisoners stumbled ahead under Stowie's firm encouragement, grumbling in low voices as he gave one of them a final shove between the shoulder blades and another kick up the backside. Archie and Ponsonby watched them go, the tension still simmering behind their eyes. Roo and Clancy now approached to admire the haul of grenades.

"Well, what've we got here then?" Clancy asked, eyeing the pile of stick grenades inside the dugout. He let out a sigh. "It looks like they were planning on taking a few of us with them".

Roo crouched beside the stash and picked one up, turning it over in his hand, as he exited the dugout.

"Don't see these up close too often...bloody lucky you two kicked their plans in the guts".

Archie, still flushed from the encounter, nodded but said nothing. The air seemed to settle around them for a moment - just men standing in the strange quiet after a fight, the ground still trembling faintly from the shelling further up the line.

The birdsong had long fled, replaced by the low hum of anticipation. Then it came.

With a shriek like tearing metal and a thunderous crack, a single artillery shell slammed into the ground just yards away.

The world exploded.

Dirt, wood, and smoke blasted skyward in a geyser of violence. Trees splintered. The shockwave hit like a fist. All four men were hurled from their feet - arms flailing, weapons spinning, lungs emptied.

A spray of shrapnel tore through the haze - and Archie cried out.

For a moment, there was nothing but ringing. Dust...shouts, muffled and panicked. Then came the coughing.

Clancy pushed himself up, spitting dirt, his ears ringing.

"Bloody hell! Is everyone alright?"

He looked around. Roo was staggering to his knees, bleeding from a cut on his temple, while Ponsonby was flat on his back, dazed but conscious.

Then a voice - raw, terrified.

"My leg...I've lost my leg!"

It was Archie.

They turned. He was lying on his back, left leg in the air - except the lower half was gone, just a jagged stump jutting from below the knee, torn uniform soaked in red. His booted foot lay several feet away, grotesquely intact.

Clancy stared, stunned.

"No you haven't, mate...it's over there!"

The joke landed with a thud, even to Clancy. Reality hit like a second blast. Archie's face had gone deathly pale, lips trembling, blood pumping fast and bright.

"Jesus! STRETCHER BEARER!" Clancy shouted.

Roo dropped beside Archie, pulled the sling from his rifle with shaking hands and looped it high above the wound. He twisted it tight with a bayonet, cutting off the bleeding. Archie whimpered.

"Don't let me die," he whispered faintly, "please, don't let me die...Mum...Dad..."

Roo tried to stay strong, but his voice was quivering.

"It's alright Arch...you're alright, mate...you'll be alright".

Captain Ponsonby, still dazed from his involuntary nap, crouched beside them, placing a steady hand on Archie's shoulder.

"You're going to pull through, Archie," he said firmly, "mark my words. You've come too far now...we all have".

He looked up at the others and spoke in a steady voice.

"Let's get him to the rear. I doubt that that was their last shell".

As they gently picked Archie up, Clancy touched Archie's good leg.

"You'll be alright, you tough bastard..."

As they moved off, Archie's head lolled back. Roo walked along side, his hand still on the tourniquet, the other wiping blood from Archie's cheek.

"You hang on now, you hear me?"

A pair of stretcher bearers arrived, panting. They eased Archie onto the canvas as gently as they could. He cried out once, and then went silent.

"You go with them Roo, and don't rush back. The rest of us will look after things here," said Ponsonby, as he looked at the barely conscious Archie, "God bless you Archie...my friend".

Roo marched beside the stretcher, his expression fixed, as he tried not to cry.

Archie blinked at the sky overhead. Clouds blurred. The sky spun.

Roo's voice, distant: "We're nearly there, mate".

But Archie's eyes fluttered closed. Everything was pain and heat and then... darkness.

The war rolled on.

The 5th of September saw the 2nd Light Horse relieved by the Wellington Mounted Rifles, marking a quiet transition amid growing signs of a broader strategic manoeuvre. As the men settled into their bivouac area, it became increasingly clear that preparations were underway for a major offensive. The landscape itself seemed to whisper of deception - every detail carefully arranged to mislead enemy observers.

Each night, units were quietly withdrawn from the Jordan Valley, their movements concealed under cover of darkness. Meanwhile, those who remained were instructed to maintain conspicuous activity during daylight hours - riding in loops, stirring up dust, and creating the illusion of continued strength on the brigade's right flank. The aim was simple - to convince Turkish reconnaissance that any forthcoming assault would originate from that sector.

To reinforce the ruse, vacated camps were left intact, their tents still pitched as if occupied. In a further act of subterfuge, dummy horses - rough looking, but convincing at a distance - were positioned throughout the valley to deceive enemy airmen conducting regular aerial reconnaissance. The entire theatre became a stage for misdirection, with every movement choreographed to mask the true axis of advance.

Malaria continued to sap the strength of the 2nd Light Horse Regiment, thinning its ranks and eroding specialist capability across key roles. The illness didn't discriminate - it struck signallers, gunners, and seasoned riders alike, leaving gaps that could not be ignored. In response, a broad programme of cross-training was initiated. Every man, regardless of prior role, was given instruction in essential skills such as signalling and the operation of Hotchkiss machine guns. The aim was simple - to ensure that no critical function was left unmanned should the advance come suddenly or the attrition worsen.

Then, on the 18th, fresh orders arrived. The regiment was instructed to prepare a dump of stores and equipment deemed non-essential to mobile operations. Anything that might slow the column - excess kit, surplus stores, or items unsuited to rapid movement - was to be set aside. The directive signalled a shift in posture from static defence and deception to readiness for manoeuvre. The men understood the implication. Whatever came next, it would require speed, flexibility, and a leaner, more resilient force.

It was two hours past mid day and the sun was high and unforgiving, casting sharp-edged shadows across the stony ground as the men of the 2nd Light Horse Regiment worked methodically, piling up excess equipment which might slow them down. Percy moved with quiet focus, sweat tracing lines down his dust-caked neck, his hands busy but his mind elsewhere.

Then, without warning, something shifted.

He walked a few paces, and then stopped. Something was wrong...somewhere.

He paused beside a pile of empty crates as a strange stillness came over him. Not fatigue. Not heatstroke. It wasn't sound or sight. Just a sudden hollowing in the chest, as if the world had tilted slightly off its axis. Percy straightened, blinked, and looked around. Nothing was out of place. Horses were tethered. Men were moving slowly in the heat, and a billy bubbled somewhere behind the cook house tent. He shook his head and tried to shrug it off, but the feeling lingered. He rubbed the back of his neck, uneasy. A tightness had crept in - like the moment before a storm, though the sky was clear. He couldn't fathom it, couldn't work it out. Just a feeling, sharp and fleeting, like a wire pulled taut then let go.

At that very second, hundreds of miles away in France, his brother Archie lay bleeding in the battered earth of a foreign field. Percy would not know for days. But something in him had stirred.

By mid September 1918, the 2nd Light Horse Regiment had been absorbed into Chaytor's Force, a composite formation commanded by Major General Edward Chaytor, a New Zealander, tasked with deception, flank protection, and ultimately, a swift and decisive advance through the Jordan Valley. Though part of the ANZAC Mounted Division, the 2nd's numbers had been thinned by malaria and attrition - so severely that by the time orders came down on the 20th the regiment was operating at a ratio of one man to three horses. They were placed in Brigade Reserve, held back but ready to move at a moment's notice.

That moment came quickly.

On that very day, the British West Indies Regiment launched the opening assault. They had been waiting for this moment - not with eagerness, but with a kind of quiet tension that had settled into the bones. For weeks, they had trained in the heat, drilled in silence. Now, it was their turn. Baker Ridge first. Then Chalk. Then Grant Hill.

Sergeant Jones didn't speak as they moved out. He didn't need to. His platoon knew what was expected. They were steady, but not hardened. This was their first fight. No one said it aloud, but it hung in the air between them.

The ground was dry and broken, the ridges low but exposed. As they advanced, the first shots came fast - sharp cracks from the Turkish line, then the rattle of a machine gun. Jonah signalled the men to spread, to keep low, to move. They did. Not perfectly, not smoothly, but with intent. One man hesitated behind a rock. Jonah crouched beside him, placed a hand on his shoulder, and nodded once. That was enough to spur him on.

The climb up Baker Ridge was slow and deliberate. Fire came in bursts. A few men dropped - one wounded in the leg, another grazed across the cheek. There was no panic, just the work of getting forward. Jonah saw a gun crew falter, then recover, saw a young private fire his first shot, then stare at the rifle as if it had betrayed him. He didn't shout. Just moved on.

By mid morning, the ridge was theirs. Chalk fell soon after. Grant Hill took longer - more resistance, more confusion - but the line held. Simultaneously, the New Zealand Mounted Rifles had taken Kh Fusail, slicing into the Ottoman flank. The enemy began to fold.

Afterward, as they regrouped, Jonah sat watching the men settle, each man quiet and somehow changed. Some cleaned their rifles, some smoked. One stared out across the valley, eyes unfocused. No one spoke of victory. No one asked what came next. They had done what had been asked of them, and no doubt would have to do it again.

On the 22nd, 'A' Squadron of the 2nd Light Horse was dispatched to reinforce the West Indians and link their right with the Royal Fusiliers' left. The terrain was broken and visibility poor, but the squadron moved fast, skirting shell-blasted wadis and pushing through scrub under intermittent rifle fire. A brief skirmish flared near a rocky outcrop - two troopers wounded, one horse down - but the line was held, and the connection made.

The following day, the full regiment advanced to Kh Fusail, taking up a rear-guard position to shield the New Zealand Brigade, now driving hard toward the Jisr ed Damieh bridge. The enemy, reeling from the collapse of his right flank, offered only scattered resistance. A few snipers lingered in the gullies, and a Turkish machine gun opened up briefly from a ridge before being silenced by a well placed Hotchkiss burst.

On the 23rd the 2nd joined the rest of the 1st Light Horse Brigade in the assault on Mafid Jozelah. The approach was fast and rough and the enemy broke quickly, abandoning positions under pressure from both flanks. Meanwhile, the 2nd Brigade took Kabr Mujahid, and the New Zealanders pushed into Es Salt, pressing the advantage. The advance continued without pause. On the 24th the column rolled forward, and by the 25th, the Auckland Mounted Rifles had severed the enemy's rail line at Zuka, while the 1st and 2nd Light Horse Brigades, along with the remainder of the New Zealanders, swept into Amman.

The campaign had shifted from deception to pursuit, and the 2nd - though depleted - had played its part. Dusty and saddle-sore, and lean from weeks of strain, they rode into Amman not as a reserve force, but as a fighting regiment once again.

On the 26th of September, the brigade moved into Wadi el Hamman without resistance. Three hundred Ottoman troops were taken there - most had already abandoned their weapons, some still dazed from the pace of the retreat. There was no fight, just surrender.

Three days later, the garrison at Maan attempted to break north. They didn't get far. At El Kastal, they ran headlong into the 5th Light Horse Regiment and found themselves cut off - no line of retreat, no support, and no supplies. They surrendered in full. Over four thousand men were taken, along with three batteries of guns. It was the largest haul of prisoners the Division had seen to date.

On the final day of September, 'A' Squadron of the 2nd Light Horse was ordered to occupy Suweileh. The rest of the regiment followed on the 5th of October. The village sat quiet, but the hills around it weren't empty. Patrols were sent out to An-es-Sir and Rumeimin, tasked with keeping the roads open and the district calm. The enemy still held pockets in the mountains - small detachments, scattered and undersupplied. They posed little threat, but they hadn't vanished.

The remnants of the Ottoman left flank, those who had slipped the net, were retreating fast toward Deraa and Damascus. Other divisions of the Desert Corps were already moving to intercept. For the 2nd, the work shifted from pursuit to control - holding ground and watching passes.

CHAPTER 14

Then There Was Light

September 1918 was drawing to a close as the morning sun beat down on Doriray Station with its usual unrelenting glare. Cicadas shrieked from the tree line, and a dry wind tugged at the yellowed grass. The winter had been bone dry, turning the pasture brittle and the fence posts to splinters. Ray Taylor wiped the sweat from his face with a dust caked sleeve. He had been working since first light, hammering posts into a stubborn, unyielding earth. Beside him, Frank - now seven – was crouched beside a reel of fencing wire, face scrunched in concentration.

He was all sinew and sunburn, a country boy through and through. Ray had started calling him "a man" not out of affection, but out of truth.

"Hold it steady, mate," Ray muttered as he lined up a stubborn length of wire.

Frank grunted, gripping the wobbly post.

"I am, Pop. But this one's buggered...it's all split at the bottom".

Ray laughed.

"Buggered is it? I don't think you should let your Mum hear you using such language mate".

Frank shrugged his shoulders.

"Sorry Pop".

Ray paused to wipe his brow again then straightened with a creak of the back, stretching. His shirt clung with sweat. He glanced down the long, rutted track that ran out to the road - and froze.

A shape emerged in the shimmer of heat. Small. Thin. Moving fast on a bicycle towards the homestead.

Ray's heart lurched.

He knew that bike. And he knew what it meant. It was young Harry Pearce the Post Office delivery boy. No one pedalled that hard out to Doriray without a reason.

A feeling of dread suddenly came over him. Ray's stomach dropped like a stone and for a second he didn't move.

"Are you alright Pop? You look a bit crook," said Frank.

"Crook? No, I'm fine, but I think we need to get to the house quick," he said as he pointed to the visitor.

But then the realisation was upon him, "Struth!...No!" shouted Ray as he tossed aside his hammer and began to run.

Dirt kicked up in clouds beneath his feet as he sprinted for the house, Frank pounding behind, breathless and confused. As they reached the house poor Harry was stood helpless with his head bowed and Lil and Doris were hugging and sobbing uncontrollably.

"What is it Dot?" asked Ray reluctantly.

Doris held out an official looking envelope.

"It's a telegram from the Army," said Doris, sobbing, "I'm too scared to open it".

Ray tore open the envelope. His eyes welled up and he choked on his words as he read the document out loud.

"URGENT TELEGRAM. Officially reported that number 3116 Sgt A Taylor 9th Battalion wounded in action 18 September 1918. Injury to left leg. Soldier being treated in military hospital. Condition stable. Please inform parents Mr and Mrs R Taylor Doriray Station Sandy Creek Kilcoy and convey deep regret and concern of their Majesties the King and Queen and Commonwealth Government".

He didn't cry. Not yet. Not in front of Frank.

He looked to the sky. Just for a second.

Then he whispered, "Hang on, Archie...", and pushed the door open.

Inside, the house was still and dim. The scent of old timber, polish, and eucalyptus oil hung in the air. A clock ticked on the wall - slow, heavy beats.

The family sat. A long pause followed before Doris managed to speak.

"It says wounded...that's not too bad, is it?"

Ray put a hand on her shoulder.

"No...not too bad," he said gently.

But the worry in his eyes betrayed him.

Doris read on, lips trembling slightly as she gripped the paper.

"Injury to left leg. Soldier being treated in military hospital...condition stable".

She sank into her chair.

"Stable," she whispered, as though the word itself could hold him together across the oceans.

Frank looked between them both.

"What is it Grandma?"

Ray gave him a tired, lopsided smile.

"It's your Uncle Archie mate, he's been...er...hurt...in the war, but he's as tough as they come. He'll be alright. We just...we just have to wait."

Outside, the sun beat down over the paddocks. The dog barked, and the post boy's bicycle rattled away, already fading into the distance.

Doris folded the telegram with slow, careful fingers and pressed it to her heart.

For their efforts in their last battle, the 9th Battalion emerged from the fighting with ten men lost and thirty three wounded - a heavy cost, though not without reward. But, despite this, they had captured over two hundred enemy prisoners, along with eight Howitzers, three field guns, and more than forty machine guns. It had been a decisive blow.

The operation, later known as the Battle of Épehy, was part of a co-ordinated push involving all three Allied armies. Along this broad front, the Australian Corps had once again served as the tip of the spear - breaking through the enemy lines deeper than any other force engaged that day. Their advance covered more than three miles across a shattered landscape of torn up fields, abandoned redoubts, and shattered enemy defences.

Among the many battalions that fought, it was the 9th alone that pressed all the way to the Line of Exploitation on the Fourth Army's front. For a unit that had borne the weight of countless campaigns since the beginning, it was a striking demonstration of strength and determination.

Though none spoke it aloud, there was a quiet sense that something had shifted. The lines on the maps were moving faster now, the resistance growing thinner; and for the weary men of the 9th, this battle stood not just as another victory, but as a defining chapter in a long and honourable fighting career.

The journey from the front to Number 3 Australian General Hospital in Abbeville, near Amiens, was a blur of jolts and morphine. Archie drifted in and out of consciousness, the rumbling of truck engines and the clatter of stretcher bearers fading into white noise. Rain tapped on the canvas above him like fingers drumming on a table top. Somewhere in the haze he remembered asking for Roo, but only a nurse answered, gently brushing the mud from his face.

By the time he opened his eyes properly, the mayhem of the battlefield was gone. He lay in a starched white bed inside a vast, high-ceilinged ward. Electric lights buzzed faintly above. Rows of wounded men lined both sides, some bandaged to the eyes, others sleeping, twitching, or murmuring in fever.

A nurse noticed he was awake and approached with a warm smile.

"Welcome back, sergeant. You're at Abbeville; *we'll* look after you now".

Archie tried to sit up, but pain surged through him like fire. He gasped and looked down. His left leg was swaddled in thick, clean bandages, but where the lower half should have been - nothing - yet; he could still "feel" his leg. The weight of that absence crushed him more than the pain.

"You've done well," the nurse said gently, resting a hand on his shoulder, "the surgeons say the amputation went clean. You've been lucky, all things considered".

Archie gave a bitter smile but said nothing. Lucky. Right.

He remained at Abbeville for a week until he stabilised, before being moved to a hospital in England.

The 18th of September had been an eventful day for another family member too. For Corporal Samuel Ford, the dawn had broken slowly and ugly over the fields near Villeret, as he crouched in a shallow scrape in the earth, the collar of his tunic stiff with sweat and dry mud, rifle across his lap. The creeping barrage had started twenty minutes earlier, and now the whole landscape shuddered under the methodical weight of British artillery.

The whistle blast came sharp and loud. Then they moved.

Sam surged forward with the rest of his platoon across the rain-softened ground. The German wire had been broken in places, and the barrage had kept many heads down, but not all. From a cratered rise just short of the enemy's forward trench, a German machine gun snarled to life.

The man to his right went down in a heap.

Sam threw himself to the ground, rolled into a ditch, and gestured to two others to swing around the flank. Crawling forward under fire, he lobbed a Mills Bomb into the machine gun nest, the blast echoing like thunder in his skull, and the gun was silent.

When they finally breached the enemy line, it was like walking through the bones of a dead giant. Trenches collapsed. Rifles snapped in half. A tangle of gas masks, boots, and shattered helmets.

They cleared dugouts one by one, finding more wounded than willing. A few fought on, but most were boys - half-starved and shaking with fear.

By late morning, the Staffords held their objective, but the cost had been steep.

The 'Blue Line' was shelled heavily on the day after the attack. The next two days were quiet, then, following three days of garrisoning the front line, the 9th Battalion was relieved by the 11th and moved back to act as support battalion.

The guns were distant now. Just a low rumble over the horizon; like thunder rolling across a far off valley. It was late afternoon and the 9th Battalion were sprawled in a shaded hollow beneath a chalk rise, resting where they could, trying to forget the last few days. The quiet here was strange - no shells, no machine gun rattle, just the buzzing of flies around their mess tins and the occasional bray of a horse in the distance. Someone was boiling tea on a tiny fire made of dry grass and splinters from a wrecked wagon.

Roo sat hunched on the grass, turning Archie's helmet over in his hands. He had cleaned the blood off days ago, but the dent where it had struck the ground was still there, stubborn and sharp edged.

Clancy sat nearby, stripping down his rifle with slow, methodical movements.

"Funny, isn't it?" Roo said. "All those battles...all the close calls...and it's one bloody shell, out of nowhere".

Clancy didn't look up.

"He's tough, Roo. He'll be alright".

Roo gave a faint nod but didn't answer. The silence between them settled heavy, like dust.

A short while later, the familiar clack of hob nailed boots on hard ground broke the quiet. Heads turned as Captain Ponsonby stepped through the scrub, his uniform neat, face drawn but calm. He carried a small satchel and wore his service revolver on the belt of his Sam Browne.

"Clancy. Roo," he said, nodding to each, "just came from Battalion HQ. Thought you'd want to hear this".

The two men straightened. Clancy slid the bolt of his rifle back into place and Roo set down the helmet.

"It's about Archie," Ponsonby said, "he's being transferred over to England".

Roo stood up fully.

"Where to?"

"Roehampton," Ponsonby replied, "there's a specialist hospital there. One of the best for limb injuries, I'm told. If anyone can get him back on his feet, *they* can".

Roo breathed out slowly, some of the tightness in his chest releasing.

"So he's made it this far...that's a relief at least".

Ponsonby nodded.

"Yes. He's out of danger. Still a long road ahead for him, but...he's alive".

Clancy grinned faintly.

"Bet he's got the nurses in stitches already".

"More likely complaining about the tea," Roo added.

"Well, if I know Archie, that long road will be a short one if *he* can help it," added Stowie.

They all laughed - quietly, cautiously, as though afraid to tempt fate. But the laughter felt good. Clean. Like fresh air in a trench.

Ponsonby paused before turning away.

"If you want to write, now's the time...we might be moving again soon".

As he walked off, Clancy nudged Roo with his elbow.

"Better get started. I reckon he'd rather read your ugly hand-writing than mine".

The war still continued, but for the first time in days, it felt like something had gone right.

Roo gave a tired smile and nodded, then reached into one of his webbing pouches and pulled out some hard tack biscuits.

"Biccie anyone?" he said as he held out the tin.

Clancy rolled his eyes and rubbed his jaw.

"No thanks mate...I like my teeth".

The conversation seemed to have dried up and thoughts of Archie hovered over them like smoke.

Stowie was amusing himself by flicking pebbles into a tin cup, a direct hit raising a murmur of a cheer for just a short moment.

From the road above came a voice: "Oy, yow lot better have hot tay or I'm gooin' straight back to the line!"

Roo's head snapped up.

"Tay? Sam?"

Sam Ford grinned as he shouldered his rifle and picked his way down into the gully, boots shifting the loose gravel. His uniform looked worse than theirs - dried blood at the cuff, his left hand bandaged, and a chunk torn from his trousers.

"I wasn't expecting to see you mate?" Roo said, climbing to his feet.

"Yow ay gettin' rid o' me that easy ar kid," Sam replied, shaking Roo's hand hard.

Roo turned his gaze to Sam's bandaged hand.

"Are you wounded?"

Sam laughed.

"No mate, I just had a bit of a scrap with some barbed wire".

"I heard that you blokes copped it rough," said Clancy.

Sam shrugged.

"No wus than anyone else. We were just up past the Sunken Road, left flank of Villeret...nasty stuff...machine guns everywhere."

They all fell quiet for a moment.

Then Stowie asked, "Where you off to now?"

"Back through to collect our second line kits. But I saw your mob were in support, so thought I'd pop by".

Roo hesitated, and then said quietly, "Archie was hit. Shell burst. Took his lower leg clean off".

Sam was taken aback at the news.

"Bloody hell...that ay good...'ow is he?"

"He's alive," Clancy added, "they're shipping him off to a hospital in England".

Sam looked down for a long moment. Then he nodded.

"Best place for 'im ar reckon...and at least 'e's away from this place".

Roo nodded.

Sam dropped onto the ground and pulled a cigarette from his tunic.

"Alright then," he muttered, "let's talk about anything but bloody war".

And for a while, they did.

After two days in support, the 9th was relieved by an American battalion. The Australians watched the newcomers arrive with mixed feelings - not out of resentment toward the fresh faced Yanks as individuals, but toward the politicians and generals who had kept them out of the fray until so late in the war. Some of the Diggers shook their heads, muttering that the Americans would now "march in for the photographs". Others, exhausted and sore, said nothing at all.

Clancy gave a snort as a clean-shaven American officer passed by.

"Nice timing, boys," he said, loud enough to be heard, "the war's nearly over...mind you don't get your boots muddy".

By 0920 hours, the handover was complete, and the Battalion marched back to Tincourt Wood, where a hot meal and rum ration awaited them.

ANZAC Leave, two months in Australia, was now being given to men who had embarked during 1914. Roo, Stowie and Clancy turned it down as they didn't want to leave Archie. They were also ever so slightly miffed that such an occurrence had taken four years to arrive.

"Thanks for staying boys," said Roo.

Clancy laughed a cheeky laugh.

"No need to thank me mate...I couldn't leave Pip here by himself, *and* I couldn't exactly turn up at your place without *you* could I?"

"Fair point," replied Roo.

"It's bad luck anyway," said Stowie.

"How do you work that out?" asked Clancy.

"Did you not hear about Cloherty from 3 Platoon?"

"Yeah...we all have...poor bloke was blown to pieces by a shell that landed in the doorway of his dug out...but what's that got to do with ANZAC leave?" asked Roo.

"He was an original Gallipoli man and he was killed whilst packing for his trip home..."

Everyone went quiet. Perhaps it *was* bad luck.

On the 25th of September orders were received; the 3rd Brigade was to move west towards the Long area, nestled between Amiens and the coast. A rumour was circulating that it would be another period of rest - and while no one was complaining outright, there were quiet murmurs and exchanged glances among the men.

Clancy smirked as the news was passed around.

"Something must be up...with all this resting," he muttered, arms folded, suspicion plain in his voice.

"Yeah," Roo added, "either they think we are *really* tired, or they're fattening us up for the slaughter".

Either way he didn't sound convinced. They had seen too many "rests" before.

The next morning, the men entrained at Tincourt Station. It was nearly the end of September, and though the sun had only just cleared the haze, spirits were high. The train was a motley string of open wagons - each one crowded with khaki-clad diggers - the sort marked "Hommes 40, Chevaux 8", just like the ones they had first arrived in, what felt like a lifetime ago. Yet despite the hard benches and cramped quarters, spirits were high.

After the recent fight and the tension that had followed, the clack and rattle of the train as it pulled away from the station at 1000 hours was a kind of music.

As the locomotive huffed to life and jerked forward with a groan of iron, a cheer went up from the troops. They waved at a group of children playing near the tracks, who shouted and ran alongside the train, grinning and throwing flowers. French women in aprons stood at their doors, smiling and waving tea towels, while old men doffed their caps in quiet salute.

The countryside rolled by slowly. Morning mists lifted off the fields to reveal a patchwork of green and gold. French villagers stopped whatever they were doing to wave as the train passed. Some cheered; others threw apples or flowers up into the wagons. Roo caught a small posy tossed by a little girl in a blue dress. He grinned, tucked it into his button hole, and gave her a cheeky salute. For many of the men, it felt like the war was slowly slipping behind them - at least for now. As the train chugged westward through the gentle folds of the Somme countryside, they soaked in the scenery. Rows of stubbled fields glowed gold beneath the autumn sun. Church spires and small farms dotted the hillsides, and in the distance, the sea of trees turned from green to amber with the season's change.

Roo leaned back against the side of the wagon, closing his eyes for a moment, the wind brushing his face. It wasn't home, but it didn't feel like the Front anymore either. It was something else, something easier to breathe.

The further west they travelled, the more peaceful everything seemed. No thud of guns, no clouds of dust to be seen, no ruin and wreckage; just quiet fields and slate-roofed villages untouched by war. It felt strange, almost unreal - like stepping out of a storm into another world.

"Reckon this is what peace might look like?" Clancy said quietly, gazing out over a patch of freshly ploughed farmland.

"Maybe," Stowie replied, "or maybe it's just the eye of the storm".

Clancy chuckled at the comment.

"You always *were* a cheerful bastard Stowie..."

The train rolled into Longpre at 1500 hours. The men felt stiff from the journey, but were still in good cheer. From there, it was boots on the ground again for the twelve mile march north to a town called Gorenflos. The men groaned, but they were used to it – heavy packs, shoulders hunched, hob nailed boots clomping in rhythm along the dusty road. The going was relatively easy, the roads lined with tall poplars and the air filled with the scent of harvest. Farmers paused to watch the column go by, their faces open and grateful. Some offered water. One old woman pressed a warm loaf of bread into Clancy's hands, tears shining in her eyes.

By the time they reached Gorenflos, they were footsore and hungry. But the sight of the billets lifted every man's spirits. The town was clean, quiet, and untouched - and the accommodation was better than anything they had known since landing in France. Quaint houses with tiled roofs, soft beds with real mattresses, and even hot water.

The CO and his staff were billeted in the local château, its white walls gleaming in the afternoon sun and its elegant windows peeking through the trees like something from another world. The Company Commanders were quartered in an annex nearby, whilst for the other ranks, there were barns and cottages with solid walls and proper bedding. For once, there were no rats, no cold draughts and no shattered glass.

Roo dropped his pack on the floor of a spotless barn and looked around with a satisfied grunt.

"If this is resting," he said, "they can keep us here all bloody year".

Clancy chuckled.

"Maybe they will".

That night, lying in real beds under dry roofs, the men didn't talk of the front or of what might come next. They shared memories of lost mates like Ten Bob, Jacko, Taff, Big Mac and Archie. There was laughter, too, at old jokes and shared mischief. But it was softer now, tempered by experience and loss, and like armies of ancient times, the men of the 9th were confident that their stay at Gorenflos would be a substantial one...their winter quarters. They might even have a proper Christmas for once.

The usual sports were organised - cricket matches, tug-of-war, and footraces - offering the men something familiar to cling to. For a time, it almost *felt* like peacetime again. Clean billets, warm meals, and dry socks were luxuries they hadn't known in months. Laughter returned to the ranks, the men relaxed, and some even dared to plan for life after the war. Letters were written with more optimism, and the sound of harmonicas and rough voiced songs filled the chilly autumn evenings.

Then, on the 11th of October, Billy Hughes, the Prime Minister of Australia, arrived for a surprise visit. A handful of officers offered polite greetings, but among the diggers, the reception was far frostier.

"I didn't see him around when the bullets were flying," Clancy said as he watched the Prime Minister being fussed over by staff officers.

"Gutless bastard..."

Roo chuckled.

"Careful, mate. That's the leader of Australia you're insulting".

Clancy spat into the dirt.

"Yeah...well, he's welcome to lead from the front next time".

But the sense of calm wouldn't last.

The middle of October for the lighthorsemen was spent patrolling, despite being ravaged by malaria. Men were weak, some barely able to stay in the saddle. There were no reinforcements, no relief. The other units weren't faring much better.

Most of Chaytor's mounted troops had shifted to Amman. The infantry had pulled back to Jerusalem to ease pressure on the supply lines, which were stretched thin and slow. The 2nd stayed put.

There was no more fighting on their flank. The enemy had gone - either captured, scattered, or retreating north.

The horses moved slowly through the scrub. Loose stones, dry wind and nothing ahead but more of the same.

Davo broke the silence.

"It's quiet...do you reckon it's over?"

Percy didn't answer straight away. He watched a hawk lift off from a dead tree before replying.

"It sure feels like it mate".

Davo nodded once.

"I wouldn't mind if it was".

Percy shifted in the saddle.

"You'd be mad if you didn't..."

Davo grinned.

"Well...there you go then...they're done...its over".

They rode on. No more talk.

On the 28th of October, the ANZAC Division assembled for a formal parade in Amman. Every unit was represented. The occasion was the hoisting of the Hejaz Flag - a symbolic gesture marking the district's transfer to the authority of the King of Hejaz. It had been one of the conditions of his co-operation - territorial control in exchange for support. The flag went up without ceremony beyond the gathering itself. The men stood, watched, and said little.

Two days later, the 2nd and 3rd Light Horse Regiments were reviewed by Gaafar Pasha, a senior officer of the Hejaz forces, alongside General Chaytor. Gaafar wore the Iron Cross on his tunic - a rare distinction for a man who had once fought for the Turks. Now he stood with the British, inspecting the same regiments that had helped break the Ottoman line.

The men noted the medal but didn't comment. They had seen stranger things in the last few months.

The war in the Middle East ended on the 31st of October. In the final phase, Chaytor's Force had taken more than ten thousand prisoners. Their equipment, transport, and rolling stock were seized intact. The collapse was total.

In just four weeks, three Turkish armies ceased to exist as fighting formations. Some surrendered outright. Others broke and scattered. What remained was no longer capable of organised resistance.

For the men of the ANZAC Division, it was not marked by celebration. The pace had been non-stop and each day had blurred into the next. The scale of the victory was clear. Its cost, less so.

The track was quiet apart from the sound of hooves. The hills were behind them now, the villages still, the war - at least here - finished.

Davo broke the silence.

"I thought I'd be more excited".

"What? About the war ending...well...here at least?" replied Percy.

"Yeah...strange isn't it?" said Davo.

"The last four years *have* been bloody strange mate," Percy answered.

"You reckon the boys in the ninth know it's over out here?"

Percy shook his head.

"I don't know mate. I haven't had a letter from Arch or Roo for months. I don't even know if they're...you know?"

They rode on a few paces.

"You think we'll get sent there?" Davo asked.

Percy didn't answer but just shrugged his shoulders.

"I wouldn't mind going home," said Davo.

Percy gave a dry nod.

"You and me both mate".

The patrol passed a broken cart by the roadside. No one spoke for a while.

"Be strange," Davo said, "if we end up finishing this thing in France".

Percy looked ahead.

"Stranger things have happened".

They kept riding. Only time would give them their answer.

On the 2nd of November, the 9th Battalion's winter dream shattered with a single order. Word came down that the enemy, having retreated for weeks, was now making a final, desperate stand in the Mormal Forest, not far from the Belgian border. The cold reality of war returned like a kick in the ribs.

Six weeks after arriving in Gorenflos, the 9th Battalion packed up once again. On the 8th of November, after a number of postponements, they marched the eight miles to Pont Remy, the men quieter than usual. There was little talk - just the sound of steady marching on packed earth and the occasional sigh as someone adjusted a sore shoulder or shifted a heavy pack.

At Pont Remy they waited - seven long hours on the station platform, crammed together for warmth under grey skies that promised more rain. Rumours were spreading like the plague; the war was nearly over, the Germans were falling back. Maybe this would be the last push. No one believed it.

The train finally arrived in the late afternoon - open cattle wagons with wooden benches and a roof to keep the rain off, if they were lucky. The ride was long, cold, and miserable. Steam hissed from the engine, and the wagons clattered and groaned across frost-rimmed tracks as they rumbled eastward into the deepening night. The countryside rolled past under a pale moon: silent villages, blackened fields, and the occasional group of French civilians waving solemnly from roadside cottages, their faces half-lit by lanterns. Some waved white handkerchiefs. Others simply stood and watched in silence.

Clancy rubbed his gloved hands together and muttered through chattering teeth.

"This better be the last bloody ride I take on one of these things".

Roo squirmed uncomfortably in his seat, his breath fogging in front of him.

"Won't be long now, mate. One last stand, they reckon".

"Yeah? Hopefully not like General Custer," said Stowie.

"Who?" asked Roo.

The Texan rolled his eyes.

"Never mind..."

They arrived at Tincourt just before midnight on the 10th of November. It had rained throughout the day and a heavy frost had now set in, freezing the mud into slippery ruts. The men stumbled off the train, stiff and exhausted, and began the short but slippery march to their billets under a sky full of stars and the distant blasts of artillery.

Each step made a crunching sound over the frozen earth, every breath a puff of steam. There was no singing now, no jokes. Just the silence of men too tired to speak, dragging themselves forward through the cold - wondering if this next stand in the forest would be their last.

The next morning, the 11th of November 1918, dawned bitterly cold. A dull grey mist hugged the ground like a shroud, and the air stung their lungs with each breath that they took. There was a strange silence hanging over Tincourt, broken only by the occasional cough or the clink of a spoon in a tin mug.

Then, out of nowhere, the stillness was shattered as a long and loud tooting of whistles rang out in the distance. Dozens of them - shrill, insistent, urgent - cutting through the cold like a knife.

"What the bloody hell...?" said Roo, already reaching for his rifle.

Confusion reigned. The men did not know what to do. Many charged their magazines suspecting that the Germans had broken through again, for why else would such a racket be occurring, if not as a warning?

Clancy quickly roused the men from whatever they were doing and formed them up ready to go. As he stood at the front of the company he spied Captain Ponsonby and the company officers heading their way.

"Here we go...COMPANY...COMPANY...SHUN!"

The men sprang smartly to attention; rifles at their sides, eyes fixed forward, breaths steaming from their mouths.

As Captain Ponsonby and the other officers approached, he wasn't hurrying, in fact, he looked almost...relaxed.

"Stand them at ease please CSM," said Captain Posonby, very casually.

Clancy gave the order.

"COMPANY...STAND AT...EASE...STAND EASY".

Ponsonby was looking very relieved and pleased with himself as he glanced at his watch and then looked up. His face, usually guarded, was open now - eyes tired but alight with something unfamiliar. Relief, perhaps...or disbelief.

Then he began to speak.

"Men... ..." he began, "the moment we have all been fighting for...waiting for...is upon us...an armistice," he held up his watch, pointing at the face, its hour hand on the number eleven and the minute hand on the six, "as at half an hour ago...at eleven o'clock, an armistice was signed...the war is over. Bless you all...and thank God".

For a few seconds, no one moved. The silence was deafening.

No cheers. No whooping or laughter. Just the sound of the wind through the bare trees and the soft groan of frozen earth beneath shifting feet.

The words hung there, suspended, like smoke.

The war...is over.

Roo glanced at Clancy. Stowie looked down at his feet. Someone muttered a soft "Jesus," under their breath, but that was all.

For a long moment, the company just stood there, as if waiting for someone to shout that it was a mistake, that there had been an error in the message. After all the years, all the battles, all the mates lost...it didn't seem real. It didn't seem fair that it had ended not with a bang, but a whistle.

As the day went on, a strange mood settled over the battalion. Not elation. Not even relief. If anything, it was annoyance that they had left a good home at Gorenflos to come here. Why now? Why had they been dragged away to this frozen dump for nothing? Why had their mates been killed or wounded in the last push? Why had any of them?

By late afternoon, as the sun dropped slowly behind the ridge, a few of the boys began to talk about home - real home - about mothers and wives, and the pubs in cities and towns. Others stared eastward, wondering if they would get the chance to march into Germany and make the bastards see what defeat looked like. But for now, they just stood around, shivering in silence, waiting for orders, unsure how to feel in a world where the guns had finally fallen quiet.

For Sam Ford who, along with the rest of the 7th Battalion of the South Staffordshire Regiment, was east of Havay in Belgium, the morning had broken grey and windless, the kind of stillness that felt unnatural - like the land itself was holding its breath. It was foggy as usual, but the mist somehow softened the shattered landscape. Samuel stood on a rise, his boots hardened with a combination of frost and mud, a lone beech tree at his back. From up here, he could see the ridgelines and battered fields littered with shell holes, broken wagons, and the occasional limp wave of concertina wire in the breeze. It was a graveyard without headstones.

Behind him, the men crouched in their shallow shell scrapes and trenches. Some smoked. Others sat hugging their knees, eyes hollow with expectation. No birds sang. Even the lice seemed to keep still.

Sam fingered the edge of a letter in his greatcoat pocket - unsent. Written the night before, it had been meant for no one in particular. A habit now, these farewell scribbles.

The platoon commander, a sandy haired lieutenant barely out of school, clambered up onto a hummock and raised one arm.

"That's it, lads," he called, his voice steady and calm despite the tremble in his hands, "an Armistice has been confirmed. Eleven o'clock this morning. Cease fire. No movement until then. Then - stand down. It's done".

"Done?" Samuel thought to himself. "That's it, just like that, the war is over?"

He felt nothing. Neither did anyone else.

Like the Aussies, there was no cheer. Just a few murmured curses, a bitter exhale or two. The men looked to each other, unsure what to do with the news. One man quietly passed a tin of bully down the line.

Samuel didn't speak. He just looked out toward the horizon, where the fog was beginning to lift, and thought of home. He wondered where Percy was now - still somewhere in Palestine maybe? And what of Roo and Archie? Was Roo safe? Was Archie recovering? Had they made it this far? He hadn't heard from them since they last saw each other in September. Letters came like ghosts now - faint, too late, and sometimes bearing bad news.

At 1059 hours a breeze stirred through the broken trees, rattling a bit of loose tin in the wreckage below.

Then, eleven.

No bang. No whistle. No shouts.

Just...nothing.

The kind of silence that felt deafening after four years of thunder.

Sam pressed his hand to the cold earth at his feet. He didn't say anything. He didn't need to.

It was over.

CHAPTER 15

The Long Road Home

For everyone the desire was strong now just to get home; home to normality. Home meant warmth, routine, peace - a world where death didn't wait at every corner. But peace or no peace, they were still soldiers - now part of an army of occupation, and there was work to be done.

At 1500 hours, the 9th Battalion formed up and marched out once again. A cold wind cut through them as they clambered onto trucks. The vehicles rumbled eastward, deeper into what had only yesterday been enemy held territory. Their destination, a small village called Mazinghien.

When they arrived, the village was silent - too silent. Not a dog barked, not a child cried. Just the cold, and the ghostly quiet of a place recently abandoned by war. Only the day before, German troops had been quartered there, but now all that remained was their mess and their dead.

The battalion's billets were two miles beyond the village, in two large, dilapidated houses that had once been stately homes. But any grandeur had long since vanished. The Australians, hardened by months and years of discomfort, still reeled at the condition inside. The stench was the first assault on their senses - stifling, clinging, and putrid.

In the outbuildings and fields nearby, they discovered the source - rotting horses, sprawled where they had died, frozen in death mid-stride or collapsed against broken carts. Worse still were the bodies of German soldiers, some half-buried in debris, others caught in grotesque poses where shellfire had taken them. No one had come back for them. They had been abandoned by their mates - forgotten, discarded like rubbish.

The Australians gave the place a name, in the way soldiers do to cope - 'Dead Horse Farm'. The joke didn't carry far, though. Even the seasoned men grew quiet. War, it seemed, had not yet finished with them, and now, in this bitter postscript to the fighting, it lingered in the stables, the kitchens, and the muddy paddocks - a final, rotting reminder of what they had endured.

It was here too that the battalion saw clear proof that not all Germans behaved in a gentlemanly manner.

The village had taken a hammering. Shellfire had left many of the buildings crumbling and scarred. The whole area seemed desolate. What once might have been a thriving farming community now felt abandoned - fields lay overgrown and silent, fences broken, and not a single farm animal in sight. The place felt hollow, like something had been drained from it.

The Aussies were shocked to see the place. They hadn't expected luxury, but this was devastation. Half-starved locals emerged from the ruins - men and women who had been seized by the Germans and forced to labour elsewhere, like slaves, now limping home. Even those who had stayed behind looked shattered. They flinched when approached, wary and beaten down, as if they expected more cruelty. Children, terrified, darted behind walls or disappeared into ruins when anyone tried to speak to them.

Worse still, prior to their departure the Germans had stripped the town of anything valuable or useful, food stocks, clothing. They had informed the population that the incoming armies would provide for them - then marched off with the lot.

"Thieving bloody bastards!" exclaimed Clancy, looking around at the hollow-eyed faces.

"Yes, I agree," replied Ponsonby, "we need to get these people fed as soon as possible".

But no orders were necessary as the Diggers had already begun to share their rations with the locals, handing out tins of bully beef and hard tack like it was Christmas. Even the roughest grub was met with teary gratitude; with some saying it was the first meat they had tasted for two years.

Roo was apologetic as he stood beside a haggard old woman who held a tin to her chest like it was gold.

"I'm sorry we couldn't get here sooner," he said quietly.

No one answered, but the look she gave him said it all.

A group of twenty five British prisoners of war emerged hesitantly out into the streets. They were a sorry sight - a ragged mob, starving, emaciated, and dressed in nothing more than stained flannel shirts and tattered trousers, their feet jammed into ill-fitting German army boots, the heels worn down to nothing. One of them held a torn scrap of a white sheet and waved it feebly at the Aussies who, at first, took them for Germans, raising their rifles instinctively. But when the figures drew closer, their gaunt faces and whispered pleas in English gave the truth away. These weren't enemies - they were brothers in arms, forgotten by the front, used up and discarded by the war.

"Jesus Christ," muttered Roo, lowering his rifle, "they're bloody Tommies".

The men stood blinking in disbelief.

"Come on, fellas," Roo called out gently, motioning for the others to help, "let's get you blokes warm and fed".

The Aussies moved quickly, guiding the prisoners away from the rubble and towards the battalion's cookhouse tent. One of the Diggers took off his own coat and draped it around a shivering man. Another passed over a crust of bread, which the prisoner devoured with shaking hands. The prisoners tried to thank them, but the words caught in dry throats.

Inside the tent, steaming mugs of sweet tea were passed around, followed by bowls of stew thick with vegetables and bully beef. The mens' eyes brimmed with tears at the first taste of real food. Between mouthfuls, they spoke of months in captivity - how the Germans had confiscated their uniforms and equipment, brutalised them, and fed them only sugar beet. Needless to say, these men were in dire need of medical attention and were soon shipped off to hospitals in the rear.

Over the next few days, the Australians rolled up their sleeves and got stuck in.

The town had been spared the worst of the fighting, but months of occupation had left it battered in other ways. Shops had been looted, the church doors were hanging off their hinges, food was scarce, water was patchy, and there was a nervous stillness in the air - the kind that lingers long after the danger has passed.

The battalion wasted no time. Men were organised into small work parties, and each took on a different task. A group from 'C' Company got the old pump working again in the main square, clearing the debris from the troughs and replacing broken handles with whatever parts they could scrounge. Others helped the villagers patch up roofs, clear the gutters, and repair doors and shutters. Several of the signallers rigged up a basic wire that let the mayor send word to the nearest French prefecture. The Quartermaster managed to scrounge extra rations from brigade stores, and for two nights in a row, the townsfolk were fed hot stew and fresh bread alongside the soldiers.

Nothing they were doing was glamorous, but that didn't matter. For the men, it was a rare chance to do something good...something useful. The general consensus was that if they were going to hang around waiting for orders, they might as well be fixing things instead of sitting on their backsides.

There were no speeches, no formal handshakes. Just quiet nods and heartfelt murmurs of *merci* from people who had survived one horror and were now rebuilding in the shadow of another.

On the 14th of November the battalion was to witness yet more distressing scenes when they marched to Bohain. The town was large and had hardly been touched by the war, but it was now the railhead for the advancing allied forces. The people here too were starving; the suffering was no less real. Children with gaunt faces and wary eyes gathered quietly at street corners, watching the soldiers arrive with a mix of fear and desperate hope.

As soon as the battalion canteen was set up, the Australians dipped into their own pockets to buy up whatever food they could and handed it out to the hungry children. Some lads emptied their entire day's pay without a second thought. It wasn't much -mostly biscuits and tinned fruit - but to the locals it meant everything.

The battalion cooks also managed to muster up a hot meal which was divided equally between the soldiers and civilian population. Mothers wept quietly as their children ate their fill for the first time in weeks. Slowly, smiles returned, and the locals began to understand that these Australians were not to be feared. A few of the older folk even offered their thanks in broken English, or simply by clasping a soldier's hand with tears in their eyes.

The battalion spent their nine days at Bohain route marching and smartening up their uniforms, drill and bearing as best as they could. Orders were to present a professional image when the time came to cross into Germany, and so they marched back and forth through the surrounding countryside, heads high, chests out, shoulders back.

Some grumbled at the endless parades.

"Why are we doing this?" one man complained. "We must have marched around this country a hundred bloody times..."

But beneath the grumbling was a quiet understanding; the war was over, but the next chapter was about to begin. The long march into enemy territory loomed, and though their boots were worn and spirits uneven, they would march into Germany not as invaders, but as victors - with discipline, pride, and the memory of hungry children still fresh in their minds.

The long anticipated day finally arrived on the 23rd of November, with the battalion forming up ready, boots polished and uniforms tidy, rifles slung over their shoulders just so. Spirits were high. This was it...the great march into Germany; a chance to show the Hun, in no uncertain terms, who they should *never* have messed with. But the order came down and the groans echoed almost louder than the Sergeant Major's voice, for their destination was Mazinghien...again.

The mood turned sour. They had already been to Mazinghien once, and now they were backtracking. The "march to glory" had turned into an awkward shuffle through familiar countryside.

Still, they soldiered on. A day or two later it was Cartignies, then onwards to Sars-Poteries, just north east of Avesnes. But the route made no sense. First they had marched west - away from Germany - then south east again, skirting the Franco-Belgian border. No one in the ranks could make head nor tail of it.

"If this is the road to Berlin," muttered Pip, "then I'm a flaming donkey".

Stowie piped up on hearing this comment and spoke just loud enough for all around to hear.

"Did you hear that fellas? I reckon ee aw, ee aw, ee aw to know better..."

As laughter rippled through the ranks, the only bright spot was the weather, which for late November had been surprisingly kind...until it wasn't. Cold rain and sleet returned, soaking uniforms and tempers. To make matters worse, their billets at Sars-Poteries left a lot to be desired. The village itself was intact, and they were thankful for the use of clean public baths, but the accommodation was another story.

The battalion's billets were located in the local glass works - glass being the village's principal industry - but the machinery had either been removed or destroyed by the enemy; the place reduced to a hollow shell. Dust and soot clung to every surface, and the draft howled through shattered windows.

Still, there were traces of beauty amongst the wreckage. Delicate glassware - bowls, vases, figurines - lay tucked away in dusty cupboards or hidden beneath broken workbenches, some miraculously unscathed. Many of these fine specimens of glass workers arts, would make their way back to Australia.

Pip held up a fine crystal vase, turning it in the dim light. It caught a sliver of sun and sparkled.

"Hey Roo, do you reckon your aunt and uncle would appreciate this?"

"They'd love it mate," Roo replied, "there's not much posh crystal where *we* live".

"You could tell 'em it's a Geerman surrender pressie".

Roo laughed.

The battalion may have grumbled, but they moved as ordered - east, west, south -waiting, watching, wondering when, if ever, they would actually set foot in the enemy's land. The war might have ended, but the wandering certainly had not.

On the morning of the 1st of December, a sudden buzz went through the billets like a jolt of electricity - word had spread that the King himself was in the area. Most of the men had caught a glimpse of His Majesty months ago, but this news still stirred something deep in their chests. Even the most cynical among them stood a little taller.

Orders came down swiftly. The battalion was to form up and march out to the Mauberge Road. There were no complaints, despite the chill in the air. Uniforms were brushed down, puttees re-tied, buttons polished with spit and sleeve. The men might have looked like they had come straight from the trenches, but they were determined to make a decent showing.

The men stood tall, slouch hats at a proud angle, as they lined the roadside in neat ranks, stretching down both sides of the route. CSMs moved up and down the line, adjusting spacing, but for the most part the men were quiet - more solemn than usual. Even jokes were kept to a minimum. It wasn't every day you got to see the King of England and the Empire.

"I wonder if he'll wave," Pip asked, peering down the road.

A few of the men wagged their eyebrows or muttered jokes as they waited, but even the usual larrikins fell quiet when the convoy came into sight. A hush fell over the Australians. As the small cavalcade rounded the bend, eyes locked forward and backs straightened. The King sat upright in the back seat, wearing his uniform, his keen eyes scanning the gathered troops. As he passed, the Aussies presented arms in a Royal Salute to their sovereign.

The King's car slowed slightly, and it was clear he had seen the Australians. He lifted his hand in a return salute. The moment was brief, but it left the men beaming with pride, as to the diggers, even that small acknowledgment felt like a reward.

"God save the King!" someone shouted nervously. The cheer rolled down the line like a bushfire.

For a few minutes, all that they had endured, the danger, mud, hunger, and the cold were forgotten.

"He looks just like he does on the shilling," Roo whispered, nudging Clancy.

"He looked right at me," Pip said, grinning as the motorcade disappeared around the bend.

"Hah!" retorted Clancy, "He was probably wondering why there was a scouse git in our ranks".

"Scouse git?" replied Pip, "I *am* coming up in the world…"

The brief spectacle was over in minutes, but the mood lingered. They marched back to their billets with heads held a little higher, their earlier weariness forgotten for a while. They had seen the King, some for the first time, and he had seen them, and moments like these reminded them that their service and sacrifice mattered; *especially* to their King.

For Archie, Queen Mary's Hospital for Limbless Soldiers in Roehampton was a world apart from the mud, blood, and stench of the Western Front. A red-brick sanctuary on the outskirts of London, where its buildings stood in neat rows, surrounded by manicured lawns and flowerbeds, serenaded by the sounds of birdsong. The hum of bees in the hedges was interrupted only by the occasional clatter of men hobbling on crutches through rose gardens, learning to walk again on polished wooden floors, fighting to get back to as normal a life as possible.

Archie sat stiffly in the fitting room, staring down at the contraption strapped to what was left of his leg. The artificial limb was clunky, brutal in its honesty - hinged at the knee, a steel brace running up the outside, and a thick leather boot that felt heavier than it looked. The orderly, a quiet fellow in a white coat, tightened the final strap and stepped back.

"It'll feel strange for a while," he said, adjusting a buckle, "but give it time. You'll be walking on your own soon enough".

Archie managed a grunt and a wry smile.

"If I fall on my face, just tell the others I was practising a waltz".

A few in the room laughed politely. A pair of parallel bars stood to his front, an aid in his journey back to walking again, but when he pulled himself upright and the limb took his weight, all humour vanished. His shoulders stiffened. Pain stabbed through his thigh. The world tilted. The bars beside him groaned under his grip. Every step felt odd...he was learning to walk again...and as he moved inch by inch, his arms shook on the bars, sweat breaking out across his brow.

He took one step. Then another.

Sweat dripped down his face and his breath was ragged. But he stayed upright. Around him, the room held its breath. Then a voice called out:

"You're doing alright, cobber! Better than I did...first time I tried, I ended up on me arse".

Archie turned to see a soldier with both legs gone, sitting in his chair, his two stumps padded and bandaged. He raised his tin mug in salute.

Each day brought small gains. The staff here were kind, efficient, and strict. The physio therapy and exercise was relentless, but so were the wounded men. In the evenings they would gather in the sitting room, smoking and trading stories. Some were dark, others absurd. One man swore he had been shot by a German who saluted before pulling the trigger.

Archie let it drift over him. He didn't join in much, and rarely spoke of how it had happened. Not yet. Instead, he watched others - some missing arms, some blind - find laughter again. There was comfort in that.

In the quiet moments, when the morphine wore off and sleep came slow, he stared out of the window at the swaying trees, wondering what life might look like now. He had a leg again, even if it wasn't his.

On that particular night, Archie sat by the open window of the ward. A breeze rustled the curtains and carried the faint scent of roses. From down the hall came the sound of laughter.

He looked down at the metal brace on his leg, resting on a low stool. It wasn't him. Not really. But it was something. A start.

He leaned back, eyes half closed, and pictured the station back home. The wide paddocks and the mobs of cattle moving through red dust and sunlight. He imagined himself in the saddle again - swinging up with a bit of help, steadying himself, reins in hand.

He'd work out a way. He'd have to.

But could he ride? Not like before - but maybe. Perhaps he would train a quiet old gelding and rig the stirrup with some sort of brace. He had two arms so could still swing a rope, couldn't he? He might not be able to run, but he could ride, and riding meant freedom.

The thought lit something inside him. For the first time since the bandages had come off, he felt like he could see it - his place in the world again. He needed a purpose before he went home.

He muttered to himself, a quiet vow no one else would hear. "I'm not done yet. Not by a bloody long shot".

Orders soon came through that the battalion was to furnish a King's Guard at the chateau where the King and his two sons were staying. It was an unusual assignment, one far removed from the mud and chaos of battle. The men selected were to mount guard in the manner of the Household Division at Buckingham Palace or Windsor Castle - a ceremonial duty.

Volunteers were called for, and a section was quickly assembled. They were drilled thoroughly, issued with new uniforms, and rehearsed until every movement was crisp and precise. Buttons were polished, rifles gleamed, and boots shone like glass. By the time they stepped into position at the gates of the chateau, they looked the part.

This was a duty for the duration of the King's stay. There was no fuss or fanfare about it. The King's Guard was relieved at regular intervals, and the men stood post in silence, eyes forward, hands firm on their rifles. When the King passed by, or one of his sons strode out into the courtyard, the guard came smartly to attention, presenting arms with military precision.

It was the first time in history that Australian troops had ever mounted a guard over an occupied royal residence, but there was no mention of that among the men. They were there to do a job - and they did it without fuss, as they always had.

It soon became clear that the ANZACs were not to have their symbolic march into Germany after all. The war was over, but rather than crossing the Rhine in triumph, the men found themselves engaged in a different kind of campaign - one filled with cricket matches, football tournaments, tug-of-war contests, and all manner of spirited sporting competitions. While it wasn't what many had envisioned after years of brutal service, it helped keep the battalion occupied and lifted morale as winter deepened.

On the 16th of December, the battalion set out once more, beginning a wintry march eastward toward Charleroi. They crossed the Belgian frontier under leaden skies, sinking into the snow as they passed through sleepy villages - Solre-St-Gery and Thy-Le-Château - the landscape whitewashed and hushed. After three days of steady marching, they arrived at their destination - Chatelet, a suburb of Charleroi.

The town, home to some twelve thousand people and shaped by its coal mining industry, greeted the Australians with an enthusiasm that took many of the men by surprise. Children waved from doorways, and townsfolk lined the streets, applauding as the troops marched in. For a moment, the men could almost believe they were heroes. Their billets turned out to be the best they had known during the entire war - dry, warm, and, most importantly, with proper beds.

Headquarters was established in the La Grande Rue, and the Aussies settled into their new role as part of the army of occupation now positioned across the Rhineland. With little official work to do, and the German threat behind them, the days passed in relative calm. The officers were welcomed with a small civic reception, but for the rest of the men, time was spent catching up on sleep, writing letters home, and enjoying the novelty of peace.

Snow fell steadily over the following days, blanketing the town in a soft silence. The Australians, now accustomed to such consistent snowfall, took to it with typical good humour. Snowball fights became the norm - not just among the troops, but between platoons, and even entire companies.

There was a local cinema in town, a modest venue with wooden benches and flickering reels. On the first Sunday night, a large group of the boys had attended a screening. As they spilled out into the street afterward, the temptation proved too strong. With the fresh snow beckoning, a full blown snowball battle erupted, with the men hurling clumps of snow at each other - and at some of the bewildered civilians standing nearby.

The townspeople didn't know what to make of it. After four years under German occupation, even a playful act like tossing a snowball at a soldier had been unthinkable. Now, faced with the rowdy Australians laughing and pelting one another with snow, they simply froze, unsure whether to flee or remain still.

"What's wrong with these folks?" asked Stowie, blinking at the hesitant bystanders.

"Fear, I suppose mate," Roo replied quietly, watching the wary glances from the civilians.

"Fear...my arse," said Clancy with a grunt. He scooped up a handful of snow, packed it tightly, and let it fly - smacking a young boy square in the side of the head.

For a heartbeat, all was still. Then the child, grinning mischievously, ducked, rolled up a snowball of his own, and fired back - hitting Clancy right in the chest.

"You little ripper!" Clancy laughed, wiping the snow from his tunic and immediately firing off a return volley.

That one brave throw broke the spell. Within moments, children, then adults, joined in the frosty melee, laughter ringing through the narrow streets. The tension that had settled over the town for years seemed to dissolve in the air. The Australians, for their part, didn't hold back - laughing, dodging, lobbing snowballs in all directions. It was a moment of pure, uncomplicated joy - something neither the Belgians nor the Diggers had known in a very long time.

From that evening on, the townspeople viewed their new guests in a very different light. The Australians were not occupiers. They were men, like them, with a sense of humour, a love of life, and no taste for tyranny. That single night of snow and laughter had done more to foster goodwill than any speech or official parade.

Christmas Day dawned bitterly cold, and the snow continued to fall in soft silence across the rooftops of Chatelet as the men of the 9th Battalion prepared for what would be their first true Christmas in peace since the war began. Preparations were underway for the battalion's Christmas dinner - the last of the war, and by far the best. Word spread quickly that the cooks were going all out. Tables were set up in the barn, which doubled as the Cookhouse, decorated with pine branches, ribbons, and anything festive that the QM staff could acquire. Fires crackled in hearths. The promise of real roast meat, vegetables, gravy, and even a pudding sparked eager anticipation. It would be a proper Christmas - warm, well-fed, and surrounded by mates. The men could hardly believe it. After everything, they had made it through, and for once, the coming day was something to look forward to.

By midday, rows of long tables were soon crowded with cheerful, noisy diggers, and the laughter and scent of roasting meat filled the barn. As per tradition, the officers and senior

"You wouldn't have it any other way mate...and you know it".

Clancy returned to his seat and looked around the hall - at the men laughing, eating, toasting one another, and telling stories that had grown taller in the telling. For the first time in a long while, they weren't just surviving. They were living, and somewhere, despite the wait, home didn't seem quite so far away.

Christmas found the 2nd Light Horse Regiment camped in Jerusalem. With most of the other units withdrawn to the coast, there were enough tents to go around, and the men settled into a very comfortable camp. The weather was now cold in the Judean hills and sleet and heavy frosts were common.

The mail arrived along with the usual parcels of food and gifts. Percy finally received letters from both Australia and the western front in which he learned the news about his brother Archie. There was even one from Archie himself who joked about being a favourite now to play a pirate character in any Christmas pantomimes at home. Percy felt numb for a while but settled for the fact that Archie was alive at least.

"It happened in their very last battle you know," he uttered out loud.

"That's *some* bad luck eh?" said Chugger.

Percy nodded.

"I just want to see him...you know...give him a hug and tell him everything will be fine".

Davo held out an open hand.

"Do you mind if I have a quick read mate?"

Percy handed him the letter and stared at Davo whilst he read.

"See...this is the Archie we all know...listen...*I should be able to walk properly soon with this artificial lower leg, well with a bit of* *practice anyways...I've done a few sketches for some straps to add to my saddle too, so with that I should be able to ride no worries...*he's gonna be fine Perce, you can almost hear it in his words".

"Yeah...you're right...thanks mate," replied Percy.

Boggy, who had been sat by the fire listening, suddenly stood up.

"What a miserable bunch you lot are...it's Christmas Eve for Christ...er...pity's sake. Look where we are boys...and Rachel...where it all began. There's a service on at the Church of the Nativity...and it's not locked this time...what do you reckon we all go?"

"I thought you didn't believe," said Chugger.

Boggy smiled.

"That old chestnut again..." Boggy replied. "I never said I *didn't* believe, I just said I didn't agree with some of it that's all...but Jesus...well he is definitely part of my life...so let's go and be where *his* life began".

The streets of Bethlehem wound in close around them, the stone pale under the winter moon. At the edge of Manger Square, the Church of the Nativity rose, old and heavy with time. The small doorway cut low into the wall seemed almost too plain for such a place, yet a line of pilgrims bent themselves to pass through.

The Australians joined them. Shoulders brushed stone as they stepped inside. The air carried the weight of candles and incense. Long rows of worn columns stretched ahead into shadow, their painted saints faded almost to ghosts. Fragments of golden mosaic still clung to the walls, catching the glow of hanging lamps.

They moved with the slow press of the crowd toward a narrow stairway. Down they went, treading on stone steps hollowed by countless feet, until the passage opened into a low chamber. Lamps glimmered there too, set about an altar of marble. Beneath it lay a silver star, fourteen points shining in the lamplight, marking the place said to be that of Christ's birth.

No one spoke. Chugger's hand found Rachel's for a moment before they stepped forward together. Rachel drew her scarf closer about her face, yet did not hold back. In her own faith men and women stood apart, but here she joined the soldiers at the altar, her fingers trembling slightly as she reached for the stone.

One by one the men followed. Hands scarred by reins, rifles, and years of war came down gently on the star, each man bowing his head in silence. Percy stood at the rear with Alfie. The boy looked to him, uncertain, and Percy lifted him so he too could reach down and touch the stone.

They remained there longer than they thought they would, the chamber close about them. In that stillness the years of hardship seemed to settle over their shoulders once more, but with it came something they had not felt in a long time - something like calm, and the faint stirrings of hope.

From the chamber they followed the movement of the crowd into the adjoining church of St Catherine. Lanterns swung from the vaulted ceiling, throwing light over carved stone and pale walls. Every pew was filled, the air alive with the murmur of many tongues, all hushed as the service began.

The Australians found places to stand along the side wall. Alfie clung to Percy's sleeve, Rachel at his other side, her eyes lifted to the altar where candles flared in rows. Chugger rested a hand lightly against her shoulder, as though steadying her as much as himself.

The chanting began, voices rising and falling in solemn waves. It was unlike anything they had known - Latin words they could not follow, yet carrying a feeling that needed no translation. The organ swelled, filling every corner, and the flicker of light caught faces bent in prayer.

The men stood very still. Boggy's head bowed, his lips moving soundlessly, Davo's hands clasped behind his back as though on parade. None of them had spoken since entering, each drawn inward to their own thoughts - the long road from Gallipoli, the dust of Sinai, the blood in Palestine, the friends they would never see again.

When the moment came for the blessing of peace, Chugger felt Rachel shift slightly beside him. In her faith she would not stand in such a place, yet she had a steady gaze and calm expression, as though she understood better than any of them what this night meant.

Alfie's small hand stayed tight in Percy's. The boy's eyes were fixed on the altar, wide with a wonder that no hardship had yet been able to dim.

The carols rose as midnight came. *Gloria in excelsis Deo...* The words echoed against the stone, the sound swelling until it seemed greater than the church, greater even than the war that had once raged beyond its walls.

For a while, they were not soldiers, nor wanderers, nor exiles from home. They were simply men and women gathered in the heart of Bethlehem on Christmas morning, bound together by silence, memory, and the faint but unbroken hope of peace.

The service ended slowly, not with applause or chatter but with the heavy quiet of people reluctant to leave. When the Australians stepped outside, the night air struck cold after the warmth of candles and bodies pressed close together. Above them the sky was twinkling bright with stars, and the streets of Bethlehem seemed hushed, as if the town itself kept watch.

No one spoke for a time. Their footsteps sounded against the stone as they made their way through the narrow lanes, joining the trickle of others heading out into the darkness.

For a while they walked in silence. Chugger glanced back once at the church, then let out a low breath.

"That was something I never thought I would see or do," he said.

"Yes, it was special. I just wish Lil had been here with me," replied Percy.

Rachel walked close beside them, her scarf drawn around her face to protect her from the cold night air. She said nothing, but when she looked toward the church one last time, the men saw respect in her expression, and something more - an understanding that cut across faiths.

Davo cleared his throat.

"I think, years from now, when we're all old and grey, we'll still remember tonight".

The others nodded. There was no argument.

The road wound away through the olive groves, dark against the stars, and they followed it in silence once more, each holding their own thoughts close.

CHAPTER 16

"Mates for Life, and Don't Forget It"

January 1919 was soon upon them; the frost clung to the fields around their billets in Chatelet, but the war was well and truly over. The 9th Battalion, once a proud spearhead of the AIF, was now a fading echo of itself - men leaving in dribs and drabs, scattered to demobilisation depots, medical transport, or repatriation ships, whenever a rare vessel became available. There was talk of a ship heading to Alexandria in January, but no one was holding their breath.

There had been no grand parade, no victory march through the Arc de Triomphe, just cold, damp mornings, waiting for names to be called...waiting to go home.

The men sat around a low cooking fire, steam rising from the billy as Roo handed around mugs of tea. Archie was fidgety, adjusting the awkward angle of his artificial leg. The steel and leather contraption was crude but functional, and he moved with a limp that none of them mentioned. His face was thinner, but his smile hadn't gone anywhere.

"It's my own fault I suppose. I should have finished my walking exercises before I escaped from the hospital".

"Escaped? You make it sound like a prison mate," said Clancy.

"Yeah, you're right. It was far from it and the doctors, nurses...well...everyone was just great," replied Archie, "but I'll get by, and practice makes perfect eh?"

Captain Ponsonby approached slowly over the frostbitten grass. He looked tired - older than he had just a few months before. His uniform was still neat, but the scuffs on his boots told the story of long nights pacing. Lieutenant Sargent followed close behind, hands in his pockets, eyes heavy.

Roo looked up and smiled at the two men.

"I had a feeling once the billy had boiled we would see you two blokes".

Ponsonby cleared his throat.

"Yes...quite...but I have some news gents".

Roo passed the two officers mugs of hot tea.

"News?"

"Yes," Ponsonby replied, pausing for a moment, "have you heard of the War Graves Registration units?'

"Yeah, isn't the Number 5 Unit working in Villers Bretonneux?" replied Archie, "I heard that they found skeletons still lying in semi-circles, webbing and uniform scraps intact, surrounded by spent .303 cases".

Ponsonby nodded.

"That about sums it up, yes".

He cleared his throat again.

"Gentlemen...they are looking for volunteers for a similar job at Gallipoli. We're going to be sat here for a few months yet, and it's on the way home...and...well...I thought you chaps would be interested".

He paused, letting his words sink in.

A heavy silence settled over the fire.

"Will you and Tomo be coming skip?" asked Clancy.

Ponsonby shook his head.

"Sadly...no...apparently we are required here".

"Well, that's a bugger mate...but I can't go without you blokes...not after all these years and... well...you know"."

"I said my goodbyes to that place on the beach years ago anyway," Roo added.

The others agreed.

He looked at each of them in turn, his voice quieter now.

"Good. That's settled then".

The sun hadn't come up yet. The camp was quiet, just the canvas shifting in the breeze and the low murmur of men who'd stopped sleeping but hadn't yet started speaking.

Chugger stood beside his horse, his hand resting on the neck he had brushed a thousand times. The old Waler blinked slowly, ears twitching, calm as ever, still strong, and still sound. He hadn't missed a step throughout the entire campaign.

The order had come through the day before. All horses over eight were to be destroyed. Not sold. Not shipped. Just put down. Too costly to keep...a burden on the public purse.

He had read it twice, then folded the paper and didn't speak about it again.

Now it was just him and the horse...old 'George'...and a quiet space behind the tents where the sand was soft and the flies hadn't started yet.

He ran a hand down the horse's shoulder, felt the muscle still firm under the hide. Over ten thousand miles they had travelled together, through heat, dust, and gunfire. Through nights where the horse had stood still while Chugger slept in the saddle.

He didn't say anything. He didn't know what words would do.

He pulled back the bolt on his rifle and chambered a round, then stepped back.

The horse turned its head slightly, as if sensing something. Chugger gave a short nod.

"Good boy...I love you mate," he said.

Then he did what had to be done.

When it was over, he sat down beside the body, arms resting on his knees.

He stayed there a while. Not crying. Not praying. Just sitting.

Davo took his mount out past the latrines, where the ground was dry and quiet.

He knelt beside her, checked her hooves one last time, and then sat with her until the sun was high overhead. When he finally stood, he looked older than he had the day before.

Boggy did it fast. No fuss, no pause. But when he came back, he didn't speak for hours. Just sat on his saddle and stared at nothing.

Percy's own horse 'Sandy' was last. He led the animal out past the tent line and gave it a final brush with the sleeve of his shirt, then stood for a while before drawing his pistol. BANG! The single shot rang out amongst the others. He didn't flinch. But when he walked back, his hands were shaking, but he didn't look back...none of them did.

As he approached Chugger, still sat with 'George', he didn't speak straight away - just stood there, looking at the horse, then at Chugger.

"They deserved better," he said.

Chugger didn't look up.

"Yeah they did. You know I thought we'd be able to take them home and keep them after the war...give him a good life you know...but these bloody politicians...happy for us to risk our lives for a war they started, and now the only thing they care about is bloody money!!!"

No one spoke of it again. But they all carried it. By the end of the day, the horses were gone, but it wasn't only the horses that had to go, as Percy was to find out when he saw a trooper leading Alfie's donkey, Bow, toward the edge of camp. The donkey plodded along, ears flicking, rope slack in the man's hand. Alfie wasn't with him.

Percy called out.

"Hey mate...where are you taking that donkey?"

The private turned, uncertain.

"The QM said to clear out anything not listed for repatriation. Said the donkey wasn't on the books".

Percy stepped closer.

"That's because he's not army issue. He belongs to my boy Alfie".

The soldier shrugged.

"Doesn't matter, sarge. They're clearing everything".

Percy looked at Bow - small, shaggy, harmless. He had never done anything remarkable. Just carried Alfie and his shoe shine kit, stood in the sun, and followed Alfie like a shadow.

"Leave him," Percy said, "I'll sort it".

He found Alfie near the cookhouse tent, sitting on an upturned crate, staring at nothing.

"They were about to take Bow," Percy said.

Alfie didn't react at first. Then he stood, slow and stiff, and walked over to where Bow had been tied.

"I am not letting them shoot him papa," he said.

Percy nodded and thought for a moment.

"There might be something else we can do".

He spoke to one of the chaplains, who made a few quiet inquiries. The Franciscans in Bethlehem had space. They kept animals for the grounds, and sometimes used a donkey in the Palm Sunday procession. They would take Bow. No fuss. No questions.

The next morning, Percy and Alfie walked Bow through the streets. At the Church of the Nativity, the priests welcomed them with quiet nods and open hands. Bow was led to a small courtyard with olive trees and a stone trough. He sniffed the air, flicked his ears, and settled in like he had always belonged.

Alfie gave him a final pat.

"Don't let them dress you up too silly," he said.

Bow blinked, then wandered off toward the shade.

Alfie didn't move, but felt a lump appear in his throat. Percy stood beside him.

"He's all you had in the world isn't he mate?" said Percy, trying to hold back his own tears.

Alfie wiped his nose on his sleeve and looked up at Percy.

"Except you..."

Percy's chin wobbled for a moment, and then he picked the boy up and hugged him tightly.

"Yes you have...and you have a family too...and we're going to love you forever...that's a promise".

They didn't speak on the walk back, but Percy saw the tears, and didn't say a word.

By late February, the war was long over, but the formalities remained. On the 23rd the men of the 2nd Light Horse filed into the ordnance stores and handed over their rifles and equipment. Steel, leather, and canvas that had been part of them for years were stacked in silence, the sound of buckles and clasps louder than the words unspoken. The ordnance stores swallowed it all, and with it, the last physical trace of the campaign.

The remaining horses departed the next day under Major Birbeck, to be handed over to the remount section in Moascar. The men watched them go in silence.

At Saint George's Cathedral in Jerusalem, the whole regiment gathered for a memorial service. The pews were full, the air still. The stone walls held the echoes of names not spoken aloud, but they were there - in the silence, in the way the men sat, in the way they looked at the floor.

On the 10th of March, Major General Chaytor made his final inspection.

He thanked the regiment for their service, bid them farewell, and left them standing in ranks that would never form again.

Two days later, they boarded the train to Kantara. The desert rolled past the windows, familiar and indifferent. At the docks, they embarked on 'HMT Ulimaroa' - a sturdy steamship which had been requisitioned and transformed from a passenger liner into both a hospital ship and troop carrier. Compared to the troop decks of 1914, it was luxury. Percy and Chugger, having paid for extra accommodation, secured cabins for themselves, Alfie, and Rachel.

The voyage was uneventful. There were deck games, boxing matches, and the kind of food they hadn't seen in years. Rachel, having never left the Middle East, stood at the rail as Colombo came into view - green hills, bright saris, and the scent of spice in the air. She didn't speak but just watched with inquisitive eyes.

At Fremantle on the 7th of April, the mood soured. Officials came aboard with the announcement that the men were apparently suffering from pneumonic influenza. None of them were ill, yet the quarantine officers inspected every man, and the regiment's own medical staff kept up the routine for the rest of the voyage, and as if war and years of dust and blood had not tested them enough, the ports of Albany, Melbourne and Sydney all held them in quarantine. When they finally reached Moreton Bay on the 23rd Brisbane lay waiting, but the order came - quarantine at Camp Lytton for seven more days. The men bore it, though bitterness ran deep.

Only after weeks of frustration did the regiment finally step ashore. Invited to march through Brisbane, they paraded for the last time, the State Governor taking the salute. That afternoon their colours were laid up in Saint John's Cathedral, and the regiment ceased to exist, dismissing at the drill hall in Adelaide Street. Yet the men knew they had been part of something larger - Gallipoli, the desert. They had witnessed the birth of a nation. They had endured its baptism of fire. They had survived, when many had not. They were home.

The platform at Central Railway Station was busy but subdued - no brass bands, no cheering crowds, just the hiss of steam, the clatter of feet, and the quiet shuffle of men who had said goodbye too many times already.

Percy stood with Alfie beside the Kilcoy bound carriage, baggage stowed, tickets folded in his breast pocket. Chugger leaned against a post, Rachel beside him, her hand tucked into the crook of his arm, whilst Davo and Boggy were off to their own corners of Queensland, kit bags slung over their shoulders, eyes searching the platform like they weren't quite sure what came next.

No one said much.

They had marched through Brisbane as a unit and now they were scattering - back to farms, towns, families, silence.

Chugger broke it first.

"So...here we are..." he said, offering Percy his hand.

Percy took it.

"Here we are..."

After all of the battles and all of the death and destruction they had seen, this was the hardest moment of them all.

"You know...I've been looking forward to this for so long, but now I don't want it to happen," Chugger announced, a lump suddenly appearing in his throat.

Percy looked around at all of his mates.

"I feel the same mate. It's strange...I can't wait to see Lil and Frank...*and* Mum and Dad...but I don't want to lose you lot either".

Rachel lingered. Her eyes shone as she knelt to hug Alfie tight. Words failed her, and she pressed her cheek to his, whispering in Arabic. The boy clung to her, not wanting to let go, until Chugger laid a hand on his shoulder. She rose then, and each of the men, awkward in their uniforms, stepped forward one by one to give her a brief hug and a quick kiss on the cheek - each clumsy but heartfelt. Rachel blinked at them in surprise. Chugger grinned, giving her a wink.

"It's the Aussie way," he said to her, "you'll get used to it".

Rachel smiled, but her eyes were damp as she hugged Alfie again, then she stepped back.

"You look after him," she said to Percy.

"I will...don't you worry," he replied.

Laughter flickered for a moment, then slipped away, leaving something deeper. The men looked at one another, nothing left to say that could match what they had been through - trenches, charges, and nights where each had held the other's life in his hands - or how much it bound them. They shook hands again, some holding on too long, promises muttered about writing, about visits, about never forgetting.

The whistle cut through them like a blade. The moment broke in a flurry of last grips and hurried words. No grand farewells - just the silence of men who had shared too much to need them.

Boggy and Davo were the first to make a move. They gripped hands hard, knuckles white, neither willing to be the one to let go.

"Reckon we'll meet again," Davo said roughly, his eyes fixed on the ground, "one way or another?"

Boggy gave a sharp nod.

"You bloody well write, or I'll come and find you".

They broke apart quickly, each turning away before the other could see too much. As Boggy swung his kitbag over his shoulder, he gave Chugger a slap on the back, and muttered, "See you when I see you".

His throat caught before he could add more, so he tipped his hat and pushed into the crowd. Davo followed, quieter, shaking Percy's hand and offering Alfie a wink before slipping away.

Rachel smiled through her tears, and together she and Chugger turned toward the train bound for Bundaberg, where he promised his sister was waiting to welcome her as family.

Percy and Alfie were now alone on the platform, and stood in silence. For Percy, the weight of all they had endured pressed down on him. They had faced hell together and somehow survived it all. They had saved each other's lives and buried too many mates. Now, with little more than a shake of hands and quiet promises to write and visit, they let go.

The whistle blew and Percy and Alfie climbed aboard. As the train pulled out, Percy leaned out of the window, watching his friends shrink into the crowd.

The train to Kilcoy rattled slowly through the dark, Percy staring out at the fields while Alfie sat pressed against his side. At the little station, lantern light picked out a familiar sight - Ray with the wagon reins in hand, Doris and Lil standing close, and young Frank waving so hard his arm looked ready to fall off.

Percy barely had time to step down before Lil and Doris pulled him into an embrace, tears and laughter mixing in equal measure. Frank leapt at his leg, and Alfie stood frozen until Doris knelt in front of him.

"Are you my new mother?" Alfie asked, his small voice carrying in the night.

Doris drew him into her arms without hesitation.

"No Alfie...I am your *Grandmother*," she replied as she beckoned Lil and Frank closer, "*this* is your Mum and brother Frank".

Lil's tears spilled, but she nodded and hugged him tight. Percy watched, his chest tight, as Alfie's wary face softened at last. Then he met Ray's eyes over Lil's head, and both men nodded before Ray slapped him hard on the back.

The wagon stood ready. They climbed in together, blankets tucked around them against the night chill. Ray flicked the reins, called out, "Giddy up," and the horse pulled them out of the station yard and off down the road, wheels rumbling steady into the dark, carrying them home at last.

For the 9th Battalion, the ending came differently, when a large draft of men, including the remainder of the company, left for Charleroi, at the end of January, travelling to the channel ports and crossing to England. Here they remained, at Longbridge Deverill, south of Warminster, until the 13th of April when they set sail on the 'Suffolk' which, coincidentally, was one of the transport ships in the first convoy which left Australia in late 1914. But on the journey home they travelled via Cape Town and Adelaide before arriving at Melbourne where the Queenslanders disembarked and entrained for Brisbane, arriving there late afternoon on the 7th of June. There was no parade or official welcome home for the 9th, as on the day that the draft left Chatelet the battalion had ceased to exist as a complete unit and would return in groups over the following months; the final men arriving in Brisbane on the 9th of September, just over five years since the formation of the Battalion. The last portion was therefore scattered to the breeze, thus marking the breaking up of a gallant band of soldiers. The men may have gone their separate ways, but none doubted the bond forged in the years behind them.

Like weeks before when the lighthorsemen had returned home, the platform at Brisbane was crowded with families, embraces, and the noise of trains shunting in and out, but for the men of the 9th it narrowed down to a small circle - Ponsonby, Sargent, Clancy, Roo, Stowie, Pip, and Archie with his walking stick and steady determination.

Captain Ponsonby gave a slow nod, clearly proud, his face calm but his eyes carrying the weight of all they had endured together.

"It has been an honour and a privilege to serve with you all, and to be able to call you my friends," he said.

There was a silence, each man feeling an ache in the pit of their stomachs.

Clancy, who had never been one to hide his feelings, stepped forward.

"Do you mean that mate...because that's what you are...our mate?"

A faint smile tugged at Ponsonby's mouth.

"My bloody oath you pack of drongos".

The men laughed and cheered at that, remembering the promise before they left Australia that they would have him talking like an Australian by the time they got back...and they had...well sort of.

"Besides," he continued, "you'll be seeing me soon enough because I've decided to open a book keeping business in Kilcoy...but I have a few things to sort out in the city first".

Clancy let out a laugh that was half sob, half joy.

"You bloody ripper!"

He threw his arms around the captain and held him hard, the kind of hug soldiers give when there is nothing else to say.

Roo and the others turned to Ponsonby and Sargent. Roo pulled a crumpled scrap of field message paper from his pocket. He scrawled his Queensland address across it and pressed it into the lieutenant's hand.

"You've been more than officers...I hope you know that. Here's our address. We'll see you again, that's a promise".

Clancy's voice wavered as he looked around the station, then back at Ponsonby.

"Mates for life...and don't forget it".

Ponsonby shook each man's hand in turn, lingering a little longer when he came to Clancy.

"You are a good soldier, and a wonderful friend Clancy McBride. Take care of each other," he said quietly.

Tears welled in Clancy's eyes. He could not speak but instead threw his arms around his captain...Freddy...his friend.

As the others stepped back, Stowie lingered. He hadn't said much all morning, just stood with his kit at his feet and his hat low over his eyes. Clancy turned to him and gave him a nudge.

"You alright, you fat bastard?"

Stowie snorted.

"I'm fine. Just thinkin'".

He looked around the platform - families reuniting, trains groaning, the city stretching out beyond the tracks. Then he looked back at the men. Ponsonby. Sargent. Roo. Pip. Archie with his cane. Clancy, standing there like he always had - loud, loyal, and ready to swing for anyone who needed it.

"I reckon Taff would've liked this," Stowie said quietly, "he'd have said it was too bloody sentimental, but he'd have liked it".

Clancy nodded, managing to suppress a tear.

"He's here, mate. You know he is".

Stowie stepped forward and shook Ponsonby's hand – firm and steady.

"Thanks for everything boss," he said.

Ponsonby held his gaze.

"No...thank you Greg...you are a brave man and a great soldier".

Stowie turned to Clancy, and for a moment neither spoke. Then Clancy gave him a crooked grin.

"Don't go soft on me now".

Stowie pulled him into a hug - brief, hard, and full of everything they couldn't say.

"I'll write," he muttered.

"You bloody better".

And with that, the circle began to break. One by one, they turned toward their trains, their families, their futures. But for a moment longer, they stood together..."mates for life, and don't forget it".

As the train rolled into Kilcoy the whistle echoed across the paddocks, as it slowed to a halt with a sigh of steam. Ray and Doris waited by the steps to the platform, their faces bright with expectation. Percy was beside them, mounted, with two extra horses in hand. He knew Roo would be eager to ride again, and Archie - though still learning to master his artificial leg - deserved the chance to see if he could.

As the carriages emptied, Pip, Clancy, Roo, and Archie stepped down. Archie leaned on his stick, his limp plain to see. Doris's breath caught, but she forced a smile and opened her arms, not wanting to let Archie go. She then gathered Pip and Clancy to her, kissing each in turn.

"Welcome to our family," she said through tears, "war brings a lot of sadness, but it has brought us two new sons *and* a grandson".

Clancy swallowed hard, unable to speak, while Pip managed only a nod before hugging her back.

Ray gripped Roo's hand and patted him on the shoulder, firm and steady. He didn't speak straight away. Just looked at the young man in front of him - the uniform, the sunburnt face, and the eyes that had seen too much.

"You've grown into *him*," Ray said finally.

Roo frowned.

"Into who?"

"Your father," Ray said at last.

Roo blinked, unsure if he had heard right.

Ray nodded slowly.

"Not just in the way you stand. It's in your eyes. In how you carry things...and he and your mother would be proud...as I am".

He gave Roo's shoulder one last squeeze, then stepped back, clearing his throat.

"Come on. Let's get you home".

Percy nudged his horse forward and held out the reins of the spare mounts.

"Brought these for you both," he said, "question is, Archie...do you reckon you can still get up there?"

Archie hesitated at first but then he jammed his stick under his arm, hauled himself into the stirrup, and with a grunt dragged his body up. For a heartbeat it looked as if he might falter, but then he swung into the saddle and sat tall, breathing hard but grinning through it. It had been easier than he had expected. He let out a breath he hadn't realised he'd been holding.

"Yeah mate...I reckon I can".

The wagon creaked under its load as Doris and Ray climbed aboard with Pip and Clancy. Roo was already astride his horse, grinning like old times. Percy gave a nod to his brother and cousin, and the three Taylor boys - Percy, Roo, and Archie - kicked their mounts forward and the horses surged out from the station yard at a gallop, side by side, leaving the wagon and the others behind on the road home.

For the first time in years, there was no war at their backs. Only the open country of Kilcoy ahead, and the life waiting for them. Just home.

At the homestead, Lil stood at the gate with Frank, and Alfie. The sound of hooves reached them first, and Lil shaded her eyes, spotting the riders cresting the rise. Frank ran ahead, shouting, "They're here! They're here!"

The horses slowed as they drew near, the three Taylor men pulling up in front of the gate. Percy swung down easily, while Archie and Roo remained mounted, their faces lit with the sheer relief of being home. Lil stepped forward, her hands trembling as she reached for Archie, then Roo in turn. No words came - only tears, laughter, and the fierce grip of arms that refused to let go.

Behind them, the wagon rolled in, Doris and Ray introducing Pip and Clancy, Lil embracing them as if they had always belonged.

In the weeks that followed, the rhythms of life began to return. The war was over, yet its marks lingered in ways no eye could see. Still, there was comfort in the simple things - the sound of horses in the paddock, the smell of bread from the kitchen, the laughter of the two boys racing through the yard.

Alfie, who had once lived by his wits on foreign streets, now had a mother and father in Lil and Percy, as well as a brother in Frank. Pip and Clancy, taken into the arms of Doris and Ray, found a home as well, with a family that called them their own, and for the first time in years, each of them knew what it was to belong.

And the three Taylor boys - Percy, Roo, and Archie - were together again. Archie still leaned on his stick, still wrestled with the weight of his injury, but he was alive, and he was home. Percy carried his quiet strength into the life he had always known, while Roo's laughter once more filled the open spaces of the farm.

They had gone to war as boys, tested in ways no one should be, surviving when so many had not; and they had come back changed. To these men they felt a clear duty to live well, to remember, and to ensure that the fallen were never forgotten. And so here, among the ridges and fields of Sandy Creek and Kilcoy, life carried on. There were cattle to muster, fences to mend, and families to raise. Seasons would change, crops would grow, and children would play. The world beyond might remain uncertain, but at this moment in time there was peace, and the promise of new beginnings. And with each sunrise over the ranges came a quiet prayer - that no war would ever scar the world again.

Two regiments, two stories, drawn to their end by the same current: the war that had made them, and the silence that followed.

Tony Squire was born in England and later made Australia his home. With twenty one years of military service, he brings both discipline and lived understanding of his writing.

His lifelong interest in military history, together with a passion for telling stories of ordinary men in extraordinary times, inspired *The ANZAC Chronicles*. Through this series he seeks not only to honour those who served, but also to capture the spirit of resilience, sacrifice, and mateship that shaped a nation.

Tony lives in rural Australia with his wife Sheila, where he continues to research, write, and preserve the stories of the past for future generations.

MORE BOOKS BY THIS AUTHOR

The ANZAC Chronicles:

"...UNTIL YOU ARE SAFE".
"TO OUR LAST MAN".
"OUR LAST SHILLING".

The Evelyn Kane Mysteries:

ESCAPE TO EDEN.
CITY OF DEATH.

Other Titles:

IN THE COMPANY OF OUTLAWS - MY LIFE WITH NED KELLY AND HIS GANG.

www.ingramcontent.com/pod-product-compliance
Lightning Source LLC
Chambersburg PA
CBHW060816120726
47909CB00006B/1952